ABANDONED PROPERTY

To Ritchie

With my thanks for being
such a delightful dinner
partner!
    Happy Holidays

        Robbie Meyyes

        Dec 2014

ABANDONED PROPERTY

---◇---

ROBERT MEYJES

Library of Congress Number: 2004091722
ISBN: Hardcover   1-4134-5115-2
                Softcover   1-4134-5114-4

To order additional copies of this book, contact:
Xlibris Corporation
1-888-795-4274
www.Xlibris.com
Orders@Xlibris.com
24228

DEDICATION

This book is dedicated to my father, Willem Christiaan Posthumus Meyjes, (1895-1966). His career as an economist and banker in Amsterdam was truncated by the German invasion of the Netherlands in May, 1940. His outspoken comments about "German imperialistic striving towards military domination" had earned him a place on the Nazi blacklist. He and his family escaped to England, arriving in August of that year. A colonel in the Dutch army during the Second World War, he became Commissioner for the recovery of Dutch property looted by the Nazis. His later career was spent in the Dutch Foreign Service; he served in Canada, France, Hungary and Greece. After his retirement from the diplomatic service, he was named the first Director-General of INSEAD, the European School of Business Administration in Fontainebleau, France.

ACKNOWLEDGMENTS

Many people have provided invaluable assistance in the development of the manuscript.

My father-in-law, William Krusen, has flown every aircraft I have referred to, either at the controls or as a passenger, and helped me work out the scenario and details for the air crash in the story.

A trio of Citibank alumni, Larry Lee, Peter Page, and Peter Sperling, provided numerous comments which immensely improved the logic and flow. If there are any errors detected in my description of banking techniques, they share the responsibility for not having caught them. Bill McKnight, also a Citibank alumnus, ran enthusiastic interference, promoted advance sales, and was always ready to lend me moral support.

Tom de Swaan was most helpful in arranging for a review of the manuscript by experts from the Jewish Historical Museum in Amsterdam. Mrs. Agaath ter Haar very kindly assisted in checking the details of life in Holland during the Nazi occupation. Count Nicholas Wenckheim made many helpful suggestions and corrected Hungarian and German phrases used in the dialogue.

P.D. Block reviewed the story with special emphasis on the segments based in Chicago. I survived Waite Rawls' probing challenges of historical veracity to both his and my satisfaction. Many others, including Barbara Martin, Kitty

McKnight, Mike Stott, Tom Touchton, Andy Herz, and Nick Gardiner were kind enough to read the manuscript and give me their reactions.

Robert Youdelman took me under his wing early on in the process and encouraged me to work on my story.

My sons, Bob and John Meyjes, cheered me on and made many constructive suggestions. They ensured that I maintained an appropriate level of restraint throughout.

This book would never have been completed without the support and hard work of my nephew, Thomas Posthumus Meyjes, who applied his boundless energy and enthusiasm to any problem on which I consulted him and who displayed extraordinarily creative gifts, unsuspected by his wife and family, including the design of the book's jacket.

Finally, my wife, Pamela, led me through the story-telling process and provided critical help when I faltered. She reviewed every page of the manuscript, patiently addressing both major and minor flaws; she is the wife and editor whom every author needs.

Fall, 2004

CONTENTS

PREFACE

This book is fiction. It is rooted in the realities of the Second World War, and, in particular, the events leading up to, and following, the German invasion of the Netherlands in 1940. The Netherlands is the official name of the country. It is habitually referred to as Holland, however, which is the name of its best known and historically wealthiest province.

Amsterdam before the Second World War was a prosperous merchant city of 450,000 people. It was a major center of international shipping, trade, insurance, and finance. It had a first-class symphony orchestra, a well-known university, and an historic city center. The religious freedom for which the city was famous allowed Catholics, Protestants, and Jews to live in respectful harmony.

Starting in 1933, German Jews began to cross the border into Holland, fleeing increasing anti-semitism in Germany. The number of refugees mounted in the late 1930's, and groups of Dutchmen, both Christians and Jews, formed local committees to provide clothing and shelter for those refugees in need of assistance. While many of them arrived penniless, a few managed to bring large sums of money and jewelry with them. Most of them, rich or destitute, felt safe in Holland and made no move to distance themselves farther from the Nazis.

Soon after war broke out in 1939, French military intelligence learned of the gradual build-up of German army units along the borders of Belgium and Holland. By early 1940, the threat was unmistakable, but the Dutch government relied on the neutrality which had kept the country out of the First World War to protect it once again. Nonetheless, Jews were being urged privately to emigrate to England or the Western Hemisphere; Holland had its own Nazis, and their parades and speeches were altogether too familiar to those recently arrived from Germany. Unfortunately, the invasion of Holland on May 10, 1940, caught everyone by surprise; the country was overrun in five days.

The five-year occupation of Holland decimated the Jewish community. The Germans also deported hundreds of thousands of non-Jewish Dutchmen to work camps and looted the country of everything that could be moved. At the end of the war, the Dutch established a military commission to recover assets found in Germany which had been owned by citizens, residents, and companies in Holland. These recovery efforts were successful in recuperating tangible assets such as machine tools, ships, locomotives, cattle, and fine art. By the end of 1945, it was believed that most Dutch property in Germany had been recovered, yet some works of art, as well as financial assets belonging to Dutch citizens and residents, were never found.

In Europe, the initial focus of post-war asset recovery efforts was not on Jewish assets per se. In the 1990's, however, a belated international effort to return so-called 'Holocaust funds' to their owners or beneficiaries has resulted in some restitution, but it has been extremely laborious to find and cull through old records dating back to the late 1930's. The practical obstacles frustrating the discovery of Jewish financial assets were, and are, enormous. Some bank accounts which remained unclaimed after the war were not necessarily Jewish, but a determination of their true origins could not be made. We will never know how much money disappeared, let alone where it ended up.

In the U.S., every state has some type of abandoned property statutes which require banks and other financial institutions to turn over to that state assets and accounts unclaimed after a specified period of time. Once the funds have been turned over to the state, the task of identifying funds specifically belonging to Jewish beneficiaries is further complicated by an extra layer of details to be investigated. Outside the U.S., unclaimed funds are handled in a variety of different ways. The example used in this story is technically feasible, but it is not based on an actual case.

The story reflects the banking environment of the early 1950's; it was more informal and certainly less suspicious of possible miscreants than it is today. Banking has undergone remarkable changes in the last fifty years. Today, it would be almost impossible for anyone to be successful in claiming ownership of abandoned funds belonging to some other person. Bank secrecy is no longer available to criminals except in rogue jurisdictions, which are being increasingly isolated and rendered ineffective. Banks are required to exercise particular care in establishing the identity and activities of their clients. Large cash transactions are now monitored by banks in a widening group of countries around the world. Banks have become participants in law enforcement, for the greater benefit of the world community.

CHAPTER ONE

———————<>———————

THE CURTAIN RISES

DECEMBER, 1939

AMSTERDAM

The postman pedaled energetically on the brick-faced surface of the narrow roadway along the canal. The saddle bags, hung over the bicycle's rear wheel, swayed from side to side as he pushed into the wind, which had picked up strength since dawn. Brown leaves whirled in eddies from the road into the murky waters. He was anxious to finish his afternoon rounds; he could feel the weather deteriorating.

He stopped the bike in front of 144, Keizersgracht. As he dismounted, he could not help but admire, as he had so many times before, the handsome façade of the old town house. He was proud of Amsterdam's historic canal district. He had been delivering mail here almost all his life. This townhouse was one of the most pleasing to the eye. A brass plate, placed discreetly on the right hand side of the large, dark green-painted door, read 'Hobbema & Seventer, Bankers, since 1835'. He bent down to retrieve the afternoon mail for Number 144 and ran up the short flight of steps. The door was opened immediately by his old friend, the head porter. He handed the mail over.

"Weather's worsening, isn't it?" asked the porter.

"Certainly is! It's typical St. Nicolas weather."

"At least St. Nicholas is present-giving time. The partners here at Hobbema and Seventer have decided to bring all their presents personally to the Post Office tomorrow afternoon."

"Well, Jan, you know I complain a lot, but I have to say that the gentlemen who run this bank are my real favorites. How is Mr. Hobbema, by the way?"

"Slowing down, I'm afraid. He comes in twice a week, though. Between you and me, it's that young Mr. Seventer who is really running things around here now. Maybe he did inherit from his Dad, but he's a real go-getter."

"Well, I have to be going. I want to be home in time to listen to the news on the radio. My wife is very upset about all this war stuff."

"Don't worry. Remind her that the Germans left us alone last time. We'll be fine."

"Thank you, my friend, I'll tell her that."

Dr. Julius Bluhm walked briskly along the canal, his head bent against the bitter, wet wind. He had been accustomed to bad weather in Berlin, but the weather in Amsterdam was worse. He had arrived here sixteen months ago, with his wife and daughter. The people whom they had met in Amsterdam had been most hospitable; his wife liked the city, and their daughter Sophie was already enrolled in a Dutch school. Yet Dr. Bluhm was beginning to feel uncomfortable.

Three months ago, in the first *Blitzkrieg* of the war, the rest of the world watched and waited as the Germans invaded and occupied Poland. The British and French, having declared war on Germany in support of the Poles, sat on their hands and held their fire. Hitler made no move to attack the French; his troops, guarding the east bank of the Rhine, played music over loudspeakers directed towards the French on the other side of the river. This was not the way war was supposed to be.

He broke his stride to check the numbers on the houses. Yes, here it was: Number 144. He walked up the steps and rang the bell. Almost immediately, the porter opened the tall door to let him in.

"Good evening, sir. I believe you have come to see Mr. Seventer?"

"Yes, that's right. I hope I'm not too early?"

"Not at all, sir. Please take a seat here for a moment. He'll be right with you."

The building which housed the banking firm of Hobbema & Seventer had been occupied for several generations by a family engaged in the shipping business. When the last of the family died, it had been purchased by the bank's partners, for whom the large, light-filled rooms and the patrician atmosphere represented an ideal facility. The hallways were still inlaid with black and white marble. The bank had offered to buy the ship models from the previous owners, and they were now displayed in the foyer, carefully protected in glass cases. In what was formerly the kitchen and servant quarters in the basement, the bank had installed a large walk-in safe, a number of safe-deposit boxes, and other facilities for processing mail and securities. Dr. Bluhm looked around the waiting room, appreciating the paintings of tranquil river scenes and ships at anchor.

He had become quite fond of this young Dutchman, Eduard Seventer. Thanks to him, he had met several influential members of the large Jewish community in Amsterdam, and the Bluhms had established pleasant social connections with them. In addition, Dr. Bluhm had been asked to lecture in the Physics Department at the University; he was surprised by the fluency with which most educated Dutch people spoke German. It was rare when his students asked him to stop for a translation from German into Dutch. His own Dutch was improving, although not as quickly as his daughter's, who was speaking it almost fluently already. But then, she had the advantage of youth.

His thoughts were interrupted by the porter, who invited him to accompany him to Seventer's office. "Mr. Seventer will be with you shortly," he said. Seventer's office was at the rear of the first floor, overlooking a well-tended, formal garden from which he could watch the first daffodils and tulips bloom in the early spring. This blustery December afternoon, however, it was already getting dark. A log sputtered in the fireplace, throwing a warm glow over the Persian rug.

Seventer strode into the room, his hand outstretched to greet his visitor.

"Dr. Bluhm, it is so nice to see you. I hope I didn't keep you waiting too long. Not very nice outside, is it?" Seventer's German was impeccable.

"No, but then it is December, so we should be expecting it. Thank you very much for seeing me. I shan't take much of your time."

"On the contrary, it is my pleasure. Perhaps you would like a cup of tea?" At Bluhm's nod, Seventer pressed a bell for the tea, and continued, "I am anxious to hear how you are settling in. I hope everything is going well?"

"We could not be more pleased; everyone has been so kind. But I asked to see you because I'm a little worried, and you have always given me good advice."

"By all means, tell me how I may be of assistance."

Dr. Bluhm settled into his armchair.

"Mr. Seventer, I am concerned that some of your compatriots are not being very realistic about the situation across the border in Germany. I know you don't feel that way, but I have noticed, particularly outside of Amsterdam, that there are many Dutch people with pro-Nazi sentiments. I was in Haarlem last week where I saw a parade of your Dutch Nazi party. It was frightening; it reminded me so much of the Brownshirts. Do you think I'm becoming paranoid?"

"No, unfortunately I have to agree with you. But you must understand that we are a neutral country, and we take our neutrality very seriously. I think the Germans understood that in 1914, which is why they left us alone then and why they will leave us alone this time. We are also a democracy, so we have to put up with these fascist lunatics in our streets."

"I understand. Yet the German border is only 100 kilometers from this city. I keep hearing rumors that the German army is building up its strength all along the Dutch border. Why should they be doing this unless they are planning to invade Holland at the same time as they invade Belgium?"

Seventer stroked his jaw. "I can certainly make some inquiries for you. Perhaps our military people have a different view of the situation." He paused for a moment. "I wonder if you should hedge your bets. Suppose the situation here deteriorates to the point where you want to move away from Holland? You would not be the first, I assure you. You must be hearing how some Jewish families, even those who have lived for generations in Holland, are sending some family members to England or to the United States."

"I've been thinking about it; you are very perceptive. My wife doesn't share my apprehension; she likes it here so much. I've been wondering whether I should send some of my money out of Holland so that we would have the means to start a life somewhere else, if necessary."

"Dr. Bluhm, I must tell you that our bank has been quite active in sending money abroad for refugees like you. We have opened accounts in London, New York, and a couple of other cities where we know the banks to be sound and reliable. You can always repatriate the funds when the crisis passes."

"You are my banker. I rely on you. Tell me, what should I do?"

"Let's see." Seventer walked over to his desk and picked up a file. "I was looking at your account before your arrival this afternoon. I would judge that you have far more money in it than you need for your lifestyle here in Amsterdam. We could easily send a hundred thousand pounds to London, or the equivalent in dollars to New York."

"I would feel very relieved knowing that the money was safe. I have nothing against London, but somehow I think I would prefer to have an account in New York. What sort of account would you recommend?"

"My banking colleagues in the United States are very conservative at the moment. Almost without exception, we have opened time deposit accounts with the banks; the interest is payable every quarter at the maturity of the deposit. Unless they hear from us, they roll the deposit over automatically and accrue the interest. They do not recommend bonds because the rates are so low. Personally, I think your investment should remain very liquid, given the circumstances."

"How do I access the account when I need to?"

"As long as you are here in Amsterdam, of course, we will be happy to convey your instructions. We have recommended that the accounts be placed on 'Hold All Mail' which means that the bank in New York does not mail out advices or statements. At your instructions, however, the accumulated mail will be sent to you whenever you desire."

"What happens if I'm ever in New York, for instance, and I need the money?"

"We will send them a letter of introduction when we open the account for you. The letter will bear your signature as well as ours. You will be required to present a suitable piece of identification, preferably your passport. We will provide you with an exact copy of the letter of introduction, also bearing our respective signatures. In addition, for good order's sake, we will give you copies of the initial deposit and the transfer instructions. We always recommend that you keep those documents readily available in a safe place."

"This sounds like a very good solution, Mr. Seventer. What is the interest on the deposit?"

"At the present time, 90-day deposits in New York are earning about 3 ½ % per annum. The advantage of a time deposit is that rates are adjusted every quarter, so you would benefit from any increase in rate levels in the U.S."

"Then let us proceed with this transaction. I will sleep much better tonight," said Dr. Bluhm with a smile.

Ten minutes later, he walked out into the darkening night, satisfied that he had done something positive to protect his little family.

Two hours later, Seventer finally rose from his desk, tidied it briefly, locked two side drawers, and turned off the lights. He glanced at his watch. He had to change for the party he and his wife Louisa were attending that evening. It would take him less than fifteen minutes to get home at this time of night.

The thought of Louisa always sent a wave of happiness and expectation through him. Seventer wondered how he had been so fortunate to find her. He had grown up in Amsterdam. The only times he had been away from the city were for vacation trips with his parents and when he had studied law at Leiden University. Since he was a teenager, he had known that he was destined to follow in his family's footsteps at Hobbema & Seventer. He was expected to marry a girl from a similarly patrician family from Amsterdam.

Even though The Hague was only 50 kilometers from Amsterdam, the two cities were distinctly different. Amsterdam was the powerful commercial and financial capital of the Netherlands; The Hague was the smaller, more aristocratic, political capital. Each city prided itself on its character. The comparisons were not always made in jest by their respective inhabitants; there was an undercurrent of mutual disdain. So it came as a surprise to Seventer when he had found himself invited by one of his Leiden classmates to a dance in The Hague. That evening, he had met Louisa van Dijck.

Louisa was a radiant blonde; her hair had a natural golden luster; her eyes were crystal blue. Seventer had asked her for a dance. Even in her high heels, she had to look up into his face; he saw a charming, smiling mouth. Very quickly, he discovered that she had a teasing sense of humor. As they waltzed around the floor, he in his white tie and tails, she in a light blue silk, full-length gown, they had looked with growing fascination into each other's eyes. She had danced easily, gracefully, clearly enjoying it.

When the dance had ended, Seventer had led her to the buffet. They both took a glass of champagne and sat down on a settee. Seventer could not keep his eyes off her. He sensed the perfect proportions of her body under the folds of her gown. They had chatted effortlessly. The voice of another young man had intruded, requesting the next dance. Seventer suddenly felt jealous. He had never experienced such an overwhelming feeling of excitement. He had determined, then and there, to see Louisa again, soon.

During that spring and summer, he had frequently taken her sailing on his boat. Even when they were caught in a rising wind, or in one of the squalls that came upon them with little notice, she had laughed as she struggled to follow his instructions. On fair days, they would take a picnic lunch and anchor the boat near a spit of land, the sails down, flapping gently in the breeze. There was never enough time for them to be together. They discovered in each other a physical attraction which surprised and delighted them.

Their courtship was as brief as convention would permit. They had been married eight months after their first meeting. Seventer, like Louisa, was an only child. Her parents, the van Dijcks, rejoiced; they had never imagined that their Louisa would find so perfect a match.

The only sad note at their wedding had been the absence of Seventer's parents, killed in a car crash in France two years earlier. The car had smashed into a tree at the side of the road. He thought that the loss would have been somewhat easier to bear if he had had a brother or a sister to share it with. Perhaps because of this loneliness, he had very quickly become close to Louisa's parents, and they had taken him in as a son. Mr. van Dijck, a lawyer retired from the Ministry of

Finance, loved to talk shop with him. Eduard Seventer felt completely at home with the van Dijcks.

———<>———

He heard Louisa call out to him as he closed the front door. "Edu, look on the kitchen counter. Some beautiful flowers arrived half an hour ago. I didn't have time to see who they're from; I'm having so much trouble with this dress."

He strode into their bedroom. Louisa was standing near the bed, her dress stretched out on it as she sewed a seam on one of its panels. From behind, he clasped his arms around her lithe, warm body. She relaxed at his touch, turned around, kissed him, and said, "Come on, Edu, we have to be going. We are supposed to be at the Carlton at 8.30."

Tonight, Louisa and Edu were attending an annual affair, a dinner for ten couples, who had been close friends from childhood days. The Carlton Hotel dining room was one of Amsterdam's most elegant venues for a brilliant social gathering. Louisa's deep green silk gown was cut low in the back. The skirt was made of overlapping panels which caused it to swirl as she moved around the dance floor. Seventer observed her with a smile; he was so proud of her. She was sitting across the table between two of his friends, who could not hide their fascination with the beautiful young woman.

The couples danced to the melodies played by the string orchestra in between the six courses comprising the festive menu. When coffee was served, the men switched seats to sit together and light up their cigars. Louisa moved over to sit with the other wives.

She tried to eavesdrop on her husband's conversation. She could see that he was annoyed about something. To his left sat Pim Laan, one of Seventer's partners at the bank. He also looked angry and was very red in the face. He pounded the table in front of Seventer.

"You have to admit, Edu, that the man has brought order, a stable currency and full employment to the country. I see nothing wrong with that. So he had to take a few drastic steps to achieve it, but everywhere you go in Germany, you see happy, well-fed people."

"I don't know how you can overlook the madness in him, Pim. Look what he did to Czechoslovakia and then Poland. Listen to his speeches. You just won't face up to it. His rantings against the Bolsheviks and the Jews are not just for dramatic effect."

"It hasn't hurt us here in Holland, quite the contrary, and that is precisely why I wish you would stop using our firm to help those Jewish refugees. Some day, there will be a price to be paid. You'll see!"

"We've been through this before, Pim. I'm not putting the bank at financial risk."

"Yes, you are, Edu. How do we know the bank won't be held liable for violations of German currency controls?"

"Dammit, Pim, I've been through this with all of you often enough. We are buying Reichsmarks legally here in Holland. If the Nazis can't stop their banknotes from leaking out of Germany, that's their problem. In fact, you know perfectly well that the Germans are buying their currency back through their companies operating in Holland. So stop fussing about it. This is no place to continue the discussion. Take it up at our next partners' meeting, for Heaven's sake!"

Seventer pushed his chair back brusquely. This was the last time that he was going to get involved with Pim socially, even if he had to put up with him as a partner. He walked around to Louisa and asked her to dance. He needed to relax.

He could see that Louisa was tiring of the loud voices and the smoke. He read the message in her eyes. It was time to say goodnight. The Seventers went around the table, promising to get together again soon. They all vowed to repeat the party next year.

Louisa and Eduard waited for their car to be brought around. Louisa could sense that Edu was still unhappy. He said nothing as he slipped behind the wheel and put the car into gear. They drove off, through the dark, empty streets.

Finally, he spoke. "I'm sorry, my love, I shouldn't have gotten into another argument with Pim," he said.

She turned to look at him. "Frankly, I think he has a point, Edu. I worry about your being so openly anti-Nazi. Too many people in Amsterdam know how you feel, and this is a small country. It really concerns me."

"Come on, Louisa, we've discussed this many times. Holland may be small, but it is still a free country. People don't go to jail for what they believe in—unlike that fascist paradise over the border from us."

"I can see I'm not going to win this argument," replied Louisa. "Just promise me that you will be careful, won't you?"

"Trust me, darling. I'm doing the right thing." He took his hand off the steering wheel for a moment and placed in on her knee. She slid across the seat towards him.

CHAPTER TWO

———————◇———————

INVASION

MAY 9, 1940

AMSTERDAM

Eduard Seventer curled his legs over the side of the bed carefully, so as not to wake up his wife. He was in a rush this morning, and he had to stop at his office before taking the plane to London. He shaved quickly while drawing his bath, then washed with efficiency. His body was well-proportioned, lean, and surprisingly muscular for a man in a sedentary occupation. He stood five foot eleven in his socks. As he dressed, he looked at himself dispassionately in the mirror. He saw an open face, with an angular, determined chin. His eyes were blue, set well apart, with little creases that hinted at an easy smile. His thick, dark-blond hair was starting to turn silver at the temples. He finished dressing, carefully adjusted his polka-dot tie, pulled on his cuffs, and buttoned his jacket.

His overnight case was laid out in his study. From the window there, Seventer looked out on the Minervaplein, the broad square in front of his apartment building. It was one of the most beautiful springtimes in the Netherlands. Whenever the clouds appeared high in the sky, in thin wispy drifts, with the wind blowing out of the east, the Dutch knew that they were about to be blessed with that rarest of events: a series of beautiful days. It had not been a very pleasant winter, nor had the early spring been any different from the usual blustery, wet, depressing pall that hung over Holland for too many months during the average year. Today, the wind was calm. A lovely, pale light reflected on the quiet surface of the canals. The muted tones of the houses shimmered in the water. In the southwestern part of the city, the sun brightened the reddish-pink hues of the new brick buildings. Seventer closed his case, and walked out of the apartment, pulling the door quietly behind him. Back in the bedroom, his wife smiled in her dream.

Louisa hated to be parted from her husband, but she felt fortunate that she could take the train to The Hague to be with her parents. Lately, with all the talk of war, her parents had become insistent that she stay with them each time Seventer left on a business trip. Last night, Louisa and Eduard had agreed that he should reduce his trips outside of the country until the international situation improved. This overnight trip to London was to be his last for a while.

Seventer parked his dark-blue Buick in the Schiphol Airport parking lot and walked over to the terminal building. Inside, with the assurance of someone who knew his way around, he walked straight to the KLM check-in counter. Having confirmed that his plane was leaving on time, he checked his case, picked up his boarding card, and walked over to the coffee stand at the end of the hall.

The radio on a shelf behind the stand was tuned to the 8 a.m. news broadcast. As usual, the news was dominated by the speculation that Germany was massing troops on the frontiers of France and Belgium. The radio announced that the Dutch Government had called up several units in the Army and Air Force reserves, although "the Cabinet of her Majesty the Queen does not see any specific threat to the Netherlands". However, the radio then went on to report that German minelayers were active in the North Sea off the coast of Holland and that the Dutch government had lodged a strong protest against this violation of international law.

Seventer was surprised. What possible reason would the Germans have to take such an aggressive step? The radio rambled on. Seventer looked at his watch. It was time to go. He walked over to the departure area, gave his ticket to the KLM agent and walked out onto the tarmac, towards the stairs leading up to the three-engine Fokker plane. Inside, he bent down in the narrow confine of the cabin and found his seat near the front of the plane. He opened his newspaper and settled down for the two-hour flight. As the plane climbed towards the west, he could see the tidy Dutch houses along the canals. The sun glinted on the lakes, ponds, and waterways which made up the gigantic Dutch water management system. It looked so peaceful.

MAY 10

LONDON

The Savoy Hotel in London stood majestically overlooking the Thames. The early morning traffic along the Embankment was barely audible inside the cosseted corridors of the huge building. Seventer had requested breakfast at 8, time enough to read the papers, dress, and then, take a short taxi ride to the City. He looked at his watch; it was 7.34 a.m. He had a few more minutes to wait for his traditional English breakfast.

Suddenly there was a knock on the door. "Just a minute," called Seventer. He hastily put on his bathrobe and opened the door.

"I'm terribly sorry to wake you, sir," said the floor waiter. He handed Seventer a copy of The Times. "There's been some terrible news during the night. Holland, Belgium and Luxembourg have been invaded by the Germans. It's terrible, sir, just terrible."

Seventer's heart began to pound. He looked at the paper, then at the waiter.

"Thank you." Silence. "Perhaps you wouldn't mind bringing my breakfast right away?"

"Of course, sir. Thank you, sir."

Seventer closed the door behind the departing waiter, and turned his attention to the newspaper. Several columns dealt with the latest posturing by Hitler, the agonizing messages between chancelleries, the reports of border crossings, knowledgeable descriptions of the composition of the respective armed forces. But there was nothing on where exactly the Germans had crossed into Holland, nor at what time, nor for what purpose. There was no indication of the reaction of the Dutch Government.

Seventer looked around the room, but there was no radio. He looked at his watch again. It was 7.48 a.m., one hour earlier than in Amsterdam. He would call Louisa. He walked over to the telephone, picked up the receiver, and waited impatiently for the operator to respond. Finally, she answered. "Good morning, Savoy Hotel."

"Good morning. This is Mr. Seventer in room 45. Could you please call Amsterdam for me?" Suddenly he remembered that Louisa had gone to her parents. "No, I mean The Hague. The number is 45122."

"I'm sorry, sir, all circuits have been busy since about 6 a.m. this morning. Should I keep trying for you?"

"Yes, please. This is most important."

Seventer put the receiver down. He paced back and forth, wondering if he would get through to Louisa. He walked over to the windows to pull open the drapes. A bright sun appeared, shining through the trees that lined the Embankment. He stood there for a few moments, wondering how such a beautiful day could start so badly.

The waiter knocked on the door. "Here is your breakfast, sir." He wheeled in a trolley and proceeded to lay out Seventer's breakfast. "Will there be anything else?"

"No, thank you," said Seventer. "Oh yes. Do you have a radio available somewhere?"

"We have one in the bar downstairs, and there is one in the headwaiter's quarters. I'm sure you could come down to listen, if you wish."

"That's very kind of you; perhaps I will. Thank you."

"Thank you, sir."

Seventer sat down and poured his coffee. A feeling of guilt came over him. Should he be sitting here, with the world falling apart, eating kippered herring? He began to think. First, he had to get some facts.

He dressed quickly. He was tying his shoelaces when the phone rang.

"Mr. Seventer, this is the telephone operator. Your call to Holland will go through in about five minutes."

Seventer continued to pace around the room. Shortly, the phone rang again.

"Mr. Seventer, I'm connecting you to Holland now."

He could hear the operators talking, then a telephone ringing, then a female voice, "*Ja?*"

"*Moeder?* This is Eduard in London. I just heard the news. Is Louisa with you? What's going on?"

"Oh Eduard, it's shocking. Thank God Louisa is right here with me. Her father went down to the office to see if he could find out more. Here she is." There was a short pause.

"Edu darling, I'm so glad you called. Where are you?"

"I'm at the Savoy. Are you alright?"

"We're fine. But we can't understand what's happening. Are the Germans really at war with us? It makes no sense."

"I don't understand it either, sweetheart. I've just heard the news, but I have no idea what it means."

"Edu, I'm scared."

"Well, obviously I'm going to cut my trip short and get back immediately. You had better stay with your parents in the meantime."

"You have no idea how much I miss you, my love. I'm so worried! Please come back quickly."

"There's nothing to worry about. I'm going down to the office here to get everything squared away and to arrange for my passage back tonight."

"Edu, please be careful. I spoke with Arie at the office in Amsterdam about half an hour ago. He is very worried that the Germans might have you on their black-list. He thinks there are people at the office who will tell them about your helping the Jewish refugees."

"Well, the Germans won't make it to Amsterdam. We will open the dikes and flood the fields."

"I hope you're right. I miss you terribly. We'll be alright, won't we?"

"Don't worry. You and I can survive anything together. I adore you, Louisa." They hung up.

Seventer hurriedly packed his case, checked the room one more time, and wove his way through the corridors of the hotel until he found the stairs. He descended them two at a time, and ended up in the front reception hall. Normally a quiet place, vaguely reminiscent of a baronial estate, it was alive with people this morning. The porter's desk was three deep with clamoring guests, most of them speaking in accented English. Seventer thought that this scene must be repeating itself in every hotel all over London. The cashier's room, set off to the side of the hall, was also unusually busy. He had to wait in turn to check out. The two clerks in morning coats worked efficiently and politely. When Seventer's turn came, his bill was made up quickly, and he wrote a check for the balance.

Outside the hotel, under the marquee, a long queue had formed for taxis. Seventer patiently waited his turn again, knowing that waiting here was still the best chance he had of getting a cab. Finally, his turn came. "Please take me to 32 Moorgate."

The driver pulled open the glass partition and asked, "You 'eard the news, guvner? They say old Winston will become Prime Minister today."

"That will certainly get Hitler's attention!"

"Where are you from, sir?"

"Holland. I know very little about what is happening there. It's very worrisome."

"Well, don't worry, guvner, we'll get the bleedin' Jerries."

The man's optimism buoyed Seventer. The taxi crossed the intersection in front of the Royal Exchange and was soon going down Moorgate, where it stopped in front of one of the smaller buildings. Seventer paid off the driver, and strode through the swinging doors under a discreet sign which read 'Mathijs Smithson & Co.'. The hall porter rose to greet him.

"Good morning, Mr. Seventer. I was so sorry to hear the news."

"Thank you, Brown. Has Mr. van Meeren arrived?"

"Yes, sir, he is expecting you. Please go right in."

Seventer opened a heavy mahogany door at the side of the hall and walked into what was clearly a 'partners' room'. Three large desks stood along one wall. Heavy, leather-covered armchairs were placed in front of them. Portfolios were stacked on mahogany shelves on the opposite wall. Two portraits of older men, their watch chains prominently displayed over ample girths, hung on either side of the door. The discreet aroma of Cuban cigars underscored the impression that Mathijs Smithson & Co. was a solid, conservative banking house.

A tall, elegantly attired man emerged through a door in a corner of the room. He appeared to be about fifty. His hand reached out for Seventer's. They spoke in Dutch.

"My dear friend," said Seventer, "I'm so glad to find you here."

"Not a great day for the Dutch, is it?" replied Jan van Meeren. "What are you going to do? Do you have any news of Louisa and her parents?"

"Yes, I managed to reach them in The Hague this morning. They knew very little; they were in a state of shock. What have you heard?"

"I'm afraid it's not good news. The Germans have punched a hole right through the Belgians and have reached Stavelot. The French are sending several divisions to the north to help the Belgians. The British are reinforcing their Expeditionary

Force in Flanders. The news from Holland is very confused."
Van Meeren continued, "I spoke to Pim Laan in Amsterdam
about an hour ago. He says the Germans have already reached
Apeldoorn. He managed to admit that you had been right all
along, by the way. He was almost speechless with rage,
threatened to kill the first German he ran into, called them
every conceivable name; you know how he is when he gets
worked up. I didn't have the heart to tell him what a blind
fool he has been."

"See if you can get him on the phone again and tell him
to close the bank for business until further notice. There is
no way we can continue to operate in these circumstances.
Also tell him to get rid of all of the evidence concerning the
Jewish accounts; they provide too much of a trail for the Nazis
to follow." Seventer paused and then continued, "Now I have
to decide what to do. The first thing is for me to get back to
Holland. Can Stella get me on the next flight to Schiphol?"

"Let's see what she can do."

Twenty minutes later, Stella returned to the partners'
room. Seventer was on one phone, van Meeren on another.
She walked over to Seventer. He signaled for her to wait a
moment, finished talking, put the phone down.

"All flights to Schiphol have been canceled," she said
without preamble. "I inquired about the ferries. They say
that the Harwich-Hoek van Holland ferry is still operating
normally. You do not need a reservation if you take the day
ferry, but that one is leaving in 45 minutes, so you'll never
make it. The night ferry is also scheduled to sail on time, but
you need a reservation, and I can't get you one. They
suggested you go to Thomas Cook's and wait in their offices
to see if something should open up. Perhaps you should wait
for the day ferry tomorrow."

"Stella, I can't risk that. Who knows whether it will be
running tomorrow?"

Van Meeren overheard this and walked over to Seventer's
desk. "You could find yourself completely unable to return if

you wait too long. Why don't you try going to Ostend or Calais or something; then you can always take a train."

"Let's look at the map," replied Seventer. Van Meeren went to a cabinet, ran his fingers through some files, and pulled out a large map of the Netherlands, the southern edge of which also showed some of the Belgian coastline.

"You see," continued Seventer as they both pored over it, "Ostend is already too far south if the Germans are advancing as rapidly as it appears they are into Belgium. Calais is even farther south. It's either Hoek van Holland, or perhaps the ferry port at The Hague near Scheveningen."

"Stella, can you see what you can do with either of those possibilities? Check to see how many other ferries might be running to some place on the Dutch coast. I've never heard of one, but perhaps there is a ferry straight to Ijmuiden near Amsterdam."

Stella nodded, clearly in control of this crisis.

"While we wait, what do you want me to do with all of these accounts that you opened recently? Suppose these German refugees get stuck in Holland?" asked van Meeren.

"Whatever you do, do not try to communicate with them; they may ask us to do something under duress. I'm sick at the thought that their nest eggs may not do them any good if they can't get out of Holland. When I get back to Amsterdam, I'm going to see if I can't persuade some of them to leave while there is still time. Oh, and while I think of it, here is one more account opening document."

Seventer took out a folder, which he opened and spread on the desk in front of him. "Here is what will most likely be the last account that you will be able to set up." Van Meeren stood behind him to look at the folder.

"This one, in the name of Max Goldstein, is probably the largest account we have opened. The old man owned a pharmaceutical company in Augsburg, and in the week after *Kristallnacht,* he agreed to sell it to a German company. They beat him down on the sale price, but surprisingly, they still paid him the equivalent of US $9,000,000 in Reichsmarks, which I was able to convert into guilders. Finally, I convinced him to send some of this money outside of Holland, and I bought Sterling and US Dollars for him. Here is a check, payable to Mathijs Smithson, drawn on Barclays, for 1,220,000 Pounds Sterling. I sent off the remainder to the Empire State National Bank in New York. Funny, isn't it, he wanted some of his money closer to 'home', wherever that might be in Europe. He said that America was in another world."

"You had better attend to your return to Holland. I'll take care of this. Maybe Stella has some news."

Seventer went along a narrow passage into Stella's small office. She was on the phone. He sat down in the only chair in front of the desk and waited, looking around the room. He noticed that she had pinned a recent picture of Winston Churchill on her bulletin board.

She ended her call and turned to him. "You may be in luck. I have you on a ferry leaving Great Yarmouth for Scheveningen this evening. You don't have much time. The train leaves Liverpool Street Station at 1.45 p.m. The train and ferry tickets are being run over by Cook's. You are scheduled to arrive tomorrow morning."

"Stella, I don't know how you do it."

"Well, just bring me some of those delicious Droste chocolates when you come back."

MAY 11

GREAT YARMOUTH

With the breaking of dawn, the ferry passengers rose early, hopeful that they would soon have a specific time of departure. It seemed as if the wait was going to continue, however; the ship was still tied to the dock.

"I'm very sorry, ladies and gentlemen, but we have been ordered to stay in port until we receive clearance from the Royal Navy," the purser had said last night as they stood around in disconsolate groups. Almost all of them were Dutch, attempting, like Seventer, to reach home. Finally they had retired to their cabins.

This morning, Seventer was pacing again, in the main salon, waiting for the purser who had promised to get them an update on the delay. At last, the purser made an appearance.

"We have just had word that we are to transfer you to a Dutch ship. The British authorities have ordered all British vessels to stay in port until further notice. Please place your luggage outside your cabin door; our staff will then collect it and move it to the other ship."

A chorus of voices arose. "Where is the ship? When will it be leaving? Is it going to Scheveningen?"

"I'm sorry, that's all the information I have at the moment."

Seventer looked around. He needed to call van Meeren

to let him know the situation. He touched the purser's sleeve. "May I make a telephone call?"

"Yes, of course, sir, but only if you reverse the charges. The telephone is in my office. You'll have to wait your turn, however."

Seventer descended the stairs to the main deck and found the purser's office. Two men were already waiting to use the telephone. Finally, it was Seventer's turn. He asked for van Meeren's number at home; he had just remembered that it was Saturday. Van Meeren took the call and accepted the charges.

"Hello, Jan. Edu here."

"Good heavens, are you calling from The Hague?"

"I wish I were. We are still at the dock in Yarmouth. The Royal Navy won't let the ferry leave, so we have to wait for a Dutch boat. What's going on?"

"I've been listening to the news since I got up. It's totally confusing, except that the Germans seem to be overrunning everything in their path. In Holland, they seem to have captured a lot of our airfields with parachutists."

"Well, surely they can't have gotten too far over the flooded polders?"

"Edu, the Germans seem to be attacking all over the country."

"Here's what I'd like you to do, Jan. Please call Louisa; she's staying with her parents in The Hague. The number is 45122. Tell her I'm on my way. We should be in Scheveningen by nightfall. I'll take a taxi from there."

"I'll do what I can. I tried to call my sister in Aerdenhout this morning; it took almost an hour to get through, and then we were cut off in two minutes."

"Jan, even the slightest indication to Louisa that I'm on my way back will make her feel better. Perhaps you can back it up with a telegram."

———— <> ————

The Dutch steamer 'Maetsuycker', 4,100 tons, had a maximum speed of 14 knots. It was on its regular run between Stockholm and Rotterdam when it was ordered by its head office to proceed to Great Yarmouth to pick up Dutch nationals returning to Holland. The captain protested that Yarmouth was a small harbor, ill-suited for a merchant vessel such as his. He requested Hull as an alternative. By 4 p.m., he had not received an answer and decided to proceed on his original course to Rotterdam. The office in Rotterdam, too understaffed to deal with the growing crisis, failed to notify the British authorities.

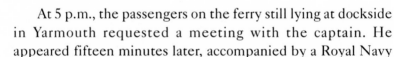

At 5 p.m., the passengers on the ferry still lying at dockside in Yarmouth requested a meeting with the captain. He appeared fifteen minutes later, accompanied by a Royal Navy lieutenant. Seventer acted as spokesman for the group.

"We cannot wait here any longer. We all have to get home. Your company must make alternative arrangements for us." Seventer sounded firm, but the edge in his voice was unmistakable.

"Please accept our apologies," replied the captain. "This situation is completely beyond our control. We have no idea what happened to the Dutch ship which was supposed to take you on. I have asked Lieutenant Horton to fill you in."

The lieutenant edged towards the center of the room. "As you will readily understand, we have been ordered to stop all British flag ships from hazarding into Dutch waters. The Germans are moving very fast and may be occupying some of the port facilities within hours. Ferry service from all English ports to Holland and Belgium has been suspended. In the absence of any Dutch ships momentarily available to cross over to Holland, I'm afraid that your only alternative is to go back to London to seek other ways of returning home. I'm terribly sorry, but that's how it is."

The ferry captain continued. "We have reserved seats for all of you on the 7.13 p.m. train back to London. The crew will assist you with your luggage. The purser and I will be available for any other assistance that you may require. I should add that the telephone circuits into London have been overloaded since mid-day. It is almost impossible to get through at the moment. I suggest that you defer trying to make your calls until you are back in the city."

The passengers broke up into small groups, their faces drawn with worry. Seventer went out on deck, lit a cigarette, and tried to organize his thoughts. He stared out at the lengthening shadows in the harbor and at the horizon beyond the breakwater. Over there lay his homeland, unreachable and under attack. Hopefully van Meeren had spoken to Louisa earlier that day, but what would she think when he didn't show up tonight? He had to find a way to get home.

MAY 12

THE HAGUE

Louisa's father, Arnold van Dijck, was up very early. He had tried to pick up radio broadcasts from Belgium, England, and even Germany, on the short wave. The only consistently clear transmissions were from London, but the first BBC news report did not begin until 7 a.m. London time. The Belgian radio was sporadic, shifting unpredictably from Flemish to French and back to Flemish. Like the French, the Belgians played classical music or military marches to fill the time. After some initial attempts, he had given up on the German stations, even though his German was as fluent as his English. Their bombastic propaganda was intolerable.

He tried to reach a cousin in Arnhem by telephone. The lines were down, he was told. A call to a classmate at the Ministry of Foreign Affairs was more productive.

"Gerrit, what can you tell me? What's going on?"

"I, for one, am sitting here destroying certain files and preparing to take others to England with me." His despair was evident.

"You're going to England? Why?"

"My dear friend, I don't mean to be rude, but the Germans are less than fifty miles away from where you are sitting. My advice is to prepare for the worst."

———<>———

LONDON

Seventer woke up slowly, unsure of where he was. His gaze roved around the bedroom. The curtains were drawn, but he sensed that there was daylight behind them. Where was he? There was a discreet knock on the door, and then the butler came in carrying a tray with a teapot of freshly brewed tea, a china cup and saucer, and the morning papers. He greeted Seventer. "Good morning, sir. Mr van Meeren told me not to awaken you until 8 a.m."

Now he remembered. The train from Great Yarmouth to London had been an hour late the night before. He had arrived at van Meeren's flat at midnight, exhausted mentally and physically. This morning he felt tense, stiff, and unrested. He had to get himself to Holland quickly, but how? He looked at the newspaper headlines. The brunt of the German attacks was against Holland and Belgium. The French border, which extended all the way to Switzerland, had not been penetrated at any point. He hurried to shave, bathe and dress. He had to go to the office and try to find another way to get back to Louisa.

———<>———

By 5 p.m. that afternoon, Seventer was still in the office at Moorgate. He had been on the phone most of the day. A two-hour wait for information at Thomas Cook's ended in complete frustration. "No, sir, we know of no ships leaving for the Netherlands." "No, sir, all ferry service has been suspended indefinitely." "No, sir, there are no flights at all." Seventer was beginning to panic.

MAY 13

THE HAGUE

"The fighting around Rotterdam intensified during the night. Dutch troops are fighting stubbornly along the Grebbe Line, protecting the capital and the North Sea coast. Flooding has stopped the German attack in many places. Our army has dislodged German paratroopers from several airfields."

Van Dijck interrupted his radio listening to answer the doorbell. Louisa had already opened the door to admit their neighbor, Frans van Breem, who stepped importantly into the front hall.

"I have some really big news. Can I show you on a map?"

"Come into the library," answered van Dijck. Van Breem and Louisa followed him into the room, where van Dijck laid out a large-scale map of the country on the writing table.

"I have just received very accurate information about the situation from my nephew, who is in charge of operations for the Port of Rotterdam Authority. In a word, our situation is critical. The Germans have broken through the suburbs of Rhenen, at the southern end of the Grebbe Line." Van Dijck and Louisa followed van Breem's tracing on the map. "Some of their units have already been spotted on the north bank of the Lek," van Breem continued, "and there is nothing to stop them from being in Utrecht by nightfall. German paratroopers hold the Moerdijk Bridge, cutting us off from any reinforcements that might have come up from Belgium. French troops that had reached Breda have fallen back towards Antwerp."

The three were silent while they contemplated their own encirclement. Van Breem continued, "However, the good news is that the Germans cannot reach The Hague or Amsterdam unless they cross the Maas River at Rotterdam. That is one part of the front which is heavily defended. The Germans have been unable to make any headway there at all."

Van Dijck shook his head. His patrician features sagged, making him suddenly look quite old. Louisa laid her hand on his shoulder in a moment of silent comforting.

"Where can Edu be at this moment? Why hasn't he called?" she asked.

"I don't want to sound like a pessimist," said van Breem, "but I think your husband must not have found any transportation back to Holland. There's nothing moving in the port of Rotterdam, I can tell you that. Anyway, if I hear anything else, I'll let you know immediately."

Van Dijck and Louisa thanked him as they accompanied him to the front door. Van Dijck returned to his radio. It was nearly noon, so he sat down to wait for the updates. Precisely at the stroke of 12 noon, the announcer came on and said, "The Government of her Majesty the Queen has just made the following announcement:

> Earlier this morning, Queen Wilhelmina, accompanied by government ministers and a number of senior officials, left for England on board a British warship. Last night, Princess Juliana, accompanied by Prince Bernhard and their children, were also evacuated to England. Her Majesty made this decision on the recommendation of her Government, believing that a prolonged struggle against the invader will be more efficiently conducted from a base in the United

Kingdom. She intends to continue the fight against
the invader until victory is achieved. General
Winkelman, Commander-in-Chief of Dutch Armed
Forces, will continue to direct operations from his
headquarters in Holland."

Arnold van Dijck sat in his armchair, immobile from the
shock. How could the Queen and her family have abandoned
them? What would happen to the country now?

———— <> ————

LONDON

In desperation, Seventer went to the French embassy.
Perhaps he could cross over to France; at least he would be
back on the continent, and he could make his way up to The
Hague. He stood in a long line of people waiting to see an
official. The air was thick with the smoke of Gauloise
cigarettes. Finally, his turn came. The official was unshaven
and haggard.

Seventer explained his situation. "Is there any way I can
reach Holland through France or Belgium?" he asked.

"You can go to France, if you wish. You will certainly
make it to Paris. From that point on, there are three ways, in
theory, for you to get back to the Netherlands. The first, by
plane, has not been an option since two days ago. Secondly,
you could try the trains, which are still running as far as
Brussels, but on an erratic schedule. Nobody knows whether
there is service from Brussels to Amsterdam. In my opinion,
whatever service there is will be suspended shortly. Your third
option is to drive. It is not realistic. Petrol is almost impossible
to obtain, and the Allied troops are not letting anyone through
unless they have a French military pass. I am not authorized
to issue one from here; you would have to obtain it in Paris. I

must add that the military situation in Holland is extremely grave. I very much doubt that there is any time left for you to try going through France."

Seventer's shoulders sagged. He took a cab back to the office. Stella took one look at his face as he walked into the partner's room, and suggested, "Mr. Seventer, shall we try to reach your wife again?"

An expression of hope suddenly crossed his face. "Yes, please. Thank you."

He read the evening paper as he waited. The Dutch were clearly being overwhelmed. He was just turning the page when the telephone rang.

"*Hallo?*" he queried. He could hear some clicking on the line, then "*Ja, hallo, hallo?*"

Seventer could not believe it. "Louisa! It's me, in London!"

"Oh, sweetheart," she replied, "It's so good to hear your voice. Are you on your way home?"

"I can't find any way to get back, but I'm still working on it. Are you and your parents all right? What's going on?"

"It's just awful, Edu. Why has the Queen gone to England? What's going to happen to us?"

"I'll be there soon. Just wait for me. We'll sort it out."

"I can hardly hear you, Edu. When did you say you are you coming home?"

"I'm trying to find a way, dearest. I will be there soon . . . *hallo*, Louisa, are you there?" The telephone crackled and went dead. Seventer slammed the headset down and ran into Stella's little office. "Stella, I just got cut off! Can you please try it again?"

Seventer returned to the partner's room, his stomach knotted with fear and tension. The telephone rang again.

"*Hallo?*" It was a man's voice. Seventer did not recognize it.

"*Hallo?*' replied Seventer, "Is this the van Dijck residence?"

"Whom are you calling?"

"Van Dijck. Have I reached 45122 in The Hague?"

"Sorry, you have a wrong number."

Seventer leaned back in the armchair. He felt sick. He was beginning to realize that he was caught in a trap, and there was nothing he could do about it

MAY 14

ROTTERDAM

The ultimatum delivered to the Dutch garrison at Rotterdam was unsigned. It called for the city's immediate surrender, failing which it would be destroyed. The Dutch refused to accept an unsigned document, and a Dutch officer was sent to the German command post outside the city to ascertain its authenticity. At the same time, 100 bombers from the *Luftwaffe* took off from airfields in northern Germany; their target was Rotterdam.

The Dutch officer was unable to complete whatever negotiations might have ensued; the bombers were already over Rotterdam. Their bombs rained down on the unprotected city. The wind spread the fires rapidly. The garrison, blanketed by billowing black smoke and orange flames, surrendered at 4 p.m. 900 civilians were killed in two hours. The historic town center was obliterated.

Later that afternoon, General Winkelman, having learned that the *Luftwaffe* was threatening to demolish the old city of Utrecht next, decided to surrender the remaining Dutch forces. The Nazis had completed their conquest of the Netherlands in five days. It would be five years, almost to the day, before the Dutch nation would finally be rid of the Germans.

———<>———

LONDON

Seventer and van Meeren sat in the latter's elegant living room facing Regent's Park. The large, double windows were open, letting the evening breeze gently ruffle the chintz curtains. It was not quite 8 p.m., but there was still sufficient light outside that they could see Londoners strolling around the lush gardens or stretched out in deck chairs, calmly reading their evening papers.

The two men were silent. There was nothing left to be said tonight. They nursed their cocktails, van Meeren occasionally eyeing his watch. In a few minutes, it would be time for the evening news on the BBC. Seventer was slouched down in his armchair, his chin on his chest. His eyes were closed. Van Meeren could only imagine what he was thinking. He felt so sad for his friend. Seventer was facing life at its worst. Holland had been overrun; his wife was unreachable; his business was closed, and his friends and colleagues were God only knew where. Here he was, sitting in London, alone except for his friend, van Meeren.

Van Meeren sighed and rose to turn on the radio. With each day that passed, the BBC became a more important rallying point for the besieged island. Seventer kept his head down; he did not want van Meeren to notice that his eyes were brimming with tears.

MAY 17

AMSTERDAM

Heinrich Wanstumm arrived in Amsterdam right behind the victorious *Wehrmacht*. German troops stood at the corners of major intersections, while the Dutch peered at them from behind shaded windows. A few people had ventured out to look for food, but most of the stores were closed. At least Amsterdam was still standing, unlike Rotterdam, whose city center had been destroyed by the *Luftwaffe* three days before. The fires had burned all night, and a huge cloud of black smoke still rose thousands of feet into the air over the Dutch coast. Resistance had quickly disintegrated. Holland was occupied by a foreign power for the first time since Napoleon had invaded the country in 1804.

Wanstumm commanded a special squad of nine Gestapo agents. They had been ordered to act as soon as Amsterdam was secure and to use the advantage of surprise in ferreting out all the Dutch on the Gestapo blacklist. One name on the list, identified as a suspect as early as 1937, was that of a Dutch banker, Eduard Seventer. He had come to the Gestapo's attention for his anti-Nazi remarks and for having assisted many Jews in resettling outside of Germany. Wanstumm sent two men to the Seventer apartment at Minervaplein, but it was unoccupied. The agents went to Seventer's office on the Keizersgracht. The office was closed.

Frustrated, Wanstumm ordered a general search for anyone with the last name of Seventer. One family member, an aging uncle, informed them that Seventer's in-laws lived in The Hague.

The two agents arrived at the van Dijck house the next morning at 10.30 a.m. The door was opened by a maid in uniform. "We want to talk to Mr. or Mrs. Seventer," one of them stated in passable Dutch.

"And whom may I say is calling?"

"Gestapo."

"Please wait here," she said, indicating that they should stay on the steps outside the house. She closed the door.

The seconds ticked by, then the door opened again. A tall, distinguished man looked at them impassively. "What do you want?"

The two men walked up the steps, brushed by him, and stood in the hall, waiting for him to close the door behind them.

"What is your business here?" van Dijck demanded.

"Do you have a son-in-law named Eduard Seventer?"

"You are standing in my hall, uninvited. I don't know who you are. If you don't leave immediately, I shall call the police."

"We are the police now. We are from the Gestapo. If you refuse to cooperate, we will have to take you with us to Gestapo Headquarters for questioning."

"My son-in-law is not here."

"Please tell us where we can find him."

Van Dijck's expression did not change. "He is in England."

The agents looked at each other. The Dutch-speaking agent said, "I hope you are telling us the truth. We know that his wife is here with you. If Seventer should be in touch with either of you, tell him to report at once to the Gestapo office in Amsterdam for questioning. There are severe penalties for not cooperating with us." The agent saluted, and turned on his heel, followed stiffly by the second agent. Van Dijck slammed the front door closed behind them. He looked worried.

The agents reported back to Wanstumm. "Are you sure that you checked properly?" he asked them coldly. They assured him that they had. He ordered a watch on the house in The Hague. Perhaps Seventer would return to Holland and try to contact his wife and in-laws. Meanwhile, he had other enemies of the Reich to round up. He was going to be very busy.

Wanstumm was 33 years old. He was Bavarian. He was old enough to remember the First World War. His father owned a butcher's store in a village near Memmingen. His mother served the customers. In 1918, at the age of eleven, he overheard his parents talking about the collapse of the German Army in the space of seven weeks. Later, he learned from his teachers that Germany was being sucked dry by the Allies, who demanded reparation payments for a war that the Germans had not started. He saw how his parents' meager savings were wasted by spiraling inflation. His father had to mortgage the butcher shop, and his mother walked to outlying farms to buy food more cheaply. He was shocked to see people begging in the streets. Wanstumm's uncle, a maker of orthopedic shoes in Augsburg, committed suicide rather than face bankruptcy.

In 1931, Wanstumm finished his apprenticeship at a food products company. He expected to be promoted to the next level, that of assistant foreman. That same year, he joined the Brown Shirts. He liked the regimentation and the security. He was also mesmerized by Hitler, the head of the Nazis, the *Nazionale Sozialistische Partei*. He became a member of the Nazi Party, and cheered when Hitler promised to wreak vengeance on all of those who had made the German people suffer. He joined his friends at rallies and admired the uniforms, the occult swastika, the marching songs, the perfectly synchronized, goose-stepping men.

His early days in the Brown Shirts were happy ones, until he began to realize that the Brown Shirts were becoming a noisy rabble led by sexual deviates and ruffians. He was quicker than most to resign, but only after he had lined up a job as a research assistant at the *Geheime Staats Polizei* (GeStaPo). He joined on May 26, 1934, at the age of 27. His parents purchased a small farm near Memmingen in Bavaria with their remaining savings, eking out a simple existence. They died of pneumonia in 1936 within two months of each other. He was the sole mourner at their funeral. Other family members did not show up because they couldn't afford the train fare. Heinrich Wanstumm was now alone in the world, but he belonged to a group, and he had a leader.

Wanstumm's first years as a Gestapo agent involved preparing files on members of the Socialist and Communist parties, German Jews, and foreigners in Germany who could become a threat to the New Order. The foreign section, to which he was transferred in 1937, kept track of foreigners who had criticized the Third Reich, the Nazi Party, or Hitler personally. While much of the work involved research and documentation, Gestapo agents were frequently involved in interrogations, searches of homes and offices, and covert operations. Wanstumm's colleagues were generally younger men who preferred police work to enlisting in the armed forces.

Wanstumm advanced in the ranks without any overt excess of brutality. He supervised the interrogation of prisoners calmly and methodically. He didn't flinch at applying additional 'persuasion'. He was considered to be above average by his superiors, reliable and efficient. His earlier association with the Brown Shirts had been questioned, but he was not alone in having resigned from that organization, and his colleagues' testimony supported his statements. He dated Aryan girls, slept with some of them, but was not ready for marriage and a family. He was an uncomplicated person, and he believed, with complete conviction, that Adolph Hitler was the savior of Germany.

He was still a middle-level member of the Gestapo when he was assigned to the Gestapo office in Duisburg. His territory included the *Gutehoffnunshütte*, the largest tank assembly plant in the Ruhr. He was also responsible for Gestapo activities along the Dutch border, only 56 kilometers away.

In late 1938, he received a number of messages from Gestapo headquarters in Berlin that the Dutch had opened their border to German Jews. His unit was instructed to implement the confiscation of all valuables carried out of Germany by these refugees. Wanstumm inspected the principal border crossings and ordered the border guards to perform body searches on every male and female refugee, since they were rumored to be hiding cash and jewelry in their clothes, and sometimes inside their bodies. He made no exceptions.

In September, 1939, the Germans invaded Poland, and the French and British declared war on Germany in support of the Poles. Wanstumm continued his job of classifying people as enemies of the state and added arrest, imprisonment, and the hanging of the Reich's enemies to his daily activities. He organized the arrest of Jews at the German border and arranged for their transportation to the new camps that were being set up to accommodate them. The Jewish migration into Holland came to a halt.

Then on May 10, 1940, with stunning speed, the German armies invaded the Netherlands, Belgium, and Luxembourg. The lightning strikes of the German *Wehrmacht*, rolling back the Dutch and Belgian armies, excited and stimulated Wanstumm. Each day, he woke up to some new, extraordinary feat of German arms, supported by what the world now recognized as the greatest air force in the skies, the *Luftwaffe*. He loved the feeling of power bestowed on him by Hitler's victorious armies.

Wahstumm was now given an important mission. Having set up his headquarters in Amsterdam, he was to ensure that his territory was, at all times, a pliant, submissive part of the Reich.

CHAPTER THREE

——————<>——————

OCCUPATION

JULY, 1942

AMSTERDAM

The city, now entering its third year of German occupation, had a threadbare look. Shortages of food and medicine were increasingly evident. The Nazis had organized a ghetto in one of Amsterdam's older quarters. Progressively, Jewish families were being moved into it, permitted to take only a bare minimum of their belongings with them. In a city where Christians and Jews had lived side by side for centuries, the very idea of a ghetto was an anathema to the Dutch. The burghers of Amsterdam rebelled; city workers went on strike to protest the tormenting of the Jews. Every morning, the city's inhabitants awoke to find fresh posters, mocking the Nazis, nailed to trees and bridges.

Hans Schuurman was employed by the tax department of the municipality of Amsterdam. Shortly before the war, he had been promoted to section head, and he, his wife Aagje, and their ten-year old daughter, Ingrid, had moved to a larger apartment at 14, Jan van Boegstraat. They had been there hardly a month when the Germans invaded. He continued to go to his office and to keep a low profile as a loyal municipal employee, but Schuurman quickly became disgusted with Nazi brutality and anti-Semitism. When his turn came to sign a form declaring that he was not of Jewish extraction, he had decided to join the Dutch Underground. His access to housing and tax records provided him with invaluable information, particularly in assisting Jewish refugee families to move into abandoned apartments.

Schuurman also observed how the Germans, aided by the Dutch Nazis, methodically, district by district, had begun to hunt down the large number of Jews living in Amsterdam. He developed a primitive, but effective, early warning system. By observing the patterns of each night's activities, he was able to forecast the location of the next day's searches with reasonable accuracy and to get a warning to those who might be affected. The Germans were nothing if not systematic.

One morning in July, Hans Schuurman realized that the street on which he lived was likely to be next on the Nazis' search list. He feigned a stomach ailment and rushed home. He had to warn Dr. Bluhm, who lived with his wife and daughter, Sophie, on the third floor, right above his apartment. The families had become friends.

He turned the key in the lock of his front door. Aagje looked up from her sewing, surprised to see him in the middle of the afternoon.

"Hans, what are you doing here? Are you alright? Are you sick?"

"I'm fine. But I've learned that the Germans are coming to our neighborhood to look for Jews within the next few days, maybe even tonight. I must warn the Bluhms." He paused. "Aagje, remember what we discussed?" She nodded.

"I'm going upstairs to see Dr. Bluhm. When Sophie shows up with our Ingrid, keep her down here."

Schuurman hurried upstairs, taking the steps two at a time. He knocked rapidly on the door. It opened into a small foyer. Julius Bluhm smiled as he recognized Schuurman.

"I'm sorry to bother you, Dr. Bluhm. I need to speak with you urgently." The smile faded from Bluhm's face.

"Please come in," answered Bluhm, closing the outer door. He led the way into the small parlor. "I am a little surprised to see you at this time of the afternoon. Is something wrong?"

"Where is Mrs. Bluhm?"

"She is resting in her bedroom."

"Good. I would rather discuss the situation with you alone." Schuurman lowered his voice. "You know that the Germans plan to move every Jewish family into the ghetto, or even to deport them to camps. Nobody will be spared. I have some information that our neighborhood will be searched soon, perhaps tonight."

"But what can we do?" asked Bluhm anxiously. "We have no place to hide. We'll have to go with the others and hope that the Germans will leave us alone in the ghetto."

Schuurman looked down for a minute and then raised his eyes to meet Bluhm's. He continued, "Once in the ghetto, you will be completely at their mercy. You know as well as I do what will happen to you. I have a suggestion. My wife and I have already discussed it. You know how fond our Ingrid is of your daughter. We will take your daughter into our apartment and hide her until better times are here."

Bluhm looked stunned. "But isn't that a dangerous thing for you to do?"

"We can handle it. Sophie won't be able to continue going to school, of course, but Ingrid can keep her up to date. It will be difficult for her. She must not be seen at all. Somebody might denounce her."

"It is a very generous idea. My wife will be relieved, and I, well, I don't know what to say. I am very grateful to you. Hopefully, it will be for just a few days."

"More than a few days, I fear, but your Sophie will be safe with us."

"I must discuss it with my wife first. If she is agreeable, what shall we do?" asked Bluhm.

"Clean out her room at once, and move everything that belongs to her to our apartment. We cannot leave a trace. Not her toothbrush, not her cough medicine. Everything must disappear. When you have finished removing everything, I want you to clean her room thoroughly. Not a single hair should be left. I know the Gestapo. Remove all pictures of her. Go through your files, and let me have everything that mentions her name. They are unbelievably thorough."

Bluhm turned to his wife who had just entered the room. She must have overheard part of their conversation. She looked disbelievingly at Schuurman, then again at her husband. He walked over to her and put his arm around her shoulder. "Mijnheer Schuurman has suggested that Sophie go to his apartment; he thinks that the Germans will come soon to move us to the ghetto. He will hide her. You know that this is what we must do."

"Julius, there are many Jewish families who are still in their homes, and they have never been bothered. I don't want Sophie away from us. Please."

"We can't take the risk. Mijnheer Schuurman is right. Sophie will be safer with them."

"Come, let us start to move her things," urged Schuurman.

Bluhm and Schuurman worked fast; clothes, books and toys disappeared down the stairs. Mrs. Bluhm overcame her disbelief and started cleaning Sophie's room. Bluhm then went through the desk in his study, looking for all documents and references to Sophie. He was sure he was going to overlook something.

He paused for a moment, staring at the thin file in his hand. What should he do with this, he asked himself. He pulled out a sheet of paper and wrote on it for a few minutes, referring frequently to the file. When he finished, he folded the sheet of paper, put it in an envelope, and added it to the other documents and letters. He went downstairs and knocked gently on the Schuurman door, which they had left ajar.

"Here are all the papers which refer to Sophie," he said to Schuurman.

"I will find a safe place for them."

"There's just one item that needs an explanation," continued Bluhm, lowering his voice. "May I show you?"

"Of course, let's go in here," said Schuurman, leading the way into the bedroom.

Bluhm opened the envelope containing the documents and letters, showed them to Schuurman, and gave him the hand-written notes he had just made. He explained, "Before the outbreak of the war, I was advised by a young Dutch banker, Eduard Seventer, to move a considerable amount of my money to America. He arranged for the opening of the interest-bearing account at a bank in New York. These are the details of the account. I have copied all of the relevant information for you. Should anything happen to me or to my wife, this money belongs to Sophie. I know I can trust you to help her claim the money."

Schuurman went over the details once more with Dr. Bluhm. He looked up and promised, "You may count on me, although I hardly think that this will be necessary."

"Who would have thought we would reach the point of hiding our Sophie?" asked Bluhm sadly. "Now, let us get ready to tell Sophie what we plan to do. The girls should be home any minute."

AUGUST, 1942

AMSTERDAM

Gestapo Headquarters was not located in the center of Amsterdam, but rather in one of the modern neighborhoods of the city, towards the southwestern edge of town. In a spate of enlightened urban development, the Dutch had built, in the 20's and 30's, modern middle and upper-class housing in a leafy, airy web of broad streets stretching towards the south and west of town, the only areas which had enough land available to support that kind of expansion. Shortly after the German occupation of the Netherlands in May, 1940, the Gestapo had commandeered an entire building. Heinrich Wanstumm's office was on the second floor.

He was frustrated by the Dutch Nazi Party's untidy execution of Himmler's orders to deport the Jews to camps in Germany and Poland. A first phase, which had been launched in April, 1942, had consisted of rounding up Jews and sending them to 'holding camps' or ghettos in Holland. The Dutch Nazis were hired by the Germans to provide the manpower to search the Jewish neighborhoods. They went about their job with more energy than method, often overlooking pockets of Jews in certain buildings in Amsterdam.

Wanstumm scanned the daily activity reports, and made sure that his own group of agents mopped up areas identified by the Jewish Council as containing numerous Jewish families.

He was particularly anxious to remove those who were recent immigrants from Germany. It would look good on his record, and he thereby avoided problems in arresting Dutch Jews whose families were well-connected in Holland and who were sometimes able to claim Aryan ancestors as a reason for being spared the deportation orders. He set in motion a series of raids, conducted at night, to ferret out these stragglers.

It was one of these that he was preparing that Tuesday morning in August, 1942. It was 3 a.m. Orders had been received from Berlin to expedite the internment and subsequent transportation of Jewish families to Germany. He had previously conducted searches in the older parts of Amsterdam; today he would start in another area known to be home to a number of Jews. He had arranged for the assistance of a company from the 371st Infantry Regiment, who had been trucked into town the previous day and had taken up positions around the targeted area on the western side of the city.

Three of his agents stood around him. Wanstumm looked again at the map laid out on his desk. He said, "We will start at this end of the Jan van Boegstraat, working our way systematically up to the Kattenplein. Each of you will take your men down the side streets here, and here. We have sealed them off. We will start promptly at 4 a.m. Trucks into which the Jews will be loaded will be waiting for you around the perimeter of the search area."

He handed out lists of names and addresses, keeping one list for himself. "You are to search every house and every apartment noted on these lists. If they do not open the doors, break them down. Make sure you collect every member of the family. They have to wear their Star of David. Allow them the usual amount of time to get dressed. No suitcases or parcels. Have them walk down to the end of the street to the truck, and make sure there are soldiers who can watch them."

"What are we to do if any of them resist?" asked one of the men.

"The use of force is permitted, of course. Just don't make too much noise. In the extreme case, you are to shoot anyone who fails to comply with the orders. Is everything clear?"

"We seal the doors, right, and then come back for their belongings tomorrow?"

"*Genau*. Make sure you get the keys to the apartments."

Outside, in the blackness of the night, the men dispersed to their cars. Wanstumm walked over to his, buttoning his leather coat against the wind. As he sat down in the passenger seat, he waved his driver on. The convoy of cars headed west along the Lairessestraat.

Within minutes they had arrived at the south end of the Jan van Boegstraat. Wanstumm took one of the agents with him, and walked over to Number 2, the first on the list. The front door, at street level, led to a foyer, where three doorbells with names under each indicated the residents of the apartment building. Wanstumm checked his list again, and looked for Goldstein on the list of tenants. He rang the bell. Seconds went by. He rang again. Then he heard the buzzer, and the front door catch released. He pushed the door open and walked up to the first floor, an agent following him closely. He rapped on the door. It was opened by a middle-aged man in pyjamas, a bathrobe hastily flung over him.

"Is your name Max Goldstein?" The question was asked in German.

The man was very pale. A look of terror spread across his face. "Yes, I am Goldstein." The question was answered in German.

"Your wife is here?"

"She is in the bedroom. I think she is asleep still."

"Get her up. Both of you are to get dressed. You are coming with us. Hurry up."

Goldstein turned, then came shuffling back. "Where are we going? What's going on?"

Wanstumm didn't answer. He just waved Goldstein on as he stepped into the living room. He looked around. The room was well-furnished. A brick-colored Kipsie Gul carpet from the Caucasus stretched almost wall to wall. Wanstumm admired it and made a note to have it taken to his office. He heard Mrs. Goldstein, tearful and questioning.

Within minutes, Mr. and Mrs. Max Goldstein appeared at the door of their bedroom, fully dressed and each carrying a bag.

"Leave the bags here," ordered Wanstumm.

"But I need my medicine," wailed Mrs. Goldstein.

"No bags. Put your coats on. Don't forget your Star of David. Let's go."

Mr. and Mrs. Goldstein preceded Wanstumm and the agent. As they reached the foyer, Wanstumm asked for their keys. Goldstein handed them over.

"Please, my wife is not well; where are we going?"

Wanstumm said nothing. When they reached the street, Wanstumm told them to walk to the end of it, and give their names to the army officer who would tell them which truck to get into.

It was already 4.17 a.m. Wanstumm liked to get these operations over with before 6 a.m. He looked at his list. The next name was Bluhm, at Number 14. Again, he rang the bell, and soon he and the second agent found themselves at a door on the third floor of the building. This time the door was opened with alacrity. Julius Bluhm was a tall, balding man with a commanding presence. He looked down at Wanstumm.

"What do you want?" he asked in German.

Wanstumm looked at his list again, and then raised his head to look into Bluhm's eyes. "Please tell your wife and daughter to get dressed. You are accompanying us. Please make it quick."

"What daughter? I have no daughter. I will go to tell my wife to get ready."

Wanstumm looked at the list to make sure. It showed Sophie as the daughter of Hannah and Julius Bluhm. The

Gestapo didn't make mistakes. He knocked loudly on the bedroom door. "Hurry up."

The door opened. He could see Mrs. Bluhm putting some things in her handbag. She was also tall and very beautiful, with a cascade of dark brown hair coming down to her shoulders.

"Where is your daughter Sophie?" inquired Wanstumm.

Bluhm looked at him fixedly. "We have no daughter. You must be mistaken."

"Show me your Dutch residence papers."

Bluhm went to a desk in the bedroom, pulled open a drawer, and extracted a bundle of papers. He pulled a document out from the rest, and handed it to Wanstumm. It was a residence permit issued by the municipality of Amsterdam, dated April 16th, 1938, in the name of Dr. and Mrs. Julius Bluhm. There was no mention of Sophie or any other child. Wanstumm decided to check this out later, but right now, he had to get these people off to the trucks. He watched the couple walk down the stairs ahead of him and out into the street. Something bothered him about these two. They were so dignified.

By 6 a.m., a small stream of people had been shepherded to the waiting trucks. Wanstumm gathered his men. Several Army officers joined them to discuss the successful round-up. Wanstumm asked for a quick check of each agent's list. With the sole exception of the missing Bluhm daughter, everyone else had been found and sent to the trucks. All told, the pre-dawn activities had bagged 43 Jews, soon to be on their way to camps in Germany.

———<>———

The next morning, Wanstumm and his men fanned out over the area that they had covered the previous day. They opened the front doors with the keys given to them. Small trucks waited outside, ready to be loaded with the belongings of the people who would never return. Wanstumm entered the Goldstein home and went straight to the bedroom. He pulled out every drawer, and tipped the contents out onto the bed. Then he went into the kitchen, and tossed the contents of cupboards and drawers onto the floor. Finally, in the living room, he emptied every drawer of every piece of furniture onto the carpet. Idly, he kicked the contents apart. It was then that he saw a wad of papers, held together with a rubber band. He bent down to pick them up, and put them in his pocket. He could look at them later in his office. He continued to look around, went back into the bedroom, and made sure that he had not missed anything.

Further down the street, at Number 14, Alois Ganz, one of Wanstumm's senior agents, was performing the same kind of search through the Bluhm apartment. He was known for having an eye for detail. Every piece of paper was scrutinized. The Bluhms had obviously kept all of their letters and documents from their lives in Germany, from which, in 1938, they had fled to Holland. Ganz sifted through the rest of the papers. There were many letters, from what appeared to be family members in Germany. There was no mention of a daughter named Sophie. There must be a mistake. This annoyed Ganz; the Gestapo did not make mistakes. He came across an official letter from a Dutch bank, confirming the transfer of a large sum of money to New York. He placed it in his briefcase, along with a number of other items.

———<>———

Two days later, at 9 a.m., Wanstumm convened all of his agents involved in the early-morning operation. He wanted to question them about belongings found in the homes of those deported to Germany. His secretary recorded the meeting.

"Good morning, *mein herren*." He looked around at the group, comfortable in his role. The agents responded dutifully.

"Two nights ago, we successfully removed 43 Jews. It took us one hour and 53 minutes to do it. On previous occasions, we have been more productive, but the areas were smaller in the old town, and perhaps there were more Jews per house. This morning, I wish to receive your reports on the contents of the apartments searched, as well as any suggestions on how we can speed up the entire process. Now, let us have the follow-up reports. Herr Ganz, will you start us off?"

Ganz consulted his notes. "Obviously, we took all the papers, such as letters, documents, *und so weiter*. We searched the clothes carefully for hidden jewelry, coins, banknotes. Anything that appeared of unusual interest, such as art, books or religious objects, we took also. Every piece of furniture was checked; we turned the chairs over to see if they had taped anything to the bottom. We checked the insides of all the sofas. Ever since the case at the Oudezijds Voorburgwal," (he had trouble pronouncing it), "we have examined the toilet bowls. We tapped the walls methodically. Sir, I have a suggestion."

"*Ja?*" inquired Wanstumm, surprised that Ganz had broken his line of thought.

"We should use dogs. They have a terrific sense of smell."

Wanstumm looked thoughtful, and said, "I do not think so. It is too much trouble training them for our requirements."

Ganz looked down at his notes, obediently subdued, and continued. "We found sets of documents which seemed to tie some of these people together. In my case, at the Bluhm home, I found some statements about deposits in a bank in America. The sums appeared to be quite considerable. I discussed it with Jaeger," he nodded his head to an agent sitting across from him, "who stated that he found similar evidence in his search."

Wanstumm looked over to Jaeger. "Please tell us what you found."

Jaeger was clearly not used to being in the limelight. He swallowed hard, then, in a strained voice, he said, "Herr

Wanstumm, as you know I speak a little Dutch. I read these papers. They are letters from a Dutch bank, acknowledging receipt of funds, to be transferred to a bank in America. These people were clearly preparing to move from Holland. Then I looked at Herr Ganz's papers. One of the receipts was identical, except for the named beneficiary, the amount, and the bank where the funds were being deposited. There is a pattern here we should investigate."

Wanstumm coughed and looked around the room. "I want all documents relating to bank accounts brought to my office after the meeting. Is that understood?" The men nodded their heads.

The meeting broke up at 10 a.m. Wanstumm hurried back to his office. As soon as the door was closed, he dialed a number on his phone. "*Ja. Guten Morgen*, Herr Weiss. This is Wanstumm. I need you to do something for me. Please examine all the bank documents which we have collected from the Jewish residences since we started the deportations. Go back as far as you can. I am specifically interested in statements and receipts for the transfer of money involving a bank in Amsterdam named Hobbema and Seventer, on the Keizersgracht. Let me have a report by tomorrow morning."

The next evening, the rain was hurling itself at the windows in waves of wind-driven fury. The freak summer storm on the North Sea had already claimed two German patrol boats; wreckage would be found the next morning on the beach without a trace of the crews. But Wanstumm was too focused on the documents spread before him on his desk to pay any attention. The search through the Jewish papers, while not completed, had yielded copious evidence detailing the activities of the bank of Hobbema & Seventer. The records showed that they had systematized the transfer of funds belonging to German Jews to banks in America and

England. Wanstumm estimated that the total amount of currency transferred for the benefit of the Jews named in the accounts on his desk exceeded US $5,000,000.

The information was complete: amounts, dates of transfers, names and addresses of banks, arrangements for identification of the beneficial owners. He decided to make a complete list in a notebook. As he worked, it occurred to him that there must have been similar accounts. Supposing he could get his hands on all of the letters; could he somehow use the information for himself? He had stumbled onto something that might prove to be valuable in the future, after the war. In the meantime, he had to find an efficient way of gaining access to any other accounts that might have been created in this manner. He had to force his way into the offices of Hobbema & Seventer.

Suddenly he recognized the Dutch banker's name. Eduard Seventer, the man who had eluded them in 1940. It was time for a visit to the man's family. He recollected that they lived outside of Amsterdam. His activity report for May, 1940 would give him the information he needed. He walked over to the shelves where he kept his files, alphabetically by year. From his 1940 file, under S, he found what he wanted.

> SEVENTER, Eduard. Partner at Hobbema & Seventer, Bankers, in Amsterdam. From a well-known Dutch family. Married June, 1938, Louisa Van Dijck, daughter of Arnold and Elizabeth van Dijck of The Hague. Home address: Minervaplein 1, Amsterdam. Van Dijcks' address: Bosstraat 11, The Hague. Parents and wife visited by Agents Luebke and Ganz on May 18, 1940. E. Seventer reported to be in England. No further action.

He reached for his telephone.
"*Jawohl*, Herr Wanstumm."
"Please come to my office."

Agent Ganz walked in a few minutes later, after knocking discreetly on the door. He stood before Wanstumm's desk.

"You will recall, soon after we completed the occupation in 1940 that you went with Luebke to The Hague. We were looking for Eduard Seventer, a hostile Dutchman. The house in The Hague belonged to his in-laws, the van Dijcks. Seventer had apparently fled to England, leaving his wife in Holland."

"I remember. We didn't see the wife, however, only the father-in-law. We put a watch on the house, but nothing suspicious seems to have occurred."

"It didn't matter then. At the very least we scared him into hiding where he could do little harm. But now I wish to learn more about him. This man managed to send large amounts of Jewish funds out of Holland. Here on my desk is evidence enough. But I want to know who else was involved and where they are now. This could bring a lot more Jews out of the woodwork. Start with the bank; here is the address. Find out everything you can. Get a team to break the locks if you have to. If you find a lot of evidence, let me know; I'll want to see it right away."

"At once, Herr Wanstumm." Agent Ganz clicked his heels, saluted, and left the office.

The next morning, Ganz stood in Wanstumm's office, glancing at his notes as he spoke. "The building on the Keizersgracht was empty. Clearly, the offices had been abandoned in a hurry. We managed to open the safe in the basement, not so difficult because the three time clocks had all run out, so we merely had to force open the lock on the grill leading to the door itself. A lot of file drawers were empty. We think they destroyed evidence of the Jewish accounts, because we found nothing relating to them."

Ganz checked his notes again as Wanstumm scribbled on a pad, his face expressionless. Ganz continued, "We did find some personnel records, including names of employees and their addresses. But for some reason, the records relating to the bank's partners were also missing. There seemed to have been three or four of them; one of them is retired, a Mr. Jacob Hobbema. We have the names of the others, but no addresses. We checked the Amsterdam telephone directory. Only one listing appears, for a Jan ten Haave. We checked the apartment; it is now occupied by a music teacher, who was assigned to it when it was declared abandoned. Perhaps the others lived outside Amsterdam, in a suburb?"

"We're wasting time," answered Wanstumm. "The one who can lead us straight to the other partners is Seventer's wife. I will interview her myself. You will come with me to The Hague."

"*Jawohl*, Herr Wanstumm."

———<>———

THE HAGUE

Wanstumm got out of the passenger side of his requisitioned Citroen and marched up the steps of the townhouse in the old section of The Hague. He rang the bell. After a few moments, a tall, silver-haired lady opened the front door. She looked down at him.

"*Guten Morgen*, Mevrouw van Dijck, I am from the Gestapo. I have come to ask a few questions of your daughter, Mevrouw Seventer. Just a routine inquiry. Is she at home?" His Dutch had become quite fluent, although the German accent was unmistakable.

Mevrouw van Dijck disappeared, leaving the front door open. Shortly, Louisa came to the door. "You wished to see me?" she asked nervously.

"Your husband has been away since May, 1940. We have reports that he is in England. Is this true?"

"I have not seen my husband for over two years."

Wanstumm stepped into the pleasant, clean-smelling foyer of the van Dijck house. A tall grandfather clock ticked softly. Louisa led him through double doors into a gracious sitting-room and turned around to face him without asking him to sit down.

"What is your husband doing right now?" The directness of the question scared Louisa.

"I have no idea."

"He worked for Hobbema and Seventer. How many partners in the bank did he have?"

"I believe there were four partners."

"Where are they now?"

Louisa thought for a moment. "I know that Mr. Hobbema was already retired in 1938. He was living in Bussum. Pim Laan should still be in Amsterdam. Arie Dorninck went to Belgium the day after we were invaded; I don't know what happened to him. That leaves Jan ten Haave, and we heard he had been captured by the German Army near Utrecht."

Wanstumm pulled out a notebook and a pen.

"What is Pim Laan's address?"

"I cannot recall the number, but he lived on the Herengracht."

"You'll have to do better than that. You are not specific enough." Wanstumm's voice hardened.

Louisa felt a jolt of fear. "I really don't remember. I think that it was near the corner of the Spiegelstraat."

"How often did you go to his house?"

"Not often. We were there for an occasional dinner or reception. His wife is an artist, and sometimes they invited people to see her work."

"So you knew them well?"

"We were friends, yes."

Wanstumm made some notes and stared at Louisa for a moment before resuming his questioning.

"Where is ten Haave's family?"

"I only remember that he was divorced and was living in a house on the Jan van Goyenkade. I only met him a couple of times."

"I suppose you don't remember his street number either, right?"

Louisa rubbed her hands together. "I'm sorry, I really don't. I never went to his home."

"So tell me how your husband aided the Jews at the bank. What did he do for them?" He barked the question.

Louisa bit her lip. "Please, I don't know what my husband did at the bank. He never spoke about his work."

"I'm sorry, Mrs. Seventer. I don't have the time to sit here and pull answers out of you. Wait here, please."

Wanstumm walked to the front door, looked into the street, and beckoned to the Citroen parked at the curb. Two men emerged. He spoke to them curtly, and they followed him into the house. Louisa was still waiting in the living-room, talking to her mother. The women looked at Wanstumm apprehensively.

"Mevrouw Seventer, you will come with us for further questioning."

Mevrouw van Dijck hobbled forward on her cane. "My daughter has done nothing wrong. She certainly knows nothing about her husband's work. Please leave her alone. My husband died recently, and I need her to look after me. My health is not so good anymore."

Wanstumm looked at Louisa's mother and smiled slightly. "She will not be gone long. If she cooperates, she will be home for dinner."

"But where are you taking her?"

"We are taking her to our headquarters in Amsterdam. Let's go, Mevrouw Seventer."

Louisa kissed her mother, her eyes brimming, and followed Wanstumm out of the room. The two agents closed the procession. Mevrouw van Dijck was left standing in the living room, rigid with worry for her daughter.

———<>———

AMSTERDAM

Louisa awoke with a start. She brushed the matted hair off her brow, raised her eyes to the walls of the little room, and slowly straightened her back. They had removed her wrist-watch, but judging from the blackness behind the dirty yellow curtains, it was night. She must have fallen asleep in the chair. Dear God, what would happen next? She had tried hard to answer their questions, but her answers didn't seem to be good enough for them.

Wanstumm's agents had kept repeating the same few questions: "What is your name? Where do you live? Where is your husband? Where is the list of Jewish names?", until she pleaded with them, "Stop, please stop; I don't know where my husband is. I DON'T KNOW!"

Louisa was thirsty. She looked around the room. It was bare except for the chair she was sitting in, a small table and a wash-basin. She got up slowly and walked shakily across the room. There was no glass anywhere, so she leaned down and turned the cold water faucet on. Nothing came out. She tried the other faucet. Nothing. She felt cold now, and her fear returned. She walked to the door and mechanically tried the knob. Of course, it was locked. Her mother would be so worried; whom could she turn to for help? The German agent had said she would be home for dinner, but it was already dark outside. What would they do to her? They had to let her go; she couldn't believe the Gestapo had brought her here, to this dirty little room.

It had now been over two years since Edu had made that fateful trip to London. She missed him so much. Their life before the war seemed so far away. The endless litany of unanswerable questions ran through her head again. Why had she not heard from him after the letter in early 1941? Could she really believe that he had tried to return to Amsterdam from London, only to be thwarted by the speed of the German advance? Would she ever see him again?

Her train of thought was interrupted by her physical discomfort. She needed to go the bathroom. She pounded on the door to get their attention. At first, with hesitation, and then with increasing strength, she slammed her fist against the door. Then, she heard a key turn in the lock. The Gestapo agent was holding a gun.

"I need to go to the bathroom, please?"

She recoiled as she looked down at the revolver.

"You'll have to wait. I will come back," he said. The door slammed in her face. The minutes went by. Then she heard the lock being turned again. Two men stood at the door. One of them beckoned to her to follow him. They turned into the corridor, walked a few steps, and the man in front pointed to a door. She went in, and to her relief found a proper toilet. There was a piece of soap on the sink. She would make the most of it.

After two minutes had passed, they knocked on the door. "*Heraus, bitte.*"

"Just a moment, I am washing my face and hands," she replied. They knocked again. She opened the door, and they escorted her back to the interrogation room. The door closed with a bang. Louisa started to cry softly.

Upstairs, Wanstumm was pacing in his office, showing some agitation, unusual for him. He felt sure she knew more about those bank accounts. First, he was going to ransack the house in The Hague, since the Seventer apartment in Amsterdam had been picked clean with nothing to show for it except a marine painting that Wanstumm had particularly liked. He called Ganz on the phone. "Get two men and take the van Dijck house in The Hague apart, top to bottom, and do it first thing in the morning."

Ganz and his two colleagues arrived in The Hague at 8 a.m. The car came to an abrupt stop in front of the house. The three marched up to the door, and while one rang the bell, repetitively, the two others pounded. Shortly, Mevrouw van Dijck opened the door, leaning on her cane, a shawl pulled around her shoulders. She stepped back as the men pushed their way in.

"We are from the Gestapo. We have orders to search your house. Go to your room, and stay there until we call you."

"But you can't do that! You have no right to come in here! Where is my daughter? What have you done with my daughter?"

Ganz grabbed her brusquely by the arm and shoved her ahead of him. She cried out in pain. "Do as you're told." He opened a door, looked in to see that it was a small den, and pushed her into it.

"Stay here until I say you can come out."

Mevrouw van Dijck started to panic. "What is happening? What do you want?" Her eyes were wide open. She raised her cane and put it through the crack in the closing door. She started screaming. Ganz jerked the door open and hit her across the face as she started to fall. She tripped on her cane and crashed to the floor, her face hitting the marble with a wet crack.

Ganz swore, then, turned to the two others. "Pull her into the den and lock the door. She'll be quiet for a while." The men did as they were told, grabbing the old lady by her feet and slamming the door closed behind her.

A dark red stain marked the spot where her face had taken the fall.

Ganz and his men were back at Gestapo Headquarters shortly after 1 p.m. They went straight to Wanstumm's office. He was at his desk, looking through a stamp collection he had taken from one of his victims. They sat down wordlessly. He looked at two more pages and closed the album.

"Quite nice, this lot. It has a good quality 'Penny Black' and some very unusual Austro-Hungarian Empires. Well," he continued as he moved the album to the side of the desk, "I hope you found something we can use?"

"Herr Wanstumm, we took the place apart: top to bottom. We found absolutely nothing relating to Jewish accounts. We did find some pamphlets distributed by the Resistance and an illegal radio. That's it."

Wanstumm remained silent, looking at each of the three men in turn. Then he got up, and asked the other two to go, leaving Ganz sitting nervously in his chair.

"Do you think we should tear the house down?" asked Wanstumm. "Maybe they bricked up the records in a wall."

"We checked every wall. In a couple of rooms we tore out the backs of the closets. The attic boards were all pulled up. I can go back with a crew and take the whole place down, but my instinct is that it isn't worth it."

"It may be faster to tear the Seventer woman apart," Wanstumm commented reflectively. "She must know more than she is telling us. And while we're at it, bring in the old woman, her mother, just to make sure."

"I should have mentioned, Herr Wanstumm, that there was an incident. The old woman died in an accidental fall in the house. She must have broken her nose because she fell flat on her face. I checked her when we left, thinking she was just injured, but there was no pulse."

"So you just left her there?"

"Well, I thought you wanted our report as quickly as possible. I can send two of my men out tomorrow morning to clean things up."

"Never mind; someone will find her. Let them deal with it. I need to work on Seventer's wife. Tell the kitchen to send me up a sandwich. Stick around. I will need you later."

Two hours later, Wanstumm and Ganz entered Louisa's interrogation room. She was sleeping on her side, her arms pulled around her chest. Wanstumm kicked her cot. She screamed as she awoke and saw them standing over her. Quickly, she sat up on the bed. Wanstumm pulled a chair up to the side of the cot. Ganz remained standing.

"We need your cooperation," began Wanstumm. "So far, you have told us nothing of value. We are not disposed to be patient. There is a war on, and we are going to win it. So let me summarize: we need all the information which you can give us about your husband's activities at his bank, and in particular, his connection to the Jewish accounts there. So far you have told us nothing. That is not good. We have several ways of refreshing your memory. Make it easy on yourself, and you can be out of here very quickly."

"But I already told you, my husband told me very little about the bank. I don't understand anything about finance."

"But you know that he was helping Jews, don't you?"

"Well, I knew about it but only in a general sense. We all felt pity for them and wanted to help."

"Were you ever directly involved with Jewish families?"

"Well, sometimes I asked my friends for clothes."

"Can you remember their names?"

"The names of my friends? Of course."

"No, I meant the names of the Jews."

"No, I didn't really know them."

"How many of your friends were helping the Jews?"

"Oh, maybe twenty or thirty."

"So are there friends of your husband's who would remember the Jews' names?"

"I don't know. It's been several years."

"How old are you?"

Louisa thought for a minute, disoriented by the change in the line of questioning.

"Thirty."

"And you are in good health, I see?"

"Yes."

"THEN-WHY-IS-YOUR-MEMORY-FAILING-YOU?" Wanstumm shouted, leaning all the way over in his chair, staring into her cringing eyes.

"I promise you, I'm telling you all I know. Really I am." Louisa was trying to shrink into her chair. Wanstumm stood up. It was time for a little pressure. He turned to Ganz.

"Take her downstairs. Get her ready. I'll be there in a little while."

———<>———

Early the next morning, Ganz stepped into the cubicle where they had left Louisa the previous night. She was lying on the table in a fetal position. The smell of urine and feces was strong. He turned on the small ceiling light. Her clothes were soiled; her hair matted and humid. One of her stockings was ripped from the thigh all the way to the foot. One hand was coarsely bandaged. She did not move. He leaned down and noticed that she was breathing in gasps.

"I wonder what the boss will do with her now?" he asked himself.

———<>———

Later that morning, Wanstumm attended a meeting with some *Wehrmacht* staff officers. Army trucks had been set on fire in the streets of Amsterdam, and a lieutenant's body had been found floating in a canal near Haarlem. Apparently the taking and shooting of ten hostages for every German killed was not having the desired effect. Also there was continuing evidence that the Dutch were managing to broadcast messages to London. Those clandestine radio sets had to be found, and the *Wehrmacht* didn't have enough resources to home in on them. The Gestapo had to provide more support. The usual whining. He barely listened. He never told them anything because the information always seemed to get passed on and misused by the *Abwehr* (German Military Intelligence), or even by the SS. Wanstumm knew better than to get involved in the labyrinthine competition between the many security organizations in Nazi Germany.

He returned to his office and climbed the stairs with his usual energy. He had a great deal to do today. He called for Ganz. "Where do we stand today?"

"Two more Resistance leaders were brought in this morning."

"Very good, Ganz. Please have the files sent up as soon as they are ready. I shall certainly want to interrogate them personally." He skimmed through the papers on his desk.

"Now what else; let's see. Oh yes, the Seventer woman. What do you think, Ganz, should we give it another try?"

"Frankly, I think it would be a waste of time. She's in bad shape, anyway. She probably doesn't know anything more than she told us."

Wanstumm thought for a minute. He drew a cigarette from his pocket, lit it, and walked around the room. "All right, Ganz, get rid of her. I want a permanent watch on the house. Seventer is too important to us. He may show up one of these days, looking for her, and then we'll nab him."

"Very well, Chief. I will see to it right away." Ganz went down the corridor to his office and gave instructions on the phone.

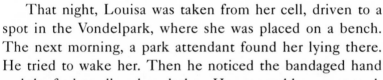

That night, Louisa was taken from her cell, driven to a spot in the Vondelpark, where she was placed on a bench. The next morning, a park attendant found her lying there. He tried to wake her. Then he noticed the bandaged hand and the foul smell on her clothes. He propped her up enough to look into her face. It was completely vacant. There was no reaction from her. He put her back down and rushed to summon help.

An hour later, he returned with a friend and a two-wheeled cart. Together, they placed Louisa on it. It took the two men over twenty minutes to reach St. Elizabeth's Hospital. The nurses helped the men lift Louisa from the cart onto a gurney. One of the nurses asked the men to step inside to give them the details of where Louisa had been found. In the meantime, a doctor started examining her. He recognized the wounds, the vacant stare.

This was not the first time someone had been brought in off the streets like this. He wondered whether she would survive, and if so, in what condition. He started preparing for a complete examination.

CHAPTER FOUR

―――――――◇―――――――

INTERLUDES

JANUARY, 1943

ORIANENBURG, GERMANY

Dr. Marlene Buthe washed her hands methodically, as she did everything. She looked into the mirror above the sink and noted the fatigue in her eyes. Her blond braids were pinned so tightly to her head that they had given her a headache. The bus ride home had taken almost an hour. It was already 8 p.m., and she still had to prepare her dinner.

The week had gone by very quickly with all of the additional work she had been assigned. She was now the deputy director at the 'Special Clinic for Psycho-physiological Research' at the Sachsenhausen concentration camp. As the only female doctor on the staff, she was unlikely to be moved suddenly to the eastern front. There, the rapidly escalating rate of casualties was forcing the *Wehrmacht* High Command to create new field hospitals at the rate of one every five days. So many promising young doctors had been transferred. Many had already been killed by Russian shells or at the hands of Russian partisans.

Marlene was pleased with her increasingly important work at the camp. The experiments she had conducted so carefully were proving that Adolf Hitler was right. Her clinical observations of Jews, Gypsies, and Slavs pointed to the irrefutable superiority of the Aryan race, as personified by the Germans and some of their Nordic neighbors. Her newest

assignment was to evaluate the quickest and least expensive
method of birth control: castration. Her only problem with the
assignment was that it stimulated her sexually. There were few
eligible German men, so she had forced some of the camp inmates
to have sex with her before they underwent surgery.

Tonight, at the end of a long week, she planned to relax,
have a good meal, listen to the nightly news on the radio,
then go to bed with the window open to the winter air. In the
morning, she planned to have lunch with her girlfriend.
Afterwards, they would go for a long walk in the countryside.

She walked back to the entrance of the little house and
took two letters out of the basket on the inside of the door.
She brought them back to the kitchen and poured herself a
glass of wine to sip while she read through them. She felt so
comfortable in this little house. When the war was over, she
would look for the perfect husband to share this house and
her life, her research, her ideals.

One of the envelopes bore the franking of the German
Army field postal system. She recognized the handwriting.
She opened it carefully, and unfolded the cheap brown sheet
of paper, neatly covered with handwriting. She took a sip of
wine as she began to read.

"Stalingrad, 9 January, 1943.

Dear Sister,

The quartermaster of our company has arranged
for our mail to be flown out on one of the planes taking
out the wounded. This is the toughest battle our unit
has fought, and we may be here for a while longer.
There has been a lull in the fighting since last night,
so this is a good time for me to write you these words.
Our letters will be collected an hour from now, so we
are all writing home quickly.

You will have read about the battle in the
newspapers at home. I do not have to describe to you

how intense the house-to-house combat has been. Our
soldiers have experienced terrible wounds, lack of
food and ammunition, but you have no idea how tough
we are. The Russians have been unable to recapture
those parts of the city which we have fortified. We are
waiting now for reinforcements. The *Luftwaffe* is
dropping us supplies by parachute.

Whenever I have a minute to rest, I think of you.
You must be doing very important medical work. In
my mind, I try to imagine the day when I will return
to Germany and be with you. You will tell me all
about your scientific experiments and achievements,
and I will bore you with stories of my battle victories.

I must close now. It is so cold that I can barely
write. My fingers are numb. When I lick the
envelope closed, perhaps my tongue will be frost-
bitten? Just a joke.

With love from your brother,
Werner."

She started to put the letter back in the envelope. Then
she heard the word 'Stalingrad' on the radio newscast, and
turned up the volume.

"The German Sixth Army continues its glorious resistance
at Stalingrad. Our troops are being successfully re-supplied by
air as they wait for Field Marshal von Manstein to link up with
General Paulus inside the city. The battle will forever shine as
one of the greatest feats of arms in German history." The refrains
of the *Horst Wessel Lied* filled the airwaves.

Marlene knew that the report could not be true. She had
heard from other doctors that Stalingrad was completely
surrounded. The wounded were no longer being evacuated by
air. She now felt sure that she would never see her brother again.

She sat back, twirling the wine glass, thinking about the
days before the war, when she had been in medical school in
Berlin. She had gone home to her parents' house in the Ruhr

once a month for the week-end. Werner, younger by three years, had just joined the Army. He was in the elite group of Panzer Grenadiers, and he looked so handsome in his uniform. Together with their parents, they had spoken of all the wonderful things that were happening to Germany since the Fuhrer had come to power.

She felt numb. Those sunny, hope-filled days were gone forever, gone when both her parents had been killed in a British air raid, gone now with her brother's disappearance at Stalingrad. Marlene raised her right hand in a last salute to them and vowed that she would live up to their expectations. They would have been so proud of her.

JUNE, 1944

TULLE, FRANCE

Within hours of the Allied landings on D-Day, the SS *Das Reich* Division, bivouacked in Toulouse, was ordered to break camp and make its way north to the Normandy battlefield. This was one of the most seasoned fighting forces in the entire German Army. It had fought valiantly in Russia and had born the brunt of the fighting, along with two other SS divisions, at the battle of the Kursk Salient the year before.

The refitting period in Toulouse had been well-used; the division again had its full complement of Panther tanks, and the officer cadre, having experienced a high casualty rate in Russia, was now re-staffed with officers transferred from other SS units. By road and by rail, this powerful force of fourteen thousand men began to make its way up through the center of France.

As some of the forward elements approached the region known as the Limousin, they were attacked by French resistance fighters. The arrival there of the main body of the Division was slowed down by the local *Maquis* who mounted night-time attacks on German encampments, railway lines, and bridges and harrassed them with sniper bullets. The situation became so serious that *Das Reich* fell behind by days, not hours, in its planned arrival south of Caen in Normandy.

On the night of June 7th, along a main road near Tulle, a small group of the French resistance placed mines which, a few hours later, destroyed three trucks and killed seven German soldiers. The next morning, reprisals were ordered by Colonel Joachim Meinhaft. One hundred men from Tulle were seized at random, and 99 were hanged or shot. Three days later, on June 10th, in a horrible repetition, but on a far greater scale, the entire population of the village of Oradour-sur-Glanes, including 190 children, was murdered by the SS troopers. Colonel Meinhaft watched from his command car while the village burned to the ground.

The Division extricated itself from the Limousin and moved quickly up through the flat, open country of the Loire valley on its way north. Colonel Meinhaft gave little thought to the brutal killings he had ordered en route. It never crossed his mind that Germany might lose the war, and that, when it did, he would become a criminal to be hunted down and tried for crimes against humanity.

CHAPTER FIVE

———————⟨⟩———————

LIBERATION

SEPTEMBER, 1944

LONDON

Four years of rationing, bombing and sacrifice had cast a grayish tinge over London: buildings were battered and unpainted, cars and buses were unwashed and rusting, and people's faces reflected their fatigue.

The elation which had followed the successful landings in Normandy and the breakthrough into the heart of France had dissipated by the time that the Germans sent their first V-I unmanned 'flying bombs', known to Londoners as 'doodlebugs', diving into south-east England. It seemed as if the Germans had an inexhaustible supply of nasty surprises.

The land war in Europe came to a standstill. Even as Belgium was being liberated, it became obvious to Eisenhower and his staff that getting across the Rhine was the key to the end of the European conflict. The Rhine, which extended from the Swiss border to the North Sea, formed a formidable defensive line behind which the Germans were regrouping.

Field Marshal Montgomery developed a plan for the Allies to break across the Rhine, known as Operation Market Garden, and presented it to Eisenhower on September 9, 1944. In essence, it called for the largest air drop of the war and the subsequent seizure of the bridges across the three arms of the Rhine. The American 101st and 82nd Airborne

Divisions were to capture the bridges over the Maas and the
Waal rivers. The northernmost target was the city of Arnhem,
which had a large, modern steel bridge across the Rhine. The
British First Airborne Division was given the task of dropping
into Arnhem, seizing the north end of the bridge, and holding
it until the arrival of land forces from the south.

Planning for the audacious attack began immediately. The
drop was scheduled for Sunday, September 17. All front-line
units were brought to the ready: the British armored forces
were poised on the Belgian border, and U.S. and British
airborne troops were assembled at airfields throughout
southern England. The Dutch military administration, lacking
fighting units to place in the front lines, was nonetheless
brought into the planning. The liberation of areas of Holland
recently occupied by the Germans required immediate relief
measures to deal with hunger, sickness, demolished utilities,
and transportation. In addition, the Dutch would need to
pursue German stragglers and Dutch Nazi sympathizers.

Harrington House was a substantial and elegant office
building of a type built in the better London neighborhoods
before the war. Along with two smaller facilities also in the
West End, it had become the nerve center of the Dutch
government-in-exile. As demands for logistical support had
grown, every available space of every floor in Harrington
House had been stretched to capacity. Desks encroached on
corridor areas, broom closets were filled with bulky telex
equipment, and temporary wiring dangled in untidy bunches
along the ceilings. Competitive jockeying for space was at a
peak and was only slightly relieved by the move of some of
the Dutch Army General Staff to Eisenhower's headquarters
on the continent outside of Brussels.

Major Eduard Seventer's office at Harrington House was
small, but some of his former colleagues from the Treasury
section were still envious of his status as a senior staff member
of the Dutch Army Military Administration. In late 1943, he
had been sent to a training camp in Northampton, run by

some very tough British sergeant-majors with no sense of humor. At the end of the seven-week indoctrination, he received his officer's commission and was given a dress uniform with Dutch Army sleeve patches and pips on the collar, a Sam Brown belt, a swagger stick, a Browning revolver with its holster, and an ID card labeled "Allied Forces-Netherlands Contingent." Then he was sent back to London, where he learned that he had earned himself a private office on the second floor of Harrington House, a decided improvement on shared space on the fifth floor.

Seventer was busy, involved, and willing to be sent on any assignment which would hasten his return to Holland. He had even volunteered for active duty in the Navy but had been turned down because of his age and lack of big ship experience. The Army's Military Administration unit, established in 1943 in preparation for the liberation of the Netherlands, was his best alternative.

He looked back on his early months in London after the fall of France in June, 1940, as the bleakest of his life. He rented a small flat near Regent's Park, on Gloucester Place. It was shabbily furnished, heated by a small gas heater which required a shilling for its feeble flame to flicker for about an hour. Thanks to van Meeren, who had advanced him the funds, Seventer purchased a basic wardrobe. Within two weeks of his arrival in London, he was employed by the Dutch Government-in-Exile in its financial affairs section. Since the bureaucratic apparatus of the government had remained in The Hague, the London-based organization had to make the best of those Dutchmen who found themselves, like Seventer, stuck in England. The hours were long, and the work was often boring. After the Blitz started in September, Seventer also learned how to put in a full day of work while having his sleep continuously disrupted by the German bombing, which generally started at 7 p.m. and continued into the early hours of the following morning.

There was some occasional relief from the dreadful monotony. London was full of Dutch people like himself, refugees trying desperately to fit themselves into a strange world of bombing, dangerous missions, and increasing shortages. Many of them, like Seventer, had left wives and families behind. The Dutch Government published a directory which noted all those who were in London without their wives. It was a small consolation for Seventer that he was not the only one to be so painfully separated. There were rounds of cocktail receptions and dinner parties which Seventer attended because he met interesting and amusing people from many countries, all at war against a common enemy. Sometimes he went to a movie or a play with friends.

His enforced celibacy was extremely troublesome to him. Yet he was incapable of the impetuous, tomorrow-we-die affairs which he often saw around him. He concentrated his mind and heart on Louisa. He still couldn't believe that he had left Amsterdam without a picture of her in his wallet; he was only going to be gone overnight, after all. He wrote to her after hearing that the Red Cross sometimes managed to get some mail delivered into the occupied territories. A letter had arrived from her at the Mathijs Smithson office early in 1941, but nothing since then.

Morale in London soared twice in 1941: the first time, in June, when Hitler made the huge miscalculation of ordering the invasion of Soviet Russia. The second occurred on December 7, when the attack on Pearl Harbor brought the United States into the war against Germany. Even though there were many more dark moments in 1942, final victory was no longer a pipe-dream. By 1944, Seventer allowed himself the occasional fantasy about his return to Louisa and their home. He had to find a way to accelerate that return.

———<>———

Seventer was at a meeting with some Belgian colleagues when he was summoned to the office of General Haarema. Excusing himself, he walked down the carpeted stairs, along the hushed corridor, and knocked on the door that said 'Deputy Chief of Staff—Army'. He walked in without waiting for an answer, and the general's secretary told him to proceed into the inner office.

General Haarema stood up, walked around his desk to shake Seventer's hand, and pointed to a chair. "Good morning, Major. Something important has come up. Would you like a cup of coffee?" Seventer was not one to refuse an offer of real coffee, which was scarce in wartime. Haarema gave his secretary the request and turned around to seat himself in a chair facing Seventer.

"Let me explain. The Allies are preparing a major offensive to capture the Rhine bridges. Once we control them, there is nothing to stop us from going all the way into the Ruhr and on to Berlin. Let me show you on the map."

Haarema walked over to a table covered with a large-scale map of the Netherlands. "You can readily understand," Haarema continued, pointing at the city of Arnhem, "that the Allies are going to pivot to the right after they have captured the last bridge over the Rhine. That is the shortest route to the Ruhr and thence, to Berlin. We are under no illusions that the liberation of north Holland is a secondary priority for the Allies. Even though the Scots and the Canadians covering Montgomery's left flank are poised to penetrate in the direction of Rotterdam, they will also have to swing to the right. Our assessment is, therefore, that northwest Holland will be by-passed and may not be liberated for weeks, possibly months, if the fighting bogs down.

"The situation in Holland is bad and getting worse. We need someone who can give us an independent assessment of the situation behind the front lines, someone who can tell us with as much accuracy as possible what our military administration units will be faced with when the remaining

Dutch territory is finally liberated. The local underground is still very effective, but their few people are too isolated to collect the facts, analyze them, and come to the right conclusions about what the situation would be at the end of the war. We also believe that the Germans have infiltrated some of our informant networks. We need new blood in the system. You are not someone they know, and Seventer, we have very little time."

Seventer felt a surge of excitement within him. After the years of frustration, he would see Louisa much sooner than he had expected. "Of course I will do whatever is required, sir."

General Haarema continued. "I need you in Brussels by tonight. As usual, the weather is not cooperating, and although we have a plane on stand-by, I can't afford any delay at all. Take only the essentials. One of our staff cars will drive you to your flat and wait for you. You will be driven to Harwich, where a Royal Navy MTB is waiting to take you across to Ostend. It will be late by the time you arrive, but another car will take you directly to Dutch Military Headquarters in Brussels. There, you will meet with Colonels de Boer and Witt."

Seventer stood up, and saluted. Haarema also stood and offered his hand. "Our thanks, and God be with you."

Seventer thought about the old-fashioned parting as he left the room.

———<>———

BRUSSELS

The camouflaged Humber came to a dignified stop in front of the bland-looking building on the Avenue de Tervuren. It was 1.02 a.m. Rain swept the broad street in periodic gusts. The sergeant walked around to open the passenger door, but Seventer had already stepped out. The sergeant, reached in for Seventer's bag, handed it to him, and bade him a polite goodnight. Seventer walked up to the front door and rang the bell. Within seconds, the door was opened by a Dutch soldier.

"Major Seventer," he said, not questioning. Seventer nodded to him, but refrained from responding. He was too tired. He had enjoyed the long trip across the North Sea in the MTB. He had never been in a boat that went so fast, the thrumming of its diesel engines overpowering the crashing of the hull through the short, steep waves. The British crew had loved showing off, although they admitted, after they had discovered that he was Dutch, that the Royal Dutch Navy also operated some of these craft, "quite well, actually." But the ride had been rough. Then, the car had crept along, with dimmed headlights, from Ostend to Brussels. It had been a long day.

At the top of the staircase, he was led into a comfortable sitting room. The lights were low, and the pungent odor of tobacco reminded him suddenly of the homeland he had left four years ago. Another door opened, and two officers entered. Both were colonels. They were in 'battle-dress', the informal uniform of the British Army, which the Dutch, amongst others, had adopted as their own. Seventer recognized de Boer immediately; he had been a successful architect in pre-war Holland. The other man was small, his face reminiscent of a beaver's. They introduced themselves: Colonel Witt was head of Dutch Military Intelligence, and de Boer was Deputy Chief of Staff of Military Administration.

"Thank you for coming, Seventer. You must be tired. We have a lot to do tomorrow morning, so we will let you get to bed. The orderly will wake you at 0630 hours." Seventer withdrew with a polite goodnight, having decided that Witt was not going to be easy to deal with.

He was awakened by a knock on the door. He took a long bath, suspecting that it might be his last for a long time. He dressed, made sure that his khaki tie was properly knotted, buffed his army-issue cordovans, and left the room. At the bottom of the staircase, he was met by the same orderly who had been on duty the previous night. In the dining room, the buffet table offered a large assortment of breads, cheeses, and jams. As he sat down, the two colonels he had met the night before walked in together. Seventer wondered what they would do in peacetime when they had to resume their separate lives.

Witt greeted him, took a sip of his coffee, and sat back in his chair. He spoke abruptly. "General Haarema informed you of the Allied plan to capture the bridges over the Maas, the Waal, and the Rhine. The attack will consist of paratroop landings near Eindhoven, Nijmegen, and Arnhem. The British XXX Corps, consisting of heavy tank formations, will punch through the Dutch border and race to meet up with the troopers in each of the drop zones, clearing the road all the way to Arnhem. You must understand that this plan requires very precise execution for all the moving parts to come together.

"We scanned the early morning intelligence reports before we came into breakfast. They were not encouraging. What we cannot understand is why the Germans have started to build up their forces around the Arnhem drop-zone without having been tipped off. Apparently some SS Panzer units have moved into the area."

"Our major concern, however, is this," interjected Colonel de Boer. "The country will soon be in a transportation gridlock. The Dutch railroad workers are preparing to go on strike. The Germans will have to move everything by road. Food and fuel will no longer be moving to the cities, and shortages will quickly become acute. We need to know how bad the gridlock will be and how long the main cities can last without being re-supplied. None of our agents can give us a feel for the big picture. We need every piece of intelligence we can get."

"Where do I begin?" asked Seventer.

"You have to get yourself to Amsterdam, where you will establish yourself. We still have two or three reliable Underground units in that area. Your objective, after making contact with them, will be to collect all the information you can about German activities, living conditions, and the effectiveness of our underground. We need particular verification of food and medical supplies. After breakfast, we will show you our list of requirements. We will also provide you with a list of contacts with radio transmitters and safe houses, which you must memorize."

"I understand," replied Seventer, "but how am I supposed to get through the lines?"

Witt exchanged a glance with de Boer and continued, "We are sending you through the front lines with a controversial character. He is an important member of the Dutch underground, but frankly, we are concerned by the ease with which he seems to be able to move around between the Allied and German lines. We call him King Kong because of his huge size. His real name is Christiaan Lindemans. He is due here sometime today. Oddly enough, he does not work for us, but for a Canadian officer in British Military Intelligence. King Kong has been instructed by the Brits to check in with us when he has finished de-briefing them. We have arranged for him to take you back into Holland late tonight. He claims that he can get you across the Rhine. After that, you'll be on your own."

"How do I know that he isn't going to turn me over to the Germans immediately after we cross the lines?"

"You don't." Witt was utterly without sympathy.

"How do I travel around inside Holland? If the trains are on strike, there are not too many alternatives, are there?"

"Use your ingenuity," Witt replied. "The bicycle is probably the only other choice." Seventer was clearly not satisfied with the answer.

"How long am I supposed to stay in Amsterdam once I get there?"

De Boer spoke up. "The Germans are showing signs of exhaustion. They cannot hold back the Russians. The British and Americans, once they are over the Rhine at Arnhem, will bring unbearable pressure from the west. It is our collective judgement that the war will be over by Christmas. Therefore, there will be no need to bring you out of Holland. Do you see?"

The room was quiet. The breakfast had been cleared. De Boer had started a pipe. Witt lit up another cigarette. Seventer knew that he had to go, no matter what the risks.

Witt cleared his throat. "Let's go to my office for the full briefing. Later this morning, you will go to see Major Koopman. He is responsible for covert operations and will give you forged identity papers. You will cross the border in your uniform, then change into civilian clothes. We are giving you the identity of Jan Flieger, a Catholic priest. Sounds silly, but you wouldn't believe how often that disguise has fooled the Germans, at least initially. I don't have to tell you that the minute you are out of uniform, you could be arrested as a spy and shot. Hopefully, the clerical garb will give you a little more protection."

Seventer squirmed. "But I'm a Protestant. Can't I at least be a pastor?"

"Sorry, we ran out of those. We only have Catholics available now." Witt paused and allowed himself a slight smile. "This afternoon, you will be studying maps to help you memorize the roads you will need to use, and we will instruct you in the use of wireless transmitters. Colonel de Boer, you and I will then meet for supper to review everything. King Kong is expected here this evening. You will leave with him tonight."

"When will the attack be launched?" asked Seventer.

The two colonels looked at each other. Then de Boer said, "Shortly."

———<>———

SOERENDONK, HOLLAND

The night was calm, with scarcely a rustle of wind. King Kong was more enormous than Seventer could have imagined. Seventer kept peering at him as they made their way through the dark countryside. The man was wearing a Canadian uniform. His shoulders were unnaturally wide, his steps long and confident, and his huge head was bent forward as he walked, like the Hollywood gorilla after whom he had been nicknamed. He was astounded by the energy of the man's movements. Seventer had to keep reminding himself that this monster was an ordinary Dutchman. De Boer and Witt were right. King Kong was some kind of a Neanderthal throwback.

As they turned a corner on the narrow, brick-paved country road, a voice hailed them from the darkness: "*Halt, wer da?*"

"*Isolde*," replied King Kong.

Two German soldiers stepped out into the road, their characteristic steel helmets outlined against the starlit sky. One of them played a flashlight on King Kong, then turned it on Seventer, who, like King Kong, was wearing battle dress but with Dutch, rather than Canadian, insignia. The flashlight waved back to King Kong.

"You just went through here this morning, *nicht wahr?*"

"Yes, now get out of my way." The two soldiers turned off the flashlight and stood aside for them to pass.

King Kong strode off down the road, followed by Seventer. They came to a crossroads. A small cottage stood to one side. They walked up to it, and King Kong opened the unlocked door. He found a candle on a table, lit it, and turned to Seventer.

"My instructions are to get you over the Rhine. I can get you through the German roadblocks and across the bridges, but after that you will be on your own. This is where you change out of that uniform. From this point on, it won't save you from the firing squad." King Kong walked through a door at the side of the room and disappeared.

Seventer brought out the black suit and clerical collar which had been prepared for him in Brussels. He was extremely worried. Which side was King Kong on? He certainly had the inside track with the Germans.

The man reappeared with a bottle of Dutch gin in his hand. His face was flushed. Even though it was a cool September night, King Kong was sweating profusely. He had torn his tie away from his collar and unbuttoned his uniform down to the belt. His thick brown hair, parted high on his scalp, stuck out on each side of his enormous skull like a pair of clipped wings. The small black eyes peered out from the oversized face. "You look stupid dressed like that."

Seventer remained silent. There was no point in picking a fight with the man. "Have a drink," continued King Kong, offering him the bottle.

"No thanks. We've got to get going."

"Don't tell me what to do," roared King Kong. "I'm the most valuable intelligence agent the Allies have in Holland." He took a long drink from the bottle. "I call the shots. Understand?" He put the bottle down on the small table and sat down. He looked up at Seventer. Slowly, he swung his beefy right arm around and pointed to a small sofa in the corner of the room. "Go over there, and sit down. I have something I need to do before we go any further." He took another drink. "What work did you do before the war?" he demanded.

"I was a banker in Amsterdam."

King Kong started to smile slowly. "I knew it! Well, do you want to know what I was?" Not waiting for an answer, he continued, "I was an auto mechanic in Rotterdam." He paused. "In Rotterdam, we didn't like people from Amsterdam."

Seventer couldn't believe he was sitting in some obscure village, somewhere in Holland, listening to this obnoxious lout. Perhaps he should let King Kong drink himself to sleep. But he knew that he still had to cross the three arms of the Rhine in order to reach Amsterdam. Bridges were heavily defended, and he didn't know where to find the ferries, if there were any. He needed King Kong. He had to put up with him a little longer.

Suddenly King Kong stood up. "Wait for me outside," he ordered.

Seventer did as he was told. The night air felt refreshing. Seventer's thoughts turned to Louisa. The events of the last few hours had given him little time to think about how close he was to seeing her. She had been so beautiful in her sleep when he had left her that morning in Amsterdam, more than four years ago. At least she was with her parents. Would Louisa understand that he had been frantic to find a way back to her? He wondered if the years had changed her as much as they had changed him. Apart from that heavily censored letter from her in 1941, he had had no other word.

Minutes had gone by without any sign of life from King Kong inside the house. Seventer walked back to the door and opened it a crack, straining to listen. He could hear muffled laughter. With his hand still on the door handle, Seventer saw the gorilla-man coming out of the side room, pulling up his trousers. He was laughing as he closed his fly. From the back room, Seventer heard a woman's voice say in Dutch, "Come back quickly, sweetie."

Seventer took a moment to grasp the situation and exploded with anger. "You stupid ape! You had a woman in there listening to everything? What the hell d'you think you're doing anyway? You have compromised my plan, and God knows what else . . ." Seventer didn't finish. King Kong lunged at him and grabbed him by the throat. Seventer could smell the man's foul breath.

"I could kill you right now if I wanted to." The huge hands tightened around Seventer's throat. "I've told you before; this is my show. You will play it my way." The hands relaxed. King Kong backed off and laughed again. "Maybe you need a woman to quiet you down, eh?"

He turned towards the little room and shouted, "Hey, *schat*, you want to take care of this pipsqueak? He's real small; it shouldn't take you long." King Kong roared with laughter. Then he grabbed Seventer's coat and shook him.

"My first job is to get rid of you. There are two bicycles outside. We still have about four hours before dawn. You will follow me. When we get to the first bridge at the Maas, I'm going to turn you over to a German soldier who works for me. He has a motorcycle with a sidecar. He will take you across the second bridge over the Waal, and then, over the Rhine bridge at Culemborg. He will claim that he is taking you to Lieutenant-Colonel Giskes, head of the *Abwehr* in Driebergen. There won't be a problem. After you are over that bridge, he will drop you off. Then you'll be on your own, pipsqueak!"

"Wait a minute. I can't walk the rest of the way!"

King Kong snickered. "Maybe you want to tell me what your final destination is? Perhaps I can help?"

Seventer realized that King Kong already knew too much. He prevaricated, "I need help to get to Utrecht. I can handle everything on my own after that."

"Utrecht wasn't in the plan. How am I supposed to get him to take you there? Do you have any money on you?"

"I'll give you fifty guilders, take it or leave it. For that, he drops me off in the center of Utrecht."

"It's a deal," answered King Kong, pocketing the money. He shed his Canadian uniform, putting on a worn, blue serge suit, and walked to the door of the back room. "*Tot straks, liefje,*" he cooed to his invisible bedmate. She replied with something incomprehensible. He roared with laughter again.

——————<>——————

UTRECHT

Seventer hadn't been in Utrecht in a long time. He was in the downtown area, where the inhabitants moved slowly through another day of occupation and hardship. He needed to procure a bicycle; there was no other form of transportation. He walked around the corner to the market square. A few stores were open. He spotted a stationery shop, walked inside, and greeted an older lady behind the counter.

"Good morning, Reverend Father."

"Good morning, Mevrouw. Perhaps you could tell me where I could buy a bicycle in this neighborhood. I don't know my way around Utrecht very well."

"You want to buy a bicycle?" The woman looked at him carefully. "And where might you be from?"

"Amsterdam," he replied truthfully.

"Well then you'd better go back there because we haven't seen a bicycle for sale in at least two years. There are two ways to get bicycles around here: steal them or inherit them. That's it. And half the time the Germans will commandeer them right out from under you."

"I see. Thank you. I suppose I will have to walk."

"Yes, I suppose you will, just like everybody else." She crossed her arms and stared at him.

Seventer realized that he would have to steal a bicycle. He walked quickly, scanning the streets for any opportunity to make off with someone else's essential transportation. He saw only one Dutch policeman along the way and no German soldiers.

The further he got from the city center, the more frequent became the rows of tidy homes with pocket-size gardens. On this early September day, the trees and lawns were still green. Suddenly, out of the corner of his eye, he saw a bicycle with tall handlebars, a man's bike, just what he needed. It was leaning against a garden fence. In full daylight, the chances of his being seen were high. There was no sign of life inside the house, so he quickly grabbed the handlebars, pushed the bicycle into the street, hopped on the seat, and started pedaling as fast as the old-fashioned machine would let him.

Every muscle in his body strained as he picked up speed. He came to the street corner, turned sharply right as two ladies started to cross in front of him and headed straight for the road to Amsterdam. He was not in the best of shape, and sitting at a desk in London for weeks on end had not helped. Now he was asking his body to perform at peak level. He felt conspicuous and was thankful when other riders came into view.

By now, the houses were further apart. He came to a fork in the road, and with some hesitation, took the narrower one to the left. It was a country lane, shaded by overhanging trees. The road to Amsterdam was the wider one which he had just left, but he feared that he might run head on into a German army unit. He wondered whether he had made a mistake in thinking this smaller road might parallel the larger one. On one side of the road the trees grew thickly, and he could not see through them. He had almost determined to double back to the crossroads when he heard the deep growl of large engines. The sounds seemed to be coming from the other side of the trees to his right. He stopped the bike and waited, listening.

Seventer heard voices close to him. The hair on the back of his neck started to prickle. They were speaking German, and he had no difficulty understanding them.

"He wants all the equipment backed into the woods and covered with brush."

"But there's nothing going on. Why bother?"

"He's worried about British reconnaissance aircraft. They've been flying over Holland these last few days."

"All right, let's move."

Orders went down the line. The clatter of tank tracks was audible. Seventer jumped off his bike, dropped to his knees and peered through the bushes. There was no mistaking the uniforms. Seventer craned his neck a little further to get a better look at the area. Now he could see at least ten big tanks, some smaller vehicles, and two command cars. This was not some small, isolated unit.

He knew he had seen enough. Slowly he backed out of the underbrush into the road. The countryside was quiet again. The Germans had shut their tank engines off to avoid any risk that a plane might observe their exhausts. Seventer knew he had to get away, quickly.

The German soldiers stepped into the lane ten yards from where he was. They held rapid-fire Schmeissers in their hands, pointed straight at him. From behind him, he heard the rustle of leaves and turned around to see several similarly-armed soldiers form up behind him. An overwhelming feeling of despair crept over him.

"*Was machst du hier?*"

Seventer realized that he had to play his role, the role of a lifetime. There might still be a chance of survival.

"I am a priest. I am going back to my church." Seventer was thankful that he had been properly coached in Brussels.

"Let's see your papers." This was the standard question in occupied Europe.

Seventer dug into his pockets. "Here you are," he answered in Dutch. In Holland, there wasn't much point in pretending that you couldn't understand German, since most people could. One of the German soldiers took his identity card, carefully doctored in Brussels by the forgers now employed by Dutch Military Intelligence.

"This says that your home address is in Maarn. Where is that?" Seventer recalled the argument about how they should pick his home town. ("Use a really obscure place. The Germans won't know where it is, and the Dutch police won't admit to not knowing.")

"It's twelve kilometers to the east from here."

"What were you doing on this road?"

"I had a meeting in Utrecht with my bishop."

———<>———

BRUSSELS

"Any word from Seventer yet?"

"Nothing yet, Colonel."

Witt got up, strode out of his office, down the hall and entered Colonel de Boer's office without knocking.

"Goddammit, we should have heard from Seventer hours ago. I knew we shouldn't have used an amateur."

"Come on, Harry, we're all amateurs. So there is no sign of him?"

"Nothing. I had Station 7 on the radio a few moments ago. They could only transmit for a minute. They say the German radio direction finders are all over the place. Anyway, they have heard nothing from Seventer and probably won't; their radius of effectiveness has been seriously curtailed."

"Maybe we should wait another day," suggested de Boer.

"Either we hear from Seventer soon, or we won't hear from him at all. Trust me."

The two men stood silently, discouraged and frustrated.

"You know what," said Witt, "I think we should arrest that creep King Kong. He is due back tonight. He could have fingered Seventer to the Germans."

De Boer thought for a minute and nodded. "I agree. Let's get a detachment of *Maréchaussées* up here to grab him. We can't afford to dither. We'll lock the guy up on suspicion and sort it out some other time."

"You had better call your friend Brigadier Sharp to tell him that his pet Dutch spy has, shall we say, met with an accident?"

For the first time in the last few days, the two colonels smiled.

————<>————

NEAR UTRECHT

At the headquarters of the 4th Panzer Division, Major-General Klaus von Bissach looked up from his desk when he heard the knock on the door. "*Herein!*" he ordered.

"It is me, General," his adjutant said as he hurried into the large, oak-paneled room. "One of our units has just brought in a Dutch priest for questioning. He was found on a side road, close to the 2nd Battalion camp. He says his parish is in Maarn. What should we do with him?"

"We're not equipped to handle this sort of thing. Turn him over to the *Abwehr*. Get rid of him."

"*Jawohl, mein General.*" The adjudant clicked his heels, turned, and left the room.

———<>———

DRIEBERGEN, HOLLAND

Lieutenant-Colonel Giskes twirled a paper-cutter between his thumb and index finger. Opposite him sat Major Fasslieb. He was consulting a file.

"There is nothing on this priest they picked up outside Utrecht. His documents look genuine. He's in good health. His clothes are worn. On the face of it, he looks and acts like whom he says he is. We are checking with the Bishopric in Utrecht. Their office is only open twice a week, so we'll have to wait till Tuesday. He says he lives in a rented room in a small town east of Utrecht, near his parish."

Giskes thought for a moment. "You'd better check out his residence. He has no family?"

"None that he has admitted to."

"Sounds like we might be wasting our time, but then, you never know. We have a lot on our plate. Speaking of which, do you have today's report on sorties flown over Holland by the R.A.F.?"

"Well, just as you suspected, something must be cooking. King Kong is going over again tonight, so we should be able to get an update from him."

"You know what, Major? I think we should have the Gestapo check out our friend, the priest. We have too much to do. They enjoy spending their time 'interviewing' people." The two men laughed.

"Put the good father in the cooler for tonight, and call them up in the morning. Tell them we are delivering a priest to them. The *Abwehr* is too busy with more important matters.

They will love that!" The men laughed again. "Wanstumm will be furious and puff up like an adder. And maybe he'll burst someday." The roar of laughter was heard all the way down the corridor.

———<>———

AMSTERDAM

In the street, the usual parade of cars drew up to the curb, deposited their passengers, and drove over to the other side of the small square to park. Wanstumm had given strict instructions that the entrance to headquarters was to remain clear for him and important visitors. His car, commandeered during the invasion of France, was a front-wheel drive Citroen with a low center of gravity, capable of turning corners at the speeds he enjoyed. It was always ready for him and was the only car permitted to park at the curb.

An Army staff car drew up. The driver got out, walked around to the rear passenger door, and opened it to let out a young lieutenant, who in turn stood aside to allow Seventer to exit the car. Seventer was in handcuffs. He was thirsty and hungry, but as he looked up, he felt encouraged. He was on his home ground. The pale sun reflected on the buildings he remembered so well. The architecture was uniquely Dutch, and in particular, so typical of Amsterdam. The red brick buildings, the white window sashes, the heavily-shellacked front doors. He was home, although he would have preferred a different way of returning. With any bit of luck, he would talk himself out of this predicament, and then, he could go to Louisa in The Hague. If the German Army and their military intelligence had shown so little interest in him, why should the Gestapo?

The lieutenant took him by the arm and led him through the front door into a narrow hall.

"My name is Lieutenant Grieb. I'm from *Abwehr* headquarters. This prisoner is being delivered to you for questioning. We've had too much to do down at Arnhem today to mess around with small fry."

The plainclothes man at the desk looked up. "The British took you by surprise, didn't they?"

The *Abwehr* officer scowled. "Don't worry. We're taking good care of them."

The Gestapo agent picked up a pen and asked, "Name?"

"Father Jan Flieger."

"Address?"

The lieutenant handed over the ID card, and the agent wrote down the information carefully. The *Abwehr* lieutenant turned to the agent and said, "Here's the file. He was picked up under suspicious circumstances. If there is nothing wrong with him, don't bother us." He saluted and went back outside to the waiting car.

The Gestapo agent turned back and looked closely at Seventer. "Age?"

"39," replied Seventer truthfully.

The Gestapo agent got up. "Follow me." Seventer followed him along the hall and down the stairs to the basement level. The agent stopped at an open door with a key in his hand. Seventer could see one bare light bulb in the ceiling. He felt dizzy from the lack of sleep and food. It had been more than two days since he had eaten anything substantial. If he could just get some fried eggs on a piece of toast and some coffee, he would be fine.

The room was dark, small, and had a strange, musty smell to it. The hours went by. His thirst was becoming almost painful. Several times, he got up to try the door handle. Every time, he knew it would not yield. He also tried calling out. There were no sounds from the other side of the door. Could they have forgotten about him?

On another floor, Agent Ganz called Wanstumm on the phone. "He has called out a couple of times. I think we'll give him another hour."

"Don't waste too much time with him," ordered Wanstumm. "My feeling is that this guy is not important."

Ganz hung up and returned to the papers on his desk. He was going to conduct the first interrogation of the prisoner. He was very good at his work. It was unusual when he failed to break someone within the first two hours. He was increasingly aware of the pressure on him to expedite his work efficiently. The case-load had been very heavy during the last few weeks. The Dutch resistance was getting bolder. More able-bodied men were needed for work at slave-labor camps. Now the Germans had to cope with a national railroad strike.

Wanstumm had become increasingly demanding and unpredictable. He had ordered the public hanging of ten men from a near-by village. It was a waste; they should have been hanged in the large public square of a city like Haarlem where the example would have had more impact. When Wanstumm was edgy, Ganz knew he had better watch out for himself.

A little later, he looked at his watch and realized it was time to go downstairs to interrogate Flieger. He rang a bell on his desk, and one of his younger agents walked in.

"Let's go and take care of the Dutch priest. Here's the file. There's nothing on him, yet." They walked down the corridor as Ganz continued to talk. "He was picked up by our troops outside of Utrecht just before the attack at Arnhem. He claims he stumbled into them by accident, says he has a parish near Utrecht. They sent him to the *Abwehr*. That snake Giskes has had his hands full dealing with the British drop at Arnhem. So he sent the man to us. Just to annoy us, I suppose, because the man is probably a simpleton." He jabbed the other man in the ribs.

"Anyway," added Ganz as they turned down the corridor to Seventer's room, "We'll find out in a hurry. Let's not mess around. Wanstumm is not in a good mood."

As they opened the door, Seventer rose from his chair. "Please, my son, may I have a glass of water, and I need to go the bathroom."

Ganz had done this hundreds of times. "You may have some water soon, but first, your name, please."

"Reverend Jan Flieger."

"Date of birth?"

"21 June 1905."

"Address?"

"Paardeweg 26, Maarn."

"Occupation?"

"Priest."

"What is the name of your church?"

"St. John the Baptist." Seventer was licking his parched lips, hoping the answers were adequate.

"How long have you been there?" asked Ganz.

Seventer tried to remember his lines. "Since 1941. My predecessor died."

"Interesting," replied Ganz. "How many parishioners do you have?"

Seventer was becoming giddy. "About sixty. It's a very small place."

"Where were you before 1941?" asked Ganz.

"In Weert." He had been warned to limit every answer to a minimum. Offering information was often a way for the interrogator to expand the questioning.

"Recite the Creed in Latin," demanded Ganz brusquely.

Seventer remembered skating with one of his childhood friends on a canal on the outskirts of Amsterdam. The day before had been quite mild, and his father had warned him about weakness in some areas of the ice. He and Jan-Carel had gone anyway. They were skating quite fast when Jan-Carel had caught his skate in a weak spot, and had gone headlong into the wall along the side of the canal. The ice had started to crack loudly. Seventer had felt panic then, and he felt it again now. Was there any Latin he remembered from school?

"Credemo in Pater santo, et su Filius, et Spiritu santu, la ecclesia Romana, la renonciata de vivos extremos, et nihil sub rosa sic transit gloria." If Ganz were a Catholic, Seventer was a dead man.

Ganz stood up. "Maybe you are a priest, but you were caught in a forbidden war zone. When you have decided to tell us what you really know, rap three times on the door." He started to walk out. Seventer rose from his chair.

"My son, I am a simple country priest. I don't know much about these things. Please give me some water, and let me go to the bathroom."

"For all I care, you can go to the bathroom right here. No water until you tell us what you were really doing near our troops." Ganz had found that sounding repetitive was quite effective in questioning suspects. It was so simple, really, breaking people beyond their capacity to function normally. Ganz had his hand on the doorknob.

Seventer called out in panic, "Please, I can tell you something interesting, but please, I need a drink of water."

"That's better," thought Ganz. He nodded to the other agent. "Leave us alone." This was routine. The prisoner would suddenly feel that the odds had gotten better. It was now one-on-one.

"We do not want to harass someone needlessly." The relief on Seventer's face was obvious. "You must help us in whatever way you can. Then we will let you go. The Germans and the Dutch are fighting a common enemy, the British and the Americans. If you know anything about them, Father, tell me, and I will give you a *laissez-passer* which will insure that you won't be arrested again."

Seventer was exhausted. Something told him that this man would let him go if he came up with some kind of useful information. What could he give him?

Suddenly, it struck him. He had an ace in his hand, but he hadn't even realized it. "There is something I can tell you, my son. But first, I need that drink of water."

Ganz left the room, stepped into the corridor and ordered his assistant to bring some water. He re-entered the interrogation room and said to Seventer, "Water is coming. Now what is it that you wanted to tell me?"

The assistant entered the room with a pitcher of water and a glass. Seventer attempted to exert enormous self-restraint, but he gulped down two glasses of water immediately. He knew that the next few moments would be critical to his gaining his freedom. He said cautiously, "The *Abwehr* has an agent who has double-crossed them; I'm sure that he is also an agent for the Allies."

Ganz could not stop a look of satisfaction from spreading across his face. This was very promising. They were going to stick it to the *Abwehr*.

"Father, anything you tell us will be held in secrecy. If your story turns out to be true, you will be granted protection by the Gestapo."

Seventer took another long drink of water. His freedom, no, his entire future, depended on his getting this right. "A Dutchman has been crossing the German and Allied lines for the last four weeks. The Allies think he is working for them. The German Army, however, gave him their passwords so that he could get back through the lines and report to them."

Ganz had an instinct that this was good information. It would put Wanstumm in a very good mood. He stood up.

"What is the agent's name?"

"Christiaan Lindemans."

"How do you know him?"

"The man's girlfriend is from my parish."

"Is she there now?"

"I'm not sure. She moves around with him sometimes. She lives with her mother, who is very upset about the situation."

"Describe Lindemans to me."

"I've only seen him twice. He is over two meters tall, weighs well over 120 kilos, age about 38, dark hair, parted in the middle."

"How do you know he is a double agent?"

"I know he works for the *Abwehr* because he bragged to me one day that he had friends at the *Abwehr* headquarters in

Driebergen. He also seems to go through the Allied lines with no problem. Just two weeks ago, he brought some American cigarettes back with him. He said he had friends in all the right places."

That's when Ganz knew that this man's story rang true.

"Stay here. I have to consult with my chief." Ganz left the room, walked down the hall, up the stairs, and knocked at Wanstumm's office door.

"*Herein!*"

"Herr Wanstumm, I think the prisoner is who he claims to be. He has information about an agent named Christiaan Lindemans who works for the *Abwehr* and who is also working for the Allies. He says the man's girlfriend is from his village. If you agree, we will get all the information on the *Abwehr* agent. I don't think the priest is harmful."

"First, get the information. Then, I will decide what we do with this man." Wanstumm's lips narrowed. "Make no mistakes. These Dutchmen are not to be trusted."

"I understand, Herr Wanstumm. I am sure you will be pleased with the results."

———<>———

DRIEBERGEN

Lieutenant-Colonel Giskes picked up the phone.

"Colonel Giskes, this is Wanstumm in Amsterdam."

"Yes, Herr Wanstumm, what can I do for you?"

"Your favorite Dutch spy has been turned."

"What are you talking about?"

"Christiaan Lindemans, alias King Kong. I bet he doesn't show up again."

Giskes laughed to himself. This was a throw-away piece of information, but he would let Wanstumm believe that he had scored a coup.

"Perhaps you will be good enough to tell me how you received this information?"

"Let's just say it was a cooperative venture. I think your people should be more careful in selecting their agents."

"We are doing a good enough job at Arnhem, don't you think?"

"That's only because the SS were there to save the Army's skin."

"You know as well as I do, Herr Wanstumm, that there is still too much information leaking out of Holland because the Gestapo has been unable to shut down the clandestine radio transmitters. That is a very serious matter. Also, you had better make sure that this railroad strike gets stopped very soon. The Army can't move over the roads; they're too narrow."

"We've already executed two of the strike leaders. If they don't go back to work, we will use more persuasion."

"Then I wish you a good day. Goodbye, Herr Wanstumm."

"Too bad about King Kong. Goodbye, Colonel Giskes."

Giskes hung up the phone. If he were transferred soon, as he had requested, he would finally be rid of that creep, Wanstumm.

———<>———

AMSTERDAM

Seventer was so hungry he felt almost nauseated by the bread and tea that they brought him. He also needed to shave and wash. He could smell his dirty clothes. Louisa would be horrified to see him in this condition.

But first, he had to get out of Gestapo Headquarters. Ganz had questioned him again for over an hour. He had promised to let him go when the 'paperwork' was completed. Turning in King Kong was a masterstroke which he was sure Brussels and London would approve of. He had exploited the festering rivalries between two of the Reich's security organizations. He was pleased with himself. Within an hour, he would be on his way, cleared by the Gestapo, legitimately free to roam the country to complete the main part of his mission.

The knock on the door was a mere formality. Wanstumm walked in, accompanied by Ganz and another agent.

"Good-afternoon, Flieger," Wanstumm said. "My name is Wanstumm. I am head of the Gestapo here. Have you had a good meal?"

Seventer sized up the man: five foot ten, thinning blond hair carefully parted and pasted down around the cold, pale face, like a mannequin in a store window. He had a thin, wiry frame, and his delicate hands, with exceptionally artistic thumbs, could have been those of a surgeon's. The voice was high-pitched and reedy.

Seventer remained seated. Wanstumm remained standing. Wanstumm leaned over and suddenly shouted, "GET UP!"

Seventer, shocked by his tone of voice, knocked over his chair as he scrambled to his feet.

"If you know about this man, Lindemans, you must have other interesting things to tell us, *nicht wahr?*"

"I told you; that's all I know."

Wanstumm slapped him across the face. "You are not telling the truth."

"Please, I told your assistant everything I know; I gave him a full description. I swear the man was crossing the Allied lines. The Holy Father knows I speak the truth." Seventer's eyes were tearing from the sting to his cheek.

"You'll have to do a lot better than that. I have found that cutting off fingers, one by one, is a quick and trouble-free way of obtaining what I need to know. Show me your hands." Seventer swallowed the mounting bile in his throat. He had to think of something, anything. But if he tried to come up with some other piece of information, they would think he had even more to tell them. No, he had to make a stand. It was his only hope now.

"You can do what you want with me. Our Lord set an example of strength and faith. I shall follow in His path. I am an innocent man."

Wanstumm turned to Ganz. "Get him ready. I will be with you shortly." He stalked out of the room.

Suddenly the air raid siren sounded. Ganz looked up in annoyance. The British were at it again. They seemed to know exactly where to drop their bombs. He glanced at Seventer and hurried out of the interrogation room, turning the key in the lock behind him. Seventer let out a breath. Could this be the reprieve he so desperately needed?

The two bombs dropped away from the belly of the R.A.F. Mosquito and curved lazily downward. They landed on the building next to Gestapo headquarters. The explosion was ear-shattering. The naked light bulb hanging from the ceiling in Seventer's cell swung backwards and forwards. Seventer could hear men running down the corridor, shouting. Doors banged. He heard more running. He could smell acrid fumes seeping under the bottom of his door. He was trapped in the interrogation cell, terrified that he might be caught in a fire with no way to escape. The noise outside subsided, followed by complete stillness. The minutes ticked by. What was going on? Should he bang on the door? Would anyone hear him? He walked over to the door, grasped the handle and started rattling it. "Hey, out there; let me out!" he shouted. Nothing. He sat back down on the small wooden chair.

Two hours later, he heard steps outside. The door opened. It was Ganz.

"Well, Father, we have decided to let you go. We have other things to do right now. If you lied, if we catch you helping the underground, we will shoot you, but only after making you wish you had never lived."

Seventer's mind reeled. What had happened? Where was Wanstumm? Could he really believe them? Belatedly, he remembered that he had a role to play.

"Bless you, my son." Seventer followed Ganz out into the corridor and up the stairs to the main floor. How was he going to get to The Hague? He had to see Louisa first.

Outside, the street was cluttered with fire engines and other utility vehicles. The fire had spread. Now, smoke was also pouring out of several windows on the top floor of the Gestapo building. Nobody paid any attention to the priest.

Seventer walked down the street, leaving the shouting, gesticulating Germans behind him. He had to get to The Hague. He knew exactly where he was. His and Louisa's apartment was only a few blocks away, but he couldn't risk going there. He headed for the main road south out of Amsterdam. By following it, he figured he had the best chance of getting a lift to The Hague. He turned right on the Michel Angelostraat and crossed several intersections until he reached the Stadion Kade. The trees along the canal were still green. He remembered his childhood when this part of the city was being built. He and his friend Jan-Carel had raced through it on their first bicycles. Now, the streets were almost deserted.

The Gestapo could be watching him. His job was to contact the underground at an address in Amsterdam, but it was safer for him to be seen leaving the city. If he were convinced that they were not following him, he would head for The Hague and Louisa.

Seventer kept turning his head at the sound of traffic. Some streetcars were still operating, and a few German Army vehicles passed by. Who could give him a ride? He continued to walk. He heard the sound of an oncoming vehicle. It was a hearse. It slowed down and stopped when the driver saw Seventer's hand signal. Seventer walked around to the driver's side.

"I need a lift to The Hague," said Seventer. "Are you going in that direction?"

"Well, Father, it's a bit of a tight squeeze in here, but we can take you as far as Wassenaar. You'll be on your own after that."

———<>———

THE HAGUE

The van Dijck house looked exactly the way Seventer remembered it: the dark-green front door, the tall windows, the elegant gable outline of the roof. The trim, however, looked the worse for wear, and one of the upstairs windows was broken. That was odd; the van Dijcks always kept their house in perfect repair. There was a wet, cold wind coming in from the North Sea, blowing the dry leaves into sodden heaps. This street, like so many others, was deserted. Seventer's heart pounded as he approached the house. Would Louisa recognize him in his tattered clothes? It had been over four years now.

He looked up at the sound of an engine and saw a German *kubelwagen* coming in his direction. He remained stock-still, holding his breath. The vehicle slowed down, looked him over, and then drove past. He glanced up at the windows again. They were very dirty, and the paint was peeling off the shutters. As he walked up the front steps, he noticed that bunches of leaves had collected in the corners of the entry. Something was very wrong.

Seventer rang the doorbell. There was no sound. He started knocking on the door. He repeated it several times, each time increasing the force behind each knock. He stood back to look at the upper windows again. Where were the van Dijcks? Where was Louisa? The door of a house further down the street opened, and an old man looked out. He made a furtive sign to Seventer and quickly retreated inside his doorway. Seventer hurried down the street and stepped into the man's house. He soundlessly closed the door behind them.

The old man looked at Seventer suspiciously. "Who are you looking for?" he inquired. His eyes were red, and he started to cough.

"The van Dijcks," replied Seventer. "Where are they? What has happened?"

"First, tell me who you are," the old man asked.

"You may remember me; my name is Seventer; I am the van Dijcks' son-in-law."

The old man looked him up and down, not quite believing that this scruffy, unwashed man in clerical garb could be Louisa's husband. But the accent was educated.

"I thought you were in London? How did you get back here?" The man pulled a soiled handkerchief from his pocket and blew his nose.

"It's a long story. But first, please tell me what's happened? Where is my wife? Where are her parents?" Seventer sounded on the verge of panic.

Van Breem took him by the arm and led him into the parlor. It reeked of tobacco smoke. There were small Persian rugs on the floor, and one was draped over a table. "Please sit down. I'm afraid I don't have good news for you."

Seventer's apprehension was clearly etched in his face.

"First of all, your father-in-law died in 1941 of pneumonia. The doctors did everything they could, but to no avail." He paused. "Then, Gestapo agents came to the house in 1942. They had some questions about your work at the bank." Another pause. "They took Louisa to Gestapo Headquarters in Amsterdam for further questioning. She never returned."

Seventer felt a stab of terror. They had taken Louisa to Gestapo Headquarters? Oh God, what had they done with her? Where was she? Where had she been for two years?

"I'm so terribly sorry, Seventer. I wish I didn't have to be the one to tell you." Van Breem pulled his handkerchief out again and coughed deeply.

Seventer sat there, saying nothing. He put his head in his hands. He tried to hold back the tears that began to slide down the stubble on his cheeks. He lifted his head slowly, swallowing hard, and said slowly, "And my mother-in-law?"

"There was a terrible accident. She was found in her house by her sister two days after Louisa had been taken away. She was lying on the floor. She had broken her nose, and apparently, a blood clot had formed in her brain."

"So she was lying there dead for two days, and no one knew?"

"Sadly, that was the case. The Gestapo came back a few hours later after taking Louisa in for questioning. They tore the whole house apart; they broke through walls, ripped up floors. It was a terrible mess. Mevrouw van Dijck was there when they came. They must have killed her."

Silence enveloped the room. Seventer stared off into space, his jaw tightening. Van Breem blew his nose again. Wordlessly, he got up, went to a cupboard, and took out two glasses and a stone bottle. Returning to Seventer, he poured some of the clear liquid into a glass and handed it to him. "Here, a little *jenever* will taste good."

Seventer took the glass and drank the contents in one swallow. He coughed. "I'll have another if I may, please."

"Good, I'll join you." They sat in silence as they drank.

Van Breem got up again, and this time he found a small tin box in the closet. "Have a cigarillo," he offered. Seventer reached out and took one. Van Breem dug some matches out of his pocket. They lit up, the blue smoke eddying around the room.

Van Breem coughed and asked, "Do you have a place to stay?"

Seventer shook his head slowly. "I was on my way to Amsterdam."

Suddenly, the two men tensed at the sound of engines. Without warning, cars and motorcycles appeared on the street. German troops and Gestapo agents came cascading out of the vehicles. Wanstumm drove up a few minutes later, got out, and marched up the walk to the van Dijck house. Orders were shouted out to search every house on the street. Other orders were given to surround all the houses in the rear.

With extraordinary speed, van Breem got up from his chair and beckoned to Seventer to follow him. "Take your glass with you. Snuff the cigar out completely. Follow me," he whispered.

Seventer was dizzy from the *jenever* and stress, and now, here was another terrifying situation. He didn't think he could cope with any more. Silently, he followed van Breem up the stairs to the attic.

"Quick! Come in here, through this little passageway. At the end, you will find a small space. Close the metal door behind you." Seventer crawled through, breathing heavily, and almost collapsed as he pulled the door closed behind him. He could barely see except for the small ray of light coming from what looked like a crack in the side of the roof where the chimney met the tiles. He heard the pounding on the door downstairs.

"*Ja, ja,*" yelled van Breem as he hurried to open the front door. Two Gestapo agents and a soldier stood on the stoop. "We need to search your house," said one of them.

"Come in, come in. This is the third time you fellows have come around. Maybe I should give you a key to the place." He laughed sourly and coughed several times. They paid no attention to him, concentrating on opening every door, searching every closet, tipping over a chest of drawers, looking under the beds. Slowly they made their way up the stairs.

Van Breem sat down in his parlor and smoked his cigarillo. He had been through this before. They had never discovered the attic space where he had hidden an Allied airman, and later, two Dutch resistance fighters, while the Germans turned the neighborhood upside down. He took another sip of *jenever* to spike his confidence. Soon, he heard them coming down the staircase. He got up to hold the front door open for them. He could hear them talking to the Gestapo chief.

"Nothing in this house, either, Boss."

"I can't believe we missed him. He must be on foot. I want two of you down in the sewers. Search everything. I want guards at the end of every street in the whole neighborhood. Nobody will move without my permission. Is that clear?"

Wanstumm turned to Ganz. "You're an idiot! Obviously this priest they just saw trying to get into the van Dijck house has to be the same fellow you just interrogated and let go in Amsterdam. It can't be a coincidence. You blew it, Ganz, blew it! He must have been Seventer, that banker I've been looking for. You let him slide out of your grasp. Now I will have to turn The Hague upside down to find him." As an afterthought, he added, "If we don't find him in 48 hours, Ganz, you will find yourself on your way to the Russian front, on foot." Wanstumm marched back to his car, got in, and drove off in a fury.

By nightfall, most of the vehicles had left. Sentries had been posted at every street corner. It was virtually impossible for anyone to move through this part of town without being challenged. Upstairs in his little cell, Seventer waited patiently for van Breem to return. Intense anguish and worry about Louisa gnawed at him. Where was she? Had they hurt her during their interrogation? How could he possibly hope to find her if they had sent her to a work camp in Germany? Could the Gestapo chief who had questioned him yesterday in Amsterdam be the same man who had interrogated Louisa two years ago? Seventer felt a cold rage building up inside.

At midnight, Seventer heard van Breem on the other side of the small metal door whispering his name. He crawled out. "The Germans have given up the active search, but the whole area is filled with soldiers. You are going to have to stay here until further notice."

"Mijnheer van Breem, I don't know how to thank you. How long do you think they will keep watch?"

"In the past, it has been anywhere from two days to two weeks. I don't think they'll be here quite as long this time because they can't spare the soldiers any more. The Germans are under pressure everywhere. They are holding out in Arnhem, but I've heard rumors that they had to give up the bridge at Nijmegen. The Gestapo doesn't have all that many agents either. I want you to spend most of your time in the attic. You must not go near the windows. You'll have to bear with me. I've done this before."

"I must get to Amsterdam right away. I can't stay in hiding very long without compromising my mission." Seventer's anguish was increasing.

"Of course, of course," said van Breem soothingly. "But first of all, I think you should shave, take a bath, and put on some decent clothes. I don't mean to offend you, but you smell awful."

"Could I have something to eat, if that isn't asking too much?"

"We have very little left to eat in this part of Holland, Mijnheer Seventer. It will be worse with the onset of winter. But you are welcome to what I have. The bathroom is the first door on the right. I will bring you some clothes." Van Breem left the room, blowing his nose.

Half an hour later, Seventer was sitting at a small table in an upstairs room on the back side of the house. His clothes were worn and ill-fitting, but clean. The food was simple: a piece of fish, smoked to preserve it far longer than nature had intended, and two boiled potatoes.

Van Breem apologized. "I have a friend who gets the fish. The potatoes are still being sold at the market, but I've heard that there will be no more this winter. Frankly, if the Allies don't come soon, I think many of us will starve."

"But the farmers still have their cows and chickens, don't they?"

"The Germans have taken most of the cows to Germany. There may be a few chickens around, but I hear that when farmers run out of feed for them, they eat them then and there."

When Seventer had finished, van Breem took the empty plate downstairs. Seventer curled up on the bed, too exhausted even to conjure up nightmare visions of his gentle Louisa at the hands of the Gestapo.

———<>———

Two weeks later, van Breem stood in the foyer of his house. He watched as Seventer came down the stairs. He nodded approvingly as he inspected Seventer's clothes. They had been especially selected for their nondescript seediness. The scuffed shoes, the battered felt hat, and the ill-fitting suit were typical of the average Dutch male's attire at this stage of the war. Seventer's identity papers had been doctored by one of van Breem's friends to pass all but the most expert scrutiny. Not that identity papers provided any protection when the Germans were conducting their round-ups. Anyone caught in their net was deported to labor camps. But Seventer needed the papers to get through the check-points that the Germans threw up at random.

The two men shook hands and said goodbye. Van Breem had saved Seventer's life. Seventer wondered whether he would ever have a chance to thank the man properly after the war was over. Right now, he had to get on with his mission. He walked down the steps to a waiting bicycle, which van Breem had miraculously produced. The metal wheel rims were covered with strips of old rubber, lashed to the wheels with piano wire.

Seventer had no illusions about what lay ahead of him. Conditions in Holland were much worse than he could have possibly imagined. The Dutch were tired, hungry, and disheartened. He would be hard-pressed to pull together a small group and to keep them actively collecting the intelligence that London needed. He was an amateur, as they all were, but the knowledge that the Canadians were already fighting in the islands south of Rotterdam would keep them energized. The end now seemed in sight.

JANUARY, 1945

AMSTERDAM

Heinrich Wanstumm was a loyal Nazi. He would give his life for the Fuhrer, but he was also a realist. The failed Ardennes offensive, he now knew, had been the last major effort of the German Army to postpone its defeat. The news from Germany was appalling. Major cities including Hamburg and Stuttgart had been reduced to rubble by the Allied air forces. The Russians were already in Poland. On January 18, the German forces in Budapest surrendered to the Russians. Eisenhower's armies were now poised along the Rhine for the final assault on the German homeland.

In Northern Holland, the Dutch, weakened by almost total starvation, barely got through each passing day, dragging themselves about, simply waiting. Wanstumm knew the end was coming, and he began to plan methodically to save himself from certain arrest at the hands of the Allies. He was still young and resourceful. He smelled defeat now, but there would be another time for a *reinigung*, an ethnic cleansing, of every enemy of the Reich. Yes, the Reich would be born again. Right now, he had to have an escape plan for himself.

The two key elements of his survival, he had decided, were money and mobility. He set about the task with his usual efficiency. He had already stashed away a substantial amount of gold and banknotes in Pounds sterling and American dollars.

The gold was in the form of coins and wafers, a bit heavy but highly marketable.

Wanstumm had also acquired a handsome collection of small, transportable art objects and an impressive stamp collection. There had been some temptations, to which he had never succumbed, to augment his holdings by appropriating larger items such as impressive antique furniture or Persian carpets. What he chose to collect must fit into his car, since that would be his most likely means of getting away. His artistic appreciation had improved as a result of Gestapo raids on private homes during his four and a half years in Holland. Other than an occasional concert, or an evening with an anonymous woman, he had spent most of his leisure hours learning about his acquisitions.

In addition, he had, at least potentially, access to a very large amount of money deposited by Jews in British and American banks. Very carefully, he had compiled a list of all of the relevant documentation, concentrating on accounts which appeared to have balances in excess of $100,000. He knew that he would be called upon to provide proof of ownership. While he hadn't worked out every detail, he was already thinking about how he would claim the accounts. After all, who knew better than he that there were no living beneficiaries?

Two other questions needed to be addressed. The first, essentially a matter of last-minute judgement, was when to leave Amsterdam in his car. The other was where to go. At least initially, he would have to go to Germany, to his home state of Bavaria. He had lost his Bavarian accent but was capable of reverting to it. The closer he got to his home town of Memmingen, the better his chance of blending into the landscape. From there, he could plan his next move. He felt sure that a defeated Germany would be a difficult place to live in for many years to come. He had also heard reports about the treatment of Nazi officials captured in the liberated areas, and he was enough of a realist to recognize that his own life was at risk if he were caught by the Allies when they liberated Holland. He had to disappear.

By the end of January, 1945, he felt confident that he had thought of every detail. He had charted the Allied advances both on the eastern and the western fronts. The northern part of Holland was rapidly becoming strategically insignificant. It would be a matter of weeks before the Allies crossed the Rhine into Germany. Holland would be by-passed, and he would be stuck behind the Allied lines. He needed to leave at once.

He decided on a credible scenario for his departure. He did not want the Gestapo to start chasing him. He called Ganz into his office. "I have just received a call from Berlin. A special meeting of senior Gestapo officers has been convened in Hamburg. I am to leave tomorrow morning. Please arrange for my car to be filled with gas, and just to make sure, add two full jerry-cans as well. I will be gone maybe three days, not more. You know what to do in my absence. Try not to screw up again."

"*Jawohl*, Herr Wanstumm. I will attend to everything."

At the end of the work day, Wanstumm left Gestapo headquarters after dark and got into his car. He checked that the two jerry cans had been placed in the trunk and drove over to his small flat. It took two trips to get all of his acquisitions into the car. Going back upstairs for the last time, he took one last look around. He closed and locked the door, certain that when his colleagues came to look for him, there would be no indication that he had fled. Once they discovered that there was no meeting in Hamburg, they would start wondering, but by then, he would have disappeared. He put on his leather gloves, turned on the ignition, and drove off towards the east of Holland.

MARCH-MAY, 1945

AMSTERDAM

The Allies were already in Germany, but they had yet to cross the Rhine north of Cologne. Holland was still at the mercy of the remaining German units. Food supplies had run out. Tulip bulbs had been added to the diet to supplement the official ration consisting of eighteen ounces of bread and one kilo of potatoes per week. Thousands of people took to the roads, pushing baby buggies, handbarrows or bicycles, many of them now without tires, scavenging for any kind of food. There was no fuel of any sort.

In a last spasm of fury, the Germans in Holland conducted manhunts, shot men at random, and confiscated machine tools, medical instruments, farm animals, and art objects. They commandeered the remaining Netherlands Red Cross vehicles and hearses and used them to transport ammunition and other war supplies. Corpses were wrapped in cloth and temporarily deposited in the churches, awaiting burial.

By early March, conditions in northern Holland had become nightmarish. The Germans had installed their last remaining V-2 rocket launchers near The Hague. The Allies bombed them almost daily, and in one terrible moment, overshot their target and destroyed a residential suburb of the city. Morale sank even further. Whenever one of their officers was assassinated, German reprisals were fierce and immediate. The remaining German forces in Holland were now boxed in, along with six million starving Dutchmen, in the north-west corner of the country. Electricity was cut off, and even the water supply was uncertain.

After leaving The Hague in October, Seventer had joined a unit of the underground operating in Amsterdam. He had lost six kilos while in hiding. His face wore a perpetually sad look, as though he were weeping inside. Every day that he survived was a day closer to finding Louisa. He was now convinced that she had been deported. A man who had been arrested by the Gestapo, and who had subsequently escaped while being transported to a holding camp in the eastern part of Holland, had told him that younger women were often sent to work in factories in Germany. Louisa was young and healthy; Seventer was convinced that she had been sent to Germany.

When the Germans issued a decree on Christmas Eve, 1944, ordering all males between the ages of 16 and 40 to register for work in Germany, Seventer arranged for his resistance unit to destroy the school building where the Germans had planned for the registration. He knew that venturing outside during the day exposed him to random seizure at a road block. At night, during the curfew, he risked being shot on the spot. He moved frequently from safe house to safe house, anxiously awaiting news of the Allies' progress. He had to stay alive. He had to find Louisa somewhere in the chaos.

Every day, people died of hunger. On March 7, the Americans crossed the Rhine at Remagen and fanned out into the German heartland, but the Allies seemed to be paying little attention to the Dutch. Whenever Seventer learned that German vans, equipped with radio direction finders, had moved to another section of Amsterdam, he sent desperate messages to London, requesting food drops. It was a race against mass starvation, and as the days passed, the situation became ever more apocalyptic.

Finally, towards the end of March, the Canadians turned towards the north-west of Holland. General Blaskowitz, the commander of the German forces, in a final act of wanton insanity, ordered what was left of the German forces in that part of Holland, about 114,000 men, to defend it at all costs. It appeared that the Dutch would be the last to be liberated from the Nazi scourge.

A new threat loomed. If the Germans blew up the huge dike restraining the North Sea from flooding the vast expanse of reclaimed land north and east of Amsterdam, irreparable harm would be done and hundreds, perhaps thousands of people, would drown. The underground sent increasingly urgent messages to London requesting immediate relief. In response to continued entreaties, Churchill advised the Dutch Prime Minister in London that he would forward the Dutch requests for emergency aid to General Eisenhower. The first Allied food airdrop took place on April 29. Dutch civilians came out into the streets to cheer on the British planes, but the Germans continued to patrol the streets of Amsterdam. The next day, Hitler committed suicide in his Berlin bunker.

On May 6, the Germans in Holland surrendered to the Allies. On May 7, Seventer joined the delirious crowds in the streets of Amsterdam, but the German military police, seemingly oblivious to the Reich's surrender, opened fire and killed 22 of them. Seventer helped move the wounded to the city hospitals. He radioed the situation to his superiors in London. They advised that the Germans in Holland were supposed to have surrendered two days ago; General Blaskowitz had signed the cease-fire document in the presence of the general commanding the Canadian First Army. Seventer informed London that confusion reigned; some of the Germans were becoming trigger-happy as they awaited orders to move to internment camps. The Dutch underground, now out in the open, tried to bring some order to the streets, but they were outnumbered by the remaining German troops.

To compound the chaos, hordes of Dutch civilians, liberated by the Allies from the camps in Germany, were beginning to make their way home. Seventer was instructed to organize reception centers for the greater Amsterdam region to accommodate the huge wave of people who would be returning there. A plan, carefully drawn up by Dutch Military Administration several months earlier, had anticipated making use of all available transportation. Towns near the German borders were designated to sort the incoming throngs. From that point, people were sent to board trains, hastily strung together by the Dutch railroads with whatever equipment was still available. Some of the ultimate destinations were without rail service, and the Dutch military pressed Allied army buses into service. Those arriving in the north, attempting to return to Amsterdam, were to be ferried across the inland sea.

Seventer wondered how he was going to find Louisa among these crowds of emaciated, sick people. The single largest concentration point was at Amersfoort, a railroad hub in the center of the country. The authorities had advised him that three thousand returning civilians would be arriving every day just from Amersfoort at Amsterdam's Central Station. The ferries would bring in an additional two thousand per day. Would Louisa ask to go to Amsterdam? Would she be too tired or too ill to realize that he would be searching for her every day? Perhaps she didn't know that her mother had died; she would surely ask to be taken to The Hague.

Seventer made up an announcement, the size of a small poster, describing Louisa and requesting that anyone with information about her contact him at the temporary headquarters of the Amsterdam Military Administration. He had to copy it by hand. Seventer asked a friend to take a few of the announcements to The Hague. One of these was to be nailed to the front door of the van Dijck house. Louisa would see it when she returned. He provided the main reception centers in Amsterdam with copies. Finally, he inserted an announcement in the first rudimentary edition of Amsterdam's principal morning newspaper.

The newly arrived members of the Dutch Military Administration, flown in from London two days later, greeted him warmly and brought him two fresh uniforms, the first new clothes he had since he had left England. He learned that he had been promoted to colonel.

Seventer was now officially in charge of military administration in the Amsterdam area. During the next few days, he worked feverishly to organize distribution centers for food and clothing, and all the while, he kept asking his colleagues and other officials to be on the look-out for Louisa. As the days wore on, he became frantic to find her. He couldn't sleep. He lost two more kilos. Surely she would be on the next train, or the next bus? Thousands had already returned; it was only a matter of hours or days before he would find her.

By the third week of May, however, intense fear had taken the place of worried anticipation. Seventer questioned hundreds of returning deportees, especially women. Were there many more people yet to come? Were there any Dutch women in the Russian zone of occupation? Would they be held up by the increasingly suspicious and intractable Russians? He called Canadian Army headquarters. Could they tell him how many Dutch deportees still remained in Germany? Could they make inquiries with the French, the British, the Americans?

On May 30, an envelope, delivered by hand, appeared on his desk. He tore it open. It was written on the stationery of St. Elizabeth's Hospital in Amsterdam. He read:

"Dear Colonel Seventer,

The poster about your wife has come to our attention. We believe we may have some information about her. Please contact me at your earliest convenience.

Yours sincerely,
Henrietta van Manen, R.N."

———<>———

After a short wait, Nurse van Manen came out to greet him. "Good afternoon, Colonel Seventer. Please come into my office." They sat down. She glanced at a file in front of her.

"What can you tell me about your wife?"

"Her name is Louisa Seventer-van Dijck. She was taken away for questioning by the Gestapo in 1942. That's all I know. She never returned to her parents' home in The Hague. I've been told that she was most likely deported to a German work camp."

"How old would she be today?"

"She will be thirty-three in June."

"How tall is she?"

"About five foot six, I believe. Tell me, please, do you have any information about her?" Seventer was becoming more anxious every minute.

Nurse van Manen looked down at her file again. "Just let me ask another question before I answer yours. Does your wife have any birthmarks?"

Seventer was tired. He did not immediately understand the implication of the question.

"She has a birthmark on her right shoulder-blade."

"Colonel Seventer, our chief of staff suggested that you come in to see one of our patients. I have to warn you that we think that she might possibly be your wife."

Seventer looked shocked. "That's not possible. How long has this woman been here?"

Nurse van Manen consulted her notes. "Since August 24, 1942."

They walked down a long corridor. The ceiling was high, and the floor was covered in dark green linoleum, giving the impression of walking through a tunnel. The place reeked of carbolic soap. At the end of the hall, she knocked on a door. A gray-haired man in a white coat was expecting them. She performed the introductions.

"Dr. Hulst, this is Colonel Seventer." Turning to Seventer, she said, "Dr. Hulst is our chief of staff. Please sit down."

"Colonel, I understand that you are looking for your wife, who disappeared in 1942. Is that correct?"

"Yes, Doctor. I have heard that she was taken by the Gestapo for questioning."

"May I ask where you were when she disappeared?"

A guilty look came over Seventer's face. "I was in England. I went on a business trip to London the day before the Germans invaded. I couldn't get back. The Germans moved too quickly. I tried every conceivable way to get back to Holland, but it was impossible."

Dr. Hulst continued, "I see. Would you please describe your wife as accurately as possible?"

Seventer did so, haltingly. His hands were beginning to shake.

The doctor consulted some notes, looked at Seventer with great pity, and said, "Colonel, you must be prepared for several different outcomes, one of them being that your wife was never here, or if she were, that she was discharged soon thereafter. However, the reason we have asked you to come here now is because we have had a young woman here since 1942. We have never been able to identify her. She has not spoken since she was brought in. From your description, there is a possibility that this young woman might be your wife. But I warn you, you should be prepared to see a woman who is little more than a cadaver. We do not expect her to live much longer."

Seventer's mouth was dry. It couldn't be Louisa that they were talking about. But he had to see for himself. All he was doing was eliminating the possibility that Louisa had ever been here. No, it could not be her. No, no, no.

The three of them climbed some long stairs to the first floor. Again, they walked down a long corridor and turned through a swing door into a dormitory. All the beds appeared to be occupied, mostly by older women. The doctor stopped at a bed in the back of the room and parted the curtains around it. A pitifully thin woman lay on her back, eyes closed. Her

hands were those of an old woman. Seventer quickly noticed
that she was missing three fingers on her right hand.

He stared, his heart racing, at the woman in front of him.
This was not his Louisa. Louisa had thick, blond hair. This
woman had thin, stringy gray hair. Louisa had a healthy,
attractive figure. This person resembled a scarecrow. Louisa
was lively and smiling. This woman's vacant face was lifeless.
Louisa always wore a light perfume. This woman exuded a
stale smell of urine.

As he continued to compare the reality with his memory,
he started to realize that this person might be, could be, Louisa.
There was something about the mouth and the ears that looked
familiar. He started to shake.

"Take your time, Colonel Seventer. We know this is
very difficult. You mentioned something about a birthmark
on a shoulder-blade. This person has one. Should we take
a look?"

Seventer grasped the side of the bed to steady himself.
He thought that he was going to throw up. This couldn't be
Louisa. He took a deep breath and nodded. The doctor
leaned down and very gently turned the woman over on her
side. Her skeletal structure protruded; her body had consumed
all of its fat. Gently the doctor pulled her gown off of one
shoulder.

Seventer's hand rose to his mouth. He gagged. He quickly
averted his eyes from the one distinctly recognizable feature
on this woman. Then, with utmost despair etched on his face,
he leaned over to touch her face. There was no reaction; her
eyes were empty, lifeless. He picked up her maimed hand,
caressed it, and brought it up to his lips. The tears welled
from his eyes, rolling down his cheeks. Gently, he placed her
hand down on the bed and turned away, his body heaving
and shaking. Nurse van Manen kept him from falling. She
helped him into the corridor. The doctor pulled the curtains
closed and came after them.

In the hall, Seventer stopped. He was trying to control his sobbing. The doctor took him by the arm. "Come with me; let's talk about it," he urged.

Blindly, Seventer was led down the hall, back to the office. Nurse van Manen excused herself, with a pat on Seventer's arm.

"Sit down, please. Can I offer you some *jenever*?"

"Yes, please. Thank you."

Doctor Hulst opened a medicine cabinet, extracted a bottle and two glasses, and poured some of the pale golden liquid into each glass. Wordlessly, he handed one of them to Seventer, who took a big gulp. The fiery liquid burned its way down to his stomach. It seemed to settle the heaving.

"Doctor, I can't leave her here," said Seventer after a few moments. "I must move her to a place where I can look after her while she gets better." He rocked back and forth in the chair. His face was twisted in an agony of horror and guilt.

"Colonel, I hate to be blunt, but your wife was severely tortured. She is not the only case of Gestapo torture I've had, more men than women, but the prognosis is never good. Your wife's physical damage was considerable, but her mind was completely destroyed. My colleagues and I feel that the damage is irreversible."

"You mean," Seventer spoke slowly, "that Louisa will never recover?"

"I'm terribly sorry, but no, I don't think she will. In fact, I don't think she will last much longer. She has been losing too much weight, and as you know, we have had very little food to give her. She cannot eat like a normal person."

"I will find food for her. I will come every day to look after her. She must get well. She has to get well." He paused, and then, swallowed. "We've had so little time together."

"Colonel Seventer, if there is anything we can humanly do, we will do it. We are just beginning to receive emergency supplies. Even so, my considered opinion is that it will be too late to make any difference. Your wife is *in extremis*. I wish I could tell you otherwise."

Seventer looked around the starkly furnished office, as if a miracle might suddenly occur to dissipate this nightmare. To think that Louisa had been here all along. If only he had known earlier, could he have made a difference? Could he have spoken to her, let her know that he was there at her side? Could she have mustered enough strength to pull through?

"Doctor, may I go and sit by her bed? Perhaps she can hear me. I have to be with her; I can't leave her like this."

"I understand. I will ask Nurse van Manen to accompany you."

Seventer rose, and held his hand out to Dr. Hulst. His voice cracked as he said, "Thank you. Thank you for your help." He left the room and slowly made his way back to the ward.

————————<>————————

Louisa died three days later.

CHAPTER SIX

—————————<>—————————

DISAPPEARING ACT

OCTOBER, 1945

MEMMINGEN, BAVARIA

The country road was slick in the cold downpour. Heinrich Wanstumm was riding his rickety bicycle directly into the driving rain. A sack of potatoes was perched precariously on the handlebars. His wet, tattered overcoat was bulging with food wrapped in soggy paper. He could hardly see a few feet ahead; he sensed where to turn.

The path off the road ran for about 100 meters up to the courtyard of a small farmhouse. Wanstumm, mindful of the many times he had tried to ride down the rutted path, walked through the mud, pushing his bicycle. His socks were wet; his boots were cracked, and he could feel the itching between his toes. He opened the door, put the potatoes down and began to remove his heavy, sodden coat. Then he leaned over to pull the packages out. One pocket contained carrots; another disgorged half a chicken.

Wanstumm felt safe for the time being in his family's farmhouse in the U.S. Occupation Zone, but he knew that this could only be a temporary haven for him. Some day, someone would recognize him. He had carefully covered his traces when he left Holland. He had abandoned his car about 50 miles away from the farm after having removed the license plates and every other identifying feature. The nearest town was Memmingen, where the Americans had a base. They drove around the countryside in groups of three or four jeeps. The G.I.'s were approachable and seemed genuinely concerned about the terrible living conditions of the local population and of the many refugees coming from further east. The Americans were acquiring a better reputation as occupiers than the British, who completely ignored the Germans, or the French, who taunted them, let alone the Russians, who now ruled East Germany with an iron hand.

Like many areas of occupied Germany, Bavaria had become a huge camp for displaced persons, not all of them Germans. They were part of the mass of homeless, stateless, and unemployed people on the move throughout Europe. They stood in long lines, desperate to obtain residence permits or new identity papers. Germans from the Sudetenland were forcibly expelled from Czechoslovakia, with no place to go. Like the Hungarians, Gypsies, Bulgarians, Ukrainians, and Poles, they wandered around in makeshift camps while the Allies tried to figure out what to do with them.

In this maelstrom of humanity, Wanstumm carefully plotted his next move. Staying in Germany was not an option; he had no illusions about the outcome of being identified, but he needed money to leave. Money was critical. With money he could buy decent clothes, pay for transportation and bribes, and obtain false identity papers.

Then, he must make the next decision: where should he go? Eastern Europe was no longer an option; the Russians had sealed the borders. With the exception of Spain or Portugal, there was no country in Western Europe that was not participating in the search for Nazi war criminals. There were rumors of Nazis leaving for South America, but he wanted to distance himself from his past. No, he was in the American zone of occupation. America would be the best place for a permanent move. The Allies would never think of looking for him right there under their noses. He decided to get a job with the Americans.

His first step was to create a new identity. He knew that it would be difficult for the Allies to check on the background of a refugee from the eastern zone. What could be more credible than a Hungarian, fleeing from the Red Army, whose brutal treatment of Axis soldiers was already well-documented? As a refugee from Hungary, he would not attract attention, and might even get some sympathy. His knowledge of the language was rusty, but thanks to his Hungarian grandmother, he could still speak it with only a trace of a German accent. He was not fluent enough to pass for a native of Hungary, but where he was going, it would not matter.

He had spent long hours reviewing every detail of his new identity: he would become Joseph Galish, born in Gyor, Hungary in 1908. Galish's parents had been killed in a highway accident in 1937 when their bus had collided with a truck. Galish was an only child. After graduation from technical school at the age of 17, Galish had been hired as a helper in a restaurant in Estergom. Galish had learned cooking from the chef, who was grooming him to become his assistant. When war broke out in 1939, Galish had been drafted into the Hungarian Army and had spent 13 months stationed at Szeged on the Romanian border. From there, Galish had been transferred to Gyor, his home town, where he was garrisoned until Germany had invaded Russia in June, 1941.

The Germans retreated from Russia in the summer of 1944, and so had their allies in Eastern Europe. Some of the units disintegrated under the simultaneous onslaught of the Russian Army and the intolerable deprivations caused by the collapsing supply system. Galish's company, attached to the German Fifth Infantry Division, started to unravel as it crossed the Pripiet marshes. Galish, miraculously spared from being wounded or killed, developed chronic enteritis. He was transported to Budapest on a hospital train. When they reached Budapest, he was hospitalized, and then sent home on sick leave. He was still in Gyor in December when the Soviet forces rushed into Hungary. The Russians laid siege to Budapest and pounded it to a smoking hulk.

Desperate not to become a prisoner of the Russians, Galish had made his way at night along the main road from Gyor into Austria. German troops had been retreating so quickly that they hadn't even noticed the stragglers, former Hungarian soldiers now in civilian clothes, who had been walking in the shadows along the same road.

Galish had walked for weeks. Food had been almost impossible to find. The German Army itself had been on short rations. Three weeks later, he had reached Memmingen, Bavaria, in the American zone. Instinctively, Galish felt that the Americans would be more generous to the refugees. Now, certain of being in the American sector, he had decided to pause and rest.

Wastumm kept rehearsing his new identity. He worried about running into other Hungarians. Although he could describe Gyor with considerable accuracy, he would be stumped if he were asked any questions about service in the Hungarian Army.

The U.S. Army base was about two miles outside of Memmingen. Wanstumm had examined it carefully. He knew that the Americans were friendly, unsuspecting people, so why would they question his story? His English was not very good, but somehow, he had to get a job with the Americans.

On October 21, 1945, Heinrich Wanstumm walked from his modest farmhouse into Memmingen. It was bitterly cold, and the wind had a sharp bite. His wool bonnet was pulled tightly down over his head. He made his way through the narrow, winding streets. The only traffic consisted of bicycles and an occasional horse-drawn cart. He walked quickly, his head down. At the other end of the town, he took the road bearing left, towards what had been a summer camp for Hitler Youth. Now he saw a fence of barbed wire around the area, with a seven-foot high gate and a wooden sentry box standing to the side. He walked up to it, shuffling slightly. The sergeant on duty came out of the guard house.

"What can we do for you?" The Americans had orders to be polite but not to fraternize with Germans.

"Do you have work? I am a good cook." His English was heavily accented.

"Dunno, buddy. Go to the cabin on the left, Unit A. Tell 'em what you want."

Wanstumm crossed the courtyard to a trailer. Three wooden steps led up to a door. He knocked without too much confidence. A very large American soldier opened the door. A blast of warm air blew in Wanstumm's face. He could not help but feel envious of the American uniform. His shirt and pants were perfectly ironed. This soldier even had a bright yellow ascot tucked neatly into his shirt. Why did the Americans have to look like conquerors? Wanstumm resisted the impulse to stand ramrod straight. Instead, he shuffled his feet again and mumbled, "I'm sorry I disturb you, sir, but you want a good cook?"

The lieutenant looked blank. Then he said, "Maybe we do. Come on in. Talk to our mess chief." He turned around and yelled at someone "Hey, Joe, do we need a cook?" At the other end of the room, a soldier in overalls walked over to them. His forehead glistened with sweat. He rubbed his hands down his dirty apron.

"What's this guy got we need? Can he cook and clean dishes?"

"Dunno. If he can improve on the stuff you're serving, he's got my vote."

Wanstumm looked from the one to the other. His thin, blond hair hung down over his forehead. He was wearing his old coat, now dried out, but still hanging down over his legs in irregular folds. The army cook shrugged his shoulders, and said to him, "Come back in the morning. You have to fill out the forms. I can't use you if you ain't legal."

Wanstumm looked at the man and nodded. He knew at that moment that he would be employed by the U. S. Army. He shuffled back to the gate and, once out of sight, straightened his back and began the long walk home to the farmhouse.

MARCH, 1946

MEMMINGEN

It had been one of the coldest winters on record. The coal mines in the Ruhr were operating again, but extensive damage to the machinery at the pit-heads, as well as the mostly-destroyed *Reichsbahn,* were major obstacles to the efforts of the Allied Occupation Forces to distribute coal to major cities and to the displaced persons camps. Some activity was returning to the industrial centers, but elsewhere the economy was all but comatose. The Allies had to provide food, lodging and above all, work, for millions of unemployed people.

The best, and therefore the most sought-after, jobs were those working for the occupying forces: secretaries, translators, plumbers, electricians, stonecutters, painters, tailors, chemists, librarians, clock repairers, barbers, maids, guides, gardeners, cobblers, skiing instructors, doctors, woodcarvers, and, last but not least, cooks.

Joseph Galish, as he was now known, had become indispensable to the 2nd Company of the 2nd Infantry Division. He seemed to have a special talent for cooking. The food served in the 2nd Company's officers' mess was rated the best in all of the Third Army command. On Friday and Saturday nights, it had become an honor to be invited to the Company's mess for a gastronomic event. Galish had made good use of local Bavarian resources, particularly game. Wild boar, matured for three days at room temperature, cooked slowly in a broth of *pflaumwasser*, mushrooms and chestnuts, was ranked as the equal of anything tasted by adventurous American servicemen on leave in the Alsace or Paris.

Galish took great pains to consult Captain Defoe about his menus. Defoe was a quiet, detail-oriented officer who had taken a special interest in Galish. Unlike many of the American officers who disliked the often unpleasant life of an occupying force, Defoe enjoyed being in Germany. He studied the German language daily and was respectful of the civilians working in the camp. Joseph Galish had struck him as being particularly deserving of his attention. He was a refugee from Hungary, with no family, and therefore, excluded from regular civilian jobs reserved for Germans. Galish had also talked Defoe into letting him use a small room on the base formerly occupied by a caretaker. Galish abandoned his parents' farmhouse. Another slice of his past was obliterated.

Defoe knew that Galish wanted to emigrate to the U.S. Galish frequently asked about life there. Defoe and others described the rules of baseball; they portrayed what the average American home looked like and how Congress worked, and they spent hours discussing the merits of American automobiles. Galish listened to Defoe and his friends with rapt attention. In reality, he thought that the Americans were incredibly trusting. He was becoming impatient to implement the next step of his plan, but he could not let it show. He knew that he needed to build a stellar record as a servant of the U.S. Army. In order to get to the U.S., he needed the convincing recommendations of decorated officers. He had to bide his time.

In the meantime, he had little opportunity to break out of the camp routine. That is, until he requested permission to go into Memmingen one evening. He was becoming desperate for some female companionship. He asked for a night off to attend a concert at the local town hall. Captain

Defoe agreed and gave Galish a pass to ride on the bus, but he told him that he would have to make it back to camp on his own. Galish was very grateful.

Galish got off the bus in the town square. He headed for a *bierstube,* a modest-looking café. After so many years away from Memmingen, Galish was not too concerned about being recognized by anyone he might have known before the war. He took a seat at a vacant table. A man walked up to him with a beer in his hand.

"*Grüss Gott,*" he said, using the Bavarian greeting.

"*Gutenabend,*" Galish replied, eyeing him questioningly.

Galish knew he had to be careful lest his own Bavarian accent become noticeable. He had practiced speaking German with his own interpretation of a Hungarian accent, but he knew that people could easily slip up when they were relaxed or had drunk too much.

"We have met somewhere before," the man said to Galish. It was a statement, not a question. Galish felt his skin prick.

"Maybe so, but I don't remember."

"Well, I do. May I sit down?"

Galish made a gesture.

"You were in Holland, *nicht wahr?*"

Galish thought quickly. He had always had a good memory for faces and voices. Who was this man? In the dim light of the bar, Galish looked at him carefully. The man was thin, of average height, with graying hair swept back from the temples. His nose was elegant, with a slightly domineering turn. His cheeks were hollow, although this could be due to recent malnutrition. Galish tried to visualize the man in a uniform, perhaps regular army, or even an SS division? How could he not recognize him?

Then, suddenly, he feared a trap. Could this man be an agent for the Allies, working undercover to ferret out war criminals? He decided to counter-attack.

"Now that I think about it, I do seem to remember you, but not in Holland. I was never there. That's what threw me off. It was Warsaw, 1943, wasn't it?" Galish had never been to Poland. The ruse didn't work.

The man smiled thinly. "You are Heinrich Wanstumm. I remember you very well. You were chief of the Gestapo in Amsterdam."

Galish stared at the man with grim intensity, like a mongoose dancing around a cobra. He had to deal with this threat quickly. Perhaps the man would reveal something about himself?

"Give me a cigarette," the man demanded. Galish pulled his pack out. "I saw you in Amsterdam in 1942," the man continued. "I was adjutant to General von Hemsdorff. We were stationed in Epe, on the east side of Holland. Von Hemsdorff provided you with troops to round up Jews. You had a reputation for thoroughness. I accompanied von Hemsdorff's men one night from Epe to Amsterdam just to see one of your operations for myself. You and I discussed the placement of the troops around the city before the operation began. It was dark, but I remember you, and I recognize your voice."

"What is your name?" asked Galish.

The man shrugged. "Joachim Meinhaft, but I use a different name now. Here, I am Gerhard Wormser. I was a colonel in the *Das Reich*."

Galish remembered. *Das Reich* was the second SS division created after the organization of the *Leibstandarte*, the first of the *Waffen SS* units. The *Das Reich* division had a reputation for brutality. This fellow was, without a doubt, extremely dangerous.

"What are you doing in Memmingen?" the man asked Galish.

Galish was annoyed with the man's impertinent questions. "I am a cook," he said flatly.

"Where?"

"In a restaurant."

Meinhaft paused, staring intently at Galish. "How informative," he murmured.

Galish finished his beer. "I must leave you now."

"Wait a minute. Let me ask you this. You've read how the Allies are hunting down every one of us. The Dutch want you; the French want me, and pretty soon, the Jews will want to settle the score, too. How are you going to survive? I don't mean as a cook; I mean as a wanted man."

"That's my business."

"Don't kid yourself. We have to stick together. We have an organization. We have already helped many colleagues to leave Europe. I myself am on the waiting list to go to Argentina. We might be able to accommodate you too."

"I have no interest in going to South America," Galish replied coldly. "I'll take care of myself. Thank you anyway." Galish rose from the table and casually dropped a U.S. dollar bill on the table. "You can pay for our beers, and by the way, my name is Joseph Galish."

Meinhaft remained seated. "We will meet again," he said.

Galish strode through the main part of town. He was extremely agitated by the encounter with Meinhaft. He walked quickly, taking deep breaths. The stores were closed, and the street lights were dim. He looked at his watch; the performance at the town hall was due to start in fifteen minutes.

Inside the hall, Galish hurried to claim an empty chair, sat down and noticed that he was still sweating. He must redouble his precautions. He could not step out of his new persona for one single minute. What was Meinhaft doing in Memmingen? How could he have let down his guard?

Galish breathed deeply until his pulse stopped jumping. He looked around the hall. It was an older crowd; there were more women than men. The women looked tired, frumpy. Some of the men were on crutches or missing limbs.

At the end of the performance, he turned to scan the room again, looking for a female whom he might approach. The crowd milled around. They were serving *ruwein* in the lobby.

He was about to give up when he noticed a striking woman standing alone. She was wearing a gray woolen dress, cut very squarely on her wide shoulders with a thick black belt at her waist. She was tall and held herself erect. Her hair was dark blond, pulled tightly back from her face. Her eyes were light blue, as hard as agates. Her Aryan face was angular, but she had large, full breasts which added sexuality to her rigid posture. Galish decided to see how receptive she might be to him. He shouldered his way through the crowd, until he was standing next to her. From his pocket, he drew his packet of Lucky Strikes, a sure attention-getter in a country where cigarettes were available only on the black market.

"Good evening, *fraulein*. Did you enjoy the show?" he asked as he offered her a cigarette.

"Yes, it was very nice. Who are you? I haven't seen you in town before." Those hard blue eyes raked him over.

"No, I work on the American base. And you?"

"I am a doctor in town. You have an accent. Where are you from?"

"Hungary. It is a long story."

"Everybody has a long story these days," she retorted. She eyed him without blinking. "Would you like a cup of real coffee?"

"Real coffee? Why not?" he answered

They put on their coats before walking out into the cold evening. He followed her along the dimly-lit street. She never looked to the right or to the left. Their shoes clicked in harmony on the cobblestone roadway. Galish could sense an aura of danger around this woman. Where was she taking him, for a cup of 'real coffee'?

After a few minutes' walk, she pulled out a key for the front door of a small house. They entered, and the door closed behind them. She never looked at Galish but just walked through to another door which led into to a small, ground floor flat. It was very warm. The furniture was typically Bavarian, solid and heavily-carved. The room was a combination living, dining and bed room. It was spotless. A tiny kitchen, the size of a closet, was off to one side.

The woman turned to face Galish. She looked him in the eyes as she took off her coat. Her gray dress clung to her body, outlining her full breasts and hips.

"Please make yourself at home. I will fix us some coffee." She stepped into the kitchen. Galish watched her move. She was powerfully built, he thought, but a little too broad-shouldered. He hadn't seen anyone with a body like hers in a long time.

She made the coffee quickly, and emerged from the kitchen with two cups on a tray. The aroma was delicious. She put the tray down and sat in the chair facing him. She leaned towards him and asked, "So, what is your name?"

He paused. "My name is Joseph Galish. And yours?"

"Ilse Huber," she replied.

He decided to open the bidding. "Were you in Bavaria during the war?" he asked.

"No. Do I sound like a Bavarian? You sound like an interrogator." Ilse retorted.

Galish stared at her. "I am a refugee from Hungary, and I work as a cook at the American base outside of town."

"Then why are some of your inflections Bavarian?"

"Perhaps because I have been here for six months."

"What did you do during the war?"

"I was a corporal in the Hungarian Army. We were assigned to the eastern front. I spoke good German. They made me a translator for the Germans."

"So why are you here in Bavaria?"

"My unit got lucky. We retreated with the Germans, and here I am." He stared at her breasts.

Ilse sipped her coffee, studying him. Slowly, she put her cup down on the tray and stood up. She walked around the table to stand over him.

"Get up." There was no mistaking the authority in her voice. "You have not slept with a woman in a long time, right?"

Galish's breathing became shallow. He stood up.

She continued, "Your story doesn't sound right, but at this moment I am interested in something else. Take all of your clothes off and go and wash in my bathroom. I like men who smell clean."

Watching her out of the corner of his eye, he moved over to the bathroom, opened the door, and closed it behind him.

He emerged naked. He looked around the small living room. She was nowhere to be seen. He walked over to the kitchen entrance, where a small light was still burning. Suddenly he felt the silk cord slip around his neck and tighten. Her knee was pressed into the small of his back. She leaned her face over his right ear. One wrong move on his part, and he wouldn't need to wonder whether his war story made any sense.

"I do not like people who do not tell the truth. Sooner or later, I will find out what you really did during the war. It would be easy to kill you whenever I want to. Now turn around." Her body looked as good as he had imagined.

Galish relaxed his body. This was going to be interesting.

One hour later, Galish started pulling on his clothes. Ilse lay naked on the bed. He looked down at her. Her long, muscular body was relaxed. Her blue eyes followed every movement he made.

"That was good. You will come back. Soon."

Galish was annoyed that the woman was telling him what to do, but he knew he must not appear to be too irritated. It might arouse her speculation about his past. He softened his voice. "I will see you again, *liebling*."

Ilse watched him leave, her eyes devoid of emotion.

APRIL, 1946

THE HAGUE

The temporary offices of the Netherlands War Crimes Commission had been installed in a gracious, nineteenth-century home away from the city center. While the individual rooms were generously proportioned, the building was too small to house the rapidly growing staff. The rooms had to be partitioned off to provide enough desk space for the investigators.

Kees Goedkamp, until recently an inspector in the Rotterdam Police Department, now Chief Inspector for the Commission, occupied a corner office. He was six foot one, thin, and dark-complexioned. A slight limp betrayed an accident sustained during the war. His face matched the rest of him, thin and long. From time to time, a grave smile would offset his otherwise formidable countenance.

Eduard Seventer had agreed to be at Goedkamp's office at eleven o'clock that morning. The train from Amsterdam had been very crowded, so Seventer had decided to walk from the station rather than wait in line for one of the few taxis. He was almost twenty minutes late when he was shown into Goedkamp's office. Goedkamp rose from behind his desk to shake hands.

"Good morning, Colonel Seventer, or is it Mr. Seventer now?"

"Mr. Seventer, thank you, as of February 28. I'm sorry to be late."

"It's hard to be on time; public transportation is still very unreliable here," answered Goedkamp with a smile. "Have a seat and make yourself comfortable." Seventer thought that he was going to like this policeman.

An older man came in with a tray, on which were arrayed a pot of coffee, a small pitcher of milk, a sugar bowl, and a plate of sugar-dusted *koekjes*. Life was slowly returning to normal, Seventer thought, except that nothing would ever be normal for him again.

"Please help yourself," urged Goedkamp.

The two men poured their coffee, passed the milk and sugar, and settled down in their chairs, with Seventer lighting a cigarette. He was smoking too much these days.

"Mr. Seventer, as you know, we are beginning to accumulate data about some of the more notorious Dutch collaborators, Nazi sympathizers, members of the German armed forces, the SS, and the Gestapo who committed crimes in Holland during the occupation. We are asking as many people as possible to help us to draw up a list of war criminals. We intend to prosecute them in accordance with international law, the Geneva Convention, and guidance from the Nuremberg Tribunal. Our task will not be easy, but hopefully, with the help of witnesses such as you, we may be able to render justice." Goedkamp stopped, waiting to see what reaction he would elicit from this little speech, which he was giving with monotonous regularity. He was not disappointed.

Seventer leaned forward. "Mr. Goedkamp, you asked me to meet with you because you had heard about my wife. Is that right?"

"Yes, we have been given hospital records, including those of patients admitted with wounds or scars that could only result from torture. Your wife was on the list."

"My wife died last year." Seventer's face looked bleak.

"Yes. I am so very sorry."

Seventer paused and drew a long breath. He continued, "She was arrested and questioned by the Gestapo in 1942 as a result of my assistance to Jewish refugees before the outbreak of war. Louisa knew very little about my work and, naturally, could tell them little of import. It seems that they remained unconvinced."

"Yes, I am aware of that."

"What you may not know is that I was also arrested by the Gestapo, two years after she was, and brought to their headquarters in Amsterdam for questioning. They did not know who I was, but one of the men who questioned me was in charge of the Gestapo in Amsterdam, Heinrich Wanstumm."

Goedkamp looked stunned. "I had no idea you had come into contact with Wanstumm. Please tell me more."

"Let me start at the beginning."

It was a quarter of an hour later when Goedkamp exclaimed, "You don't know how lucky, if I may be permitted to call it that, you were to be at Gestapo headquarters on that particular day. The R.A.F. planned a pin-point bombing raid on the building when London learned that a leader of the Dutch underground was being held there. He managed to get away in the confusion. A village priest was small fry by comparison." Goedkamp looked at his watch. "Would you mind if we have *broodje*s brought up here for lunch?" At Seventer's nod Goedkamp stepped into the anteroom to give his secretary the order.

Seventer described his growing fear at finding the van Dijck house empty, the German patrol car that slowed down to look at him, the meeting with van Breem, the sudden arrival of the Gestapo. "I should have expected that the van Dijck house would be watched." Grimly, he related learning of his in-laws' deaths and van Breem's description of the Gestapo taking Louisa away for further questioning.

"After two weeks spent hiding in van Breem's attic, I made my way back to Amsterdam where I established contact with one of the remaining underground units. Every day, I kept looking for Louisa. I had almost convinced myself that she was in a German work-camp, but after the end of the Occupation, I finally found her in St. Elizabeth's Hospital." He paused. "She had been there, in Amsterdam, all along. If only I had known." Seventer's voice trailed off. He walked over to the window and looked down into the street below. Quietly, Goedkamp made some notes.

Seventer turned back and continued, "I have heard that Heinrich Wanstumm disappeared from Amsterdam in early 1945. He had an associate who was involved in Louisa's case. Mr. van Breem recognized him when they came to look for me. He was one of the men who had taken Louisa in for questioning, and who had gone back to search the van Dijcks' house later. I think his name was Ganz. He was at Gestapo headquarters when they brought me in. Both he and Wanstumm interrogated me."

"Yes, we have a file on the man: Alois Ganz. He was captured and is currently imprisoned here in The Hague."

Seventer suddenly tensed. "Ask him what they did to my wife; he knows. He can tell you everything about Wanstumm."

Goedkamp exclaimed, "This is invaluable, Mr. Seventer, invaluable. Would it be possible for you to describe Wanstumm?"

"He is not the kind of person one forgets," replied Seventer. "He is very cold, with a shuttered face. He displays no emotion. Make no mistake about it, Mr. Goedkamp. If I knew how to go after this man, I would find him, and I would kill him."

"I don't think that you are the killer type," replied Goedkamp quietly.

A faraway look appeared in Seventer's blue eyes. "Let me describe the charming Herr Wanstumm. He was about five feet nine or ten, quite thin, but with wide hips. His dark-blond hair was thin, brushed back from his forehead, with a part near the middle. He had small blue eyes. His face was not handsome, not ugly. His ears were quite close to his head. His hands were very delicate, with long thumbs. His voice was thin and reedy."

"Did you notice anything else? Did he wear glasses, for instance?"

"No, I don't believe so."

"And you saw him just once. Is that right?"

"Yes, at Gestapo Headquarters."

"Now tell me a little more about Wanstumm's interest in you, and therefore in your wife."

Seventer experienced an overwhelming feeling of guilt every time he thought about Louisa. "In 1937, I became involved with a group in Amsterdam which provided assistance to German Jews who were seeking refuge in Holland. As a banker, I handled their finances and arranged to get their money out of Holland, mostly to England and the United States."

"Do you think that the Germans found any Jewish documents confirming the transactions at your bank?"

"I'm fairly certain that my partner, Pim Laan, managed to destroy most of our copies. He escaped to the Dutch East Indies, where his parents lived. After the war, he decided to stay in the Far East, and he now works in Singapore. He wrote to me a few months ago confirming that he had burned all of the documents. However, I have not a doubt that Wanstumm found the letters we had given to our clients in case they should ever go to the U.S. or England. They would need to present some confirmation of the account." He added bitterly, "Of course, Wanstumm knew that there was no chance of any of these people surviving to claim their accounts."

"So Wanstumm figured that your wife was the best chance he had to learn more about your pre-war transfers of Jewish funds?"

"Exactly. Except for old Mr. Hobbema, who knew nothing about our day-to-day business since his retirement in 1936, my other partners were no longer in Amsterdam. Jan ten

Haave was in a prisoner-of-war camp somewhere in Czechoslovakia. Arie Dorninck was in hiding in Belgium. Louisa was Wanstumm's only solid lead."

Goedkamp fell silent as he reviewed his notes. He said, "Mr. Seventer, we are also putting together a data base of people who were deported to concentration camps from Holland during the war. Your Jewish clients were almost certainly rounded up and taken away. Do you have any personal recollections of them?"

"I remember some of the names, yes. Perhaps I could write them down for you, but it will be difficult for me to recollect details with any accuracy."

"I understand. Perhaps something will occur to you that might be helpful to me." Goedkamp changed the subject. "Tell me, Mr. Seventer, what are your plans now?" he asked.

Seventer looked down. He had neverly properly answered the question, even to himself. "I cannot stay in Holland. There are too many memories which obsess me. I have no close family left here. I can't re-open the bank in Amsterdam; I don't have the capital; my former clients are no longer there; my former partners have found other employment, or are dead, or retired." Seventer paused. "I have decided to accept a position with Mathijs Smithson and Company in London. My family had a minority shareholding in the firm. During the war, London became a second home to me."

"I see. That's natural under the circumstances. Would you be good enough to let me know where I can reach you?"

"Of course."

"I will be in touch. I can't thank you enough for your help."

The two men shook hands, and Seventer left the room, weighed down by his guilt. If only he had not gone to London that day. If only he had been able to shield Louisa from the consequences of his determination to help the Jewish refugees. Now, the refugees were dead. Louisa was dead. And he would never be able to deal with the loss.

OCTOBER, 1946

MEMMINGEN

Ilse Huber and Joseph Galish found mutual satisfaction in a once-a-week coupling, but it was hardly an affectionate relationship. Cruelty excited both of them. On the base, Galish made no secret of his assignations. He felt it would help him in preparing his immigration file for the U.S. if he were known as a 'regular' guy. Americans, he had discovered, could be very prudish, but having a steady girlfriend was 'O.K.'.

Galish was very worried that Captain Defoe, his mentor, would be transferred back to the U.S. He had asked him one night, after having served a particularly good dinner, whether Defoe would be leaving soon. Defoe was in a good mood, and decided to confide in his friend 'Joe'.

"So many guys wanted to get home that Washington became concerned that there wouldn't be enough of us to occupy Germany. I was on the list to be repatriated in August, 1945. That's how the numbers worked, but I have 're-upped' twice. I like it here in Bavaria. It's a beautiful part of Germany, and I'm interested in learning the language. Maybe I'll stay in Europe after I get out," he continued.

"So will it be possible for you you to help me with my immigration papers?" pressed Galish.

"As a matter of fact," answered Captain Defoe, "I have good news for you. I was speaking to our adjudant yesterday. You know, the guy with the thick glasses, and he told me that we should go ahead and prepare your petition. He has heard that some of the other divisions have helped people working for them, and the requests have been expedited through the War Department in Washington. Come to my office before you report to the kitchen tomorrow afternoon, say about 4 p.m., and let's go through the paperwork."

Galish wiped his hands on his stained apron, grinned, and shook Captain Defoe's outstretched hand.

"Many thanks, Captain. I will never forget this."

"Joe, you've been through a lot, and we like to do what we can for you guys to give you a fresh start."

The next night, as Galish lay next to Ilse, he thought back to his conversation with Defoe. A fresh start; he liked that. Americans were so naïve; they took people at face value. Running into Meinhaft had been an unpleasant surprise. Since their chance meeting, Galish had stayed out of his way, but if Meinhaft had recognized him, others could too.

His ticket to a new life with financial independence, maybe even real wealth, lay hidden in his worn G.I. duffel bag: the list of accounts opened by Hobbema & Seventer for the Jews whom he had sent off to the camps, knowing they wouldn't return. The banks in England and America wouldn't keep those accounts open for ever. He had to have a detailed plan to claim the accounts, and then, he had to act as quickly as possible. But first, he had to get out of Germany.

Lately, the urgency of his move to the U.S. had so concerned him that he had been unable to sleep. He diligently practiced his English, training himself to add five new words to his vocabulary every day. He knew that the German authorities, gradually re-asserting control over civilian affairs, had already begun requesting information from the U.S. Army on the status of all civilian workers on their bases. He knew that his name would be included. It was only a matter of time before the Germans would discover that there was no record of a displaced person number for a Hungarian refugee named Joseph Galish. It was time for him to move on.

DECEMBER, 1947

MEMMINGEN

By all accounts, the officers agreed that chef Joe Galish's Christmas dinner was the most delicious that they had ever eaten. The fresh turkeys had been flown in from the U.S., as had the cranberry sauce. Galish had carefully selected the potatoes to produce a perfectly smooth puree. No one knew where he had found the small, sweet peas and the tender white onions. His stuffing was a departure from the traditional American blend of flavored bread crumbs. This one consisted of mushrooms, sausage meat, eggs, chopped herbs, and chestnuts. It got rave reviews.

The mess had been lavishly, if somewhat garishly, decorated by the women who worked in the base laundry. They had obtained four Christmas trees, one for each corner of the room and had wound yards of red ribbon around them. White stars, cut out of cardboard, were stuck all over the walls. The overall effect was festive, *gemütlich*, as the Bavarians called it. The mood at the base was upbeat, even though the men would, of course, have preferred to be back at home with their families.

Joseph Galish was happy for a different reason. Captain Defoe had called him in on December 24. "Joe, I have a Christmas present for you. I have just received word that you have permission to go to the U.S. Consulate in Frankfurt, where your immigration papers are waiting for you." Captain Defoe beamed.

Galish put on a passable imitation of a grown man on the verge of tears. "This is the most wonderful Christmas of my life," he mumbled. "I will never be able to thank you enough, sir."

"You will have to buy your passage on a ship," continued Defoe. "I suggest you go to a travel agent in Frankfurt after you have picked up your papers. They can arrange it for you."

If only Defoe knew that he was helping a war criminal to escape, legally, to the U.S., away from the investigations still being conducted by the War Crimes Tribunals. Galish's master plan was working.

"Captain, perhaps when you return to the U.S., we can get together so that I can thank you properly."

"I'll look forward to that, Joe."

———<>———

Nothing had bothered Galish so much as how he was going to part from Ilse. They had become quite used to each other. In a way, they needed one another. Still, he could never reconcile Ilse by day, a doctor with a growing practice, with Ilse at night.

She had once hinted at a future together, but while he had been titillated by her erotic perversions, she meant nothing to him. In fact, he was relieved that the U.S. Army had restricted him to barracks six days out of seven.

That night, he decided to tell her about his upcoming departure from Memmingen.

"I will be leaving Germany soon, Ilse. I have received my papers, and I am going to America."

He glanced at her. Her face remained impassive.

"Within the next few weeks," he added. She still said nothing.

Suddenly she swung her legs over the side of the bed, stood up, and looked down at him. "Why are you going to America? What are you running from?" The cold blue eyes were as hard as marbles, assessing his words.

He didn't like her prying. "I just want a simple life, a little restaurant of my own, away from all the terrible memories of war and destruction."

"So you feel sorry for yourself?" She was really being argumentative.

"I feel sorry for all of us. At least you can still live in your own country, but I can never go back to mine as long as the Communists are in power in Budapest."

Ilse paced across the floor; her naked body was lithe and athletic. Her stomach was as flat as a board. Her thighs descended from her crotch in a perfectly angular sculpture. He knew that it would be hard to find another woman who could arouse him the way she had. But first, he had to get out of Germany, with no strings attached.

She walked over to the tiny bathroom and slammed the door closed. He got off the bed and finished dressing. She came out wearing a dark brown bathrobe.

As he picked up his coat, Ilse came to stand in front of him, a contemptuous look on her face. "I shouldn't have wasted my time with you," she spoke coldly. "You think you can get away from the past. You think you can begin again. Well, you will never get away from your past." She ran an arm up behind her head and pulled her long blond hair into a bun.

"Ilse, I have to go now. The last bus to the base leaves in fifteen minutes."

"I am sure that your real name is not Joseph Galish. I know that you are not Hungarian. You are German, just like me. You have betrayed the Reich. It doesn't matter now. But someday, it will matter." Her voice was as brittle as new ice. She turned away.

Galish shrugged, put on his coat, and walked out into the night, closing the door behind him.

JANUARY 1948

MEMMINGEN

Galish packed his few belongings into his worn G.I. duffel bag. The most valuable items went in first. The Jewish bank account documents, the stamp collection, the gold coins were carefully arranged around the bottom of the bag. It was painfully little to show for his years in Holland. He had traded a few of the gold coins for the forged documents he had needed to establish his new identity. He had regretfully left behind the art objects, buried deep in a field on his farm just before he left it for the last time. Perhaps one day, he would return to Bavaria to recover them. He folded his clothes, carefully washed and ironed, and placed them in the bag. On top, he placed two English grammar books and a pair of American army boots. He was riding the 6 p.m. bus into town to take the overnight train to Frankfurt.

As he stood waiting for the bus, a few of the civilian employees on the base came up to wish him good luck. One of them, an old man who had lost his son at the battle of El-Alamein, clasped him by the shoulders and said, "I hope you have more luck than most of your generation." One of the older ladies kissed him on each cheek. "You will marry a fat woman and have six children." She roared with laughter, as did several others around her.

Suddenly, Meinhaft appeared at the bus stop. Ever since their first meeting almost two years ago, Galish had worried about the one person in Memmingen who knew who he really was. He had carefully avoided him. Meinhaft's open admission that he had been a senior officer in one of the most notorious SS divisions might be a useful piece of information, if the need arose. Galish looked at him warily. Meinhaft walked over to him, a piece of paper in his hand.

"You are leaving us?" Galish wondered how Meinhaft had found out that he was leaving Germany.

"The overnight train to Frankfurt."

"Let me give you this address. Some day you may need a friend or two from the past."

"Thank you, but I won't."

Meinhaft laughed. "You are deluding yourself. You and I are Germans, first and last. We may have lost this time, but we will never lose again. We are survivors. We need to stick together. Here, take this."

Galish looked down at the piece of paper. It read: "Sr. Gerhard Wormser, 126 Avenida de la Republica, Buenos Aires 12, Argentina."

"This is where you can contact me," added Meinhaft. "I too will be leaving Germany soon. We have an organization. You might need us, and I might be able to help you." His smile did not reach his eyes.

Galish carefully folded the piece of paper and put it in his wallet. Then his curiosity got the better of him. "Why are you going to Argentina?" he asked.

"My dear comrade, it must be obvious to you that the Allies are on the lookout for us. We cannot stay here. We must go where we have friends, or where people do not care who we are or where we came from. I don't know your plans, and it is better you do not know mine. Good luck. Until we meet again. *Auf wiedersehen.*" Meinhaft walked away quickly.

The bus arrived, and the waiting knot of people boarded it. The banter inside was good-natured. One older fellow had observed how heavy Galish's bag was and said, "I bet he has a lot of Ami cigarettes stashed in there to bribe his way into first class."

"He'll never get into first class; he doesn't have enough bags." More laughter.

"Hey, Galish, are you taking that cold fish of a lady doctor with you?" Someone tittered from the back. Silence. Galish stared straight ahead; he had to play his role to the end. He gritted his teeth as sudden anger seized him. He recalled the times when he had killed someone for less reason. Tonight, he felt the same tight sensation. In the old days, he would have taken the stupid shit and pumped his lungs full of gasoline, watching his victim writhe as his esophagus and larynx closed up, burning and choking him at the same time. He willed himself to show no emotion.

The bus came to a stop at its usual place in the town square. Galish waited in his seat until the others had gotten off. He would soon become a vague memory for them, just another Hungarian refugee who had made good meals for the Amis. Galish pulled the duffel bag down from the rack, nodded to the driver, stepped off the bus, and walked towards the train station.

CHAPTER SEVEN

―――――――＜＞―――――――

DEAD ENDS, NEW LIVES

FEBRUARY, 1948

CHICAGO

Joseph Galish got off the train at Union Station. The platform led to an enormous hall. He walked in the direction of a sign that said 'Way Out'. Looking around, he saw a cavernous corridor leading to three revolving doors and two side entrances. There were very few people around, probably because it was 11.30 at night. An old, skeletal black man was shuffling in the opposite direction, a cloth coat pulled tightly over his shoulders. Galish had seen very few black people in his life. They made him uncomfortable. His pace accelerated towards the revolving doors, and as he pushed the heavy glass around, he felt the bite of a bitterly cold wind.

Galish might as well have stepped out into the Antarctic. Snow dust swirled around his feet. There was almost no traffic. He stopped to look at the piece of paper which he had pulled out of his pocket for the third time. It read: 4524 North Skokie, Chicago. He was to ask for Theodore Radinski.

He stood shivering on the sidewalk, watching for a taxi. Soon, a dilapidated LaSalle, painted a bright red, stopped at the curb. A black man with white hair was at the wheel. He turned his window down a fraction. Galish asked if the man knew where 4524 North Skokie was. The black man grinned and said, "Yessir, just get in, sit back and relax."

The address on Skokie turned out to be a two-family house built of yellow brick, with a pocket-handkerchief garden in front of it. Drifts of dirty snow lay against the side of the house. It was now past midnight. Galish paid the driver and added a $1.00 tip, then stumbled, exhausted, up the walk. He rang the bell. There was no answer. He rang it again. He heard the shuffling of feet. The door opened a crack.

"What do you want?" a man asked.

"My name is Galish, Joseph Galish. Captain Defoe sent me. Are you Mr. Radinski?"

The man behind the door seemed uncertain. He was having trouble waking up. "Oh yes, yes I am. Patrick sent you. Come in," he said, as he took the chain off.

"I'm very sorry to be arriving so late. I had no idea the train would be delayed."

Galish looked around him as he walked in. The furniture had a heavy, dark, middle-European look. The curtains and carpets were also dark. A small window, high in the wall, was made of cheap, multi-colored glass.

"My name is Radinski, Theodore Radinski," the man said. "Everyone calls me Ted." He extended a pudgy hand which felt damp to the touch. He was wearing a dark blue satin bathrobe.

"Pleased to meet you," said Galish. "Thank you for receiving me." He bowed slightly. "Since it is so late, we will talk tomorrow. Now, perhaps you will show me to my room, and I will go to bed. I am very tired."

"Of course. You have been travelling for days. Is this all the luggage you have?" he asked, looking down at the duffel bag.

"That's it," replied Galish curtly.

Radinski led the way up the narrow stairs, turned at the landing and opened a door leading to a small bedroom. A hint of mothballs suggested that the room was used infrequently.

"The bathroom is over here," Radinski said, waving a hand towards another door. "Make yourself comfortable. Is there anything I can get you? How about a drink, or something to eat, maybe?"

"You are kind, but no thank you. I will see you in the morning. Can you wake me before you leave the house?"

"Certainly. Tomorrow I can be a bit later than usual at the office. We need to talk about finding you a job. I promised Captain Defoe I would help you," Radinski added importantly.

They said goodnight, and Galish closed the door to his bedroom.

The next morning, Galish was surprised to find himself awake at 7.45 a.m. The sun was streaming through the sides of the curtains. He swiveled out of bed and walked over to the window to push the curtains aside. The sun's brightness was reflected by the thin carpet of snow. Galish squinted as he examined the surroundings of the house. A small back yard led to a low wooden fence. A few scattered bushes completed the perimeter. Behind the fence appeared the upper portion of a similar house.

Galish was downstairs half an hour later, dressed in his dark brown jacket and trousers. He wore a clean shirt and one of his three ties. His shoes were dark brown lace-up boots which he had traded for a pound of coffee two years ago. He looked around the living room and walked through it into the kitchen. He called out for Radinski. There was no answer. He inspected the kitchen, looking for a cup of coffee. Just then he heard the front door open. He turned to face Radinski as he walked into the kitchen carrying a large brown bag. Radinski looked surprised to see him standing there.

"So, you're awake! Good morning, Joe. How did you sleep?" Radinski asked, placing the shopping bag on the counter.

"Very well, thank you."

"Let me show you where everything is," continued Radinski. "Since I live alone, I keep things very simple. Fortunately, they invented instant coffee during the war, so let me get you some."

Galish followed the other man's movements carefully. Radinski was about five feet eight; he was corpulent, with a boxy frame. He was probably in his early sixties. He was dressed carefully in a dark suit, a white shirt, and a wide, flowery tie. Galish thought the shoulders of the jacket were too wide, but perhaps the man wanted to enhance his physique.

"Please sit down, and let me get you some breakfast." He shuffled around, opening drawers and cabinets in the little kitchen. "You see, my wife died three years ago. I didn't want to move. I've been here for thirty years, and I'm used to everything. My auto parts business needs my constant attention. By the way, it is such a pleasure to have someone to stay with me."

Galish decided to let the man ramble on. He had no interest in Radinski's background, but Galish's future in the U.S., at least in the early stages, was very largely dependent on this man's goodwill. He therefore pretended to appear interested.

"Please don't go to any trouble. My needs are very simple."

"No, please. Sit down and tell me about yourself. I have been expecting your arrival. How was your trip?" He continued to prepare the coffee as he spoke. Galish disliked inquisitive people, but he had to satisfy the man's curiosity.

"Captain Defoe told you the facts. I am a refugee from the Communists, probably like a lot of other new arrivals here in the States. I have no family left in Europe. I need to get a new start in life." Galish attempted to look sad. "We all need to look to the future."

Radinski tasted the coffee, his eyes never leaving Galish's face.

"It must have been terrible in Europe during the war. I have a cousin in Milwaukee whose parents, like mine, were born in Poland. He helped another cousin get into the country

last year. It was pretty tough getting through Immigration."
He paused. "How do you like your coffee?"

"With milk and sugar, please," replied Galish.

"At least you are able-bodied. Weren't you wounded at
all?"

"I was evacuated from the Russian front when I got severe
dysentery."

"Jeez, you were lucky, I suppose. Well," said Radinski
looking at his watch. "I will have to leave you. This afternoon,
you and I have an appointment with a friend of mine. His
name is Peter Faber, and he owns a factory in downtown
Chicago. He said he might be able to give you a job."

"That will be fine," answered Galish. "What kind of a
job?"

"They make bakery supplies, you know, like syrups and
decorative candies. I thought that would fit in well with your
cooking skills."

MARCH, 1948

MEMMINGEN

The *bierstube* was very busy on Friday nights. Gradually, some degree of normalcy was returning to the town, even though shortages were still the rule, not the exception. The bar was packed with the usual patrons, many of whom had just collected their weekly pay checks. Meinhaft was one of them. He had already downed two beers, and was well into his third. Tonight, he was not going to worry about spending too much money. It was one of his last nights in Memmingen. In two days, he would be leaving on a circuitous route to Argentina. Everything was ready. He would be joined on the journey by a former colleague, also a senior officer in the SS *Das Reich* division. They were wanted men, and they had to disappear.

Meinhaft looked around the room and decided that he was not going to miss the Fatherland. He had not seen his wife since he had gone on a short leave in early 1945. Now, she was unreachable inside East Germany, and there was absolutely no chance that he would be permitted to cross into the Russian Zone. Besides which, applying for travel documents might expose him to questions which he did not want to answer. No, he had to make a clean break. His wife would undoubtedly assume that he was dead.

A woman's voice spoke up behind him.

"Good evening, Herr Wormser."

He turned around and recognized the woman whom he had seen several times with Heinrich Wanstumm, alias Joseph Galish. She was as tall as he was, he noticed, and her blond hair was pulled tightly away from her forehead. Under her black coat, he sensed the unusual width of her shoulders.

"Good evening to you, Fraulein. Will you join me in a beer?"

"Thank you, I would like that."

"Have you had any news from our friend Galish?"

"No, I haven't," she said abruptly.

"I see. Well, I haven't seen you here lately," commented Meinhaft.

"I generally come earlier. To tell you the truth, it is not easy for a single woman when the bar becomes crowded with drunken men."

"Certainly. But you are a little later than usual tonight?"

"Yes, but to be perfectly honest, I came late to look for you, Herr Wormser." There was a slightly clipped edge to her voice. Meinhaft said nothing while he leaned over to take the beer passed to him by the waitress. He handed it to Ilse.

"And how may I be of help, Fraulein?"

"I have prepared a little supper at my home; perhaps you would enjoy a home-cooked meal?" Meinhaft looked at her carefully. She had been Galish's girlfriend until his departure two months ago. What was on her mind? Obviously, something she didn't want to discuss in public. He might even get her into bed. He decided to accept her invitation.

They finished their beers and walked out into the clear, cold air.

"It is not far," she said. He kept up with her, noticing that she moved with considerable grace and strength. They turned into a narrow street. She stopped at the little townhouse, unlocked the front door, and led the way into her small apartment. Meinhaft looked around, guessing how she and Galish had spent their hours together. In the corner of the room, a table was laid with two place settings.

"Please make yourself comfortable," she invited. "May I serve you a wine with dinner? It is a simple white wine from near Stuttgart."

"*Bitte*," he replied.

Ilse emerged from the small kitchen with a bottle and two glasses. She poured the wine carefully, then presented him with a glass, raised hers and said, "*Prosit!*" They clinked glasses. Ilse continued, "I have already prepared dinner. It is in the oven."

"Wonderful. Now, Fraulein, perhaps you will tell me how I can help you?"

She stared into her wine glass, then raised her eyes towards Meinhaft. He had never seen Ilse so close up. She had a strong, angular face, but it was the eyes which fascinated him. Ilse seemed nervous; her eyelashes flickered, perhaps to hide the impenetrable blue irises.

"Herr Galish told me a little about you."

"Oh, I hope he spoke well of me?"

"He said you had been in the SS."

Meinhaft sipped carefully from his glass. He did not answer.

"Herr Galish said that you have contacts in South America."

"Why do you want to know?"

"Herr Wormser, I need to get out of Germany, permanently."

After a moment of reflection, Meinhaft asked, "Why didn't you ask Galish for help?"

"Herr Galish didn't want any encumbrances. It was too complicated, he said."

"Perhaps because he didn't tell you who he really was."

"I knew he was not Hungarian. I could tell that he was German."

"Well, Fraulein, I must tell you that you were having an affair with a former Gestapo officer, whose real name is Heinrich Wanstumm." Ilse stared at Meinhaft; then, a slight smile hovered over her lips. She said nothing. After a pause,

Meinhaft continued, "So tell me why you must leave Germany?"

"Let me serve dinner, and I will tell you." She placed the dishes on the table, lighted the two candles and sat down again, facing him. "*Mahlzeit!*" she said as she picked up her knife and fork.

"Delicious," said Meinhaft. He looked at Ilse, letting his eyes run appraisingly over her body.

"Herr Wormser, what I am about to tell you, no one else here knows."

"Before you tell me," interjected Meinhaft, "You have to realize that your chances of getting away to South America are not good. Most of the routes have been compromised by informers."

She chewed a mouthful, swallowed, and replied, "Anything is better than staying here in Germany. I am from the Ruhrgebiet, from Oberhausen to be exact. I trained as a medical technician. During the war I worked in a clinic near Berlin. We did reconstructive surgery. At the end of the war, I was given a chance to go south, towards the Alps, where I was told we would be safe. Our car broke down near Memmingen. I have been here ever since."

Meinhaft looked at her and smiled thinly.

"Please, Fraulein, tell me, what did you reconstruct at this clinic?"

She looked at him without a change of expression. "We performed surgery on SS officers who had been horribly disfigured. Almost all of them came from the Russian front."

"Then what happened?"

"What do you mean? We ran out of medical supplies. We could no longer perform even the most basic blood transfusions. We were forced to close the clinic."

Meinhaft sat back in his chair. He looked at her for a few seconds, and then, he lifted his eyes to the ceiling.

"Fraulein, you must think I am an idiot. It is possible, but just barely so, that I might believe your story. But if I had, then you would not have needed to bring me here to persuade me over dinner. Patching up wounded SS officers is not a crime. Unless you tell me who you really are, and what you are really afraid of, I cannot and will not help you." He sat back and stared coldly at her.

She looked at him, her eyes flickering slightly but never wandering away from his mouth. He hated people who looked at his mouth; the scar there had never healed properly. The seconds ticked by. She rose from the table and paced around the small room, back and forth, like a caged tiger.

"Very well. My name is not Ilse Huber. It is Marlene Buthe, *Doctor* Buthe. My chief at the clinic was Professor Dietrich Sommer. He recommended me to a surgeon, Professor Auguste Hirt, head of the Anatomy Institute at the University of Strasbourg. He was conducting some research into the characteristics of the Jewish brain. My role was to handle the corpses of Jews and to prepare their heads for examination. Those heads that we did not work on immediately, I put in hermetically-sealed cans filled with a preservative fluid, for future examination."

Meinhaft pushed his chair away from the table as she spoke. He wiped his mouth and threw the napkin down on the table. "Enough, Fraulein, I don't want to hear any more."

She continued relentlessly. "My expertise became known to Himmler. He wanted someone like me to assist in medical experiments at Sachsenhausen. I was good at my work there. Then the doctors became concerned about the rapidly-approaching British. When they fled, I decided to go south to Bavaria; everyone was talking about Hitler's move to Berchstesgaden. I ended up here in Memmingen. No one knows who I am. My family died in the war. I have not communicated with friends or former colleagues. There is no trail. Herr Wormser, I must get out of Germany before they find out who I am."

Meinhaft lit a cigarette. The smoke curled lazily towards the ceiling. "I will have to give this case some thought. There are very few people who can avail themselves of our arrangements. We had one man who pretended to be a member of the Party, who claimed he had killed socialists in the early days. We found out he was lying. He ended up in the middle of a road, run over by a truck. I will have to check your background and obtain agreement to let you use our facilities."

"When will I know if you can help me?"

"Soon. Someone else will be in touch with you. They will ask you questions. They will probably want physical proof of your claims, such as letters, ID cards, whatever." He was not about to tell her that he would already be long gone.

She went over to a small desk, wrote something on a piece of paper, and returned to the table. "Here is where I can be reached during the day. I have about 600 dollars and some gold coins and jewelry. Will that be enough to cover the cost of the trip?"

"Frankly, no, but if we decide to sponsor you, we will make arrangements for you to reimburse us later, after you have arrived at your destination."

"Herr Wormser, you have no idea how relieved I feel. Please, will you have a little dessert and a glass of liqueur, or something else?" Ilse leaned towards him; the inference was clear.

He watched her carefully, unable to reconcile the contradictions in her behavior, her appearance, and her story. He wondered whether Galish had been able to sort it out. Maybe he had left her behind for a good reason.

Half an hour later, he took his leave, and went home to his small apartment. He already knew that he would recommend her to the organization. She had been a loyal Party member. They had taken very few women out, but she knew too much. He resolved to get up early to start the process.

APRIL, 1948

THE HAGUE

Kees Goedkamp had just moved his staff to much more appropriate offices on the outskirts of The Hague, closer to the International Court of Justice. There was a large, dry basement in which they could store the rapidly growing collection of documents and files concerning German criminal activities in the Netherlands during the war. The files were organized according to groups active from 1940 until the final liberation in May, 1945. The largest group was the Dutch Nazi Party, followed by the Gestapo, then the SS, the SD, and finally the German Army, including the *Abwehr*. A special section had also been created for Dutch citizens who had collaborated with the Germans, and who, while not guilty of specific crimes, had acted as informers on their own countrymen.

Every Wednesday, Goedkamp chaired a meeting of his department heads. The meeting was an opportunity to monitor progress and to share among his colleagues new information which could be useful to them. Their work was painstaking and required careful assessments of the reliability of the information. An indictment had to withstand the rigors of legal procedure. They could not afford to be sloppy, let alone to be accused of unsubstantiated witch hunts.

Anton Hardewijk was in charge of the Gestapo files. He was an energetic young lawyer who had graduated from

Leiden University. He had served during the war with the Royal Netherlands Navy as navigation officer on a corvette. He was well-liked for his openness and his ready smile. It was his turn to report at the meeting.

"We have finally been able to complete the profile of Heinrich Wanstumm, the head of the Gestapo in Amsterdam. We have several witnesses who could recognize him, and we therefore have a composite description of the man. We finally got lucky when digging through some of the files from the Gestapo offices in Amsterdam. It's fortunate that the Germans have a penchant for orderliness and bureaucracy. Wanstumm was born in Bavaria, near a town called Memmingen. We know that he disappeared in January, 1945, because he was reported missing by his assistant, a fellow named Ganz. His service car disappeared at the same time. It had an extra load of petrol when he left. We can assume that he went to Germany, since, by then, there was really no other place he could have gone. Our guess is that he went into hiding, and he may have assumed another identity. At this point looking for him is like looking for a needle in a haystack.

"We have extensively documented his activities, including the torture of Dutch civilians and the deportation of Jews. There is no question in my mind that he should rank in the 'most wanted' category. We are ready to submit his name and dossier to the Allied War Crimes Tribunal for their consideration, but given the fact that he spent almost the entire war here in Holland, we feel that we should be the ones to go after him."

"Well done," complimented Goedkamp. "I want to re-emphasize, as you pointed out, Anton, that just because Wanstumm has vanished, and the trail is growing cold, it doesn't mean that we should give up on him. Like much police work, progress often depends on the correct interpretation of an apparently trivial event or fact. In the case of Wanstumm, for instance, we should make sure that he did indeed surface in Germany. I want this checked out. Anton, you might go to his home town, Memmingen, and ask questions, just in case he left some trace there. Are you aware of any relatives he might still have there?"

"No, but there may be people in Memmingen who remember him. Who knows? We can check the town records. I'll go as soon as I finish the depositions I have arranged for this week."

"Let me find out what you will need to travel by car into southern Germany. Memmingen is in the American Zone, and you will need a special pass." The meeting continued with the remainder of the reports.

———<>———

MEMMINGEN

Goedkamp called one of his friends at Dutch Army headquarters, who in turn arranged with the U.S. military for a pass, as well as for an introduction for Hardewijk to the commander of the local U.S. Army base. Given the difficulty of finding good train connections, Goedkamp had also decided to let Hardewijk drive one of the staff cars.

Hardewijk found the drive easy enough. At the Dutch border, he linked up to the *autobahn* at Dusseldorf, then drove straight down through Frankfurt and Stuttgart to Ulm. He marveled at these highways, built during Hitler's regime for military purposes. His car, a well-maintained Packard and reputedly the best car in the pool, lapped up the road at eighty miles an hour. At Ulm, he got off the *autobahn* and took a variety of country roads to Memmingen. It was already 7 p.m., and he was tired and hungry. In town, he found a *gasthaus* called the Golden Ox, and after a mediocre meal, he went immediately to bed, anxious to get an early start in the morning.

Breakfast the next day was as mediocre as the meal the night before. The atmosphere in the hotel was funereal. He told the sullen owner that he would be back that night and would therefore keep the room. Before leaving, he remembered to ask the man for directions to the U.S. base. He drove out of the town's narrow inner streets and found the road to the base. He passed through the gates after the usual scrutiny of his papers and parked the Packard near the headquarters building.

The office inside was spartan, tidy, and hot. A sergeant looked up from his desk.

"Good morning," said Hardewijk. "I am from the Netherlands War Crimes Commission. Here is my pass and a letter of introduction to your commanding officer."

The sergeant scanned the documents, rose from his chair, and handed them back to Hardewijk. "Thank you, sir. Colonel Armistead is away from his desk, but he should be back in about fifteen minutes. Would you care for a cup of coffee?"

Hardewijk nodded and took out his notes to review. The colonel arrived a few minutes later. The sergeant spoke to him briefly as he entered the room. Armistead turned to Hardewijk, shook his hand, welcomed him to the base and showed him into his office.

"Mr. Hardewijk. I'm sorry. How do you pronounce your name?" asked the colonel.

"The Dutch w is like the English v, but don't worry about it," smiled Hardewijk.

"Please have a seat. What can we do for you?"

"Thank you for seeing me, Colonel. At the Commission, we are responsible for investigating and prosecuting those who committed war crimes on Dutch territory during the war. My particular area of responsibility is the Gestapo and its activities during those years."

"I see. Well, you're not the only country, I can tell you. I've had visits from the French, some of the Nuremberg staff, and inquiries by the Belgians. My territory only covers western Bavaria, however, so I may be of only limited help to you."

"On the contrary, sir. Let me explain," said Hardewijk. "The Gestapo chief in north-west Holland, who had his headquarters in Amsterdam, has been identified as a major war criminal. We have been able to document many of his activities. We have tallied well over one hundred deaths of Dutch citizens for which he can be held personally responsible. He was also actively engaged in the deportation of Jews, mainly from Amsterdam. The case against him is so strong that we have forwarded it on to the Allied War Crimes Tribunal. In the meantime, we are continuing our own investigation. He disappeared from Holland in 1945. One of the few facts we have is that he was born here in Memmingen."

"So you think he might be around here somewhere?" asked Colonel Armistead.

"No, we think he is long gone. But when he left Amsterdam, somewhat precipitously, in 1945, he could only have gone to Germany, and the chances are that he came here. He may still have family here."

"I see. Well, it looks like you'll need to get into the town records and so forth. How's your German?"

"Whether we like it or not, Colonel, most Dutchmen speak it. Mine is good but not perfect."

"Okay." The colonel rose from his chair. "I'm going to assign Lieutenant Goodrich to you for a couple of days. He will make sure that you get the information, if it is available."

"Many thanks, Colonel. I have my own car, which will make it easier."

"As you wish. Lieutenant Goodrich will meet you in five minutes outside my office." They shook hands.

Lieutenant Goodrich arrived promptly. They introduced themselves and decided to head first to the Memmingen town hall. It was located just off the main square and was surprisingly fresh and attractive-looking. Inside, however, the usual drab grayness of officialdom dominated. Hardewijk followed Goodrich up a broad staircase and into a long room with a counter at one end with stacks of files arranged behind it.

They walked up to the middle-aged man behind the counter, who took one look at the American uniform and decided to be of service.

Hardewijk explained his objective in reasonably fluent German. "We need information on a Heinrich Wanstumm. He was born in Memmingen and is approximately 40 years old."

"Well, if you don't mind waiting, I'll have to go through the registry of births. They are organized by year. You say 40? That means 1908. Let me look."

He retreated to the back of his domain. The shuffling was audible. Goodrich and Hardewijk sat down on a pair of rickety, upright chairs. They exchanged information about each other to pass the time. Hardewijk liked this bright, energetic young man.

The man returned, shaking his head. "I'm sorry, there is nothing. Are you sure it was Memmingen?"

"Yes," answered Hardewijk, "but I'm not sure about the year. Try 1907 or 1909."

The man shuffled off again. The minutes went by. Then they heard him walk back, more quickly this time.

"I may have what you need." He was holding a battered brown paper file, which he placed on the counter. "A Wanstumm, Heinrich, was born on June 12, 1907 at the maternity clinic here. His parents are listed here," he pointed with a dirty finger. "He seems to have been an only child. The address given is outside of town, a farmhouse on the Donauweg. Here, perhaps you want to copy it down."

"Do you have a marriage certificate for him?"

"I would have to know what year he was married."

"Don't you cross reference the marriage to the birth certificates?"

"Only if the certificates were both delivered here. If he requested a marriage certificate in Hamburg, for instance, we wouldn't know."

"All right. Now tell me, where can we find educational records?"

"You'll have to go to the schools. We don't keep those here."

Hardewijk turned to Goodrich. "I think we're through here for the time being. I want to go and see this farm."

The Packard purred along the rain-slick road. Hardewijk had asked Goodrich to find the American Forces Network on the radio, and they were now listening to a tune by Phil Harris. They counted off the miles until they came to a fork in the road at the village of Insingen, where they had been told to turn off onto a country lane. Hardewijk slowed the car; Goodrich was trying to decipher the man's instructions on how to reach the Wanstumm farmhouse. Soon, they saw a modest building, fifty meters off the road. The Packard turned into the rutted drive. There appeared to be no sign of life. Goodrich suggested blowing the horn. After an interval, a buxom woman emerged from the house. She stood there, glaring at them.

Hardewijk got out of the car. "We are looking for Heinrich Wanstumm," he said.

"And who are you?" she asked with palpable hostility.

Goodrich decided to get out of the car. She saw the American uniform.

"He is not here," she informed them in a more cooperative voice.

"And where might he be, then?" asked Hardewijk, the excitement rising inside him.

"*Weiss nicht.*"

Goodrich decided it was time to lean on her. "He may be indicted as a war criminal," said the American in German. "People who help him escape from the law will also be prosecuted." This was delivered in very poor German, but she got the gist of it immediately.

"He lived here after the war, but he didn't pay his taxes. The state put this house up for sale, and we bought it."

"So you have no idea where he went?"

"They say he went to work for the Americans."

Hardewijk and Goodrich looked at each other, stunned.

"What did you say?" asked Hardewijk.

"That's the rumor, anyway. You should ask Frau Schmidt, in the village. She lives above the bakery. I heard her talk about it."

The two men walked back to the car quickly. "Is this possible?" asked Hardewijk. "Do you Americans employ locals?"

"Lots of them, but we screen them pretty thoroughly first."

They arrived in the village, and parked the car in the narrow street opposite the bakery. They rang the doorbell. Upstairs, a curtain parted. Soon the door opened, and an old woman stood facing them, her hands pulling a shawl tightly across her shoulders.

"Frau Schmidt, we're sorry to bother you," said Hardewijk, "but we need some information. Did you know a Heinrich Wanstumm, whose family owned the farm up the road?"

"Yes, but not very well. I remember his mother. She shopped at the bakery."

"What happened at the end of the war? Did Wanstumm come back here?"

"I think so. I worked at the American base for a few months as a cleaning lady, and I saw him there two or three times."

"Are you sure?"

"I remember. I was so surprised because I recognized his face. At first I couldn't think who he was. Then it came to me. But I left soon because I broke my hip."

"So you saw him working there at the American base?" asked Goodrich.

"I don't know whether he was working there."

"Just to make sure we are talking about the same man, can you describe him?" asked Hardewijk.

"Average height, quite thin, blond hair."

"How old do you think he was?"

"Late thirties, it seemed to me."

They thanked the woman and took their leave. Goodrich scribbled her address in a notebook.

It was four o'clock by the time they returned to the base. They had agreed that Colonel Armistead should be briefed on their day's activities. Goodrich and Hardewijk had to wait a few minutes for the colonel, who was on the phone. Then Goodrich said, "Sir, we have come across something that may require further investigation. We thought we should let you know first."

They recounted the day's events. When they had finished, Colonel Armistead looked at them thoughtfully.

"So it's just possible that Wanstumm may have been on this base. However, does that mean that he was working for us? At the very least, we should establish whether he is still here. You should have Frau Schmidt take a look at the photos of our present local staff, excluding the women of course. Lieutenant, please arrange to have her come in tomorrow. Hardewijk, I should like you, if you will, to look at the work files of all the men, between 25 and 40 years of age, who have worked at the base. If either you or she recognizes Wanstumm, we could narrow the possibilities down to a few leads and take it from there."

They stood up. Tomorrow's work was cut out for them. Hardewijk paused on the way out. "Colonel, before I start in on the files tomorrow, I should like to go to the town hall again, this time to ascertain when taxes on the Wanstumm farm stopped being paid and when the farm was sold off. This might bracket Wanstumm's presence here."

"Good idea. When you get back, we will have all the files at your disposal."

———<>———

Unlike the past few days, the next day dawned bright and sunny. After eating the same bland breakfast at the *gasthaus,* Hardewijk walked over to the town hall. In a large room at the top of the stairs, he found the man in charge of the archives, who recognized him immediately.

"Guten Morgen," Hardewijk said. "I need information on the Wanstumm farm. I understand it was sold at auction to pay back taxes on it. I would like to know when the taxes stopped being paid, where the tax notices were sent, if they were not sent to the farm, and when the farm was finally sold."

"I'm afraid we will have to go upstairs for that. My colleague can take care of you. Please come with me."

They walked up the next flight of stairs, and entered a large room not unlike the one downstairs. A white-haired man listened to the request, looked at Hardewijk, and said, "We can't give out that information."

"Why not?"

"It is against the law."

"What law are you referring to?"

"The German law, of course."

Hardewijk was almost six feet tall. His normally pleasant face darkened into a scowl. He leaned over the counter. "Until further notice, you are occupied by the victorious Allied forces." He pulled out his official ID. "See this? I have the authority to put you in jail on suspicion of war crimes. The only way you are going to avoid that is by giving me the information I want. Do you understand?"

The white-haired man stepped back two paces behind the counter. His face was ashen. The man's colleague had beaten a hasty retreat down the stairs, terrified of getting mixed up in this.

"Jawohl, I am sorry. Forgive the misunderstanding. Now let me see, could you please write down the name of the farm and the owner?"

Hardewijk waited while the man disappeared into the aisles of dilapidated file cabinets. Fifteen minutes went by, then twenty. Hardewijk was getting fidgety. He heard nothing, and wondered whether the man was still there. Suddenly, the fellow reappeared, holding several files.

"It seems that the farm in question was owned by Emil and Anna Wanstumm. They died, and it passed to their son, Heinrich, in 1936. The taxes were paid regularly until 1944. After that, nothing was paid on time for one reason or another. But a payment for taxes in arrears was received in early January 1945. The payments became regular again until February, 1946, when they stopped completely. Early last year, a final notice was sent out by the *Steueramt*. When no reply was received, the property was sold publicly. It now belongs to the Hugen family."

"Let me see." Hardewijk pored over the documents, irritated at having to decipher the Gothic script. He made some notes as he worked his way through the dense, impractical lettering.

"I have enough for now. If I need anything else, you will be delighted to help me, *ja?*"

Hardewijk stalked out. He got back in his car and drove out to the base, where he parked the car near the administration building. He entered and asked the first person he saw, "Could you tell me where I can find Lieutenant Goodrich?"

"Are you Mr. Hardewijk, sir? Let me take you to the conference room he has set aside for you. The files you requested are on the table, sir. He will be along a little later. My name is Corporal Parsons, sir. There's a buzzer on the table in case you need anything."

Hardewijk sat down at the conference room table in front of a large pile of personnel files, clean and properly labeled. He started going through them quickly to establish that the employees were indeed between the ages of 25 and 40. Each folder contained a header sheet, to which was pinned a passport photo. Quickly, Hardewijk started eliminating the overweight, the ugly, the dark-haired employees. It was hard to believe so many local men had worked, or were still working, on the U.S. Army base.

Of the men whom he decided to review more carefully, he eliminated all of those who were born after 1914. This left him with four men who seemed to fit Wanstumm's description, until he noticed that three of the four were German nationals. The fourth was a Hungarian refugee named Galish. He eliminated that one. That left three men: one was born in Augsburg, one near Hanover, the third was from Munich. Unless they had lied, not one was from Memmingen.

Hardewijk rarely smoked, but Goodrich had offered him a pack of Lucky Strikes yesterday. He groped in his coat pocket, found them and some matches and lit a cigarette. He was doing something wrong, but he wasn't sure what. He tried to think the way Wanstumm would have thought as Germany collapsed in 1945. He would have left Holland. He seemed to have done that successfully. He would have gone to a familiar place: Memmingen. It appeared that he had indeed been here. Wanstumm was anything but a fool; he knew he was a hunted man. He would have shed his identity, and then he would have tried to remove himself as far away as possible from the investigations conducted by the Allies. Getting out of occupied Germany was almost impossible, but some evidence was accumulating that a number of Nazis had fled to South America, taking a round-about route through Italy, then to Spain, from which passage was more easily arranged. Why would anyone like Wanstumm have taken the risk of working for Americans? It made no sense.

He was aroused from his reverie by the entrance of Lieutenant Goodrich, accompanied by Frau Schmidt. They shook hands politely. Frau Schmidt looked around her in wonderment, and began to loosen her wool overcoat as she felt the effect of the overheated room. The two men hovered over her courteously, both realizing that she might become a key witness in their search. Hardewijk invited her to sit down.

"Thank you so much, Frau Schmidt, for coming down here to help us with a few questions. You told us that you saw

Heinrich Wanstumm here on the base. It would be very
helpful if you could identify him for us. Would you be so kind
as to look through these pictures and see whether you
recognize anyone?"

Hardewijk passed along the group that he had selected,
consisting of the three men. Carefully, she opened each file
and looked at the pictures stapled to the front pages. After
the first attempt, she went back to each picture, spending
more time on the man from Hanover. She pursed her lips, her
left hand brushing away a strand of gray hair that kept falling
over her left eye. Then she started shaking her head.

"I'm sorry, they are not Heinrich, I don't think. Maybe a
little bit this one (the man from Hanover), but the chin isn't
right." She looked at them, shrugging her shoulders.

"Never mind," said Hardewijk, equally disappointed. He
continued, "Is there anything special you can remember about
the man who you think was Heinrich Wanstumm?"

"No, not really, it was one of those things. You recognize
a face but you don't know from where. Then you remember
later. Perhaps I made a mistake?" She was sounding
increasingly unsure of herself.

"Well, thank you very much for coming in, anyway,"
said Hardewijk. They accompanied her to the door. After
she left, the two men sat down and said nothing for a
moment. It would have been such a coup to have been able
to identify Wanstumm.

"Just because she failed to recognize him in these pictures
doesn't mean that he wasn't on the base, right?" asked
Goodrich. "He may have changed more than she realized,
fatter, thinner, balder, who knows? Maybe we should have
her look at all the pictures of men who ever worked here."

"These pictures are poor quality. Our experience is that
they are rarely of any use in making a positive identification
unless we have a second source which provides a match-up,"
commented Hardewijk. "We have to assume that he was here
at some point. It's the best lead we have. But the next phase

will take a lot of time. I have to get back to Holland and review this with my boss."

"Then I guess we'd better bring Colonel Armistead up to date."

———<>———

THE HAGUE

Hardewijk returned to The Hague too late to stop by the office. He called Goedkamp from the garage, where a suspicious mechanic walked around the Packard to make sure that it was still in perfect condition. Goedkamp told Hardewijk to have a good night's sleep; they would meet first thing in the morning. Hardewijk walked home. It was a bit of a hike, but it felt good to get some exercise. He rented rooms from a widow, who was very small, very thin, and very attentive to his needs. She shopped for him, took care of his laundry, and once a week, she cleaned his apartment. Some day, she hoped that he would have time to entertain a young lady. At the moment, he had other things to preoccupy him.

Next morning, Hardewijk was in his office at 7.45. He quickly arranged his files and notes, then walked up the flight of stairs leading to Goedkamp's office. He knocked carefully on the door, heard a greeting, and walked in to find Goedkamp in his shirt sleeves, smoking a cigar.

"Good morning, sir," said Hardewijk, "I have quite a lot to report to you."

"Coffee will be here in a short while," replied Goedkamp, "so make yourself comfortable, and tell me about it." He leaned forward to be sure not to miss anything.

"It is pretty certain that Wanstumm went back to his hometown in 1945. He may have found a job working for the Americans. Then he disappeared."

"Do you have a positive identification?" asked Goedkamp.

"Sort of, but not really. We have an old woman who thinks she saw him in the area and on the base. The U.S. Army keeps pretty good files on whom they employed at the base. We have been through them, but we were unable to match any of the personnel records with him. Frau Schmidt looked at some of the photos which we thought were most likely to be a match with Wanstumm's description."

"She didn't spot him, did she?" asked Goedkamp.

"No, she didn't. She said that she was confused."

"Of course she did. It happens every time. You put one hundred pictures in front of someone and ask them to identify the suspect. On the first pass, they come up with five likely candidates. Then they go back and start worrying about the nose, the eyebrows, the hairline. They go back to look at other pictures. Sometimes they ask to go through the whole collection. Finally they tell you that it might be "one of those two", but they really can't be sure." Goedkamp wasn't angry, just resigned. "So what do you think happened to Wanstumm?"

"Sir, I think he is no longer in Germany. It's just a hunch though. He had a lot of nerve going to work for the Americans, and I think it gave him time to prepare his next move."

"So where did he go?"

"Who knows? Perhaps he went to South America, or Africa. Perhaps he's still somewhere in Germany, but my hunch is that he's nowhere near Memmingen."

Goedkamp thought for a moment. "So why would he want to risk exposure, working for the U.S.? How many other Nazis are suspected of having done this?"

"None sir, at least not among our list of suspects."

"Then find out from the Belgians, the French, the Danes, and the Norwegians whether they have any names on their lists of suspected war criminals who appear to have worked for the U.S. in occupied Germany. I want to know whether Wanstumm was part of a pattern, or whether he was an exception."

"Right away, sir."

"Hardewijk, we've opened several new files during your trip to Bavaria. I want to follow up quickly on the most likely leads." Goedkamp looked down on his desk. "I can't have you spending another week on Wanstumm if I can pull together a watertight case on two others in the same amount of time." He paused again. "We need results, and with every passing week, the trail becomes more difficult to follow. I want you to prepare a proposal for the next steps on Wanstumm, but in the meantime, I want you to study the new files and initiate appropriate follow-ups. We have limited resources, and if I don't use them properly, we will still be chasing Nazi war criminals thirty years from now."

The coffee had not come, so Hardewijk retreated to his office, wondering what the new files held in store for him. He could not get his mind off Wanstumm.

JUNE, 1948

THE HAGUE

The phone on Goedkamp's desk rang just as he was walking into his office. He lunged at it as he swiveled around his desk and sat down in the large wooden chair.

"Mijnheer Seventer, how nice to hear from you. Where are you?" A pause. "When can we have lunch? Tomorrow? Great. Where? The Vieux Doelen? Very well. I'll be there at one o'clock."

The next day, they shook hands warmly and walked into the elegant dining room. They ordered their meal and then chatted about recent events. However, Goedkamp could see that Seventer was preoccupied.

"Kees, if you don't mind my using first names, I'm terribly frustrated. I simply can't forget about Louisa." Goedkamp knew this was coming. He nodded. "The picture of her haunts me. I don't think I'm mentally unhinged, but her death preys on me because there has been no closure." Another pause. "You are the only person who can find Wanstumm. I realize that you have many other cases to pursue. Perhaps I just need to know that you have done all that you can to find the man."

Goedkamp took a sip of wine before answering. "Funny you should ask. Just last month, I sent one of my best men to Germany, looking for any trace of Wanstumm. He appears to have been in Bavaria, near his hometown of Memmingen in 1945, but like most of the others, he has disappeared."

"So, you are sure that he returned to Germany from Holland?" asked Seventer, suddenly alert.

"We can't prove it. We have absolutely no leads. There was even a rumor that he went to work for the Americans at their army base down there. That is really very far-fetched, but we are seeing strange coincidences as we look for these criminals."

"Well, what brought him to mind more forcibly," interposed Seventer, "was my recent review of the dormant accounts at Mathijs Smithson in London. Some of these, it turns out, were accounts that I had opened for my clients when I was still in Amsterdam before the war. It breaks my heart to see the money, carefully saved over the years, held in a safe place, tragically useless because the beneficiaries disappeared during the war. I checked with one of my colleagues at another bank we used, the Winchester Bank, and they report having similar accounts, in addition to those that we helped set up."

"What will eventually happen to all this money?" asked Goedkamp.

"I really don't know. We will probably hold it for years, just because there is always the off-chance that a beneficiary will turn up. Ultimately, it's anybody's guess. The best outcome would be to turn the funds over to a Jewish charitable organization. I wouldn't put it past some of the banks to take the money for themselves. That is the practice of some banks in Europe. The good news is that a few of the beneficial owners have turned up in the last two years. We can only keep hoping."

Goedkamp was scowling. "It makes me so angry that these scum of the earth remain unpunished." He took another sip of wine. "The problem is that we have very limited resources with which to look for a very long list of people.

There are weeks, Edu, when we solve one case, only to open two more based on new evidence. I'm afraid it will take quite a while to find some of these ex-Nazis. Some will never be found."

The two men finished their wine in silence. Finally, Seventer spoke up. "Kees, I have recently had a talk with Jan van Meeren, the senior partner in our firm. He knows me better than most. He has stood by me ever since the first days of catastrophe in 1940. I told him that I needed to do something, anything, to try and find Wanstumm. He agrees that it would not be a problem if I took a few weeks away from the office now and then. That's why I'm here, Kees; I want you to put me to work to look for Wanstumm. At least I will have done something. You won't have to pay me. I'm sure I can get the right security clearance."

Goedkamp looked hard at Seventer. "Okay, I know you want justice to be done. I have trouble enough with the bureaucracy; I'll have to be careful about raising the issue of using you. You are certainly one of the most reliable witnesses available to us; you have seen Wanstumm face-to-face. I think I could make it stick." They both relapsed into silence.

Seventer came out of his reverie. "My German is pretty good. Why don't you let me go down to Bavaria and follow whatever traces your man found down there?"

"Edu, I don't need convincing. Just give me a little time. You can't imagine the turf battles I have to fight, and I don't need another one. How long are you going to be around?"

"I'm going to Amsterdam this evening for a business dinner. Tomorrow I have a number of meetings there, and then I will probably take an overnight ferry back to London. I'm staying at the Amstel."

"I'll leave a message to bring you up to date. Be patient. I think this might work."

———<>———

Three days later, Seventer picked up the phone in his office. It was nearly 5 p.m. "Seventer speaking."

"Halo, Edu, this is Kees Goedkamp. How are you?"

"Fine. I've been hoping to hear from you."

"Well, I'm afraid I don't have very good news. I've run into that bureaucratic nonsense I warned you about. The Ministry of Foreign Affairs is refusing to accredit you as a member of my staff on the grounds that you are a permanent resident of the United Kingdom. Can you believe such idiocy?"

"I know our ambassador here very well. Let me have a chat with him."

"No, I'd rather you waited. My boss has started a procedure to put a stop to this once and for all. You are not the first problem we've had with them. It may take a while. There is nothing I can do in the meantime. I'm so sorry. I know how much this means to you."

FEBRUARY, 1949

LOGAN AIRPORT, BOSTON

The Transcon Airways DC4 trundled down the windswept runway, seesawing slightly as the pilot maintained its heading. It began to rise ponderously into the air, the four engines clawing for speed. Captain Hagstrom was worried about the cold front that was forecast to pass through his destination at Chicago's Midway Airport within the next five hours. The flight had been delayed two hours already by a broken magneto in the #2 engine. Now they were scheduled to arrive at 11.30 p.m.

The flight was only half full. Captain Patrick Defoe, 2nd Infantry Division, sat in a window seat, towards the back of the tourist class compartment. It was the final leg of a long trip which had started in Memmingen, Bavaria, four days ago. He ordered a bourbon and water from the stewardess. He was still wearing his uniform, but in less than a week, he would be demobilized. It felt so strange to think of himself as a civilian after five years in the army. His mother would be waiting for him at home in Elgin. He had made no plans except to visit classmates and a couple of officers who had served with him. He wanted to go back to Europe. Germany, in particular, appealed to him, but he had not found a way to shift to civilian life there. He would have to sort it all out in the next couple of months.

The flight droned on. After dinner had been served, Defoe put his head back and fell asleep. Violent bumps and jolts woke him up. The stewardesses were checking seat belts, reassuring the passengers that this turbulence was not unusual. The captain announced that they were approaching Chicago's Midway Airport. The turbulence increased. Defoe heard a woman trying to repress a small cry of fear. He could see that heavy snow was now streaming past the plane windows.

The TIG Airlines Lockheed Lodestar, completing its flight from Lincoln, Nebraska, had descended to 3500 feet when the pilot realized that he had been instructed to hold at 4000. He pulled back on the joystick to correct his altitude, and plunged into the belly of the descending DC4. The shock of the impact crushed the Lodestar's cockpit, and as it dropped away from the DC4, it turned lazily to the left, and continued the turn until it had completed a full spiral. It fell in the middle of the Chicago Sanitary and Ship Canal near the Argonne National Laboratory.

Captain Hagstrom knew immediately what must have happened. His co-pilot started shutting down non-critical electrical systems to prevent fires from spreading. A large slash in the cargo hold was drawing in the freezing air at 160 mph, and was causing the plane to veer strongly to the right. Hagstrom realized that he would need all of his 5,000 hours of flying experience to save the flight. He radioed the emergency to the Midway control tower on 118.7 and requested clearance for an emergency landing.

"This is Transcon 418 requesting 31L approaching from the south east."

"418, you can't have 31L, we have snow ploughs on it. Use 31R."

"Midway Tower, get them off; 31R is too short, I need all the runway I can get."

"Roger, 418, can you circle while we clear?"

"Negative. I'm coming straight in."

The DC4 approached rapidly from the south-east, side-slipping as it was buffeted by the winds. Hagstrom knew that the faster he put the plane down, the less the risk of a catastrophic finale. He registered the location of the KIDZI marker, confident that he was still on course. His altitude had fallen to 1500 feet, lower than the 1800 called for at the marker.

The control tower was urging all planes and vehicles to move at once as far as possible from the runway. As he broke through the cloud cover, Hagstrom saw the ploughs gunning their engines to escape from his flight path. The DC4 hit the tarmac so hard that it seemed to bounce right back into the air. It careened down the runway at 130 mph, and its right wing clipped the last of the snow ploughs. The wing sheared off at its root in the side of the fuselage, and with a shrieking sound of metal, tore out the seats on the right hand side of rows 12, 13 and 14. Patrick Defoe was instantaneously ejected. Later, he was found lying in the snow, his neck broken, still sitting in his seat.

JUNE, 1949

CHICAGO

The truck backed up to the loading dock of the Hocker and Balz Company building on West Hubbard Street. The driver jumped down from the cab, and walked to the rear of the receiving area into the cramped office used by the foreman.

"Hi, Steve. I got a truck load of goodies for you."

"Mornin', Kaz, I'll get a couple of the boys down to help you."

Steve dialed a number, and waited patiently while the phone rang. "Morning, Joe, Kaz is here with a delivery, let's see, mainly butterscotch pellets, chocolate sauce, a lot of almonds, and more marshmallow than I've ever seen. Most of it should go to the third floor, but shall I send the almonds up to five?" Steve listened attentively, then said, "OK, boss, you got it."

Upstairs, on the second floor, Joseph Galish put the phone down. He called out to his secretary, Elaine. "Get me Mr. Faber, will you?"

He waited while she made the connection. He hated this place, but he was earning $390 a month as vice president. The business consisted mainly of stocking bakery supply items, which they ordered wholesale and then resold to retail bakeries. The margins were very good. The company was liquid, and Mr. Faber was making a solid profit, but Joseph Galish was a mere hired hand, although he had a title which impressed small town bakery owners. He despised Mr. Faber.

Galish lived in a one-room apartment in the Polish area of town, commuted to work on the El, and saved $85 every month, which he put into a savings account at the Plains National Bank. He was alive; he was safe, but he was poor. It would be another three years before he became eligible for U.S. citizenship. He was now 42 years old.

The only satisfaction he had these days was reading about the unbridled thuggery of the Soviets. The western Allies had been so naïve about the Russians. Hitler had warned about the threat of communism starting in the 1920's. Now perhaps his Fuhrer would be vindicated. But he had to keep quiet. He had read about the prosecution of war criminals, and he had no doubt that his activities in the Netherlands had been documented. But they would never find him here in Chicago, of all places. He had to be patient.

At ten minutes to five, everyone left the building. He left ten minutes later. He walked down to Wells Street, where he took the train to his home on McKinley. His evenings were mindlessly boring. He walked through the front door of his small apartment and picked up the mail on the floor. As usual, it was just a bill and some advertisements. He threw it all on the kitchen table.

From his briefcase, he extracted the maps and brochures he had picked up at a travel agency downtown: the Bahamas, Bermuda, Costa Rica, Panama. Even if he could only dream, at least he could dream with a purpose. The dream would one day become reality, and he must have his plan ready. He walked over to a wall cabinet, pulled out a bottle of gin, and poured it into a glass. He added two ice cubes. The fire of the alcohol burned his throat. Parts of the plan were already in place. He had to learn more about banking, though, before he could ever hope to execute raids on the Jewish accounts.

He had to get himself employed at a bank. He knew that he was making a good impression on the officers at Plains National Bank, where his company did all its banking business. He had even met Harold Strickland, the president of the bank, on two occasions. It was Galish who had come up with the idea of having Faber host a lunch for the bank to thank them for their continued good service over the years. It had worked beyond his expectations.

He was also trying to decide what he would do after a successful raiding of the Jewish accounts. He thought he could clear over $4,000,000 after expenses. With money no longer a problem, he would go to live in a country with a warm climate. He reminded himself to research extradition treaties between the Netherlands and the countries he would try to visit in the next couple of years. Once settled in some tropical paradise, he might finance a restaurant. He had occasional visions of a beautiful woman with a body like Ilse's, but he had become so accustomed to casual sexual encounters that he could hardly imagine what it would be like to have someone around him all the time. Marriage was not a high priority, he realized.

Ultimately, he would have to make one final move to eradicate his past. He would need to change his name again after he left the U.S. He took another sip of his drink. Under his bed, in a locked suitcase, he kept a growing number of files on various aspects of his plan.

Tonight, he wanted to review the travel brochures and make notes about various countries. He slid the suitcase out, unlocked it and found the file entitled "Countries to Consider". He took it over to the kitchen table, sat down, and opened the brochure on top of the pile.

The photos of Bermuda were very attractive, until he noticed the Union Jack flying from the top of a building. He found a page called "The Facts". A few caught his attention:

- British Possession. Governor appointed by His Majesty the King.

- No visas required for visitors staying up to one month.
- Residency permits restricted. Inquire at any British Consulate.

Bermuda was not at all suitable. He despised the British. The next brochure was about the Bahamas. He moved quickly past the pictures of golden beaches to the text. Same problem: another British possession, another Governor.

Costa Rica appeared to be a clean, quiet little country. He looked through the brochure quickly. Maybe he should go there for a short vacation just to check it out.

Finally, he opened the Panama brochure. It prominently featured the Canal connecting the Pacific and the Caribbean and emphasized the country's geographical location as a crossroads between east and west, North and South America. Panama offered international banking and other offshore financial services. This sounded much more promising. The currency was the U.S. dollar. He read that any one could open a U.S. dollar account in Panama and benefit from the country's bank secrecy laws. The brochure said little about the weather, but judging from the pictures, it looked quite tropical. His mind was made up. He would visit Panama at the next opportunity. He took another sip. It was all beginning to fall into place.

OCTOBER, 1949

NEW YORK—OTTAWA, CANADA

The Schuurman family disembarked in Brooklyn, New York from the M.S. Schiedam, one of the Holland-America Line ships that had been recently refurbished for service on the North Atlantic. It was a 19,000 ton ship which combined cargo with a 150 passenger capacity. The Schuurmans traveled in two cabins, one for the parents, one for Ingrid and Sophie. There was only one class aboard the ship. The two girls quickly discovered the pleasures of an Atlantic crossing: sleeping late, playing ping pong, eating good food, and best of all, flirting with the Dutch crew. On the third night, the Captain arranged for a dance after dinner, to the tune of records played on a turntable by the young, red-faced purser. With the exception of the watch and the engineers, the entire ship's company and almost all of the passengers had put on their finest for this celebration of their impending arrival in the New World.

The girls were in great demand. Ingrid's blond hair was bobbed and framed her round face to advantage. Sophie did not look remotely like her 'sister'. She had grown to be tall like her parents, and her lustrous, dark brown hair fell glamorously to her shoulders. Her features were rectangular and could have been forbidding were it not for the quick smile of her generous mouth. Both girls stayed up until dawn.

The morning arrival in New York harbor was an extraordinary experience for them. Never had they seen such tall buildings. The customs and immigration formalities took a long time. Mr. Schuurman had arranged to spend the night at a hotel in New York before boarding their train to Canada the next day. The hotel on West 58th Street, between Fifth and Sixth Avenues, was comfortable, but noisy. They soon realized that the entire city was noisy. They stood in awe of the skyscrapers. After dinner at an Italian restaurant, the girls insisted on walking to Rockefeller Plaza.

The following morning, the taxi dropped them off at Grand Central Station. They needed a redcap to help them with their bags. The train with the enormous cars was unlike any train they had ever seen in Holland. They arrived in Montreal late at night, where they stayed at another hotel. Mrs. Schuurman had been very pleased to show off her French when they had ordered dinner. The next day, they took a train to Ottawa, where Schuurman had been offered a job in the city's ordinance and zoning department. As they approached their final destination, their excitement began to turn to anxiety.

Ottawa was pleasant enough, but the Schuurmans were unsettled by the unfinished look of the streets, the wooden telephone poles leaning at angles, and the jumble of houses and stores outside the business district. The City of Ottawa personnel department had rented the top floor of a three-story wooden house for them. It was situated on a large street leading to Rockliff, a wealthy suburb. They settled in quickly, Schuurman into his new job, Mrs. Schuurman into the task of creating a new home, and the girls into improving their English as quickly as possible. They registered at the consular section of the Dutch Embassy, a routine which they would probably have overlooked except for the fact that they needed to decide fairly soon on employment for the girls, and they had been advised that occasionally the embassy could be a source of jobs.

Now, two weeks after their arrival, life was beginning to run smoothly. Schuurman was delighted with his job, even though he had to brush up quickly on his school French to deal with the French-speaking section of town on the other side of the Rideau River. Ingrid was enrolled as a nurse-trainee at one of the local hospitals. For Sophie, the search was more difficult. She had shown excellent writing skills at school in Holland and was now undergoing a crash course in English writing at the local high school. It meant special tutoring and therefore an extra expense, which worried Sophie, but the Schuurmans were determined to give her the experience.

Since that summer night in Amsterdam in 1942, when the Gestapo had taken Sophie's parents from their home, there had never been a question that she would remain with the Schuurmans. As conditions grew worse in the city in late 1944, the Schuurmans had decided to go into hiding with Schuurman's sister in the small town of Bussum. The risk of someone in Amsterdam denouncing Sophie as a Jew had become too great.

In 1947, the Schuurmans officially filed for her adoption with the Amsterdam municipal court. Her name was changed to Sophie Bluhm Schuurman. When they had first considered the possibility of immigrating to Canada, they asked Sophie whether she would prefer to stay in Holland. Her response was unequivocal. She would go wherever they went. They were all the family she had.

————<>————

Tonight, the Schuurmans had decided to introduce her to a fact of which she had been, for obvious reasons, unaware. She was now nineteen. After dinner, they told Ingrid that they had a special matter to discuss with Sophie. Ingrid could stay, they said, but she should probably use the time to study. Ingrid took the hint.

The three of them sat around the kitchen table. Mr. Schuurman coughed slightly and began, "Sophie, we have decided that it is time for you to know that your father made some unusual financial arrangements during his stay in Amsterdam. I'll try to make it simple. Like many other Jews, your parents felt that they would be safe in Holland. However, your father was advised by a Dutch banker to move a great deal of his savings to a safer place, and he arranged to open an account in New York. To protect you, in case he was some day unable to use the money in the account, he showed me the documents and wrote down the details for me. Unfortunately he kept the originals, which have disappeared, but I have all of the information you need. The money now belongs to you.

"A few days ago, I spoke with a friend at the Royal Bank of Canada about how we should proceed. He said that it might be quite complicated, since the bank in New York would have to be satisfied that you were the legitimate beneficial owner. Sophie, that money will make a big difference to you. For instance, it could pay for you to go to university. But it will take time to sort it out."

Sophie had cupped her face in her hands. She looked perplexed. "Is it really worth the bother?" she asked.

Schuurman looked at her carefully. "There is probably half a million dollars in the account today."

Silence descended on the little kitchen. The Schuurmans looked at each other, and back at Sophie, as she dealt with the improbable number. She could not put it into any recognizable context. She had never had more than twenty dollars in her purse. The Schuurmans were frugal, and she had never heard of anything costing more than one hundred dollars. A winter coat that Mrs. Schuurman had recently bought for her had cost $45. Slowly she began to understand that she was wealthy. In a whirl, she started to fantasize about what she would do with it. She would buy her dear adoptive mother a fur coat, a new wool coat and matching hat for Ingrid, a pair of those big, fur-lined boots which she had seen in a store for Papa Schuurman. Slowly, a smile crossed her face.

"This is so exciting. Think what we'll be able to do with the money!"

"Just a minute, Sophie. Your enthusiasm is understandable, but we have to claim the money first. Will you come with me to the Royal Bank of Canada tomorrow? I would like you to meet Mr. McClain, with whom I have discussed this matter."

"I have two classes in the morning, and I promised to help one of my new friends with a project over lunch. Can we do it at two o'clock?"

"Mr. McClain said he would prefer the afternoon, so I'll let him know. We will meet at his office on Parliament Street. The number is 103." Schuurman wrote the address on a piece of paper and handed it to Sophie.

"Does Ingrid know?" Sophie asked.

"No," replied Schuurman.

"Well then, I must tell her immediately," said Sophie as she rushed out of the kitchen.

Schuurman looked at his wife. "I hope that we will be successful."

The following afternoon, Hans Schuurman and Sophie Bluhm Schuurman were ushered into Jack McClain's office at the Royal Bank of Canada. McClain extended his hand in welcome and invited them to sit down. Sophie looked around the walls at the hunting prints and at the photographs of his family. It was altogether a warm, pleasant room.

"Sophie, your father has told me the story of your family. I'm sure you've heard it before, but I hope you won't mind if I say how terribly sorry I am to hear about your parents."

"Thank you, sir," she said with a slight smile.

"Your father may not have told you that I know Holland quite well. I served in General Crerar's First Army, which liberated the northern part of the Netherlands in 1945. I have to tell you that we found some pretty shocking conditions there. The worst part was the starvation. We simply could not believe our eyes. Anyway, I am delighted to welcome you and your family to Canada."

"Thank you, Jack, for seeing us," said Schuurman. Sophie was still getting used to the easy use of first names in this country. Schuurman continued. "I have explained to Sophie that she has a claim on her father's account in New York. I told her that it was going to be quite laborious to assert her right to the funds. Would you mind explaining what you advise us to do?"

"I would be delighted. At least, we're not looking for a needle in a haystack. Sophie, your adoptive father has shown me the information which your real father gave to him. The first issue is whether the bank in New York will even admit to the existence of the account. Without any formal documentation, they are under no obligation to reveal anything to you at all. However, if they get so far as admitting that the account exists, then you have to deal with the second issue, which is to have the bank recognize you, Sophie Bluhm Schuurman, as a claimant. Your adoptive father can prove beyond a doubt that you are the daughter of Julius and Hannah Bluhm."

"The third issue, therefore, is whether the bank will accept circumstantial evidence of the disappearance of your parents. We are on tricky grounds here. Canadian and U.S. law are quite similar, but I have advised your father to retain a lawyer in New York. This may be a little expensive, but it will help your case with the bank if you have reputable legal advice."

"There's something else. Your account is at the Manhattan National Bank in New York. I happen to have some very good connections there, and I will give you a letter of introduction which, at the very least, will ensure that they give you a fair hearing. All the banks have had some experience with accounts in the names of Jews who disappeared during the war, so your situation is not completely unusual. There is considerable leeway in the treatment of these situations, however, so we might as well create as much initial goodwill as possible."

"Since we have to see the people in New York on a weekday, I'll have to take a couple of days off," said Schuurman. "Jack, can I get back to you on when we might be able to go to New York? I'm still new at my job, so I have to request a leave when they can accommodate my absence."

"That's fine with me, Hans. Don't forget to take all of the documents, including Sophie's adoption papers translated into English and so forth. The more evidence you can produce, the better. If you give me a few days notice, I will get in touch with my colleagues at the Manhattan Bank." They rose and shook hands. Sophie took Schuurman's hand as they walked out into the street.

DECEMBER, 1949

LONDON

"I've been looking all over for you," Stella said accusingly. Seventer winced. Everyone at Mathijs Smithson was intimidated by Stella, Seventer as much the other partners. Fortunately, she had decided to take a motherly interest in him, ever since that day in 1940 when he had arrived in London. She was always a step ahead of Seventer, attending to the smallest details of his life. But Stella was worried. Seventer had not remarried, even though the war had now been over for four years. She had never, ever heard him mention his late wife, not once. No, this was not normal, especially for such an attractive gentleman.

Seventer came to an abrupt halt in front of her desk. "Sorry, Stella, the meeting took much longer than it should have."

"I have several messages for you, but one is particularly important. Mr. Goedkamp in The Hague wants you to call immediately."

Seventer moved quickly to his desk in the partners' room. Stella had already placed the call. The line was ringing.

"Hallo, Goedkamp speaking."

"Kees, this is Edu Seventer in London. You called?"

"Yes, my friend. You probably thought you would never hear from me, right? Well, a little Dutch obstinacy always helps. You have been appointed a special consultant to the

War Crimes Commission. If you are still interested, I have something for you to do in connection with the Wanstumm case."

———<>———

MEMMINGEN

The U.S. Army base in Memmingen had a new commanding officer, Major General Robert Wright. Goedkamp had put in a request to the U.S. Military Attache in The Hague for assistance to be provided to Mr. Eduard Seventer while in Memmingen. As Seventer sat waiting in General Wright's office, he marveled at the courtesy and efficiency of the U.S. Army. He had taken a train to Augsburg, where the general had a car and driver waiting for him. He had been shown to his quarters on the base, spartan but comfortable.

General Wright walked into his office. Seventer stood up, impressed by the man who stood towering over him.

"Welcome to Memmingen, Mr. Seventer. I gather this is your first visit?"

"Yes, General. I really appreciate your putting me up during my stay."

"No problem. I have been briefed. I noted that you were a colonel in the Dutch Army during the war and that you are acting as a consultant to the Netherlands War Crimes Commission?"

"Yes, that's right."

"Well, to be perfectly frank with you, I can't believe we employed a major war criminal. What are the facts?"

"We are looking for Heinrich Wanstumm, head of the Gestapo in the north of Holland. He was born on a farm near Memmingen, and at the end of the war, he still owned the farm. The family who bought his farm not too long ago stated that he was here in 1945 or 1946.

"An elderly woman who did cleaning on this base also claimed to have seen him here several times, and she guessed that he had worked here at some point. We showed her a few photos from your personnel files which we thought corresponded to the description that we have. She became confused and unable to make a positive identification. Mr. Hardewijk, the Dutch investigator who came here last year, ran out of time on this case. During the last few months, he has been closing the files on a number of other war criminals, whom we have successfully brought to trial. However, we keep coming back to this case because Wanstumm was responsible for some of the worst offenses in our country. I'm here to attempt to make some progress on this case."

"Mr. Seventer, thank you for the update. I am told that since we established the base here in August, 1945, we have employed over 1,200 locals in various capacities. We have maintained records on all of them. I'll be blunt; I am going to ask you for a favor."

"Certainly, General."

"This is a ticklish issue for us. It is very hard for us to accept that a major war criminal could have inadvertently worked for us. I will provide any assistance you may require to sift through all this information, anything at all. I would also appreciate your discretion. I have assigned Lieutenant Reitell to work with you. Before you discuss a possible suspect with anyone else, please review the case with me first."

"Of course, General." Seventer realized how embarrassing this search could become for the U.S. Army.

Early the next morning, Lieutenant Reitell knocked on Seventer's door. "Breakfast, sir?"

Seventer joined the youthful officer at the mess hall. They took their places in the line, and Seventer proceeded to pile his plate full of scrambled eggs, sausages, pancakes, and toast.

"This is wonderful," he enthused. "In Holland, we like to eat a large breakfast, but nothing as enormous as this!"

Reitell led them to a table away from the center of the mess.

"Mr. Seventer," Reitell said as he sat down, "I think you realize that we are all a little spooked at the idea that an important war criminal may have been working for us. The general is really steamed up."

"Your general has already impressed on me the gravity of the issue. Now, lieutenant, I will need every single file of every man who ever worked on the base through the middle of 1948. I have to set aside every suspect. Anton Hardewijk did it before, but he may have missed someone, although I doubt it. I need to make sure that we have missed nothing."

"I have asked our administrative section to pull all of the files. So as soon as you are finished, sir, we'll get down to business."

They walked over to the administrative building. The conference room had a long table piled high with files.

"Are these in any particular order?"

"Let's see; they seem to be arranged alphabetically."

"I think it would be best if you start with the A's and re-sort them for me by date of hire. We are really interested in the period August, 1945 through April, 1948, because Wanstumm was sighted, and then disappeared, before Hardewijk's visit last year. That should eliminate a good number of files."

The two men worked in silence for a while. The A's hired before April, 1948 totaled 17 names. Seventer worked carefully through each of them. Only one of them seemed to correspond to Wanstumm's general description. He put it aside. The B's yielded two files, the C's none. They broke briefly to get some coffee and went back to work. The D's had four interesting files, the E's one, the G's two. Seventer recognized one of them, that of Joseph Galish, a Hungarian, from Hardewijk's notes. Hardewijk had rejected it last time because of the nationality. Seventer read the file carefully.

The man was in fact stateless, claiming Hungarian nationality, born in Gyor in 1908. Seventer looked at the photo closely. "Lieutenant, could you get your hands on a magnifying glass? This face fits our description, but I need to get a better look."

"Hang on. Let me see if we have one."

While Reitell was gone, Seventer re-read Galish's file. The fitness reports were written by a Captain Patrick Defoe. The last one was dated December, 1947. "Joe has had another good year as officers' mess cook. He is reliable, friendly, and always willing to prepare something special. He will be missed. We wish him well in his new home."

Seventer scratched the side of his nose. The picture of Wanstumm as a cook just did not fit. Yet this Galish had materialized out of nowhere at the end of the war. Reitell returned, brandishing a magnifying glass.

Seventer bent over the file, moving the magnifying glass around over the photo. The grainy quality was even more obvious, but he also saw more clearly the squarish, plastic face, the light-colored hair combed almost straight back, parted slightly off-center. Seventer's heart began to beat a little faster.

"Lieutenant, this Joseph Galish may have claimed to be Hungarian, but he matches our description. We need to talk to this Captain Defoe who was his sponsor. Can you see where we might get hold of him? He should be able to tell us where Galish's 'new home' is."

When Reitell returned, Seventer had made it through the J's. Six additional files had been put aside for further scrutiny, including one of the three that Hardewijk had selected for the old woman to look at last year. He looked at his watch. It was nearly one p.m.

Reitell said, "Defoe went back to the States early this year. He gave his mother's home near Chicago as a forwarding address. We have someone in the States trying to reach her by phone. In the meantime, how about a bite to eat?"

After lunch, they sat down at the table to continue the tedious sorting of the personnel files. By four o'clock, they were down to the W's, and half an hour later, they were finished. In all, they had 51 files to review more closely.

"I think that we should take a break," said Seventer. Looking at the files had given him a headache. Even so, Seventer felt a surge of confidence. He was now convinced that Galish and Wanstumm were one and the same man.

———<>———

THE HAGUE

A stale smell of cigars hung around Goedkamp's office. Seventer was becoming edgy waiting for him. Goedkamp stormed into the room, without saying a word to Seventer. He threw himself into the chair behind his desk, reached for the phone, and dialed. "Hello, Mr. de Ruiter, please." Seventer knew that this was the Minister of the Interior. "Yes, good morning, sir. Goedkamp here. I've just returned from Foreign Affairs. They had the nerve to summon me to an emergency meeting. They have put a ban on any further travel of my people to foreign countries. They say that they have had complaints about what they call 'snooping', and they want every investigation outside our borders cleared with them first. I can't work this way." Goedkamp listened for a few moments.

"Good. Thank you, sir. I will tell them." A large smile appeared on Goedkamp's face. "May I quote you, sir?" He hung up and turned to Seventer.

"So, Edu, you didn't hear this conversation, by the way. Now tell me, what happened in Memmingen?"

"I think we have a prime suspect, but nothing I can prove." He described his laborious review of the personnel files, and his selection of the three who most closely fit Wanstumm's description.

"The most intriguing one is Joseph Galish, simply because there is no way we can verify where he was before 1945. The resemblance to Wanstumm is greater than any of the others. I just feel in my bones that it's him. It sends shivers through me when I think of being questioned by him that night at Gestapo headquarters in Amsterdam. Of the other two, one has been found near Memmingen, clearly not our man. The other is currently being questioned by the Americans."

The phone rang. Goedkamp reached over to get it. He listened, looked up and said, "It's for you, Edu, from Memmingen." Seventer grabbed the receiver.

"Seventer speaking."

"Hi, this is Lieutenant Reitell. Thought I had better let you know right away. Captain Defoe, you know, the fellow who signed off on Galish's file? He was killed in a plane accident near Chicago in February. Now what do we do?"

"Damnation. Can you believe it?"

"I told the general. He has instructed me to get the names of others who may have known Galish when he was here. A long shot, but who knows?"

"Well, anything you can do would be much appreciated. Thank you, Lieutenant."

"What happened?" asked Goedkamp after Seventer hung up the phone.

"Our best lead to Galish's whereabouts died in a plane accident earlier this year," said Seventer.

JUNE, 1950

CHICAGO

Joseph Galish turned into the driveway of the large house. The attendant greeted him as he opened the door of the Studebaker and handed Galish his claim check. Galish walked into the front hall, where the reception had just begun. He was annoyed that he had to waste his time at a wedding reception, and he was annoyed that the receiving line was moving so slowly, but his face showed none of his distaste.

At last, Galish stepped forward to greet the young couple, introducing himself. The bride and groom had no idea who he was. Then the bride's father, Harold Strickland, noticed Galish and enthused, "Joe, how nice to see you! This is my wife, Mary Lou. Mary Lou, this is Joe Galish. He is vice president and chief financial officer of Hocker and Balz, one of our best clients!"

Mary Lou smiled vaguely. Galish walked towards the bar. He ordered a Coca Cola and turned to survey the guests. The Gestapo would have been proud of him. He blended perfectly into the festive crowd.

Ten minutes later, a heavy hand descended on his shoulder. It was Strickland again. "Joe, my boy, I'd like to talk to you for a moment. Let's go into the den." Strickland pointed to a deep armchair. "Sit down, boy, and make yourself comfortable." He walked over to a table, and returned with two cigars, offering one to Galish. "Here are matches and a cutter."

Galish knew that this was part of the interview process. Carefully, he snipped the end of the cigar and slowly brought the lighted match to it, playing the flame around the rim of the cigar.

Strickland continued, "I've been observing you for a while, and I'm very impressed by the way you have handled the H and B relationship with my bank."

"Thank you, Mr. Strickland. That's very nice of you to say so."

"If you don't mind my asking, Joe, how old are you?"

"I've just turned forty-two, sir."

"Have you ever thought of getting married?"

"Well, as you know, it is only since I came to the U.S. that I have been able to lead a normal life. Now that I have a regular job, I will be getting married one of these days, when I find the right girl."

"Good thinking." A pause. "Joe, the world is changing. It's getting more international."

Galish puffed on his cigar. "Yes, sir, foreign customers are doing more business with the U.S. I wish there were more opportunities for advancement at Mr. Faber's company."

"I know what you mean," replied Strickland. He paused, then said, "Joe, you have done an outstanding job at H and B, but I think you may be outgrowing it. Am I right?"

"Well, to tell you the truth, I have been thinking of other possibilities. Of course, I would not want you to repeat this to Mr. Faber. He has been very good to me."

"He is a good man. But between the two of us, I don't think his business will do as well in the future. Have you noticed the growth of supermarkets? They are selling more baked goods directly to the customers. H and B's base of independent bakers will have a hard time surviving, and so will H and B."

Galish saw where this was leading. He opened the door another crack. "To tell you the truth, Mr. Strickland, I have been hoping to use my administrative experience in a job where I could also use my language skills."

Strickland leaned over and dropped his voice. "You are familiar with my bank. We have an enviable record, and our location is well-suited to develop business with local companies that are getting into the import-export business. I have been thinking of setting up an international department. Joe, I would like you to join us as its new head." Strickland leaned back to observe the effect of this announcement.

Galish did not hesitate. "Why, Mr. Strickland, what a great idea! I'm flattered that you would even think of me." It was now time to be modest. "But I have no banking experience, except, of course, what I have learned as one of your customers."

"We can take care of that. We'll set up a little program for you to learn the key procedures. Don't forget, I have people who can assist you. What do you say?"

Galish knitted his brows. "I will have to think it over, if you don't mind. I want to make sure in my own mind that I would not be a disappointment to you."

"Joe, my boy, I think that is wise, but I want you to get started soon. Perhaps you could call me in the next few days. I'd like for you to come over to the bank for lunch and meet some of the people you will be working with. We can also talk about salary. I was thinking of $8,000. How does that sound?"

"Mr. Strickland, that sounds very attractive. I am really interested and grateful to you."

"Well, let's re-join the party, shall we?" They walked out side by side, with Strickland's arm around Galish's shoulder.

Galish left the party two hours later. After parking his car in a nearby garage, he unlocked the door of his small apartment. He looked around. The furniture was used and

needed recovering. The carpet was threadbare. The small
windows looked out on a busy commercial neighborhood. At
night, unless he kept the window curtains tightly drawn, the
neon signs above the stores cast a fluttering, fluorescent glow
into his bedroom.

"I have to move out of this dump," he muttered to
himself. It was not a fit home for the brand-new head of the
International Department at the Plains National Bank.

JULY, 1950

NEW YORK

The temperature had reached a high of 96 degrees the previous day. This morning, even though it was only 9.30 a.m., it had already climbed to 85. Hans Schuurman, unused to these high temperatures, was squirming in his suit. He could feel the sweat running down his neck into the collar of his shirt. Sophie, in contrast, appeared cool and elegant in a navy sleeveless dress, bought the day before on Madison Avenue. A small dark blue hat was perched on her head, and she wore white gloves. Last week, she had celebrated her twentieth birthday. She looked, in a word, little short of spectacular.

Fortunately, the head office of the Manhattan National Bank was air-conditioned. Schuurman began to cool down as they sat waiting for their appointment. In spite of the heat-induced discomfort, he looked fit and younger than his fifty years. Canada had agreed with him. His work was interesting, and he had already been promoted once. He felt a little ambivalent about being in New York with Sophie. She had become as much his daughter as Ingrid. Yet here he was, assisting her in accessing a substantial sum of money which would inevitably give her a sense of independence from the Schuurman family. In a way, he was envious. Such a fortune would never be his, and he would never be able to offer his wife and natural daughter the luxuries which would now be within Sophie's grasp. On the other hand, this fortune could never make up for the loss, under horrific circumstances, of her parents.

The door to the conference room opened, and three men walked in. The older one introduced himself: "Good morning. My name is Jeffrey Husband. I'm responsible for our Auditing and Potential Loss Department. These are my colleagues, John Drum and Herb Satterly. In a moment, we will be joined by Ted Biggart, whom you met last December. Please have a seat. By the way, we do have cold drinks if you would prefer them to coffee." The two younger men busied themselves with the beverages, carefully calculating which particular seats around the conference table would give them the best vantage point from which to admire the attractive young lady.

The door opened again, and Ted Biggart entered the room. He shook hands warmly with Schuurman and Sophie. "Welcome again! It looks like there may be some progress on your situation, Miss Schuurman. Let me have Jeff begin."

Jeffrey Husband leaned forward in his chair, consulting a file in front of him. His voice was as thin and dry as his demeanor. "As you can imagine, we have reviewed the facts of the case very thoroughly. The reason we have asked you to meet with us today is to give us, face-to-face, your confirmation of some of the account documentation.

"Miss Schuurman, we agree that you appear to have a claim on the account of your father, Dr. Julius Bluhm. As we have explained, we have already turned the funds over to the State of New York, as the abandoned property law requires. However, the Manhattan Bank is prepared to assist you in processing your claim. You must understand that the state will have to be satisfied that you are the sole rightful owner of the funds.

"Now if you will permit, let me ask you a few questions. Mr. Schuurman, can you describe for us again the documents you were shown by Dr. Bluhm, from which you obtained the information which you shared with us?"

"Certainly," replied Schuurman. "There were three forms. One was a receipt from the bank in Amsterdam, Hobbema and Seventer, for funds initially deposited with them in their Dutch guilder account. The second was the confirmation of a transfer from that account in Amsterdam to an account at the Manhattan Bank in the name of Dr. Julius Bluhm. The third was the copy of the original letter from Hobbema and Seventer to your bank, introducing Dr. Bluhm, advising that he had recently moved to Holland from Germany and that he wished to have a 90-day revolving interest-bearing account. I took careful note because Dr. Bluhm was insistent about safe-guarding this information for his daughter. One of the managers of the bank in Amsterdam, Mr. Eduard Seventer, signed the letter, along with Dr. Bluhm."

Husband consulted his file. "Can you tell me the amount of the transfer to our bank and the date?"

Schuurman looked at his own notes. "The amount was $312,000, and the date of the transfer was December 14, 1939."

Again, Husband checked in his file. He nodded. "Now, if I may, I would like to ask Miss Bluhm some questions."

"My name is Schuurman, sir." Husband's face reddened slightly.

"I apologize. For the record, may I have your full name?"

"My name is Sophie Bluhm Schuurman. I believe you have seen my birth certificate, my adoption papers, and my Dutch passport."

"Yes, I have, thank you." Husband's two colleagues were clearly fascinated by Sophie's command of the situation. She was smart as well as beautiful, they thought.

"We don't question your claim, Miss Schuurman. Our problem is simply this: there is no evidence that your father, Dr. Julius Bluhm, is not alive somewhere today. If we retrieve the account from New York State and pay it over to you, we are liable to him should he request the funds."

It was time for Ted Biggart to intervene. "Miss Schuurman, you know that before escheating an account to the State, we are required to advertise in the newspapers that an account has remained unclaimed for a certain period of time. To save money, at periodic intervals, we group a large number of such accounts together, and advertise using the smallest possible print. Your father's account was included in one of these advertisements. There are some people who specialize in reading these announcements. They would have noticed that the balance in the account was much larger than average. They try to locate the beneficial owner and attempt to extract a commission for having found the account for him.

"Well, we advertised your father's account *after* you and Mr. Schuurman contacted us last December. Therefore we *know* that you did not come to us because of any information in the papers. I'm sure that Mr. Husband will agree with me that the only remaining issue is how to transfer the account to you. I know it sounds terrible, but we have a responsibility to your father in the unfortunately unlikely event that he might have survived."

Sophie's composure cracked. All this talk about her father had sounded so academic until Biggart raised the possibility that her father might still be alive. Could he be somewhere in Europe or perhaps Russia, in a hospital, or in a home for the sick and handicapped? Her deep brown eyes filled with large tears. She tried to choke them back. The two younger men in the room squirmed with embarrassment.

Schuurman's irritation was apparent. "Gentlemen," the Dutch accent was more pronounced under stress, "I think we can agree that Sophie does not need to be reminded of the terrible tragedy. As you know, my wife, my daughter and I were witnesses, with Sophie, to her parents' deportation from Amsterdam."

Biggart spoke up again. "Miss Schuurman, Mr. Schuurman, all of us in this room are very mindful of your dreadful loss. We have discussed the situation, and I think we have a proposal for you which makes a lot of sense, given the circumstances.

"We are going to request the State to return the funds to us. We will provide them with the requisite statement that we have found the beneficial owner. We will open an account in the name of Sophie Bluhm Schuurman, as custodian for the estate of Julius Bluhm. You will agree, in a side letter, to leave the original account opening balance untouched in the account for five years. The accrued interest will be yours to use. At the end of that time, we will acknowledge that the waiting period for any legitimate claim will have expired, and the balance of the account will revert entirely to you, Miss Schuurman, with no restrictions."

Schuurman glanced at Sophie. She had dried her eyes. There was a heartsick look on her face. Then she turned to Schuurman. "*Papa*, you decide," she said softly.

"I think these gentlemen have spent a lot of time to help us, and their proposal makes sense. You should give them the authority to go ahead as they suggest."

The two younger men in the room were obviously disappointed that the meeting was coming to an end. Husband stood up, gathering the documents into his file. "Miss Schuurman," he said, "Mr. Schuurman, forgive my earlier insensitivity. We are very pleased that you are a client of our bank, and we look forward to being of service to you." A thin smile appeared.

Schuurman and Sophie shook hands all around. One of the younger men had a hard time letting go of Sophie's hand. She rather enjoyed it.

CHAPTER EIGHT

————————⟨⟩————————

UNWANTED INTERFERENCE

SEPTEMBER-OCTOBER, 1952

CHICAGO

The Plains National Bank stood at the intersection of Curtis and North River in suburban Chicago. It was a boxy, sandstone building, with large ground floor windows. The main floor was laid out predictably enough; teller cages ran along one wall of the banking hall, and the platform, with officers' desks arranged symmetrically, was on the other side of the hall. An elevator led up to the second and third floors. The second floor housed the operations departments of the bank. The third floor contained the executive offices and the dining room. A large vault, with a generous number of safe-deposit boxes, had been built in the basement. Plains National was a cornerstone of the local community, but over the years, it had developed a customer base from many parts of the north and west sides of Chicago.

Joseph Galish had been at the bank for over two years. He had not taken a single day of vacation, anxious to prove to Harold Strickland that Joseph Galish was a key member of the bank's management team. He had recently moved into an office on the third floor. The plaque on the door read 'Joseph Galish, Assistant Vice President, International Department'. Galish even had a secretary, Mrs. McCarthy, who sat in a room next to his which she shared with another executive secretary.

Today, Strickland had organized a lunch for the Chicago Development Association, a group of civic leaders who provided a forum for the Mayor's office to explore new economic and social initiatives. The topic was 'New Export Markets for Smaller Companies'. Three members of the association, an aide from the Mayor's office, and heads of four local companies were expected to attend. Strickland was to host the lunch. Galish was expected to say a few words.

All morning, Galish had struggled with his little speech; he was worried about his lack of formal education. He decided to blame it on his imperfect English.

The guests arrived promptly. Strickland prided himself on the bank's dining room, a luxury few banks of his size could afford. He believed that the conviviality of a meal made for better business relations. The luncheon's subject was introduced by one of the members of the association. He related progress made to date, then went on to emphasize the importance of support from the banking industry.

Strickland took the opportunity to explain the creation of the bank's international banking department with the hiring of Joseph Galish. "Joe has had hands-on experience in international business before coming to us. He was born in Hungary and speaks several languages. Thanks to him, we have been able to accommodate new financing needs for our customers. Joe, would you say a few words to these gentlemen about some of our new initiatives?"

Galish had written out a few notes, but he barely glanced at them as he described new programs in trade finance, including some export insurance plans. He added that the Plains National Bank had hired two recent college graduates and that one of them was currently in New York, attending a training program organized by the National City Bank for its correspondents.

The presentation was well received. At 1.30 p.m., when the meeting broke up, one of the bank's clients came up to Galish.

"*Koszonom szepen!*" he said in Hungarian. "Where are you from?"

Galish had known that this would happen some day. He had always dreaded the eventuality, but he had perfected his reply to avoid any challenge. "From Gyor," he replied in accented Hungarian, "but my parents moved to Vienna after the First World War," he continued in English.

"What a coincidence!" said the client. "My family was also from Gyor. We lived on the Theodorus Utca. Do you know it?"

"I remember the name. It's on the north side of town, right?"

"Exactly, near the cathedral. Well, we'll have to get together. Are you married?"

"One thing at a time, I always say," answered Galish. "I've been too busy learning English, banking and so forth." He laughed thinly.

"My wife is also from Hungary, from Budapest. You must come for her goulash. It's the best in Chicago."

"I would love to." Not if he could help it.

When Galish returned to his office, he found a message from Strickland. He wanted to see Galish as soon as he returned. Joe walked down the hall, through the glass doors, into the carpeted area of the executive suite. Mrs. Kranach sat at her typewriter outside the door leading to Strickland's office. "He's expecting you," she said.

Galish walked into the large, ornate office.

"Come in, Joe, come in. I had a call from Gil Parsons. He was the man sitting to your left at lunch. He's head of Turbine Combustions, remember? Well, you really impressed him. He suggested to me that it would be much easier handling his international transactions through a local bank, namely ourselves, rather than having to go through the big boys on LaSalle Street, let alone the New Yorkers. He thinks it would be good for the bank, for you, and for a company like his, to give you some first-hand experience with the banks overseas that he deals with through us. He suggested that you should take a trip to South America, where he has a lot of customers. You could kill several birds with one stone by seeing banks and some of his customers as well. He's willing to split the cost of the trip with us. I have to add, Joe, that I'm proposing Gil to join our board of directors. What do you think?"

"It sounds very interesting, sir."

"Joe, call me Harold, okay?"

"Yes, Harold, thank you. When do you think I should do this?"

"Gil tells me that it's springtime down there, a good time to travel. He specifically wants you to go to Venezuela, Brazil, and Argentina. I have no problem with that. I think you should take a good look at where we do business and where our customers have their customers."

"You know, Harold, that I don't speak Spanish?"

"I know that, but many businessmen down there speak English, or maybe you can use your German. Let's not worry about that. Just take a look at the possibilities, prepare an outline of the trip and what it might cost and get back to me in a couple of days, okay?"

Galish closed the door to his office. This was a distraction he didn't need. He had been developing his plan to raid the Jewish accounts, and he knew that time would start to run out. On the other hand, he had become concerned about the expenses he would have to incur to execute his elaborate plan. He was still saving as much money as he could but his savings would never cover his future expenses. Perhaps he could develop some additional business on the side on this trip.

Venezuela, Brazil, Argentina. He thought of Meinhaft, the SS colonel in Bavaria. He had carefully retained the piece of paper with Meinhaft's address in Buenos Aires. He would write to him as soon as his travel plans were firmed up. Meinhaft might be a useful contact.

———<>———

BUENOS AIRES

Galish had been advised to go to Argentina first and was grateful for the suggestion. From his hotel balcony, he looked out on the Avenida del Atlantico. The broad avenue had wide sidewalks which were filled with people strolling in the evening air. He was amazed by the prosperity of Argentine life, the numerous American-made automobiles. He was also impressed by the uniforms. The peaked caps were particularly familiar. They reminded him of Germany. Obviously, the Argentinians took their armed forces seriously. His first impressions were excellent.

It was 7 p.m. He was becoming a little nervous, waiting for Meinhaft to call. He had written to him, giving him the name of his hotel and the date of his arrival. He wondered what Meinhaft would look like now. Tomorrow, he had a busy day, with five appointments including a lunch organized by the Banco del Rio de la Plata.

At ten minutes past seven, the telephone rang. The operator, in excellent English, announced a call for him.

Meinhaft was jovial. "This is your old friend from Memmingen. How are you? It has been a long time, *nicht war*? I have reserved a table for us at a restaurant not too far from your hotel. You are free for dinner, aren't you?"

"Of course."

"Argentinians eat late. Take down the address. I will meet you there at 9 p.m. And don't forget, my name is Wormser." He laughed.

Galish dressed carefully, aware of the impression he wanted to make. He looked at himself again in the elevator mirror. If anything, he thought, he looked younger than in the stressful days before his departure from Germany. His body was still thin but strong, his hair still blond, slicked back, and carefully parted slightly off center.

The hotel concierge explained how to get to the restaurant. He walked along the streets, excited by the sights and sounds of an unknown city. After three years of hard work, he suddenly felt relaxed. He arrived at the restaurant with five minutes to spare.

"*Buenas noches, señor,*" welcomed the maitre d'hotel. "You have a reservation?"

"*Señor* Wormser has reserved, I believe."

The man looked at his book, his pen scrolling down the entries for that evening. "But of course. They have not arrived yet. Would you like to wait at the bar?"

He walked up to the bar and ordered a dry martini. *They??* Who else was coming? His mind had begun to wander, when suddenly he heard, "Joseph, it's you!" He turned, and in the space of two seconds realized that he was looking at Ilse, more beautiful than he remembered her, accompanied by Wormser. Galish had always prided himself on his poker face and his instant ability to cope with the unexpected. This encounter was putting all his resources to the test.

"Ilse, what a surprise to see you here!" What the hell was she doing here?

"My dear colleague, how nice to see you again!" enthused Wormser. What did he mean, "colleague"?

"Shall we go to our table?" asked Ilse. Galish picked up his drink and followed them.

The maitre d'hotel came up to Ilse. "*Buenas noches,* Señora Wormser." Señora Wormser? Really?

They followed the maitre d'hotel to their table and arranged themselves comfortably in the corner booth, with Ilse sitting between the two men. Wormser ordered a bottle of Argentine red wine.

"So, Joseph, it's been a long time. You're looking very well!" said Ilse. She put her hand on his arm for a moment. Galish felt the electricity.

"Thank you. Both of you are looking extremely fit!" answered Galish.

"The climate agrees with us," affirmed Wormser.

The waiter arrived with the wine. Wormser tasted it. The waiter filled the wine glasses, and they drank to each other's health.

"Tell us what you are doing, Heinrich," asked Wormser.

"It's Joseph," said Galish softly. "Well, as I wrote you, I am head of the international department of a bank in Chicago. Very interesting work. Now they have asked me to travel also to call on customers."

"Are you married, or do you have a girl friend?" asked Ilse, a slight smile on her face.

"No, I have been very busy." They were playing some kind of game, Galish thought.

The waiter interrupted with their menus. Galish suggested that they might order for him to introduce him to the local dishes. Wormser and Ilse reviewed the specials with the waiter and then ordered. Galish was surprised by the fluency of their Spanish.

"You have obviously acclimatized yourselves very well to Argentina," he commented.

"We have been made very welcome here. People don't ask too many questions," replied Wormser. Galish could feel Ilse's eyes on him. "But tell us, how is it in the U.S.?"

"Good. People work very hard. I don't like the weather in Chicago much; it gets too cold."

"You should move to a warmer climate," suggested Ilse.

"Perhaps some day, I will," agreed Galish, taking a sip of wine.

While the waiter brought their appetizers, Galish watched the Wormsers. A decidedly odd couple: the SS officer and the whatever she was or had been. Ilse wore a tight fitting black dress which outlined her broad shoulders and full breasts. Her blond hair was rolled up around her face, outlining the cheekbones. He thought about the body he knew so well.

"I suppose you go to New York on business once in a while?" asked Wormser.

"Occasionally, perhaps three or four times a year," replied Galish.

"But you could go there more often, if you needed to, right?"

Galish wiped his mouth on his napkin, and took another sip of wine. "I suppose so. But I don't expect to be going there in the next few months."

They fell silent as the waiter cleared the appetizer plates.

"Joseph, as a banker, you know all about traveler's checks, right?"

"Of course."

"We have a proposition for you. Let's wait until the waiter has brought us the main course," he added, looking across the room.

Galish quickly glanced at Ilse, trying to read what was coming next. Her face was expressionless. The steaks were still sizzling in the cast iron skillets placed in front of them. Wormser ordered another bottle of wine.

"So, as I was saying," continued Wormser, "we have a project for which we require your help. You must realize that there are quite a few survivors of the Party here in Argentina. Many of us have done quite well; others are in need of financial assistance. Many are still hiding in Europe, and we have to get them out. All this costs money."

Galish said nothing. He didn't like the way the conversation was going.

"So, after consulting with the head of our group here, we have concluded that the Party needs a substantial injection of funds, and it must be in U.S. dollars." Wormser stopped a moment to take a bite of his steak. "It is not easy getting hold of dollar currency down here. The most liquid and available U.S. money is in the form of traveler's checks. Argentinians buy them from their bank ostensibly to pay for expenses on trips and vacations. The truth of the matter is that they hoard large amounts of the checks because they are as good as money, and they have no expiration.

"You must know, being a banker, that there are four issuers of U.S. dollar traveler's checks: American Express, Thomas Cook, Bank of America and the National City Bank. The latter has by far the largest market share in Latin America. The traveler's checks are shipped from New York on consignment to the National City branch down here. The bank picks up the shipment after it has cleared customs, and transfers it to a bonded warehouse, where employees of the bank break it up for distribution to the various local banks that sell the checks. Are you with me so far?"

"Of course," replied Galish.

"We have one of our group inside the Post Office. Our plan is to pick up an entire shipment before it leaves customs for transportation to the warehouse. We can only do this if we have information on the size and date of shipment. We have only one shot at it, so we need a big shipment. We will need at least ten hours to pull the team together to handle the operation. Do you see what I am getting at?"

Galish had an awful premonition. "Yes, but your plan is unworkable. There is nobody in New York who can get you the information."

"Yes there is: you. All you have to do is to figure out how to get hold of the information. You then call us on the public telephone to leave no trace of the call. The rest is up to us."

Galish put his knife and fork down carefully on his plate. "Listen to me. I know how things work in the U.S. I don't have a prayer of pulling this caper off, so I suggest you come up with some other plan." He looked at Ilse. Her eyes were without expression.

Wormser leaned forward across the table and said coldly, "There are two reasons why you will do this for us. The first is that we will pay you 10% of the take. The average shipment is $2,000,000; you will receive $200,000 of that. The second reason, Heinrich, is that you will not be safe in the U.S. after we have advised the authorities of your real identity. It's that simple."

Galish pulled a handkerchief from his pocket and blew his nose. It gave him a few seconds to think. He knew there was no way out. "If I do this, I do it on my terms. How is the money going to be paid?"

"The entire shipment of traveler's checks will be sent to a safe place in Switzerland. You will have to go there to pick up your cut."

"I won't do it for 10%. You must think I'm stupid. I take a firm $300,000, no matter what the size of the shipment. I want the name of the consignee in Switzerland *before* I call you with the information. And finally, I want to meet your boss here to make sure that the Party is involved, not just you."

"I'm afraid we can't do that." said Wormser coldly. He turned to Ilse, looking for her support.

"Yes, we can, *liebchen*," she countered. "It would be good for Joseph to meet the boss. I'm sure that it will stimulate his patriotism."

"Now, I'd like to go bed, if you don't mind," said Galish, rising. "I have a busy day ahead of me tomorrow."

Wormser also rose. "You won't mind if we finish our meal," he said. "I'll leave word at your hotel about the meeting."

Galish nodded curtly and turned on his heel.

———<>———

The next evening, Galish was waiting in the lobby of his hotel. He saw Ilse walk in and went to meet her. "You are very prompt," he said.

"And you look very good in your American business clothes," she commented. "I have a car waiting for us. I hate to be melodramatic, but we require all visitors to be blindfolded on their way to meet the boss, a simple but essential precaution."

They climbed into the recent model Mercedes. The chauffeur and another man got out to open the rear doors for them. Once inside, Ilse picked up a scarf lying on the seat and tied it carefully around Galish's head. "Just relax, my dear," she said. Her hand strayed a little longer than necessary on his thigh. He sat back, his mind concentrated on picking up sounds. He was not optimistic, but it was good practice.

The car came to a stop after a ten-minute ride. The blindfold was removed, and Galish saw that they were outside a high, vine-covered wall. The men escorted Ilse and Galish through a large metal door, across a garden, and up the stairs into the foyer of an impressive villa. Ilse led the way to double doors in the center of the hall, which she threw open with a slight flourish.

Galish thought that he had stepped into a Bavarian mansion. The dark, heavy furniture was highly polished and reflected the many lamps set around the room on small tables. On the wall, he recognized two Flemish masterpieces, one a van Dyke, the other by Pieter Brueghel. There was no mistaking them. In a corner, he spotted a small van Gogh, from the painter's Dutch period. Several superb old master drawings were grouped on another wall. A large Tabriz covered the dark wood floor. Galish was reminded of the beautiful art which could have been his if he had better planned his disappearance from Holland. He knew immediately that art of this quality could only have been shipped to Argentina by someone with the best contacts in the Reich.

"Quite beautiful, isn't it?" asked Ilse. She walked over to a sofa, sat down, and crossed her long legs. Galish noticed the photographs in silver frames on the piano. He could not resist walking over to look at them. The largest photo, signed in the bottom right hand corner, pictured Reinhard Heydrich, General in the SS, standing in an open car. It was dated April, 1942, a month before he was gunned down by Czech patriots. The next photo was of Heinrich Himmler. Several other photos were of groups of SS officers. Galish noticed a picture of one of the most beautiful women he had ever seen. She wore a feathered boa around her shoulders. Finally, he stopped before an autographed picture of the Fuhrer, framed in silver with a black swastika medallion attached to the top center of the frame.

Galish turned on his heel as he heard the doors open. He saw Wormser, who stood a step behind a short, stocky man in his mid-sixties. The man's face was crude, the eyes too closely set, the cheeks puffed out in a caricature of a squirrel, the skin moist and pale. The hair was thin, slicked down over the squat, brutish head. He wore a double-breasted suit, pulled tightly over a prominent stomach, his back arched to maintain the semblance of a decent posture. Eau de cologne permeated the air around him.

Galish realized immediately who he was and snapped to attention. Ilse and Wormser saw the recognition in Galish's eyes. That's when they knew that the traveler's check caper was going to happen.

MARCH, 1953

NEW YORK

It was the second time this year that Galish was visiting New York. The weather was crisp, the skyscrapers outlined against a clear blue sky. Ostensibly, he was here for the Latin American Commercial Association's annual trade show. Strickland was very proud of the way the Plains National Bank was making a name for itself in international banking. Galish had invited Strickland to come east for the closing trade show dinner, where Senator Fulbright was going to be the guest speaker, but unfortunately Strickland was tied up. That suited Galish just fine. He needed to visit the National City Bank again. Their traveler's check department held the key to his independence. He simply had to get the information that Wormser and Ilse wanted.

After the gala dinner at the Roosevelt Hotel, Galish called Rita, who confirmed that she was expecting him. He had met her on one of his previous trips to the city at a bar on Third Avenue. She had taken him to her small apartment, where she had wasted little time in taking off her clothes. He had left her 45 minutes later, fifty dollars poorer but very satisfied with the range of her sexual talents. Tonight, she had not disappointed him. It was almost one a.m. by the time he returned to his room at the Dorset Hotel. His first appointment was at the National City Bank at 10 o'clock the next morning.

He decided to have a nightcap and ordered a cognac from room service. It would help him think out his plans for tomorrow.

Ever since his trip to Buenos Aires, he had wrestled with the dilemma. If he failed to help the Party, he risked exposure. Ruthless as he had become during his years in the Gestapo, he knew that the Party in Argentina would stop at nothing to destroy him. Over time, they would bend, and then break him. He had to satisfy them. For a while, he had considered stringing them along until he was able to execute his plan to raid the Jewish accounts. After that, he could vanish with his money. But he now realized that the Party organization was more watchful and better organized than he had expected. He had to find a way to tip them off about a major shipment of traveler's checks.

Jane Dougherty was expecting him when he arrived at 55 Wall Street the next morning. "Welcome back to New York, Joe," she said. "You brought some nice weather with you."

"Right. Not like last time, eh?" he replied. He followed her through the back door of the building, and across the street to 20 Exchange Place, where the Traveler's Check Department occupied the eighth and ninth floors. Jane's office on the ninth floor was small but comfortable. She poured two cups of coffee.

"So, how's business in Chicago?" she asked.

"Good, good," he replied. "In fact, we may have to order some more checks sooner than I thought. The larger denominations are quite popular. I think a lot of the checks are being sent behind the Iron Curtain to help out family members."

"Interesting you should say that. We have noticed some slow-down in the redemption rate for checks sold to immigrants from eastern Europe. It's pretty obvious that some of these checks are being hoarded."

"Nice for you, isn't it?" commented Galish. "You make a lot of money on the float, right?"

"Well, let's put it this way; traveler's checks are probably one of the most profitable products at the bank today. That's why the competition from American Express, and even Thomas Cook, is so tough. For them, the checks are a bigger part of their revenue stream."

"You really dominate certain markets, don't you, such as Latin America?" asked Galish.

"Sure, but we can't sleep on our laurels."

"How often do you have to send checks down to Latin America?"

"It varies. This is the fall season down there, so we are past their vacation time, but the branches need to replenish their stocks right now. In fact, we have a large shipment leaving today for Rio de Janeiro; there's a lot of business between Carnival and Easter."

"Yes, I noticed in our own bank that Argentina becomes very active at this time of year."

"Correspondent banks are another of our major markets, of course."

"Tell me; I'm curious. Do you send smaller shipments more frequently, or larger amounts, less often?" asked Galish.

"Good question. We tend to send the bigger shipments to places like Rio or Buenos Aires because of the distance involved. Here in the States, when your bank, for instance, runs out of checks, I can get some to Chicago very promptly. In some of the foreign countries, we can run into lengthy delays, like post office strikes. The fastest we can get a shipment to Rio is four days. So we have to be prepared to give them plenty of stock. To give you an idea, our average shipment to Brazil is about $2,000,000 worth of traveler's checks. The branch then takes care of distributing the checks to our local correspondents. We have to compete by giving excellent service."

"You know, Jane, I have never actually seen such a large shipment being prepared. It must take a lot of work."

"You bet. Come along," she said, rising, "I'll show you."

They walked down the corridor, through a door which led to service stairs, down one flight, and onto the eighth floor. They entered through a heavily locked door. Half of the entire floor was an open room. At one end were metal stacks, like a library's, where boxes of checks were arranged by denominations. In the middle of the room, people sat around four long tables, rearranging bundles, checking a master sheet listing the shipment totals.

"This smaller lot is destined for the Sumitomo Bank in Tokyo. Most of their demand is for business travel, very little personal stuff, very little hoarding. The denominations, therefore, break down into roughly equal parts of $50's, $100's and $500's, with very few $10 or 20's. Now over here," she said as they moved to the center of the room, "We are preparing a really large shipment for Rio de Janeiro."

"Very impressive," commented Galish. "Tell me, why are they breaking open a few of the bundles?"

"They do that to verify, on a spot-check basis, that the serial numbers on the checks correspond to the printer's invoice. We check every tenth bundle. When we send the checks out, we keep a verified listing of every serial number on every check. When a check gets stolen, we can verify that it is still outstanding and that the number corresponds to the denomination claimed. We issue a replacement immediately. We refund a loss faster than anyone else in the business, as you know."

"So how long does it take them to prepare a large shipment like this one?"

"This will be ready by tomorrow at lunchtime," Jane replied. "We will do a complete re-count of all the bundles, then a sign-off to make sure that there are no gaps in the serial numbers, and finally, we will package them into cardboard boxes, seal them, and take them to the main Post

Office on lower Broadway in an armored car. The Post Office then assumes responsibility to get the shipment out to Idlewild for the next flight out to Rio."

"How many of these really large shipments do you handle in a week?" asked Galish.

"Let's see," said Jane as they walked over to a supervisor's desk. Jane picked up a red folder and opened it. "Last week, we did four of them, but three were for domestic clients. This week, we did one on Monday, to St. Louis, then this Brazilian one, and now it looks like we have to have another big shipment ready to go to Argentina later today. That's it, about three or four a week."

"That's what I call organization! Which way does the shipment fly down to Buenos Aires? That's an awful long way, isn't it?"

"The shipment will go out on a flight to Miami on Friday, then on a flight from Miami to Panama and from there on a Panagra flight from Panama to Buenos Aires via Cali and La Paz. If the shipment makes all the connections, it will arrive five days later in Buenos Aires. Panagra's pretty reliable. That's how we do it."

"Jane, this is most interesting. I really appreciate your taking the time to show me how your department works. You run a very efficient operation." Galish was elated. He now had the exact information that Wormser required.

When he returned to his hotel room before dinner, he wrote down on a pad of paper exactly what Jane had told him. He looked at his diary. If all went well, the shipment would arrive in Buenos Aires on Tuesday, March 26. He had seen the boxes; he would call Wormser from the post office on Pine Street tomorrow morning. He had done the job they had asked him to do. Now he could get on with his own business.

APRIL, 1953

CHICAGO

Galish opened the second-hand suitcase he had bought to replace the G.I. duffel bag and took out the yellowing documents. He placed them carefully on the dining alcove table. He brought a lamp over from the desk; the overhead light was too dim for this kind of close-up work. He had a clean pad of paper in front of him. He began to sort the documents by city: Boston, Philadelphia, New York, London.

He began with Boston. There were two accounts at the Pilgrims National Bank and three at the Back Bay National Bank. He knew he could only raid one account at each bank, so he selected the accounts with the largest balances. In Boston, this yielded the accounts of David Levi at the Pilgrims, with a balance of $411,000 and the account of Jacob Roth at the Back Bay Bank, with a balance of $344,100. He examined the documents in his possession: he had copies of the account opening letters from the Bank of Hobbema & Seventer in Amsterdam. The letters were very similar, requesting the opening of an interest-bearing account with a periodic rollover of principal and interest. The letters also requested the bank to 'hold all mail', since the beneficiary might be changing his address in the near future. Galish permitted himself a thin smile; he had made sure of their address changes.

He scrutinized the documents for the Levi and Roth accounts. There was nothing unusual about them. Eduard Seventer, the partner in the Dutch banking firm, had signed the copies which he had given to the depositors. The copies also bore the signatures of the beneficial owners.

The next set of accounts had been opened with banks in Philadelphia. Galish laid them out carefully, and selected one at the Philadelphia Exchange Bank, one at the Bank of Commerce, and one at the Carnegie Bank and Trust. The accounts were opened with balances of $ 189,000, $397,000, and $231,000, respectively, for a total of $817,000. He had no idea how much interest they would have accrued by now.

The third set of accounts was in New York banks. He noticed that these had somewhat larger balances. The accounts in London, however, were the real blockbusters. One account in London was larger than the combined three accounts in Philadelphia. London was the mother lode. If he were successful in claiming the smaller accounts, then London would be the bonanza. It was better to practice his drill on smaller accounts in places like Philadelphia and Boston, in order to prepare himself for the big leagues in New York and London.

The banks in London presented a special problem, however. The British still had exchange controls, which meant that an account in pounds sterling could not be converted into another currency without specific approval from the Bank of England. He had learned that there had recently been some relaxation of the rules in favor of non-residents of the United Kingdom. Nonetheless he would have to be prepared for some delays in moving the funds, and any delay could mean additional risk.

He wrote down the names of each depositor and each bank on the pad of paper. Then, he added the address and telephone number of each bank, which he found in Polk's Directory of Banks. If there were references to the Jewish depositor's business activities in the letter, he noted those as well so that he could rehearse a few sentences. His future partner, posing as the depositor, would have to appear knowledgeable about his former business in Europe, although he could pretend not to speak English.

He put his pen down. He was beginning to worry about finding a suitable partner. Galish imagined that the banks would be least suspicious if the man claiming to be one of the depositors looked to be about sixty years old, with graying hair and Semitic features. He would also have to speak German, since by definition all of the depositors were refugees from Germany. Galish could take no chances that one of the bank officers happened to speak German. He would have to step up his efforts to find a suitable impostor. His entire scheme depended on it.

Galish continued to sort through the letters. By the time he had finished, he had targeted a total of seven banks in the U.S. and two in London. Total balances in the U.S., excluding interest, were nearly $2,700,000. The London accounts should yield, at $4 to the pound sterling, slightly over $3,000,000.

He tore off the page, and on a fresh sheet, drew three columns: name, company, and bank. For the first name, David Levi, he wrote 'Antilles Container Corporation, 5611 West Dubuque Avenue, Chicago'. The closest bank was, (he consulted his pocket diary), the West Lincoln State Bank in Chicago. The next depositor was Jacob Roth. Galish gave him the 'Elegance Jewelry Company, 3110 North Orleans Street, Chicago'. In the third column, he wrote 'Warsaw National Bank'. He continued until he had completed columns for all of the U.S. accounts.

He puzzled for a few moments about the London accounts. Then he decided to use the same routine: Chicago-based corporations, Chicago area banks. The state of Illinois was a unit banking state, which prohibited banks from having branches. As a result, he had a large number of banks to choose from in the Chicago area. He also knew from first-hand experience that these small banks could not afford quality staff, and it was therefore easier to hoodwink them into opening accounts for phony depositors. He would send his future partner to each bank with a small opening deposit and a board resolution appointing himself and his financial advisor, (Galish, using another name), as signers on the account. All that would be needed after that was to fund the account with the transfer from the targeted Jewish account.

Within days of the transfer's arrival, Galish would request the bank to send the bulk of the money to an account in Panama. From Panama, he would transfer the money to an account in Switzerland. He made a note to open both of those accounts. He realized that he needed to raid the Boston accounts first to generate enough cash to open the Panamanian and Swiss accounts. Together, they required about $100,000 in opening balances.

Galish knew that he could not afford even the smallest mistake. He arose from the table, carefully put all of the documents back into the envelope, clipped his work papers together, and attached them to the outside of the envelope. It was time to go to bed.

MAY, 1953

CHICAGO

It was the fourth restaurant Galish had visited on Chicago's north-west side in the last week. He examined the exterior carefully, to make sure that it appeared to correspond to the description in the Yellow Pages as 'Polish' or 'Hungarian' or 'German' or 'Czechoslovakian'. He had narrowed the search for his 'partner' to Chicago's east European neighborhoods because he needed a German speaker above all. This particular establishment was called the Brenner Café, and had fake timbered walls and heavy oak tables. The atmosphere was *gemütlich*, and the place even sported an accordion player in Tyrolian dress.

Having requested a table from which he could observe the whole room, he ordered a beer and a first course. Galish studied the patrons, one by one. The most obvious targets for his scrutiny were older men eating alone. He had not completely eliminated men in their sixties sitting with women who most likely were their wives, but it was more difficult getting into conversation with them. The first three restaurants which he had visited had yielded only one likely prospect, an aging Ukrainian. It became very clear to Galish, however, that the man had a severe drinking problem.

He was becoming discouraged. Should he advertise in 'The Sun Times' for an acting role for an older man? He thought that this might be a more efficient way of unearthing candidates than looking for them in bars and restaurants. Then he noticed a man sitting at the bar. From behind, he looked to be in his early sixties, stockily built. Galish watched him for a few moments. The man was looking down at the bar, lost in thought. The bartender paid no attention to him. Galish called the waitress over and told her that he would feel more comfortable eating at the bar. Could she serve him there?

The man did not look up when Galish installed himself on the stool next to him. Galish opened the conversation. "Good evening. Nice weather for Chicago."

The man looked up at him. There were pouches under his sad eyes. He needed a good shave. His white shirt's top button was undone, and the cheap, wide tie was pulled down. "It's okay, I guess." The accent was not pronounced, but the man was not a native.

"Will you join me in another round?" asked Galish.

"Thanks. A Budweiser will be fine."

The round was served up, just as the waitress brought Galish's main course, adding a knife and fork around the plate. Galish raised his glass and said, "*Gesundheit!*"

The man looked at him more carefully and asked, "Are you German?"

"No, Hungarian by origin," replied Galish. "How about you?"

"Polish, from Silesia. I've been here a long time."

"So you speak German as well?"

"I went to a German school."

"Well, I also speak German. Many Hungarians do. My name's Velec, Joe Velec," he added, leaning over to shake hands.

"Banichek, Arthur Banichek," the other replied.

"*Sprechen sie noch flussig Deutsch?*" asked Galish.

"*Meine Frau ist auch vom Silezien, wir sprechen Deutsch zu Hause.*"

"You work in the neighborhood?" asked Galish, switching back to English.

"Wish I did. I'm out of work right now. I'm a stationery salesman by trade."

"That's tough," commented Galish, pleased at the way the conversation was developing. He paused to continue his meal.

"What about you?" Banichek asked.

"I'm a consultant in the food business. Lots of travel involved, unfortunately."

They relapsed into silence. Galish tried again. "Once in a while I hear of part-time work. A few days or even a week, and it pays very well."

"How well?"

"Several thousand dollars for a couple of days work. Tax free. Let me be frank. My friends pay cash because they don't want the competition to find out what they are doing."

Banichek was sitting up, appraising Galish as he spoke. "I could do with some extra money. My wife is bedridden with arthritis."

"Tell me, Arthur, would it bother you that some of their activities could be considered illegal?"

"What kind of illegal? I'm not the criminal type, know what I mean, but I can live with some things."

"Well, if you take any of these jobs, you could become an accessory. Maybe you better think it over."

Banichek looked into the bottom of his glass. "Joe, may I call you Joe? You look like a good guy. I'd like to hear some more. I really need the cash."

"Okay, Arthur. Why don't you give me your address and phone number, and I'll be in touch with you if they have a job for you." Banichek wrote the information on a piece of paper which Galish had torn out of a notebook.

"I really appreciate it," said Banichek. Galish settled his bill, shook hands with Banichek, and walked out into the busy street.

———<>———

A few days later, Galish drove his car to an auto wrecking contractor on the south side of Chicago. He entered through a gate on which a sign had been posted: 'Parts, Used and Reconditioned'. To his right stretched a wall of derelict cars. To his left was a long shed. He parked, locked his car, and entered the dark, untidy room. A buzzer sounded as he crossed the threshold.

A very large man in overalls emerged from the back. He wore a Caterpillar Tractor cap. His hands were beefy and grease-stained.

"Hi," he said. "Can I help you?"

"Good morning," replied Galish. "I understand that you might have some vehicle identification plates for sale?"

"Nope. Who says so?"

"A friend of mine has a problem. He needs to change his car's ID, know what I mean?"

"Who sent you here?"

"I found you in the Yellow Pages."

The man looked at Galish suspiciously. "And who are you?" he asked.

Galish was relieved. For a minute he thought the man wouldn't deal. "My name is Joe Velec. I'm just trying to do someone a favor."

"Yeah, right."

"Assuming that you did have some plates for sale, and I realize you don't, would you take $300 in cash for one?"

Now he had the man's attention. "Well, once in a while, I have some."

"Okay, I'd like to put in an order for one. After that, I'll need a driver's license. How much do you charge for those?"

The man came around the counter. He took Galish by his lapels. He spoke very quietly. "And then I suppose you'll be wantin' a police badge?"

"Look, I'm for real. I'm a serious buyer. I'm in the market for other things too."

The man released Galish. "One thing at a time. I'll see if I can get you the plate. If your money's good, we'll talk further. Come back tomorrow." Galish knew the man was not willing to take too many chances. Nor was he.

———<>———

The following afternoon, Galish returned. It was after five. He walked into the small office. The buzzer sounded, and the big guy came in from the back room, along with a small, weasel-faced man in large shoes. Weasel-face was the first to speak.

"So, mister, you wanted a VIN plate?"

"Yes, and I have $300 in cash here if I like the looks of it."

Weasel-face handed a plate across the counter. Galish picked it up, examined it carefully, turned it over, rubbed it, and said, "It's good. I'll take it. Maybe you heard I want some other stuff?"

"Yeah, like a driver's license," said Weasel-face. "What state?"

"Illinois."

"Whose face?"

Galish took the risk. "Mine, and another guy's."

"It'll cost you."

"How much?"

"$500 for the two."

"It's a deal," said Galish. "What do you need?"

"Two good passport pictures for each of you. Write the names, addresses, birth dates, color of eyes, hair, height, on a piece of paper for each photo. Then sign the paper at the bottom a couple of times. Use black ink. The job takes time, say about a week. You'll have to pay cash up front."

The big man had remained silent throughout this negotiation. He now came from behind the counter and looked belligerently at Galish. "We take good care of good customers. Bad customers get a big headache, got it?"

"I understand. I will be back soon, gentlemen, and I may have some more business for you. Good night." Galish walked out of the stuffy office. He had a feeling that the quality of the licenses would be excellent.

Two days later, Banichek put on a clean white shirt, a brown sports jacket, dark brown pants, a flowery tie, and brown lace-up shoes. He wore a hat even though the temperature was supposed to reach 82 degrees along the lake. He arrived early at the main entrance of the Art Institute, on Michigan Avenue, where 'Velec' had suggested they meet. The more he thought about their conversation in the restaurant, the better he liked the prospect of making some money, under the table, quickly. Life had become very difficult lately. His savings were rapidly being depleted; he had needed them for living expenses ever since his wife had become bedridden. He had tried to do everything himself, but sometimes he needed someone to come in to sit with her. His job interviews had taken him as far afield as St. Paul. The two-day trip had cost him $60 for a practical nurse.

Now, he was out of a job. He was also bored. At sixty-four, he was somewhat overweight, and the absence of a regular schedule was debilitating. His only relaxation was going to the neighborhood bar for a drink. His car needed a complete overhaul, which he kept postponing due to the expense. It sat, dusty and unused, on the street in front of his house.

Galish appeared out of nowhere and tapped him on the shoulder. "Good day, Arthur," he said.

"Nice to see you, Joe," Banichek answered.

"I brought us some sandwiches for lunch," continued Galish. "I thought we might sit in the park; it's such a pleasant day."

"Fine with me," said Banicheck.

They walked from the Art Institute towards the lake. Grant Park was filling up with people taking their lunch break under the leafy trees in the warm sunshine. Galish and Banichek found an unoccupied bench and unwrapped the sandwiches and two Coca-Colas.

"Hope Coke's okay with you?"

"Fine," Said Banichek.

Galish opened the conversation. "Arthur, what I am about to tell you will do one of two things for you, depending on how you want to look at it: either it will land you in jail or it will make you financially very well-off. You will go to jail if you tell any one about what you hear from me. Do you want me to go on or shall we stop right here?"

"Joe, just promise me we won't harm anybody, okay? No physical stuff, no violence, okay?"

"Arthur, you have my word that there is no chance of that taking place."

"Okay, Joe, then let's hear it."

Galish finished his sandwich, took a sip of his drink, and wiped his mouth carefully with a paper napkin. "I have some documents which I intend to use to take money out of some bank accounts. I happen to know that the owners of the accounts died years ago. Therefore I am not robbing anyone. You can't rob dead people. So, I have decided to take the money for myself. Are you with me so far?"

"Are you serious?"

"Yes. Now here's where I need you. The only way the banks will pay out the money is if someone shows up pretending to be the long-lost owner. These accounts belonged to German Jews who died during the war. You will have to act the part of the owner of the account. I will be your financial advisor. It will take a lot of rehearsal between us because your performance must be perfect. There must be no slip-ups."

"But, Joe, how am I going to prove that I am someone else?"

"I'm working on that now. Our names will change with each account. I need you to spend a lot of time on this, getting ready. Do you have the time?"

"I do. I told you I'd lost my job. The only thing is that I can't leave my wife alone for very long, not more than a couple of days."

"Well, we may be able to work that out. But you will have to travel some. Of course, you will always be with me. So, what about it? Do you want to help me and earn a little extra money?"

"It sounds like you know what you're doing, Joe, but tell me, what are you going to pay me for this?"

"The deal I have in mind is this: I will give you ten percent of the amount we collect from each account. For instance, if the balance in an account is $100,000, you get $10,000. Most of these accounts have larger balances. You could make more than $200,000, if we are successful. How does that appeal to you?"

Banichek looked flabbergasted. His mouth hung open. He looked at Galish closely to make sure that he wasn't kidding. "Joe, that's more money than I've ever made in my whole life!" Banichek thought for a minute. "How are you going to pay me?"

"Listen carefully. I want you to go to a bank, not one where you bank now, and open a savings account. All they will require is your name, address and signature. That is the only record they will ever have of the account. You will receive a passbook. The funds I owe you will be wired to your bank for deposit to your savings account. The bank will notify you by mail when the funds arrive. Then you need to take them your passbook to record the deposit. If a bank officer ever questions you, just say a relative in Europe sent you the money. You don't have to give them any details. There is really no way you can be linked to me."

"That sounds pretty simple," said Banichek.

"Yes, but you will have to play your part perfectly. If you agree, we need to get started right away. I need twenty passport pictures of you. You're looking pretty good today, Arthur. Do you want to come with me right now to one of those passport photo places over on Jackson? It's not far away. How about it?"

"Let's go," said Banichek, rising from the bench.

That evening, Galish drove out to the auto wreckers. The big guy was in the office. "Oh, it's you again."

"Now you listen to me. I'm about to give you guys more business than your crummy little operation has made in five years. Get Weasel-face in here. I want to talk to him." The big guy debated about whether he should punch Galish or go get Weasel-face. He decided on the latter.

Weasel-face came in, three minutes later. "So you're back?"

Galish knew that they were hooked. "I have here two sets of photos and complete descriptions of two people. I want two Illinois drivers' licenses. Here's $250. Think you can do it?"

Weasel-face looked at the photos. "I said $500 up front."

"And I say if the licenses are any good, and I mean first-class, you not only get the other $250, you get a lot more business."

"Okay, come back next Saturday. In the afternoon."

Galish arrived at the wrecker operation promptly at 4 p.m. the following Saturday. Weasel-face was alone in the office.

"Good afternoon," said Galish. "You have the licenses?"

"Sure do." Weasel-face sounded friendlier. "Here you are. Best work I've ever done."

Galish took them over to the door. "I want to see them in the daylight." He examined them carefully, rubbed his thumb down the sides, and bent them. Then he pulled his real license from his wallet and placed it side by side with the two forgeries. They were perfect. "Okay," he said as he walked back to the counter, "these are pretty good. Here's the other $250. Now I want you to get me some passports."

Weasel-face smiled slightly. For the first time, Galish noticed that the man was missing two front teeth. "Passports is a big deal, mister. Only a few people know anythin' about them. I'll have to ask around, know what I mean?"

"You do that. Tell your friend that I need about twenty of them, maybe more. I want U.S., Dutch, and maybe Swiss. I'll pay top dollar for a really good product."

"Mister, the last time I got one of those passports, it cost the guy $1,000. You got that kind of money?"

"No problem," replied Galish. He pulled out ten $100 bills from his coat pocket. "Here," Galish said, pulling two of the bills from the wad and handing them to Weasel-face, "take this just for asking around."

"How do I get in touch?"

"You don't. When are you here alone? I want to talk to you, not to that fat sidekick of yours. I don't want him around."

"Like today, Saturday afternoon."

"OK, I'll be here next Saturday."

NOVEMBER, 1953

LE BOURGET AIRPORT, PARIS

The Aerolinas Argentinas flight taxied smoothly to its parking space. The stunning blond woman in first class was the first passenger off the plane. She wore a tailored suit of dark blue silk, with white lapels, and carried a smart alligator handbag and an old-fashioned, black leather document case.

The line at passport control was short. The man in the blue uniform looked casually at her landing card, then at the passport, stamped both documents with a flourish, and handed the passport back. She walked through the hall upstairs, down to the baggage claim area on the ground floor.

A silver-haired man passed through passport control a few minutes behind her. He also had an Argentinian passport. He followed her down to baggage claim, careful not to come too close to her as they waited for their respective bags. His suitcase came before hers, so he pretended to be waiting for a second one. She hailed a porter when hers arrived. The silver-haired man watched as she approached the customs counter.

"*Passeport, s'il vous plaît.*" She handed it over to the customs officer. He turned each page carefully. He appeared to be asking her questions. He searched her handbag, removing the contents and opening them. He then nodded to the porter to place the large suitcase on the counter. She opened it with a little key. The customs inspector conducted a thorough search, and closed the case again, apparently satisfied. Finally he asked her to open the document bag. He looked inside, pulled out some books, newspapers and magazines. Suddenly, he put both his hands inside the bag, and removed what looked like a folded sweater. He placed it on the counter and unfolded it. Several objects fell out. The inspector put them back in the bag, and despite her protests, led her through a door marked *Douanes Françaises*. The door closed behind them.

The silver-haired man went through customs and joined the taxi queue outside the terminal. Upon his arrival in Paris, he placed a call to Buenos Aires from his hotel room. He spoke briefly, in German. He then placed a second call to a company by the name of Cartoscope, Gmbh, in Stuttgart. The conversation, equally brief, was also in German. Finally, he walked down to the rue Washington to a travel agency to change his ticket for a flight back to Argentina.

DECEMBER, 1953

GENEVA

Their bicycle tires hissed as the boys pedaled along the wet, black-topped road. They swayed from side to side as they pedaled harder up the hill towards the large, cross-timbered house. They turned in at the gate, both exaggerating a controlled skid, then came to a dramatic stop at the front door. Jean-Luc led the way into the house, throwing his jacket on the floor. Not to be outdone, his friend Armand imitated the gesture flawlessly. They ran up the broad stairs into Jean-Luc's room.

"What do you want to do this afternoon?" asked Jean-Luc.

"I don't know," replied Armand. "What about showing me your father's gun?"

"Perhaps I better make sure that Mother isn't home." Jean-Luc left the room, went downstairs, called out for his mother, and then came running up the stairs again. "It looks clear; follow me."

They crossed the upstairs hallway and entered his parents' bedroom. Jean-Luc moved over to a tall chest, bent down, and pulled open the bottom drawer. All they could see were caps, gloves, scarves, all neatly arranged. Jean-Luc moved his hand down through the clothes very gently, trying not to disturb the orderly appearance. A puzzled look came over his face. He probed more towards the corners: no gun.

"Strange. He always keeps it here."

"Try the next one," Armand suggested, pointing at the drawer above. Jean-Luc closed the bottom drawer carefully and opened the one above. The boys stared, not comprehending. The entire drawer was filled with what looked like money, but they were not Swiss francs. For some moments, they gazed in silence. Then Jean-Luc reached down to pull out a stack of notes which were tightly bound in a special wrapper. The wrapper read 'National City Bank' and 'Traveler's Checks'. The notes were in denominations of $100. The boys looked at each other.

"How many of these things do you think there are in this stack?" asked Armand.

"I don't know. It feels pretty thick, maybe a hundred?"

"Wow! What is this? Do you think it's a kind of money?"

"I don't know. Maybe it is," answered Jean-Luc.

"Why would your father have so much of it?"

"I have no idea," Jean-Luc replied. "Maybe we better leave the room before my mother comes home and finds us here."

The boys went downstairs, into the garden, and tossed a ball around until it was time for Armand to go home.

———<>———

Mme. Frossard was a large, contented-looking lady. Her life was straightforward and rewarding, at least by Swiss standards. Her husband had a successful career; her son Armand was a reasonably hard-working young lad with little inclination to get into trouble. Every evening, including this one, she started preparing the evening meal at about 6 p.m., to be sure that her two men would be properly fed at the proper time.

Inspector Michel Frossard left early in the morning and generally came home about 7 p.m., unless there was an emergency at police headquarters, which did not occur very often because he had deputies to take care of such matters. As chief of the Canton of Geneva's Criminal Investigation Department, he was fully in control of his life and the lives of all those around him. He was the model for a Swiss policeman, reliable, stubborn, proud of his career, proud of the Swiss Army, proud of the Swiss way of life. Crime was an anathema to him. Criminals must be caught and sent to jail to ponder the error of their ways. No foreign criminals should be allowed into Switzerland to pollute the environment which he and his colleagues spent their lives protecting. Inspecteur Frossard knew he did an excellent job. Returning home to his wife and son was a pleasurable experience which was a fitting and proper end to his hard-working day.

He hung up his coat, walked into the kitchen, kissed his wife, and asked, "Where is Armand?" He was not particularly concerned about Armand's whereabouts, but he was slightly irritated when Armand was not immediately available to greet him. Fortunately Armand had learned that his father insisted on specific routines, including the gathering of the small family when he arrived home, as if to reassure himself that their familial cell had survived unharmed since early in the morning. Within a few moments, Armand entered the kitchen and hugged his father. Mme. Frossard bustled about serving the dinner.

Towards the end of the savory meal, the Inspector genially asked his son, "And how was your day today, Armand?"

"Fine, Papa. We had a Latin composition which I think I did well on."

"Weren't you supposed to have soccer practice today?"

"No, it was called off because our coach had to go to Montreux for a funeral or something, and nobody else was available to coach us."

"So what did you do after school?" the Inspector queried. He liked to account for everybody's time.

"Jean-Luc invited me to his house, and we hacked around."

"What is his house like? I saw his father once in the driveway, and he didn't look very Swiss to me," said the Inspector.

"Very nice," Armand replied.

"How is Jean-Luc's mother?" Mme. Frossard asked.

"She's okay. Actually, she wasn't there today."

The Inspector's brows moved a shade down on his forehead. "You mean you two were there all alone?"

"Well, yes, but we didn't do much except play ball and stuff."

The Inspector knew that he had to fill in the blanks here. "So tell me, you spent over an hour just playing ball?"

"Well no, not really." Armand had a very concerned look on his face. He eyed his father carefully. He played with the bread on his plate. Finally, he let out a breath, cleared his throat, and said, "I did see something at Jean-Luc's that was kind of strange." He didn't want to mention the gun, which Jean-Luc had told him was illegal. "We found all this kind of money in packages, all wrapped up. Jean-Luc didn't know if it was money or what, but I guess his father must be pretty rich to keep it in a drawer like that."

"What kind of money?" Frossard asked.

"Well, it wasn't Swiss francs. It had something about 'national' written on the wrapper."

"You say there were packages?"

"Papa, the whole drawer was full of them."

Inspector Frossard put his elbows on the table, rubbing the sides of his nose with both hands. "Armand, try and remember exactly what those notes looked like. What color were they?"

"Sort of blue with black letters, I think."

"Was there any writing that you can remember?"

"Well, across the top was something like national, oh yeah, city bank."

"Did you see any numbers?"

"Yes, they had 50 and 100 on them."

The inspector was silent for a few minutes. Then he said, "Armand, I don't want you to discuss this with anyone at all. Is that clear? This is very strange. Do not talk about it even with Jean-Luc. If he mentions what you saw, pretend you don't remember, and you don't care. Is that understood?"

Armand knew when to heed instructions, particularly from his father. Mme Frossard cleared the table, and Armand went upstairs to his room to do his homework, wondering what all this fuss meant.

————<>————

The next morning, Inspector Frossard arrived at his office a few minutes before eight. He walked into the small, rather cramped room, hung his coat on the back of the door, walked over to the chair behind the desk, and reached for the phone. "Good-morning, Paul, please get me Chief Inspector Junot at Interpol in Lyon." He put the phone down and started sifting through the files that his assistant had prepared for his review.

Generally, Frossard spent about an hour briefing himself on the current cases under his supervision by going through these files, which had been updated the previous evening. This was his way of establishing his day's priorities. Usually, by 9.30 a.m., he had completed his review and had decided on a series of actions, which he then jotted down in a small, lined notebook he had purchased for himself, since the Geneva Police Department did not stock this particular item. This morning, the routine was interrupted by the call he had put through to Lyon.

"*Bonjour, cher collègue,*" Frossard said, "I am desolated to bother you so early in the day. How are you?"

Chief Inspector Henri Junot, now second-in-command at Interpol, was a veteran of the *Quai des Orfèvres*, the famed criminal investigation unit of the Paris Police Department, named after the building along the Seine which housed the unit. He had agreed to go to Interpol for no more than five years, after which he wished to retire to his property in Normandy, there to perfect the distillation of his private brand of Calvados. The Interpol job was interesting, he had to admit; it involved some travel and considerable use of his excellent English, learned as an intelligence officer at de Gaulle's headquarters in London during the Second World War. He enjoyed contacts in other countries; making the acquaintance of Frossard had been a particular pleasure, and they respected each other's complete professionalism.

"I am well, my friend, although we have had some terrible weather lately. Perhaps you got some of it in Geneva?"

"Unfortunately we did. It has cleared up a bit now."

"Anyway," continued Junot, "what can I do for you this morning?"

"I have run into a perplexing problem," replied Frossard. "I need some advice. Do you have a minute?"

"Naturally. Please go on."

"My son Armand was playing with a classmate at the classmate's house yesterday. By chance they opened a drawer in the parents' bedroom. They found what Armand described as packets of strange money, a whole drawer full, neatly bundled with paper wrappers. Armand describes them as having a blue background; the lettering is black. He remembers some of the words on the notes as 'national' and 'city'. The denominations appeared to be 50 and 100."

"U.S. dollars?"

"He was not sure."

"As a guess," Junot opined, "they sound very much like National City Bank traveler's checks, and the reason they come to mind is that, by an extraordinary coincidence, we are working on a major case right now involving the theft of a large amount of them. What would be your guess as to the number of packets?"

"Armand stated that the entire drawer was full of them; that could be twenty or thirty packets anyway. I was prompted to place this call to you because of the quantity of packets and their strange hiding place."

"They are dollar checks, presumably. In our current investigation, the bank has informed us that their traveler's checks have 100 notes to a pack, so the drawer may contain several hundred thousand dollars! That, *mon ami*, is definitely not normal."

"So, *cher collègue*, what do you recommend?" asked Frossard.

"If I am right, we may have an unhoped-for break in our investigation. I'll make arrangements for a quick trip to Geneva. You and I should go over a couple of pending cases anyway. I'll let you know the details as soon as I have them."

"Excellent. I shall look forward to having you here. Why don't you plan to stay with us? Mme. Frossard would love to see you again, and you know she can guarantee you a good meal!"

"I would enjoy that very much. Let me get my ticket, and I will call you back with the details."

The train station in Geneva, especially after nightfall, was damp, empty, and gloomy. Between bursts of static, the PA system announced incomprehensible arrivals, departures, and changes of platforms. Chief Inspector Junot walked through the echoing halls, down the steps, to the street. His initial surprise at not seeing his friend Frossard quickly gave way to relief when he spotted him waving from across the road. He got into the car, shook Frossard's hand, and the car took off.

"I am happy to see you," Junot said.

"My apologies for not meeting you on the platform. The traffic, for a Sunday night, is terrible."

"Any further news?" Junot asked.

"No. I told Armand to keep absolutely quiet about this. He can be trusted. What do you want to do tomorrow morning?"

"I have been thinking about it," Junot replied, "and I think it is essential that we get your son to go back to his friend's house to collect some serial numbers from those banknotes."

"Armand would probably be delighted to become a police accomplice!"

"Can we talk to him at breakfast? Maybe it won't be possible for him to go over to Jean-Luc's house tomorrow."

"Let's give it a try," replied Frossard. "Now let's enjoy the dinner that Marie has prepared for us. I have a little wine from the Vaud that you might enjoy!"

The next afternoon, Armand and Jean-Luc ran for the bicycle racks, straddled their bikes, and made their usual dramatic turn out of the school gates. As they pedaled along, Jean-Luc yelled at Armand, "So where should we go?"

"Let's go to your house; my mother is not in a good mood today. I don't want to go near the house until it's time for dinner."

The boys arrived at Jean-Luc's panting for breath, each one having tried to best the other in the race.

"So what do you want to do today?" Jean-Luc asked.

"I don't know. What about your father's gun, what happened to it?"

"I don't know. Let's go upstairs. Mother isn't home, and I don't think she'll be back for a while."

The boys made their way up to Jean-Luc's parents' bedroom, and Jean-Luc opened the bottom drawer. He pushed his hands under the clothing, and again came up with nothing.

"Maybe your father placed it in the drawer with the money," Armand suggested.

Jean-Luc closed the bottom drawer and then opened the one above it. The boys marveled at the perfect symmetry of the packets, neatly tucked side by side, exuding the unique smell of freshly-printed ink.

"Wow!" said Armand, as he picked up one of the packets. "They feel so new." Suddenly he panicked. His father and Chief Inspector Junot had asked him to get the serial numbers on any packet he picked up. Just the top banknote would do. He looked in horror: two letters, three digits, then three more digits, then three more digits. How could he remember all of these numbers?

Stalling for time, he brought the packet up to his nose. "They smell so inky," he said. In the meantime, his mind was racing to memorize: HE911, (that was easy), then 147, then 086. He repeated the numbers silently and then turned to look at Jean-Luc out of the corner of his eye to see whether he had one more minute to repeat the numbers to himself. Jean-Luc was just staring at the money, not comprehending.

Suddenly, they heard a door closing downstairs. Quickly, they closed the drawer, turned on their heels, and fled down the corridor back to Jean-Luc's room.

"Jean-Luc, are you up there?" called his mother.

"We're upstairs, and we're coming right down." The boys ran into the kitchen where Jean-Luc's mother was putting away some groceries.

"*Bonjour,* Armand," she said, "How is everything?" Armand noticed that her dress looked very fancy for a weekday afternoon.

"Fine," he answered, "Well, I should be getting along, Jean-Luc."

"No rush," said Jean-Luc's mother, "you can stay as long as you like."

"Thank you, Madame, but I have some homework to do." He was terrified that he would start to forget the numbers he was trying to memorize.

"Yeah, why don't you stay a bit longer?" asked Jean-Luc.

"Thanks, but I have to go." Armand ran out of the front door to his bicycle, leapt onto it and turned around to shout to Jean-Luc, "See you tomorrow at school."

Armand kept running the numbers through his head as he pedaled furiously back to his house. "Let's see, HE911, 147, then 096. No, was it 086? Oh no, I have forgotten the last three digits! Stop right now. Get home. If you worry about it, you will make it worse." He was home in record time. He ran upstairs to his room and wrote the numbers down on a sheet of paper. He looked at them again, convinced that he had inverted some of them, afraid that they were completely wrong.

Inspector Frossard arrived home at the usual time, accompanied by Junot. They walked into the foyer, removed their coats, and then Frossard asked his usual question, "Marie, where is Armand?"

This time Armand was waiting for them in the kitchen. "Here I am, Papa. Good day, Chief Inspector," he answered.

Mme. Frossard fussed around the table in the dining room, anxious to have everything in perfect order for their distinguished guest. The first course was already on the table: a slab of *foie gras de canard*, with small triangles of toast on a side plate.

"This is outstanding," opined Chief Inspector Junot. "Madame, you always offer me a feast!" A toast was proposed by Frossard, and the four settled down to the serious business of eating. It was not long, however, before Frossard turned their attention to Armand.

"Armand, as you know, I have made you my personal assistant in a case that has the Police Department somewhat puzzled. The Chief Inspector is here because the case may have international ramifications."

Armand looked down on his plate, his mind bubbling with excitement at the thought that he could be an important police helper in solving an international robbery.

"Did you manage to get any numbers from those banknotes?"

"Yes, Papa, I wrote them down when I got home; they are upstairs in my room."

"Excellent, Armand. Please get them for us, and then you can describe the place where you found them to the Chief Inspector."

———<>———

PARIS

Inspector Paul Ladurée picked up his phone. "Ladurée," he said curtly.

"This is Junot. I've just returned from a trip to Switzerland."

Inspector Duree changed his tone quickly. "Oh, Chief Inspector, how was your visit, *mon ami?*"

"I am desolated to bother you, *cher collègue*," Junot began. "Quite by accident, we have stumbled across a very large hoard of stolen U.S. traveler's checks in Geneva. The man whose house they have been found in is a French national who has been living in Geneva for six years. We are not sure what his occupation is, but he has legitimate residence papers. Interpol can seize the traveler's checks because we have been notified that they were stolen. However, we need to find out more about the people involved. The Swiss authorities have started watching his house. Nothing suspicious appears to be going on. It is the sheer size of the amount of traveler's checks that has us puzzled. An educated guess would be about two million dollars."

"Tell me about the Frenchman," asked Ladurée.

"His name is Gérard Christian Lejoin. He states that he works for a German company named Cartoscope, Gmbh. in Stuttgart. He has a French National Identification Card, the details of which match his passport. But, here is where it gets bizarre. His name is also registered as an Argentine national in the Canton of Zug."

"That seems to be a coincidence, don't you think? There are many Frenchmen in Argentina, and his name is not terribly unique."

"The cantonal authorities in Zug made an inquiry. The address he gave them exists, a small apartment, but he has never been seen there. He is not registered for any kind of occupation; he does not own a car, and he has never filed a tax return."

"That still does not prove that he is the same person as your wealthy Frenchman with the same name in Geneva."

"Except for the fact that the dates of his registration in the cantons of Zug and Geneva are identical."

"That does appear to be a strange coincidence," Ladurée admitted. "I shall start an inquiry tomorrow morning on this fellow, Lejoin. Is it possible that Lejoin had access to some very high-class counterfeit passports and workpapers?"

"We have to assume that he did," replied Junot.

"Something has just occurred to me," said Ladurée. "Recently, at Le Bourget airport, we seized an extraordinary collection of fake passports, some of them Argentine, from a woman who had just arrived on a flight from Argentina. One of our customs guys had one of those hunches; she was sleek, well-dressed, just a little too sure of herself, as if she had been through customs every week of the last six months. Her luggage was of good quality. She had an Argentine passport.

"Anyway, he asked her to bring her bags over for inspection. You know how dogs can smell fear on someone? Our guy told me he could sense her stiffening. He asked her to open the largest case. The contents were quite conventional. He then asked to search her handbag. She had a lot of jewelry, various currencies, and lots of cosmetics. Normally he would have stopped at this point, feeling that she was just what she seemed to be, but he could still smell her fear. Her other bag was an old-fashioned leather document case, with bulging sides and a big clasp at the top, a bit like a country doctor's satchel. It seemed out of keeping with her appearance. The Customs inspector asked her to open it. It contained magazines, some books, and underneath, wrapped in a sweater, he found a large collection of passports, about thirty of them, issued to both men and women, and all apparently valid."

"What did the woman say about them?" asked Junot.

"She said she had no idea how they got into her bag. We've put her in the cooler until we can figure out what all this means."

Junot reflected for a moment, and then said, "Can you give me a list of the names, nationalities, birthdates and perhaps copies of the photos on those passports?"

"Let me see." Ladurée opened a file on his desk. "There are four Paraguayans, five Uruguyans, six Argentines, and six Venezuelans. Five are women. However, some of the photos appear in more than one passport. There are actually only five men and two women if you go by the photos. Our experts rate them as the best forgeries they have ever seen. We have started cross-matching names, birth dates, birth places and so forth, to see whether we can establish a pattern, but as you know, that's a long job. I will also send you the details about the woman we arrested. You and I don't believe in coincidences, *n'est-ce-pas?* Now, tell me a little more about the traveler's checks."

"We know that the checks were stolen from the Post Office in Buenos Aires. They were a consignment from the issuing bank, National City Bank of New York, to their branch in Buenos Aires. As you know, blank traveler's checks are just as good as cash until they are signed by the buyer. They make a very tempting target."

"How can someone in Buenos Aires have known about the shipment?" Ladurée asked.

"The bank is convinced that the gang received information from someone in New York. The FBI has launched its own investigation, but so far, without turning up any useful leads. It seems as if further progress in this case will depend on pursuing the inquiry in Geneva. We are therefore going to arrest Lejoin and see if he can lead us back to the rest of the gang."

Ladurée promised to check out Lejoin's background.

GENEVA

Unlike their counterparts in many other cantons of Switzerland, the Genevois police preferred French cars for their official transportation. Two black Citroens, each containing four men, snaked out of Police Headquarters at 4.12 a.m. A slight drizzle added to the dismal atmosphere. They drove quickly and silently to the *quartier* where Lejoin had his home. Both cars came to a stop a short distance away from the house. Three officers sprang from the second car, and Frossard, accompanied by another detective, got out of the first. The two cars then moved away, one coming to a stop at the end of the street, the other turning into the alley at the back of Lejoin's house. Frossard, followed by his man, opened the gate on the street and walked quickly up the steps to the heavy wooden door under the *porte cochère*. The other three spread themselves around the back and sides of the house.

Frossard, his large frame outlined against door, pulled on the long handle at the side of the door. A bell jangled inside. For a few moments, there was no sound. Then a light was turned on upstairs. A second light went on in the hall downstairs. From behind the door, a man's voice asked in French, "What is it?"

"Police. Let us in." Frossard's voice was calm, just giving an order. The front door opened immediately. A medium-sized man, in bathrobe and pyjamas, stood there. Frossard showed him his identification, which the man appeared to be too dazed to examine carefully. Frossard entered.

"Is your name Gérard Christian Lejoin?"

"Yes, but . . . what is this . . . at this time of the night . . ." Lejoin was shuffling backwards down the hall, as if the weight of this imposing officer of the law was pushing him against his will.

"We have a warrant to search your house. Who else is in the house tonight?"

"Just my wife and son," Lejoin replied.

"Please have them come downstairs. The house is completely surrounded, so do not attempt to escape." Lejoin hesitated, and then turned to climb the stairs hurriedly. Frossard could hear voices upstairs, floors creaking. A very attractive woman, in spite of her nighttime attire, a young boy and Lejoin came back down the stairs. The woman looked warily at Frossard. They went into the living room and sat down obediently as the two policemen followed them.

"We apologize for this early morning visit," said Frossard. "Please stay here with my assistant. I am going upstairs to conduct the search authorized by the examining judge."

Frossard left the room, climbed the stairs, and, on the upstairs landing, looked around to get his bearings. He opened every door as he walked down the hall. He soon arrived at what he assumed was the master bedroom, with a large bed in a state of disarray. He looked around the room, trying to visualize his son's description of the chest of drawers. To his left he saw an early nineteenth century French three-drawer chest with a marble top. He walked over to it, bent down, and opened each drawer, starting from the bottom. He had to pull hard on the second one. It was stacked almost to the top with traveler's checks. He started pulling out a few of the neatly wrapped bundles. They were identical, all $100 denominations, and all had been issued by National City Bank in New York.

Frossart riffled through a bundle. It appeared to contain 100 checks. So each bundle was worth $10,000. He started counting the bundles. The drawer contained 46 bundles: $460,000. Where was the rest, if this was part of the $2,000,000 heist in Buenos Aires? He left the bundles on the floor, turned and headed back down the stairs. He entered the living room, where his men were sitting with the Lejoin family. To Lejoin, he said, "I'm afraid you will have to come to the station with us for questioning. You may consider yourself under arrest."

Frossard went out into the hall, through the front door, and called out to his men to come in. He gave instructions to search the house from top to bottom. Back in the living room, he said, "I'm very sorry, Mme. Lejoin. You and your son will have to stay in the house until you receive further instructions from us."

She looked at him. "Does that mean Jean-Luc cannot go to school today, with *your* son?"

"Of course, he can go to school. And you may go out shopping if you need to, but we must be able to reach you at a moment's notice." She shrugged her shoulders, put her arms around her son, who looked stunned by the rapidly unfolding events, and both went back upstairs. Frossard watched her leave, her bathrobe swaying gently from side to side. He turned to one of the police officers who had just emerged from the kitchen. He carried a cardboard box. Inside was another batch of traveler's check packets. He put them down on the hall table. Frossard counted them. Thirty bundles of 50's: $150,000 total.

"Keep searching," Frossard ordered his men.

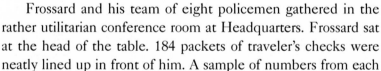

Frossard and his team of eight policemen gathered in the rather utilitarian conference room at Headquarters. Frossard sat at the head of the table. 184 packets of traveler's checks were neatly lined up in front of him. A sample of numbers from each bundle had been telexed to New York. The bank had promised to call back to confirm that these were all genuine checks, part of the lot mailed to Buenos Aires earlier that year.

As the men waited, Frossard gave further instructions. "First of all, I want a complete dossier on Lejoin and his family. I have already been in touch with the French police, who have started to investigate his background. I want to know what he does, where he came from, who his wife is, where she came from, etc. Contact our colleagues in Bonn and get all the information you can on this company he works for, Cartoscope, Gmbh. You may assume that all of their current documents are forgeries."

Frossard continued, "I want a complete profile of their friends and business associates. Inventory all their mail; check the telephone numbers which they keep around the house; where they bank; where they shop; look for travel patterns. I want to know where she goes during the day-time. Check all their clothing, where it comes from. Check the medicine cabinets. Ruel, you are in charge of that part of the investigation. Start immediately. We have left three men around the house to make sure we can track her during the day. Even if she stays at home, go through everything. She's tough. Don't take any guff from her. Tell her we can nail her as an accessory. But right now, I want her to think she may not be implicated."

He returned to his office and placed a call to Junot. "I think we should arrange for the woman still in *détention préventive* in Paris to be arraigned by Ladurée on suspicion of trafficking in forged documents. The longer we can keep her in the cooler, the better our chances of going back to the source."

"I agree," replied Junot. "I don't want to report back to the Argentine police yet. I don't want one word of this to leak out to anyone. Our best chance of finding out who else is involved is to keep absolutely quiet. That's why I'm beginning to think that we should bring Lejoin's wife in as well. Hopefully she will not have had a chance to tip anyone off yet."

"She may have done it by phone, but I doubt it," replied Frossard. "We've had her phone tapped since about 5.40 a.m. We might be better off requesting her to tell everyone that her husband is away on a business trip. If she cooperates, etc., etc. Even so, I don't think we have much time."

"Then you should concentrate on questioning Lejoin," said Junot.

Lejoin, by now wearing a shirt and casual pants under a car coat, was ushered into a bare room at police headquarters containing only four straight-backed wooden chairs and a table.

This had to be a basic model for all interrogation rooms in all police stations all over the world. Even the naked light bulb hanging directly over the table was straight from the props department.

Lejoin was invited to sit down. Adhering to good police procedure, Frossard and the accompanying Swiss officer remained standing. For a few moments, Frossard said nothing and just looked at Lejoin, who was clearly trying to control his fear. The raid had been so sudden, after so many weeks of thinking that they were going to get away with stealing the traveler's checks. He was utterly unprepared for the dramatic change in his fortune.

He was also worried about his wife. Lejoin must have been a reasonably good-looking man when he was in his twenties, but he had put on weight and looked unfit. Mme. Lejoin had been pressing him to start spending the money. He repeatedly explained to her that he was under an obligation to his associates not to cash the traveler's checks.

As a French national, Mme. Lejoin could not obtain a work permit in Switzerland. She arranged with a studio to teach Latin dances and was paid in cash by her customers. The studio took a small percentage for its expenses. She had started to spend more time out of the house. Her clothes became more daring. Lejoin was jealous, but he had no proof. She would not do anything silly now that they were so close to so much money, even though they had to share it with his 'friends'. He had told her that their share would be $200,000. It appeared to have calmed her down for a while.

"Please state your name," the Swiss policeman asked.

"I've already told you. My name is Gérard Lejoin."

"And what is your occupation?"

"I represent a German company that makes card-sorting machines."

"What is a card-sorter?" asked Frossard.

"They are cards which are widely used in business. You punch holes in them for a number or letter, so you can have name, address and financial information on a single card. Then when you want to look at all of your customers whose names begin with B, for instance, you put all the cards in, and the spindles on the machines sort out the ones beginning with B."

"What is the name and address of your employer?" asked Frossard.

"Cartoscope, Gmbh., Friedrichstrasse 120, Stuttgart, Germany." The Swiss officer wrote it in his notebook.

"Where are your customers here in Switzerland?" asked the Swiss policeman.

"My territory is Geneva, Lausanne, and a few companies on the French side of the border."

"Where is your office?"

"I work out of my house. I'm always on the road, you know."

For a moment, Frossard remained silent. Then he moved off to a corner and whispered to the other policeman. They came back to the table. Frossard leaned back in his chair, crossed his legs, and pulled out a package of cigarettes. He favored the Humphrey Bogart way of lighting a cigarette; he could do it without ever taking his eyes off his victim. As he blew his first puff across the table, he pushed the pack over to Lejoin.

"Help yourself."

"I don't smoke."

"Very well. Now let me tell you what the situation is. We have found, in your home, almost $2,000,000 of negotiable traveler's checks. We have confirmation from the issuer, the National City Bank in New York, that the numbers on the checks found in your home correspond to those on checks stolen from the post office in Buenos Aires a few months ago. In fact, it appears that you have in your possession almost all of the stolen checks. The Argentine police have confirmed the circumstances of the theft. After customs clearance, a post office employee set the shipment aside in a storage area pending verification of the addressee. He filled out forms the next day consigning the packages to an import-export agency. Nobody checked the change of destination. The packages vanished, as did the employee. So tell us, how did you manage to do it?"

Lejoin sat very still, thinking. This was it. How could they have found this out? "I refuse to make a statement. I must speak with my lawyer."

"Fine," stated Frossard. "What is his name?" Lejoin was silent.

Frossard looked up at the ceiling, then back at Lejoin. "Let me explain something to you. You are facing a trial. At the end of it you will be sentenced to at least seven years in prison. Do you understand?" Lejoin said nothing.

Frossard continued. "You did not pull this off by yourself. We have some of the names of those involved, but not all. We need to know who in the U.S. tipped you off that the shipment was on its way. May I emphasize that your cooperation might lessen the severity of the charges against you, and your prison sentence will reflect those changes."

Lejoin knew that he had little room for maneuver. He had been such a fool not to take his share and run. Perhaps he could still recover something from this disaster.

"How do I know that you will help me if I tell you anything?"

"This one is quite easy to break," thought Frossard. "M. Lejoin, let's be practical. We need you to give us a complete account of the theft from beginning to end, all of the details, all of the people. Do you know who the contact was in the U.S.?"

"No, the only person who would know is an Argentine."

"What do you know about him?"

"Not much. He lives in Buenos Aires and has some kind of art business. He comes to Geneva every couple of years. I've sold some gold coins to him. He asked if I would be interested in a deal that would make me rich. He was the one who gave me my instructions."

Frossard stopped to think for a moment. It sounded simple enough. "You are making this very tedious, Lejoin. We have other things to do."

The Swiss policeman moved over slightly, so that the light from the overhead lamp lit up the lower half of his face. It was time to play bad guy. "We have already given you more time than is customary here in this country. We do not pamper criminals here. We do not serve gourmet food in prisons. We make prisoners work. No cigarettes, no alcohol, no nothing. Families are allowed to visit once a month. You are in prison to be miserable, to want desperately never to commit a crime again. Is that clear?"

Lejoin had been forced to turn his neck at an awkward angle to look at the Swiss policeman. He was feeling ill. He wanted to get this over with. "The guy in Argentina was named Gerhard Wormser."

Inspector Frossard stood inside the terminal gate. Swissair flight 538 from Buenos Aires via Dakar (Senegal) was expected in on time. Although it was already 8.30 a.m., it was still dark outside. It had snowed lightly the night before. The wind had come up, lowering the temperature further. By early morning, Geneva was in the grip of a wet, raw dawn. Frossard had arisen very early. He had been picked up at his house by two other Geneva police officers. At Cointrin Airport, another carload of policemen had met them. They were taking no chances.

The telegram from Lejoin had been sent three days before:

> "Gerhard Wormser, 126 Avenida de la Republica,
> Buenos Aires. Come immediately. Cable your flight
> and arrival time."

The return cable had arrived the next day:

> "Gérard Lejoin, 14, rue du Moulin Vert, Genève.
> Have booked seat on SR 538 arriving 9.10 a.m.
> Sunday, December 13."

It was unsigned. Perhaps Wormser was nervous and had forgotten to do so; perhaps he wanted to remain anonymous. Either way, it made no difference to Frossard. He was drawing the big fly into the spider's web.

The DC6 taxied slowly towards the gate, its navigation lights blinking in the dull morning light. Frossard looked around the gate area and nodded carefully to each of the five *Genevois* policemen dispersed throughout the waiting hall. A few minutes later, the gate door opened, and the first-class passengers began to stream out, a little disoriented after a 23-hour flight at 19,000 feet. Amongst them, supposedly, was G. Wormser. Frossard felt confident that he would be able to recognize him.

Even so, he almost missed him. He had been expecting someone younger, more athletic. Wormser looked middle-aged, unshaven, grumpy, and ready to start an argument. He wore expensive clothes. His shoes were brown suede. His hair was dark with graying streaks. He strode towards the booth for non-resident passports. As he came within a few feet of it, he felt an arm grip his shoulder and a voice said, "This way, *monsieur*. Please cooperate."

Later that morning, Frossard sent out a teletype to the attention of Inspector Junot at Interpol headquarters:

> "Re: Theft of Traveler's Checks Shipment: This morning, we apprehended Gerhard Wormser. Argentine national, German origin (stop) age 56, medium build, graying hair, blue eyes (stop) named by Lejoin as key man in Buenos Aires (stop) refuses to talk (stop) assume you will advise your contacts at FBI re this development (stop) both Wormser and Lejoin being held on a charge of receiving stolen goods (stop) will call you tomorrow to discuss other issues, including continuing coordination with FBI. Regards Frossard."

CHAPTER NINE

———◇———

CASH REGISTERS

DECEMBER, 1953

BOSTON

Logan Airport had been crammed into a narrow spit of land surrounded on three sides by water. It was very exposed to wind, rain, and snow and was difficult to reach by road. To make matters worse, a newly-arrived traveler had to hire a taxi with no meter and travel through winding, pot-holed streets into a narrow tunnel which led into even more congested streets. Galish and Banichek were huddled in the back of the cab, turned away from each other as they looked out at the dirty streets in this dismal part of Boston. They were dressed in dark suits and each carried a small overnight bag.

The cab finally came to a stop in front of the Somerset Hotel. Galish paid off the driver and strode into the hotel lobby. Banichek followed him, visibly out of breath. At the reception desk, Galish stated that he had a reservation in the name of Grolz for two single rooms. The clerk handed him a form to complete.

"Will you be staying just the one night?" he asked.

"We should be able to complete our business in a day, thank you," replied Galish. "We have reservations on a 6.10 p.m. flight back to Chicago tomorrow evening. At what time should we leave downtown to make our flight?"

"We recommend at least one hour before departure. For rush hour, add twenty minutes to get through the tunnel."

"Thank you. I will settle our bill now," Galish added, counting out the required cash.

"Do you need a bellboy for your bags, sir?"

"No thanks. We just have our overnight cases."

The next morning, Galish and Banichek took a cab to the head office of the Pilgrims National Bank. They walked through the somber, imposing entrance, generously supported by marble pillars. The reception area was glass-enclosed; behind it, two men manned the telephones. One of them looked up and greeted Galish. "Good morning, sir. How may I help you?"

Galish pulled out a piece of paper. "We have an appointment with Mr. Nicholas Bottomley. My name is Grolz, and I am accompanying Mr. Levi."

"Certainly, sir. One moment please." The man placed a call, spoke briefly, and replaced the receiver. "You may go to the third floor, sir. Mr. Bottomley is expecting you. The elevators are to your right."

Galish and Banichek arrived on the third floor to find an earnest young man waiting for them. He strode forward.

"Mr. Grolz, Mr. Levi?" he looked at them questioningly.

"I am Grolz," stated Galish. "This is Mr. Levi. He does not speak much English, so I am here to assist him. I am his accountant in Chicago. Here is my card." Bottomley took the card. It read: Franz Grolz, CPA.

"Come this way, please, gentlemen." He preceded them down a dark corridor and into a plainly furnished conference room. "Let me take your coats. The closet is right over here." He busied himself with coat hangers and then invited them to take a seat.

Bottomley opened the conversation. "Mr. Grolz, I wasn't entirely sure what you wished to discuss with us." Bottomley checked some notes in a file. "You said that Mr. Levi has an account with us and that he wished to transfer the funds in that account?"

"Let me explain," said Galish. "Mr. Levi is a resident of the Netherlands. In 1938, his bank in Amsterdam, Hobbema and Seventer, opened an account in his name with your bank. Obviously Mr. Levi could not communicate with you during the war. The documents confirming the opening of the account disappeared when Mr. Levi went into hiding, and he has only recently been able to recover them. He now wishes to use the funds in connection with his business."

"I see. It has been a long time since Mr. Levi's account was active. Let us start at the beginning: could you give me the full name and address of the account, the number of the account, the amount and date of opening, and any signing and mailing instructions?" His pen was poised over a pad of paper.

Galish turned to Banichek, said something in German, and pulled some papers out of his briefcase. "Let me see. My client's full name is David Victor Levi. Here is a copy of the letter requesting the opening of his account which was sent to you by the bank in Amsterdam. As you can see, they remitted to you an initial deposit of $411,000 by cashier's check drawn on their account at the Irving Trust Company in New York. On the original of the letter received by you, you will find Mr. Levi's signature, just like the one on this copy."

Bottomley read the letter attentively. "May I take this for a moment, so that we can look for the original in our files? It goes without saying, as I'm sure that you will understand, that I will also require some piece of identification, preferably a passport."

"Of course," answered Galish, sliding a passport across the table. Bottomley picked it up. It had a plain blue cloth cover. The passport number was punched through it and through every page inside. On the first page, it read 'Kingdom of the Netherlands'. On the second page, Bottomley saw a grainy photo of Levi, his name spelled in full, his date of birth, his place of birth, the date of the passport's issuance, the place of issuance, and the period of validity. All the entries were made by hand in script. Bottomley passed it back to Galish.

"Please hold on to this while I search our files. Can I get you a cup of coffee while you wait?" Galish translated for Banichek and accepted for both of them. Bottomley closed the door behind him. Galish and Banichek did not look at each other. They remained completely motionless as the minutes ticked by. Finally Galish looked at his watch. It had been a mere ten minutes since Bottomley had left the room.

Someone knocked on the door and opened it without waiting. A neat young woman in a black dress smiled at them and put a tray down on the table. "Here is your coffee, gentlemen. Can I bring you anything else?"

"No, thank you," answered Galish. She retreated quietly. The wait continued. Banichek pulled a handkerchief out of his pocket and wiped his brow. Then he leaned over, and poured some milk into one of the cups with a shaking hand. He added two teaspoons of sugar and stirred the cup vigorously. Galish watched him, his face expressionless. He also picked up a cup of coffee. Banichek sipped noisily and then put the cup back down with a clatter. Galish looked at his watch again.

Suddenly, the door opened and Bottomley came in, clutching his file and some additional papers. "Thank you for being so patient," he said unnecessarily. "I had some difficulty finding the information. Mr. Levi, your account has been transferred to the Dormant Accounts Section, and it was therefore a bit more difficult to get to it." Grolz translated, and Levi merely grunted.

Bottomley continued. "This is a bit unusual. When accounts like yours are deemed to be dormant, we assume that the beneficial owner is no longer capable of exercising his property rights, for whatever reason. After eight years, we cease paying interest on the balance. After a very long period of time, we make a judgement on what we should do with the funds. Your account was about to be reviewed for further disposition."

"What do you mean, further disposition?" asked Galish sharply.

Bottomley squirmed. "It all depends on the situation. Suffice it to say that we have located your account, and it now shows, with accrued interest, a balance of $502,304. This is a sizable amount. May I ask what you intend to do with the proceeds?"

"That will be for Mr. Levi to decide," answered Galish. "Mr Levi is a refugee who suffered greatly during the German occupation of the Netherlands. He would like to be spared any further aggravation. We would appreciate your cooperation in following his instructions."

Apparently, Mr. Bottomley had never been spoken to this way. He reddened, looked down at the papers on the table and then looked up again. "May I ask where Mr. Levi would like us to transfer the funds?"

"Here are the details," answered Galish as he pulled out another sheet of paper. It read: 'Antilles Container Corporation, 5611 West Dubuque, Chicago, Illinois. Account 2114-338 at the West Lincoln State Bank, Chicago, Illinois'.

"Very good," said Bottomley, "I will have the transfer request prepared for Mr. Levi to sign. Mr. Levi, may I trouble you for your passport again? I will need to show it to my boss, who has to approve a transfer of this size." He left the room again. Fifteen minutes later, he returned.

"We have added the interest due since we stopped accruing it in 1946. It adds another $117,000, at 3% compounded quarterly. That's quite a lot of money, don't you agree?"

Galish translated for Banichek, who managed a small smile. Since his commission from Galish on the transaction was ten percent, he had just made a further $11,700. Bottomley passed the transfer instructions over; the top sheet was backed by two carbon copies. Galish read the instructions carefully, explained them to Banichek, and offered him a fountain pen. Banichek positioned the document carefully, and signed 'David V. Levi' very slowly, then slid it back across the table to Bottomley.

"May I see your passport again, Mr. Levi?" he asked. Galish passed it over. Bottomley opened the passport on the page with Levi's signature, compared it to the transfer instructions, nodded in approval, then checked the account opening file and looked at the signature on the bottom of the original letter from Hobbema & Seventer. He frowned slightly.

"Mr. Grolz, this signature does not quite conform, although I see the similarities."

"Of course it doesn't. Mr. Levi signed that letter in 1938. He was 16 years younger. How do you think your signature would look after so many years, including five years of deprivation and fear spent in hiding in occupied Holland?"

Bottomley swallowed and admitted, "Of course, I see your point. My apologies. Well, I think that takes care of everything. We are sorry that you won't be a customer of ours in the future, Mr. Levi, but we understand the circumstances."

He handed a copy of the transfer instructions to Galish, who placed it carefully, along with the rest of the documents, inside his briefcase. They rose, put their coats on, and followed Bottomley back down the corridor to the elevator.

As the door opened, they shook hands, thanked him for his help, and stepped into the elevator. They were the only passengers. As the door closed, Banichek hit Galish playfully in the stomach, scarcely containing his elation. For the first time in weeks, Galish permitted himself a smile. They had pulled it off perfectly.

———<>———

Galish had ascertained that the Back Bay National Bank building stood within two blocks of their first visit. Since they were still early for their appointment, they stepped into a coffee shop. They sat down at a booth, away from the few other patrons. The waitress brought their order which included a glazed donut for Banichek. Galish looked at it disapprovingly.

"Pretty good, weren't we?" commented Banichek through his first mouthful.

"It was well-planned and well-executed," replied Galish. He was beginning to regret that he had offered Banichek a 10% commission. He should have remembered about the accrued interest. Banichek had just made a cool $61,900 this morning, and he was about to make a lot more. All that money was bound to go to his head, and he wouldn't be able to handle it. Galish made a mental note to re-negotiate Banichek's compensation, particularly if they were going to be as successful with the other accounts as they had been on the first one.

Galish paid the check, and they made their way to their next appointment. The bank entrance was only a little less imposing than the previous one. This one favored granite and heavy wrought iron. The banking hall was busier, with a long line of teller stations on either side of the polished marble floor. A sign in gold lettering invited visitors to the information desk at the rear of the hall.

Galish gave the receptionist their names and said that they had an appointment with Mr. James Clark in the International Department. A phone call elicited the fact that Mr. Clark would be right down. They stood waiting, and in a few moments Mr. Clark approached them. He was short and bald and impeccably dressed in a navy blue suit, a white shirt, and a blue tie.

"Good morning, gentlemen. Which one of you is Mr. Grolz?" Galish introduced himself and turned towards Banichek, and said, "I would like you to meet Mr. Jacob Roth. He speaks only a few words of English, and I am here to assist him."

"Very good," said Clark. "Please come this way." They followed him to a door at the rear of the banking hall, which opened into a conference room. He invited them to take off their overcoats and to make themselves comfortable.

"Mr. Grolz, in preparation for our meeting, I have pulled together whatever documents we have regarding an account which you say Mr. Roth opened before the war. I was surprised to note that it has been inactive since it was opened in January of 1939. Could you tell me a little about the circumstances, and why, after all this time, Mr. Roth has decided to activate it?"

This fellow was not going to be a pushover like Bottomley, Galish decided. "Certainly, Mr. Clark. Let me explain to Mr. Roth what you have requested so that he won't be left wondering."

"Of course, please do." Galish proceeded to tell 'Roth' in German that he was going to go over the facts with Mr. Clark. 'Roth' nodded his head.

"Mr. Clark, as you will have noted from the correspondence which led to the opening of the account, Mr. Roth emigrated with his family from Germany to Holland in 1937, fearing persecution from the Nazis. He transferred his successful jewelry business from Frankfurt to Amsterdam. His bankers in Amsterdam, Hobbema and Seventer, recommended that he keep a significant portion of his liquid assets in U.S. dollars, and he arranged for an account to be opened with your bank.

"In early 1940, fearing an invasion of Holland, he moved his family to Paris. Fortunately, they were able to escape before the Germans reached the French capital. They went into hiding in a small French town near the Pyrenées. At the end of the war in 1945, Mr. Roth returned to Holland and re-opened his business there.

"During the war, Mr. Roth lost the documents relating to his account here with you. Hobbema and Seventer closed its doors in 1940, and the partners destroyed all of the evidence relating to their accounts. It was most unlikely that he would have remembered the details of his account, but he had the good fortune, a few months ago, of finding this letter and receipt when he recovered some of his company records from before the war."

"I must say it is an extraordinary story!" exclaimed Clark. He looked at Mr. Roth more closely. What he saw was a tired old man with bags under eyes that had seen too many horrible events. He said gently, "May I see the documents which Mr. Roth recovered?"

Galish pulled papers out of his briefcase. "Here is Mr. Roth's copy of the account opening letter which you received and the receipt from Hobbema and Seventer. As you will have noted, all statements were to be sent to the bank in Amsterdam, so unfortunately we do not have any with us. Ironically, this was a procedure recommended by the bank in Amsterdam to restrict access to the information."

Clark read the documents very carefully. He looked up. "What is Mr. Roth's current address and citizenship?"

"He lives at this address near Amsterdam, and he is a naturalized Dutch citizen." Galish handed Clark a visiting card bearing Roth's name.

"May I see his passport?"

Galish handed it over. Clark turned the pages carefully. He peered carefully at the U.S. immigration stamp and the visa on the facing page. "So Mr. Roth has been in this country for three weeks?"

Damn, thought Galish. "That's right. He was recommended to me by one of his clients in Chicago. I arranged for Mr. Roth to see some prospective clients in the Midwest, so we have been traveling a bit. This was our first opportunity to come to Boston."

Clark continued to scrutinize all the documents. After a while, Galish interjected, "Is anything wrong?"

"Mr. Grolz, you must understand that the bank has certain procedures which must be observed. Perhaps you can explain to me why the signature in the passport looks a bit different from the signature on the original letter from Hobbema and Seventer?"

"It's the same signature," Galish replied. "Don't forget that there is a time lapse between the two signatures." He turned to

Banichek to explain the problem. They had rehearsed this many times. Banichek muttered, glowered at Clark, and undid the button on his shirt cuff, pulling the sleeve up to reveal what appeared to be a deep red gash on the inside of his forearm. He said something to Galish, who explained to Clark, "Mr. Roth is upset. As you can see, he suffered a serious wound to the arm during their escape from Paris. It healed poorly, and it has affected the mobility in his wrist. He has trouble writing."

Clark was visibly embarrassed. "I am terribly sorry. I didn't mean to upset Mr. Roth. He's been through so much. Please explain that to him."

Galish spoke rapidly to Banichek. Banichek inclined his head to Clark and said, "Thank you." Clark smiled, relieved that he had corrected his blunder.

"And now, gentlemen, I need to know what you would like to do with the account. Since it's been inactive for so long, we stopped accruing interest on it years ago. In fact, it's a good thing you came when you did, because after a long period of time, we have to decide what to do with funds that are unclaimed."

"Mr. Roth would like the balance transferred to an account he has set up in Illinois to accommodate his diamond-trading business. It is account 2113-410 at the Warsaw National Bank, Skokie, Illinois in the name of Elegance Jewelry Company, 3110 North Orleans Street, Chicago, Illinois."

"Gentlemen, you will have to bear with me. According to the original letter from Hobbema and Seventer, the account had an opening balance of $344,100. The balance today will be considerably larger due to compounding of interest. I'm sure you won't object!" Clark was now very relaxed, having feared the worst at the beginning of the meeting.

Galish had a hard time not showing his elation. "We have to catch a plane back to Chicago," he said. "We don't want to rush you, Mr. Clark, but we would appreciate it if we could complete the formalities as quickly as possible. We will wait here, if you don't mind."

"Not at all. It is nearing lunch. Would you like a sandwich, or something? I'm sure you will find it more comfortable to eat here while you wait."

The door of the conference room closed behind Clark. Banichek broke out into a huge smile. Galish stared him down, his index finger over his mouth. Banichek did not take the rebuke seriously. He was not very smart, but, the way he figured it, it sounded like he had made at least $35,000 in the last hour, not to mention what he had made at the other bank. That was more than he had made in the last five years, and it was not taxable.

A black-clad waitress came into the room and offered them a choice of a ham and cheese or an egg salad sandwich and coffee or tea. Galish asked for ham and cheese on rye. She wrote the order out carefully, and turned to Banichek.

"I'll take the ham and cheese also, on white, with tomato and lettuce. Hold the mustard."

"And to drink?"

"Two iced teas," Galish ordered.

Galish glared at Banichek. He waited for the woman to leave. "You imbecile! You could have ruined the whole deal by speaking English."

Banichek looked stunned. He suddenly realized that he would have given away their game if Clark had been in the room.

They were just finishing their sandwiches when Clark came back into the room.

"Your bank in Chicago confirmed the name, number, and authorized signers on the account. They were surprised by the amount of money involved in this transfer, which greatly exceeds the current balance in the account."

Galish remained ice-cold. "I would have been glad to furnish you with the details of that account, if you had asked me."

"Please don't take offense, Mr. Grolz. You will agree that we have to take certain precautions on behalf of our clients. Well, if we may continue, I have been able to bring the value of the account up to date, and I have therefore prepared a transfer form for Mr. Roth to sign authorizing the transfer of the balance to the account he has indicated. Here, please check the details," he said to Galish, "And ask Mr. Roth to sign the form."

Galish moved closer to Banichek, so that they could read the transfer instructions together. After a few moments, Galish looked up and said, "Will you provide us with the calculation showing how the original balance of $344,100 became $538,750? Mr. Roth will need it for the Dutch tax authorities."

"Of course," said Clark. "It will take me just a minute. Not all of our customers are concerned about reporting their tax liabilities! I will also have to get a colleague to review the transaction and initial this transfer form. It will only take a few moments."

Galish and Banichek made their flight at Logan in plenty of time. They had barely exchanged a word between them since the sandwich episode, when Banichek almost gave everything away. In the space of about two hours, Galish had grossed $1,158,054. After Banichek's commission, he had netted $1,042,249.

Galish smiled to himself. If he could milk similar amounts from the New York, Philadelphia, and London accounts, he could accumulate over $5,000,000. He would definitely have to reduce Banichek's commission, and he would have to keep the idiot from making another mistake during their interviews at the other banks. Galish leaned his head back against the seat-rest, closed his eyes, and thought about hot, sunny beaches and a woman like Ilse lying next to him on the sand.

---------<>---------

NEW YORK

Agent Brian Samson had recently been re-assigned to the New York office of the FBI. He had made a name for himself in the Boston office as a tough, relentless investigator. He was developing a reputation for his handling of embezzlement, fraud and other types of financially-related crimes. Samson was a very large man. His dark brown hair was carefully combed. His neck was wide. His shoulders were gigantic. He wore dark blue suits with trousers that were a little too short and a little too wide. His shirts were always white. His shoes were always perfectly shined.

Samson didn't need his alarm clock on this gloomy December morning. He wanted to review the file on 'National City Bank, Traveler's Checks, Theft of'. New information had just come in on the case, and he knew that getting out of bed at 5.30 a.m. would give him a head start.

He arrived at the office at 7.12 a.m. The FBI was not the kind of organization to commend anyone for arriving early. It was what you had to do when the job required it. Samson had looked briefly at the file on the previous day. It appeared that the Swiss and French police had done a pretty good job of developing information. Two of the principal suspects were sitting in jail in Geneva. A woman was still languishing in a French jail 'on suspicion'.

Other pieces of the puzzle still eluded them. Who knew about that particular shipment, on that particular day? Who had tipped off someone in Buenos Aires? How had their heist come together so smoothly? The whole scheme had been well-planned, probably rehearsed. Someone in the U.S. was involved, but who? It had to be someone who knew banking, someone on the inside. In addition to Samson, the New York office had five agents working part-time on the case, and the National City Bank had assigned its best inspector, supported by a host of supervisors in various operating areas of the bank.

Samson sat down in the straight-backed chair in his 'office', a work area with a six-foot partition on three sides. He looked at the incoming telexes. The FBI had 24-hour telephone and telex service. He time-stamped each one as he read it. One of them, from Junot in Lyon, was of immediate interest.

"Samson, FBI New York: Our birds are singing. Wormser insists he was contacted by German-speaking person in Buenos Aires who was transmitting information from third person in U.S. (stop)

Information developed by Swiss police as follows. The German company allegedly employing Lejoin does not exist. The Cartoscope address in Stuttgart is vacant office, but P.O. Box is active (stop) We have asked German Federal Police for surveillance (stop) French police have discovered that Lejoin's real name is Henri Lemaire. During WWII he was member of French *Milice*, a fascist para-military group set up by Vichy France to assist Germans (stop) French authorities are expected to seek Lejoin's extradition from Switzerland."

Samson pruned the telex with his scissors and placed it carefully inside a manila folder. After that, there wasn't much he could do until the meeting at National City Bank later that morning.

The conference room on the sixth floor of 55 Wall Street had been taken over by the FBI. For the last few days, they had been interviewing officers and staff of National City Bank. Albert O'Rourke, a vice president in the bank's Special Claims Department, had been assigned full-time to the FBI team. He was a well-built man, 6 foot 3 and 260 pounds. He had an open, friendly face and was rarely at a loss for a joke. He was an 'operating' man, in the parlance of the bank, which meant that he had come up through the unglamorous back office. He knew his domain, and everyone in the bank trusted him.

O'Rourke had selected the people to be interviewed. During coffee breaks, he would regale the FBI agents with amusing anecdotes from every department at the bank. When the witnesses were in the room, however, he would stay quiet, interjecting a question when he thought that one of the agents had overlooked something. This morning, they were questioning the last person on the list.

Jane Dougherty was a 23-year veteran of the bank and had worked in the Traveler's Check department for the last five years. O'Rourke felt confident that she, as much as anyone else, would be able to shed some light on how the traveler's checks theft could have occurred. She had just returned from vacation in San Diego; her testimony had been eagerly awaited by the investigating team.

Brian Samson, the senior FBI agent, stood up when Jane walked in, shook her hand, and introduced his colleagues. Jane appeared flustered despite her suntan. This interrogation was taking place at the wrong time of her work day; many of her calls were with overseas correspondent banks, many in Europe, and by noon New York time, they were going home for the day.

"Jane, we hope that you may be able to shed some light on this affair," said Samson. "We have established, almost without question, that there is no way that the gang in Buenos Aires could have gotten the information on the consignment of the traveler's checks unless someone here in New York had given them the details. We have not ruled out, for the time being, the involvement of any bank staff. We are still questioning others involved in the shipment.

"However, we keep coming around to the following question: was there someone here, perhaps a regular visitor, who could have seen that particular shipment being prepared? Who is likely to have been here at that time? A couple of your colleagues, Nick and Howard, for instance, feel sure that you had a visitor or two in the room on that Thursday. It was a few days before the American Bankers Association annual meeting, and there were a lot of bankers in town. Do you recollect any one visiting you?"

"We always make an effort to show our good correspondent banks around," replied Jane. "It's good for business."

"Yes, we understand that some banks are major sellers of your traveler's checks."

"Well," Jane continued, "we treat those banks very well when they are in town. We show their people around; we take them to dinner or a Broadway show or something. Most of the time we get pretty senior people; it's not unusual for a bank president to visit us. I've been trying to remember who may have been here at that time. I took some operations guys from a bank in Columbus to dinner the night before. We went out, and it got rather late. I remember being mad at myself because I had a lot of work to do the next day. We get rather large orders for traveler's checks at the beginning of the summer tourist season, and we were backed up on preparing deliveries. The next morning, I discovered that we were also going to have to show a couple of 'visiting firemen' around."

Samson asked, "And you didn't make a note in your agenda book or anything?"

"I usually write down the bank's name, but that morning, I was just too busy. Now, I've been scratching my head as to whom it may have been. To the best of my recollection, we had two visitors. I know both of them well; one was John Kelly, President of the Milwaukee Bank and Trust Company. The other one is a vice president of a bank near Chicago, the Plains National Bank in Plains, Illinois. I looked through our records. Both banks have been selling our traveler's checks for a long time. We showed them around a bit; people are pretty impressed when they see all those checks lying around."

"So you told them what you were doing with the checks?"

"Sometimes we show them how we prepare a delivery. Among bankers, it's not unusual to show off a bit and tell them the sizes of shipments being sent to banks around the world. It makes them feel good about their decision not to sell American Express checks. Know what I mean?"

"Okay," said Samson. "Let's get their exact names and addresses. We'll run a check on them."

"You don't really think either of those men could possibly be involved, do you?" asked O'Rourke. "I mean, what does a banker from Milwaukee, Wisconsin or Plains, Illinois have to do with Buenos Aires?"

"Beats me," replied Samson, "We have no choice but to follow every lead." Just then the phone rang. O'Rourke moved to pick it up. "Call for you, Brian." He handed the instrument over to Samson.

"Samson speaking."

"Hi, this is Pondexter. We just got some stuff in from Geneva that might interest you. It's on the teletype."

"Just read it to me, if it's not too long."

"Okay. It's from Frossard. Here goes."

Samson whispered to the others. "Bear with me. I'm getting an updated message from Geneva."

Pondexter's voice sounded very important. He read the telex to Samson:

> "Have finished interrogation of Wormser (stop)
> Argentine national of German origin (stop) Served in
> German Army during WWII (stop) Arrived in Argentina
> in 1948 (stop) Says he received shipment details from
> an unidentified American banker who wanted $300,000
> of the haul (stop) American has not yet been paid."

"Terrific," said Samson. "This is beginning to make sense. Keep me posted. Maybe you had better get back to them and say that I will be putting in a call to them tomorrow. Many thanks, Chuck." Samson turned to Jane. "Now tell me again about those guys who were here on May 5."

———<>———

CHICAGO

The FBI office was located on the corner of Clark and Jackson. Joe Welch was the local agent in charge of the 'Traveler's Checks Caper', in FBI parlance. He was delighted to be involved in such an exotic affair. He had been bogged down in a kidnapping case across the state line in Indiana. The dreary urban scene, at the beginning of what was going to be another of Chicago's long, cold winters, had depressed him. That case was almost solved. Now, Washington had requested that someone with local experience be assigned to do preliminary background investigations on two Chicago area bankers. Welch had been chosen. He went home and had two beers to celebrate the new assignment. Even though the investigation was a local affair, it had some distant, mysterious connection with a world thousands of miles away. This was much better.

He had organized two folders, one for each of the bankers he was going to investigate:

> 'John D. Kelly. President, First Milwaukee Bank and
> Trust Company. Joined the bank in 1946 after service
> in the U.S. Marine Corps (Lieutenant). Graduate of
> Mundelein College, Chicago, 1942. Born, Peoria,
> Illinois on February 1, 1920. Father Horace J. Kelly,
> employed by the Chicago and Northwestern Railroad.
> Mother, Anna B. Kelly, born Smith. Married, three
> children. Lives at 1330 Superior, Milwaukee,
> Wisconsin. Secretary, Wisconsin Bankers Association.
> Trustee, St. Christopher's Parochial School.'

The other folder contained similar particulars, although much shorter:

> 'Joseph Galish. Vice President, Plains National Bank,
> Plains, Illinois. Born in Gyor, Hungary, June 12, 1908.
> Entered the U.S. in 1948. Joined the bank in 1950.
> Naturalized U.S. citizen, 1953. Unmarried. Lives at
> 2234 North Liberty Street, Lincoln Park, Chicago,
> Illinois.'

Joe Welch looked at these two names carefully, and sighed, a little disappointed. He checked their fingerprint records. Both of their prints were on file, a requirement for all employees of nationally chartered banks. There were no comments. He checked the credit reports he had asked for. Kelly had a mortgage on his house and a home improvement loan at another bank in Milwaukee. His bank references were conventional. His charge accounts were current. He owned a Hudson.

Galish appeared to have no debts. This was probably not unusual for a bachelor. He owned a Studebaker. His apartment was rented. He appeared to have no retail charge accounts. His utility bills were paid promptly. This was not the stuff of exotic international intrigue. But, who knows, he said to himself, this could lead to something more exciting.

He called the bank in Milwaukee first, and arranged to see Mr. Kelly that afternoon. Then he called Galish's office. His secretary said he was out of the office on a business trip. He would not be back until next week. Could he make an appointment for the earliest time Mr. Galish could see him? What was this in reference to? A new account. Good, Thursday morning at 9.30 a.m. would be fine. In the meantime, Welch decided to check out Galish's residence, just to verify that his information was correct. Welsh could get there in thirty minutes, if the traffic on Dearborn cooperated, and then continue on to his appointment in Milwaukee.

The weather was definitely not cooperating. It rarely did in Chicago at this time of year. Joe Welch was a bachelor. He had almost married a nice girl from New York, but she hadn't wanted to move to Chicago. Welch had a dream about southern places and southern women. Maybe this case would provide the opportunity. Then again, it might not.

His car was parked in the garage underneath the Federal Building. Very few people had access to this garage. He gunned the car up the ramp, and turned left on Clark, left again on Jackson, left again on Dearborn, and headed out to Lincoln Park. It took longer than he had expected.

Galish's apartment stood on a wide, tree-lined street. Most of the buildings in the neighborhood had a solid, sober appearance, typical of the 1920's. Welch parked his car and made sure the FBI special ID was on the dashboard. He walked up to the front door. Inside the entrance, he checked the names of the tenants. Mr. Galish resided on the fifth floor. He wondered what Mr. Galish did on weekends. Did he have any family in the Chicago area? Mentally, Welch began to make a list of questions he needed to ask Galish the following week. The more Welch thought about it, the more curious he became about Mr. Joseph Galish.

On an impulse, he decided to check out the garage across the street. Galish must park his car somewhere in the neighborhood. He probably drove to work, since there was almost no other way of getting to Plains from Lincoln Park. He would want to have the car very accessible.

Welch crossed the street and walked into the garage's office where the attendant sat in a chair listening to the radio. "Hi, I'm looking for some information."

The attendant swiveled slowly in his rickety chair, looked at Welch under hooded eyes, and said, "Who's askin'?"

Welch pulled out his FBI badge, and stepped closer to the man. "The FBI is asking. I have a few questions. It will only take a few minutes."

The attendant's eyes popped open, but he tried to act casual. "Oh."

"Do you have a parking customer by the name of Joseph Galish?"

"Yep."

"What kind of a car does he drive?"

"Studebaker."

"Is the car here right now?"

"Nope."

"Do you know where Mr. Galish is?"

"Nope."

"When did he drive it away?"

"Excuse me, Mister, gotta take care of this car pullin' in." The attendant walked over to the driver's side of the incoming car. He gave the man his receipt, then sauntered back to where Welch stood waiting.

"I asked you, when did he leave?"

"About 6.30 this morning."

"Does Mr. Galish drive to work every morning?"

"When he's around. Leaves at 6.30 a.m. prompt. We git hell if the car's not on the ramp."

"Does he travel a lot?"

"Well, he told me last month that someone broke his rear view mirror while his car was parked at the airport. He must get around."

"You've been very helpful. If you can think of anything else, you'll give me a call, right? Here's my card." The attendant took the card as if he were receiving communion. He slipped it into his shirt pocket, awed by his sudden acquaintance with the nation's premier law enforcement agency.

Welch returned to his office late that afternoon. The trip to Milwaukee was uneventful. Mr. Kelly, chief executive of the Milwaukee Bank and Trust Company, had turned out to be a short, boisterous Irishman who laughed at every joke he told, and he told many. He was delighted to meet an FBI agent and appreciated how much the agency had helped banks all over the country over the years.

Yes, he remembered visiting the National City Bank offices earlier that year. He remembered stopping by to see Jane Dougherty briefly. Kelly had given Welch a tour of his bank, introduced him to the senior lending officer, the head of operations, and the bank's cashier. Welch had been trained not to jump to conclusions, but it was hard for him to see how John Kelly could have been a part of an international traveler's check caper.

Joseph Galish was another story. Welch sat at his desk, alone in the FBI office except for the duty officers. He picked up the Galish file. He decided to file an inquiry with the Immigration and Naturalization Service for a copy of Galish's immigration records. He made a note to examine Galish's personal bank records. He was looking forward to meeting Galish next week.

A few hours later, the report was on his desk. It was the standard INS profile:

> 'Galish, Joseph. Entered U.S. through Ellis Island, New York, February 12, 1948. Sponsor: Captain Patrick DeFoe, 2nd Infantry Division, U.S. Army. Born Gyor, Hungary, 12 June 1908. Height: 5.10. Weight: 155 lbs. Hair: blond. Eyes: Blue. Displaced Person ID # 65993738, issued by Allied Control Commission, Germany, September 18, 1945. Naturalized U.S. citizen, 1953.'

———<>

The following Wednesday evening, a taxi drew up in front of Galish's apartment building. Ilse Wormser paid the driver, got out, pulling her small overnight bag behind her, hurried up the steps, and pressed the buzzer for Galish's apartment. No answer. Surely he would be home from work by now. She pressed again. A man's voice came over the speaker.

"Yes?"

"Joseph, it's me, Ilse."

Silence.

"Who?"

"Ilse, from Buenos Aires."

Silence, then, "Fifth floor, 5-B." The door clicked open.

She picked up her suitcase, walked through the foyer, and opened the door to the elevator. On the fifth floor landing, Galish was waiting for her. His face was a mask.

"This way," he ordered, making no effort to greet her. She followed him into his apartment. He closed the door behind her.

She put her suitcase down, walked up to him, and kissed him on the cheek. "Don't be upset with me, Joseph. We are in terrible trouble. I had to come."

"Ilse, you cannot stay here. I've just returned from a trip. I have very little time. Why don't you tell me briefly about your problem." He motioned to her to sit down. She removed her hat and coat. She was wearing a well-cut beige wool dress which emphasized her figure. She sat down in an armchair, leaned back, crossed her long legs, and passed a hand across her eyes.

"I'm so tired, Joseph. It's been such a long trip from Buenos Aires."

"You should have let me know that you were coming."

"Perhaps I should have, but it was all so confusing; everything happened so fast."

"What are you talking about?" asked Galish, his eyes narrowing.

"Somehow the Swiss police discovered the traveler's checks. They traced them back to us in Buenos Aires."

"Where is your husband?"

"They arrested him in Switzerland. He's in jail there." Galish said nothing. She looked at him intently. "Can I please have something to drink?"

"Will water do?" he asked bitingly.

"Anything, Joseph, anything at all." He went to the kitchen and returned with a large glass of water.

"Ilse, you have made a mistake in coming here. I am a very busy man. I'm getting ready to go on another trip overseas. Please be brief." She sipped her water, eyeing him from over the rim of the glass. She could feel him looking at her legs.

"Joseph, you must help us. I must get Gerhard out of jail."

Galish's face remained stone hard. He had come such a long way since his disappearance from Holland in 1945. His plans were now beginning to pay off with huge dividends. A horrible foreboding came over him. This goddamn bitch was going to ruin it all. He should never have helped them.

"You have a problem. There is nothing I can do."

"Please, Joseph, we still need money for the Party. We miscalculated. We had bad luck. Now, poor Gerhard and another colleague, Lejoin, are in a Swiss jail, and Ursula is being detained by the French police. We need you to come up with a solution."

"Get someone else to help you."

"Joseph, or should I say Heinrich, you are very highly thought of in Buenos Aires. The Party remembers your good work as head of the Gestapo in northern Holland. I told them that you would know what to do."

Galish knew at that very moment that Ilse represented the greatest threat to his survival since he had escaped from Amsterdam in 1945. He had to get rid of her. She had to be silenced. At once.

"Let me think about this. I understand what is at stake." He rose. "Why don't you take your bag into my bedroom?" Ilse got up from the armchair. As she did, she smoothed down the sides of her skirt. She followed him into the small bedroom. He opened a door. "This is one of the nice features of an American home, a large bathroom." He left her.

The idea of a woman who knew about his past, taking a bath in this apartment, was unsettling to him. Half an hour later, she came out of the bedroom. She had on his bathrobe. He knew immediately that she had nothing on underneath.

"You have not had any dinner?" he asked.

She walked up to him, put her arms around his neck, and drew him towards her. "You have no idea what it means for me to be here alone with you."

They made love violently. The strength of her body amazed him. Her nails bit into his back and scratched remorselessly down his spine until she drew blood from his buttocks and his thighs. Her blond hair came loose from its clips and covered his face. He was beginning to gasp for breath. Ilse grasped his lower back in a lock, her shoulders heaving. He moaned, hoping she would not notice that he had not the slightest inclination to come to orgasm. He needed to preserve his strength.

Her long legs held him in a scissor grip. He rolled her over, grabbed her left leg, and pulled it up high in the air. She released her arms from around his chest, and spread them outwards across the bed. Quickly, his hands closed around her throat, and his thumb found her epiglottis. He pushed hard and broke her windpipe. Her hands were beating on his head now, pulling at his hair, tearing at his ears. The pressure on her throat increased. Her face began to redden. He looked down at her bulging eyeballs as he raised himself higher over her thrashing body. Beads of perspiration formed under his chin and started to trickle in between the sparse blond hair on his chest. His hands relentlessly crushed her throat until her convulsions lessened, then ceased altogether.

Slowly, he released his grip. He stared into her lifeless eyes. Pushing himself off the bed, he stood up, suddenly repelled by the stench of sweat and death. He ran to the bathroom, turned on the shower and washed himself briskly. Much as he would have liked to, he could not linger under the soothing spray of water.

Still toweling himself, he walked into the kitchen and poured himself a glass of wine. He stood there, organizing his thoughts, knowing that every detail must be perfectly worked out. He looked at the clock. It was almost 9.30 p.m. He tried to visualize the routine that had worked well for the Gestapo. He had to remove any evidence that his apartment had been the scene of a crime. He realized that he could not remove the body by himself. There was no way he could just walk out with Ilse's body flung over his shoulder. He had to dismember her and place the pieces in sealed containers. Tomorrow morning, he would have to drive over to the Sears store on Fullerton to buy some coolers.

He had the whole night to dispose of her body. Methodically, he began to assemble the items he was going to need. He opened one of the drawers in the kitchen, and selected a long, thin knife. He found the whetstone, moistened it lightly, and carefully honed the knife to a razor-thin edge. From his tool box, he extracted a small saw. His mind was always a step ahead of the task.

Still naked, he picked Ilse up from the bed and noticed that her sphincter had opened involuntarily in the last convulsions of her life. Damn, he would have to change the mattress. He dropped her into the white porcelain bathtub. One of her arms flopped against the wall. He moved it. It felt satisfyingly dead. He gripped the knife, turned on the cold water, and started an incision just under the line of her jaw, working towards what he believed was the location of the carotid artery. When he cut through it, he recoiled at the sudden spurt of blood. The gushing subsided quickly. He continued cutting until he reached the sinews surrounding the spinal column.

He paused a moment, and leaned his bare chest against the side of the tub. Her eyes were still open. He raised himself up and started the cut on the other side of her jaw. He reached the spinal cord. He flushed the knife under the running water and picked up the saw. Her blood continued to ooze from the opening around her neck. He sawed into the gristle, then into the spine, holding her head with the other hand as it began to move loosely with every cut of the saw. Suddenly, the head separated. He picked it up by the hair, amazed that it weighed so much. He placed it upright, balanced between her legs, to let all the remaining blood drain out.

During the next hour, he clumsily amputated her arms and legs. It was extremely hard work. In removing the thighs, he had cut deeply into the lower organs. The stench was overpowering. He surveyed his work and decided that he had done as much as he could. The torso still looked very bulky, but, hopefully, Sears had a cooler large enough to accommodate it. He made sure that the tub drain was open and checked to make sure that all of the blood had drained from each piece of the body. He got up, stretched and decided it was time for another glass of wine.

The Sears store opened at 9.30 a.m. Galish called the office to report that he had a terrible cold and would not be coming in to work. Mrs. McCarthy reminded him that he had an appointment with a gentleman named Welch for a new account opening. Galish asked her to call Welch to advise him that Galish was sick. She apologized for not having taken Welch's telephone number when the appointment was made; there was no way to reach him. "Never mind," said Galish, "you can re-schedule the appointment when he arrives."

He drove to the Sears store. He was the first customer through the door. He was out again twenty minutes later. It was snowing hard, and he felt the car skidding underneath him as he backed it up to the dock. He handed the warehouseman his receipt and loaded the coolers into his car. Two of the coolers fit through the rear doors onto the back seat, and the third just barely made it into the trunk. They had to tie the trunk closed. Galish drove home very carefully, staying in the freshly-laid tracks laid down in the snow by drivers ahead of him.

He made two trips to get his purchases up to his apartment. Fortunately, his neighbors had already left for work. He took the first cooler into the bathroom. It was time to start packing the body parts. The arms and legs fitted into two of the coolers; he sealed each cooler with duct tape to keep the smell from permeating the apartment.

He used the third cooler to pack the torso. With a little pressure and pushing, he managed to get it to fit quite snugly. That cooler was similarly sealed.

Now he had to worry about Ilse's head. The chances of any police force in the U.S. identifying the head using dental records from Argentina, let alone from Germany, were non-existent. Yet his Gestapo training and sense of orderliness were such that he had to follow the procedures which he had learned. He shaved Ilse's head as an additional precaution and placed it in a plastic pail which he covered with an old towel and sealed with duct tape. Finally, he went through the apartment to make sure that he had not forgotten any of her belongings.

Laboriously, he carried the three coolers, the pail, and Ilse's suitcase downstairs, one by one, making sure that he was not observed. Carefully, he placed one cooler in the trunk and the two others side by side on the back seat. He placed the pail on the floor of the front seat of the car.

There was little traffic at that time of the morning. He drove cautiously through the northern suburbs, then accelerated to just under the speed limit, watching for patches of ice and snow. He crossed the Illinois-Wisconsin border and continued for a dozen miles further. There was no traffic; all around him, on both sides of the road, he could see nothing but dense woods. He looked for a suitable place to stop. In spite of the snow, he found a small road leading away from the highway. He turned into it, worried that the snow might prove too deep for the car. He stopped when he felt the wheels beginning to lose their grip. Then he opened each cooler and removed the contents, which he threw into the snowy undergrowth. To rid the coolers of any tell-tale blood, he used handfuls of snow to scrape the insides clean and replaced the coolers in the car. There would be no connection between them and the dismembered body now lying in its final resting place under the thick blanket of snow.

Galish backed out onto the highway, the wheels spinning occasionally. Fortunately the snow would soon hide his tire marks. Now he had to get rid of the head. He drove about two miles further, and then, satisfied that he wouldn't be seen by traffic, stopped, unsealed the pail, and flipped the head into the middle of the road. He got back behind the wheel, put the car in gear and aimed his front wheel at the head. He drove over it once, backed up, and drove over it again. Ilse's head, now an oddly shaped oval, lay in the brown slush at the side of the road. He cleaned out the pail with snow and threw the towel across to the other side of the road.

Galish made a u-turn and started the drive back towards Chicago. He had only one more thing to do. He turned onto a secondary road and followed it for about a mile, then pulled the car over to the side when he spotted an open area nearby. He removed Ilse's overnight bag from the trunk, made a fire with some old newspapers, and threw the last of Ilse into the flames: her hair, her passport, her clothes, and finally, the leather overnight bag. He watched to make sure they were totally burned.

As he drove back to Chicago, he wondered who Ilse really was. German, yes. From the northern part of the country, yes. A background in health services, yes. Intelligent, certainly. Sexually depraved, most definitely. And clearly so dangerous to him that he had no other choice. Wormser, languishing in a Swiss jail, would not miss her for some time. Eventually, the other Germans in Buenos Aires might start wondering about her whereabouts, but Galish felt sure that it would be some time before their suspicions were aroused. By then, he would be long gone. He drove on, content that he had eliminated this ghastly threat to his future in his usual efficient manner.

Joe Welch parked his car at the side of the bank building, away from the street where the ploughs were already creating mounds of snow. He struggled out of the car, pushing the door open into gusts of wind. Taking care not to slip on the snow-covered ice, he walked briskly around the corner to the Plains National Bank. The receptionist directed him to an office on the third floor.

Upstairs, he found the door labeled 'Joseph Galish, Vice President, International Banking'. It was ajar, so he knocked on it and entered at the same time. The office was empty. He walked out, down to the next office in which two secretaries sat, both of them typing.

"Good morning, ladies, I'm looking for Mr. Galish. My name is Welch, and I have an appointment with him."

"Good morning, sir, I'm Mr. Galish's secretary." She rose from her chair. "I'm very sorry, but he called in sick this morning. I cancelled all his appointments, but all I had was your name, and I didn't know where to reach you."

"That's okay, but I really need to talk to him. Can you give me his home phone number?"

"I don't think he's answering his phone, sir. We've already tried twice. Let me write it down for you. Perhaps you can get through later."

Welch was angry. He was wasting a whole morning, in a snow storm, chasing some weird guy around Chicago. He really needed to get some better assignments. He was about to leave when he suddenly stopped in his tracks.

"Tell me, does Mr. Galish travel in his job?"

"Oh, yes, sir. The international department has grown a lot under his supervision."

"Can you tell me where he travels to?"

"Well, he goes to New York a lot, and overseas, too."

It was time to push his weight around. "You are . . . ?"

"Mrs. McCarthy, sir."

"Mrs. McCarthy, could you follow me for a minute?"

She looked surprised. The other secretary looked up from her typewriter, frowning. Welch led her into Galish's office, closed the door, and pulled out his FBI badge. Mrs. McCarthy's eyes widened. "This is strictly between us, Mrs. McCarthy. My name is Joe Welch. I'm an agent in the Chicago office of the Federal Bureau of Investigation. I would like to ask you some questions. Please sit down." She sat down, very suddenly, in the chair in front of Galish's desk. He moved around and sat down in Galish's chair.

"We are conducting a routine inquiry. Mr. Galish's name has come up as a source of information. In his absence, I wonder if you could tell me a little bit more about his travels."

"Well, of course, er, sir."

"Can you tell me exactly, when and where, he has traveled in the last year?"

Mrs. McCarthy thought for a moment. "As I said, he goes to New York a lot. Probably every three months. I would have to check our records to tell you exactly. He goes to see our correspondent banks there."

Welch started making notes. "Which banks?"

"Well, the Irving Trust and National City Bank."

"What kind of business do you do with them?"

"I'm not an expert, Mr. Welch. National City Bank helps us with our Latin American credits and traveler's checks, of course."

Welch had the feeling that his morning might not turn out so badly after all.

"Can you tell me a little more about the traveler's checks you buy?"

"We are one of the biggest sellers of their traveler's checks in the northern Illinois area. They take good care of us."

Welch paused for a minute and then continued, "What about Mr. Galish's trips overseas?"

"He's only been on two, I believe. He went to South America, let's see, a little over a year ago. Then, in July, he went on a shorter trip to Mexico and Central America."

"Where did he go in South America?"

"I'm trying to remember. I typed up his call reports. It was Brazil, Argentina, and Venezuela; yes, that's right."

"Would you be able to tell me whom he saw in Argentina, for instance?"

"I can show you the call reports, if that's what you mean. But I'm getting a little nervous about giving you any more

information without an okay from someone here at the bank.
I hope you understand."

"I understand. Mrs. McCarthy, I don't need to bother you
any more today. How long have you been at the bank?"

"I've been here seventeen years, sir."

"Well then you know that, since Plains National Bank
has a federal charter, we, the FBI, have jurisdiction over all
investigations involving this bank. I am going to leave you
my card, and if you have any questions, please call me at our
office downtown. I must ask you to keep this discussion strictly
to yourself for the time being. Thank you for your assistance."

They got up. Welch smiled at her for the first time and
extended his hand. "You have been a great help," he said.

She smiled a little, relieved that she could go back to her
work.

As soon as Welch returned to his office, he picked up the
phone and called Samson in New York. He described his visit
to the bank. "Brian, this guy Galish looks increasingly like a
suspect to me. He's a loner; he's had opportunity, and we
really know nothing about him before he came to this country.
He's supposed to be sick, but he doesn't answer his phone.
After I left the bank, I went back to the garage where he
keeps his car. The car's gone. We need to check his
background more thoroughly. All I got from the INS was the
standard report."

"Great work, Joe. I'm looking at a copy of the INS file
here. Let's see, he came here courtesy of the U.S. Army. I'm
going to get Washington to run down this Captain Defoe and
see what he knows about Galish before he came to this
country."

"Brian, let's make sure they send us a photo if they have
one. I think I'll also ask the personnel director at Galish's
bank for a photo. That way we can see whether he has
changed much."

"Be careful you don't spook Galish in the process,"
Samson warned.

———<>———

While Galish was driving back to Chicago, he concentrated on how best to rid himself of the coolers. A large neon sign by the side of the road provided the answer; he decided to drive into a supermarket parking lot and dump the coolers there, but he had to make sure he wasn't observed. He parked between two other cars and waited for a while. He could hear a snow plough, but it was too far away to see what he was doing. Galish pulled the coolers out of the car and stacked them neatly lengthwise between his car and the next one. Quickly, he drove off, his rear view mirror confirming that no one could have seen him.

He looked at his watch and realized that he was not going to make it back to the bank before it closed. He found a service station and pulled up to the telephone booth. He dialed Mrs. McCarthy's number.

"Plains National Bank, Mrs. McCarthy speaking."

"Hi, Mrs McCarthy, it's Joe Galish. I'm at the pharmacy picking up some medicine. It's too late for me to make it into the office today, so I'll come in early in the morning. Is there anything special I need to know about?"

She hesitated slightly. "Well, not really. I'm glad you called, though. I don't know whether I should be telling you this, but it turned out that Mr. Welch, the man who wanted to open the new account, is actually from the FBI. He was asking all kinds of questions."

"What kinds of questions?" prompted Galish, his nerves suddenly alert.

"Well, he just wanted to know where you have been traveling and things like that. He told me not to mention it to anyone else in the office. I haven't said a word, but it seemed a little strange."

Galish thought for a brief second. "Don't worry about it. I'm sure that I can take care of his questions. Just put all my mail and files on my desk for tomorrow morning. I'll come in early. See you then." He hung up, but stayed in the booth. Galish picked up the phone again and dialed. After a few rings, he heard Banichek's voice.

"It's me," Galish said. "We're going to have to change our plans a bit. Do absolutely nothing until you hear from me again. When you do, be prepared to go on a trip which may take five or six days. I won't be able to give you much notice."

"Joe, you know I can't leave my wife for that long. Where am I supposed to find someone to look after her?"

"With all the money you will make on this one, and it will be the biggest of all, you can afford all the nurses in Chicago. You call whatever agency provides round-the-clock nurses and put them on stand-by. I'll call you in a few days to make sure you've been able to get this organized, okay?"

He wondered if the FBI man was watching his apartment. He had to get into it. He worried that now, after all his meticulous planning, he was about to walk into a trap. He decided to park his car three blocks away, made sure that he was legally parked, took his overcoat out of his suitcase, locked the car, and walked slowly down his block, scanning all the cars along the sidewalk. If someone were watching, he would be sitting in a car; it was too cold to be standing around.

Galish walked the block twice. Not a sign of life. It was dark and cold, and the wind was blowing in angry gusts. He decided to chance it. He walked back to his car, but instead of taking it to the garage, where they might also have staked him out, he found a spot on his block. He might need to get away quickly.

He opened the front door of his building, got into the elevator and went up to the fifth floor. Not a sound anywhere. He opened his apartment door and stepped inside. So far, so good. Now, he had to work fast. He systematically packed his travel bags, including all the files, documents, and false identity papers which he had meticulously prepared. He added an extra suitcase to accommodate the clothes and supplies which he would need for the next several weeks. A careful search of his apartment would yield nothing but the profile of a hard-working immigrant. Everything would be consistent with his official description.

He had developed a plan for just such a contingency: first, they would hit the two New York banks. He would then wait on the east coast, staying at hotels under assumed names, until he had the reservations for his and Banichek's flight to London. He assumed that he would need two or three days to hit the London banks. After that, he would send Banichek home by himself, and he would take a plane to the Bahamas. In Nassau, he planned to relax for a couple of weeks, organizing the last of the transfers from the various temporary accounts in Chicago to the master account in Panama in the name of Holger S.A. Finally, Georg Johann Braun, a Swiss national, a.k.a. Joseph Galish, a.k.a. Heinrich Wanstumm, would settle down to a life of comfort and security, basking somewhere in the tropical sunshine.

———<>———

NEW YORK

The next morning, Samson was advised by the Pentagon that Captain Defoe had died in a plane crash. Would the FBI like to have a copy of Galish's personnel report when he worked at the U.S. base in Memmingen, Germany? Fine, they would airmail a copy promptly.

The next day, a copy of Galish's employment record at the U.S. Army base arrived on Samson's desk. The covering letter got his attention.

"Dear Mr. Samson,

We herewith attach a copy of the file of Joseph Galish, a displaced Hungarian national who was employed here at the base as a cook, from November, 1945 to January, 1948. As you can see, he received consistently outstanding rating reports.

However, you should know that an inquiry was conducted in 1948/1949 by the War Crimes Commission of the Netherlands, located in The Hague. Their investigators were interested in Galish due to his resemblance to a senior Gestapo agent wanted for criminal activities in Holland during the war. Nothing ever came of it. You may wish to contact the Dutch authorities in this connection.

Yours truly,
Lt. George T. Curran, U.S. Army"

Samson picked up the phone and dialed the Chicago office line. "Agent Welch, please," he asked.

"One moment please." Some clicks, then, "Welch speaking."

"Joe, this is Brian. Let me read you the covering letter from the U.S. Army Bureau of Personnel which I just received."

"Go ahead." Joe let out a whistle when Samson came to the closing. "What's the next step?"

"Ask his secretary for a complete listing of all Galish's absences from the office in the last twelve months," concluded Samson. "Arrange a meeting with their head of personnel. Tell him to keep quiet. I want that photo from the bank's files. Also, get a record of his phone calls and bank statements."

Samson loved it when things began to fall into place. He decided not to waste time following up on the Dutch inquiry. Even if Galish were a suspected war criminal, that might have no bearing on the man's involvement in the traveler's check caper. Samson was in the business of bringing to justice individuals who had committed crimes within the jurisdiction of the United States. Keep it simple, he said to himself.

CHAPTER TEN

———————◇———————

THE FINAL ACCOUNTING

JANUARY, 1954

NEW YORK

The two men emerged from the Gotham Hotel on 53rd Street. One was stout, in his sixties, a black coat wrapped tightly around him and a black felt hat pushed down on his head. His face was puffy, his eyes slightly bloodshot. The other appeared to be about forty-five, lean and fit. His clothes were unremarkable. They stood on the curb until a Checker cab stopped in front of them. As they seated themselves, the younger man gave the driver his instructions. "Please take us to 155 Wall Street."

155 Wall Street was an imposing building of a style frequently found in the New York financial district. The best materials had been used in its construction. The doorway was designed to inspire confidence. Galish and Banichek entered a cavernous, double-height entry, and Galish approached a security guard.

"We have an appointment with Mr. Tom Jaspers."

"Certainly, sir. Please go to the ninth floor. The elevator is on your right."

The two men walked over to the elevator bank and entered an elevator. The doors closed, and they rose in silence to the ninth floor. As the doors opened, the elevator operator said, "Please step to your left, gentlemen."

A silver-haired receptionist looked up at them from behind an ornate reception desk. "How may I help you?" she asked.

"We are here to see Mr. Jaspers."

"Do you have an appointment?" she asked superciliously.

"Yes. We are from Chicago. The name is Josef Rosenfeld."

"Please have a seat. I will let Mr. Jaspers know you are here." Her voice sounded nasal and insincere.

Within five minutes, a thin young man, properly attired in a Brooks Brothers suit and a rep tie, emerged from a side corridor. He walked vigorously over to them. "I'm Tom Jaspers, and you must be Mr. Rosenfeld." His head swiveled from side to side to make sure he was talking to the right man.

"I'm Laszlo Velec, Mr. Jaspers. This is Mr. Josef Rosenfeld, whose English is not very good. I am his financial advisor, and I will translate for him."

"Thank you. Please follow me." Jaspers led the way to a conference room situated midway in a long corridor. "Please sit down, gentlemen. Can we offer you a cup of coffee?"

"Thank you," said the younger man, "That would be very nice." Jaspers rang a bell and a uniformed waiter came in to take their orders.

"Now, Mr. Velec, what can we do for you?"

"Mr. Rosenfeld has just recently arrived in the U.S. from Holland. In 1940, he sent some money to this bank for deposit. He would like to transfer it to his new home in Illinois."

"You say the money was sent in 1940? That's a long time ago. Can you tell me something about the circumstances?"

"Certainly. Mr. Rosenfeld fled from Germany with his family and settled in Holland in 1938. He was advised to move his family money to a safe place, such as the U.S. Unfortunately he and his family were unable to get out of Holland when the Germans invaded in May, 1940. His entire family, excepting himself, perished at Auschwitz. He remained in hiding in Holland, where he decided to stay after the war and where he became a citizen in 1947."

"What a shocking story!" said Jaspers. "People in the States have no idea what went on over in Europe."

"That's true," replied Velec. "Please let me summarize for Mr. Rosenfeld." Velec turned slightly in his seat and spoke in German to the older man. Meanwhile the uniformed waiter brought in a pot of coffee on a tray with three elegant china cups.

"Thank you," said Velec. "As you can imagine, this is not easy for Mr. Rosenfeld. However he has decided to set up a branch of his pharmaceutical business here in the States, and he plans to use some of the profits for various Jewish causes in memory of his wife and two children."

"A most worthy cause," concurred Jaspers. "Now let's try and find this account. What details do you have?"

"We have here a copy of the letter of introduction sent to your bank by a Mr. Eduard Seventer, at the time a managing partner of Hobbema and Seventer, Bankers in Amsterdam." Velec handed a rather tattered and yellowing paper across the table to Jaspers.

> Mr. George Sandman, Esquire
> Vice President
> Empire State National Bank
> 155 Wall Street
> New York, New York
>
> Amsterdam, 14 June 1939
>
> Dear George,
>
> Attached you will find a check for U.S. $514,000 drawn by us on our account at the Chase Bank in New York City. These funds are to be deposited in an interest-bearing account with you in the name of Josef Rosenfeld, one of our good clients. I hereby authenticate his signature at the bottom of this letter.

Since he will be traveling a great deal, he wishes his account to be placed on 'Hold All Mail'. Should he wish to withdraw the funds, he will come to your offices, and along with a copy of this letter of introduction, he will present suitable identification. He is a citizen of Germany, currently living in the Netherlands.

With many thanks for your attention to this matter, I remain,

Sincerely yours,
Eduard Seventer

Signature of Mr. Josef Rosenfeld:

Jaspers put the letter down. "Well, this certainly should help. Did we confirm receipt of the letter and give you a reference or account number?"

"That is possible, but Hobbema and Seventer closed during the war, and we have been unable to locate such information. We do have the receipt for the original deposit at the time the account was opened in Amsterdam." Velec turned to Rosenfeld and asked in German, "Mr. Jaspers is asking whether you have any confirmation of the account opening from his bank?" Rosenfeld answered something in German.

"No, nothing has turned up, he says. However, we do have the receipt from the Dutch bank acknowledging the opening of Mr. Rosenfeld's account with them." Velec passed it across the table.

Jaspers looked at it carefully and asked, "I apologize having to ask, given the circumstances, but does Mr. Rosenfeld have any identification with him?"

Velec translated for Rosenfeld, who reached wordlessly into his jacket and pulled out a passport, then handed it across to Velec, who handed it to Jaspers. Jaspers leafed through the document. It had a plain canvas cover, with a series of numbers punched through its top border. The second inside page was elaborately engraved, with the words 'Kingdom of the Netherlands' in bold script. The third inside page had a photograph of Josef Rosenfeld. Underneath was his signature, which looked very much like the signature on the letter of introduction. On the fourth inside page Jaspers found, in Dutch, French and English, the date of birth, place of birth, date of passport issuance, and expiration date. Finally, on the next page, Jaspers found a visa from the U.S. Consulate in Rotterdam, granted for multiple entries into the U.S. with stays limited to periods of three months.

"Well, this certainly seems to be in order. May I keep it for a moment to show my manager? He also has to approve the transfer," said Jaspers as he rose from the table. "You said that Mr. Rosenfeld wished the funds to be transfered to Illinois?"

"Yes, that's correct. Mr. Rosenfeld would like to have the funds transferred to his bank in Chicago."

"Very well. I will first have to locate the account. You realize that it most likely has been moved to the inactive accounts department. Fortunately that unit is located in this building, where we also have all the non-resident accounts. Please be patient."

Jaspers left the room. The two men said nothing, and sipped their coffee. The older man was clearly ill-at-ease in his heavy black woolen suit. The room was too hot for such a heavy suit. The younger man sat ramrod-straight, his eyes roving around the room. The minutes ticked by. From outside the large window came muffled street sounds. Ten minutes later, after a knock on the door, a waiter walked in.

"Would you gentlemen care for some more coffee?"

"No, thank you," replied Velec.

The minutes went by again. Finally the door opened, and Jaspers came back into the room. "You are very lucky, Mr. Rosenfeld," he said. "I just learned something very interesting from our inactive accounts department. New York State has a statute which applies to 'Abandoned Property'. The concept is that any property deemed to have been abandoned for a statutory period of ten years becomes the property of the State. Normally, a claimant with appropriate proof of ownership can obtain repayment by New York State even after it has been seized. However, many people never try to reclaim their money.

"As a matter of fact, we are somewhat concerned here at the bank that some Jewish accounts have been taken by New York State with insufficient efforts made to locate their owners. Normally, accounts dormant for over ten years fall into the category of those that banks have to report to the state authorities. We have not made any particular effort to report such accounts. New York State has not audited us for inactive accounts since the war. It seems that your account is therefore still with us. The balance has grown considerably due to the compounding of interest since 1939, and it is now $804,760."

Velec turned to Rosenfeld to explain. Rosenfeld merely nodded.

"Thank you, Mr. Jaspers, for this explanation. We are very grateful to you. Could I please give you the name of the company account to which the funds should be sent?"

"By all means."

Velec took a piece of paper out of his pocket. "Please send Mr. Rosenfeld's money to the North Shore Commercial Bank at 2423 North LaSalle, Chicago, for the account of Pilot Research, Inc, at 3334 West Mohawk, Chicago, Illinois. The account number is 43-9007-8." Jaspers shuffled some forms on the conference room table. Very methodically, he filled in names and numbers on the withdrawal and transfer instructions. Then he assembled the originals carefully, and handed them over to Rosenfeld.

"Mr. Velec, perhaps you will be good enough to translate these forms for Mr. Rosenfeld. When he has reviewed them thoroughly, please ask him to sign in the spaces indicated."

Rosenfeld carefully unscrewed the cap on his fountain pen, and with Velec's help, signed the transfer instructions. Jaspers thought Rosenfeld appeared somewhat flustered by the formalities. "That should do it, gentlemen," said Jaspers. "The funds will be credited to your account in the next five days."

"Thank you, Mr. Jaspers, and on behalf of Mr. Rosenfeld, I must say that you have been very sensitive to his needs."

Velec arose from his chair. Rosenfeld followed, a bit halting, beads of sweat pearling on his brow. He looked at Jaspers from under slightly hooded eyes. "Thank you," he said, "I thank you."

Jaspers looked slightly embarrassed. "I am very glad we could help you," he said.

———<>———

The next morning, a slight drizzle was falling on New York City. The Manhattan National Bank building on Pine Street, built of New York granite, was solid and imposing. Galish and Banichek exited the cab and crossed the sidewalk towards the entrance. Inside the building, they looked for the elevators. The early morning crowd of clients to the Bank was sparse, and they reached their floor non-stop. They stepped out into a paneled reception area with a deep red carpet. The receptionist sat at one end, encased in a cylindrical booth made of rich tropical wood. The younger man stepped up to her.

"Good morning. My name is Holtz, and I am accompanying my friend, Dr. Bluhm, who has an appointment with Mr. Wayne Jahns."

"Yes sir," she replied, "Please take a seat." She then consulted a small directory, dialed someone named Alice to inform her that "Mr. Hootz and Dr. Boom" were there to see Mr. Jahns. The receptionist came over to them and took their coats to the closet. Galish and Banichek sat down again. Galish picked up a magazine which turned out to be the Manhattan National's latest annual report. Banichek sat staring into space.

Within a few minutes, a somewhat overweight gentleman came through the swinging doors behind the reception area, and introduced himself as Wayne Jahns. They walked through the doors and entered a small conference room.

"Please sit down. Welcome to the Manhattan Bank," Jahns said. "I understand that you have just arrived from Chicago?"

"That's right," replied Galish in his slightly accented English. "As I told you over the phone the day before yesterday, I am here to translate for Dr. Bluhm, who has only recently arrived in the U.S. from Holland."

"And I understand that Dr. Bluhm wishes to access an account that has been on our books since 1939?"

"Let me explain," said Galish. "Dr. Bluhm is a refugee from Nazi Germany. His family was deported. He alone managed to survive the camps. Before the outbreak of the war, he and his family moved from Berlin to Amsterdam. They thought that they would be safe there. A Dutch banker who had been recommended to Dr. Bluhm by another Jewish refugee advised him to send some of his funds either to London or to New York for safekeeping, just in case. As it turned out, this was good advice. Your bank was a correspondent of Hobbema and Seventer, the bank in Amsterdam, and you, therefore, opened the account in Dr. Bluhm's name."

"After your call, I checked our records for a Dr. Julius Bluhm," Jahns replied. "Unfortunately, I was unable to locate an account in that name. Then it occurred to me that it might have been transferred to inactive status. I did indeed find a record of an account in that name. The address was 'Hold All Mail'. However, this account was escheated to the State of New York in 1949."

"What do you mean?" asked Galish, a frown on his face.

"New York State, like most states in the U.S., has a statute under which any unclaimed property 'escheats', in other words, reverts, to the state after a specified number of years, in this case, ten years. It is our policy here at the Manhattan Bank to comply with the law even though it is not always enforced. However, you should know that we can assist you in establishing a claim on the funds. The statute stipulates that if a claimant can prove ownership, and if the circumstances are credible, then the State is obligated to return the funds."

"Please give me a minute to explain all this to Dr. Bluhm." Galish turned to Banichek, and proceeded to describe the situation in German. Banichek interjected a couple of times, in what sounded like a very exasperated manner. His upper lip was perspiring. Galish turned back to Jahns.

"Dr. Bluhm is very upset. He wants to know how long it will take for him to get his money."

"Well, he will have to file the claim, which must be notarized. We are also required to file a separate statement on the origin and nature of the account, including our verification of Dr. Bluhm's identity. Since the balance in the account was considerable, it is possible that New York State will want to meet with Dr. Bluhm and take a statement from him. After that, I am told that the procedure may take four to five weeks before payment is actually made."

"This is very annoying," Galish said. "Dr. Bluhm is a resident of Holland. He is traveling to Chicago, where he has some relatives. He is an old man and not in good health. How can he be expected to make trips to New York? Is there not a way for you to expedite this?"

"Well, let me make some inquiries for you. Where can I reach you?"

"We are staying at the Gotham Hotel. However, we must return to Chicago tomorrow night. We had hoped that you could expedite this matter."

"I will see what I can do. I'm really sorry about this, you know." They got up, and Jahns accompanied them to the reception area. The receptionist fetched their coats. They shook hands with Jahns and turned towards the elevator.

———<>———

Room 1214 at the Gotham Hotel faced Fifth Avenue. It was still drizzling, and in the dusk, the city lights sparkled in the wet reflections of the windows. Galish looked out into the dark, lost in thought, only the occasional flicker of his eyes showing any kind of life. He had been annoyed to find that the hotel was full and that they would have to share a room. He preferred to keep his distance from Banichek.

Behind him, stretched out on one of the beds, Banichek lay with his eyes closed. His shirt was open at the neck. His breathing was heavy, a bit irregular. He looked larger in a supine position than he did standing up. A faintly porcine odor emanated from his body.

The room was decorated in what the hotel trade probably referred to as 'modern baroque'. It was comfortable but beginning to need renovation. A longer stay would be depressing. Galish and Banichek had each adopted a corner of the room, where each had stowed his small travel bag. A small electric clock on Galish's side of the room ticked quietly. It was 4.38 p.m. when the phone rang. Galish turned quickly at the sound. In a few quick steps, he was at the nightstand.

"Hullo?"

"Mr. Holtz? We have a call for you."

After a few moments, a voice came on. "Hello, Mr. Holtz?"

"Speaking."

"This is Wayne Jahns, Manhattan Bank."

"Oh yes," replied Holtz. "I was looking forward to your call."

"Well, I'm a little confused. Did Dr. Bluhm make a request for the funds three years ago?"

Galish's eyes narrowed slightly. "I'm afraid I don't understand."

"Well, it seems that a claim has already been filed on behalf of Dr. Bluhm."

"But that's absurd," said Galish. "Who can possibly have done so if Dr. Bluhm didn't?"

"Unfortunately, I'm not at liberty to reveal those details to you right now. You must understand that we have an obligation to our clients, whoever they may be, to keep their affairs confidential. I'm just wondering whether there may not be someone else, also by the name of Julius Bluhm, who also had an account with us."

"Well, as we told you today, we have all the details you will need to identify both Dr. Bluhm and the account. I'm sure that it can be straightened out."

"Well, you see, Mr. Holtz, the problem is that the State of New York has already paid out the money. I called our legal department, and they made an inquiry on your behalf with the State of New York. That is when we were informed that the balance in the only account we have ever maintained in the name of Dr. Julius Bluhm, originally opened at the Manhattan in 1939, was indeed escheated to New York State. However, it was reclaimed and subsequently paid out to the beneficiary."

"I'm afraid there must be some terrible mistake," said Galish. "What can we do?"

"I have been advised by our legal department that you should come in for a meeting, at which all the details you may have will be reviewed for submission to New York State. Can you come in tomorrow morning?"

"Let me speak with Dr. Bluhm, and I will call you first thing in the morning."

"Good, I think a meeting with our lawyers will help us untangle this situation quickly. I would appreciate it if you would call me first thing in the morning. Good night."

Galish hung up the phone. He looked over at the bed where Banichek appeared to be sleeping He walked over to him, and in a manic burst of energy, he seized the side of the mattress and tipped Banichek onto the floor.

"You are going home," said Galish, "now."

"Where are you going?" asked Banichek, frightened, trying to get up off the carpet.

"I will inform you later."

It was nearly noon the next day, and Holtz had not called. Jahns looked at his watch again. He called the Gotham Hotel.

"Room 1214, please."

"One moment, please." The telephone operator came back on the line.

"What is the name of your party, sir?"

"Dr. Bluhm and Mr. Holtz."

"I'm sorry, those guests checked out last night."

He decided to call Ted Biggart, a senior vice president in charge of the mid-Manhattan region. Jahns had noted in the Bluhm file that Biggart had been the original point of contact when the Bluhm account was re-activated.

"Mr. Biggart's office," answered his secretary.

"Is he there, please? This is Wayne Jahns at Head Office."

"Just a moment, please. He's finishing a meeting." After a few moments, Biggart came on the line. "Biggart speaking."

"Ted, this is Wayne Jahns in the International Division."

"Oh, hi, Wayne. How are you?"

"Fine. I've got a peculiar situation on my hands. Do you recall an account that had escheated to the State of New York a few years ago? The client was Dr. Julius Bluhm, from Holland. I see in the file that you were instrumental in helping his daughter claim it back from the state. I note that we now have an account 'in custody' for Dr. Bluhm. Do you recall the circumstances?"

"Oh, very well. His daughter came in with her adoptive father, a Dutchman by the name of Schuurman. They were able to prove convincingly that her natural parents had been deported to Germany and were presumed dead. We made it possible for her to access the account, with an arrangement that would give her father some protection should he lodge a subsequent claim.

It was a large amount of money. By the way, the daughter was very intelligent and attractive. She lives in Canada."

"At the time, do you recall any other accounts under the name of Julius Bluhm which you might have run across?"

"Absolutely not. We cross-checked his name with every account. This was not just a small savings account, you know. Why are you asking?"

"Well, yesterday, I had a visit from two men, one of whom claimed to be Dr. Julius Bluhm. He was accompanied by a younger fellow who translated for him. They had documents clearly linked to the account."

Biggart greeted this with silence as he thought of the implications. "Wayne, I think we need to get together with Jeff Husband. Something's not right. Where are these guys?"

"Well, the reason I called you is because they were supposed to come in for a meeting with our lawyer this morning. When they didn't show, I called their hotel. They checked out shortly after I called them yesterday to tell them that the account had already been claimed. I think we should get together and talk this one over."

The meeting was set for 4 p.m. that afternoon. Biggart arrived in the room at the same time as Jeffrey Husband. Jahns was already there, with a significant number of documents spread out on the conference table.

"I have already briefed Jeff," said Jahns to Biggart.

"What do you think, Jeff?" asked Biggart.

"They sound like impostors to me, but I need to understand the nature of the documents they had with them."

Jahns thought for a minute. "They handed me a copy of a letter from the bank in Amsterdam, asking us to open the account. It was initialed by the bank manager and signed by Julius Bluhm. They also had a copy of the original transfer instructions."

"I must tell you," said Husband, "I would have been very concerned that we had paid out the account to the wrong beneficiary, but the fact that these guys skipped out so fast makes me think that they were suddenly scared off by the fact that a beneficiary had appeared and had already claimed the account. What I don't understand is how they could have known about the account in the first place."

"We haven't considered the possibility that this really could be the girl's father, who doesn't know that his daughter is alive," suggested Biggart.

"That's a very long shot, Ted," said Husband. "However we can't completely exclude the possibility. You know, I think we need some help here. Let's call it attempted fraud. I'll call the FBI to see what they think."

The next morning, they met in the same conference room. In addition to yesterday's participants, Husband had called in Trevor Sawyer, representing the bank's law firm. There were two agents from the FBI, a senior agent, Brian Samson, and a younger man. Samson looked around the room, assessing everyone. "Gentlemen, I understand you have an attempted fraud?"

Biggart, as the senior bank officer in the room, decided to start the discussion. "Mr. Samson, thanks for coming over. We have run into a strange situation, and we would appreciate your help in interpreting the facts. We are indeed beginning to think that fraud may be involved. If I may, I would like to have Jeff take you through the details."

Husband cleared his throat, shuffled his papers, and proceeded to recount the series of events, culminating in the telephone discussion during which Jahns advised Holtz that the account had already been claimed. Jahns then gave a brief description of the men and added that the hotel operator advised that they had checked out less than an hour after his phone call to them the previous evening.

Samson sat stonily in his chair, chewing his cigar. Then he sat up. "That's great. So you let the cat out of the bag? It didn't occur to you that you needed to keep them on a string?"

"Of course it did," complained Jahns. "I told them to come in yesterday morning to see whether we couldn't straighten it out."

"If these guys were impostors, all you did was to tip them off that their scheme was unraveling. Now they're gone. No real names, no addresses. I bet they paid their hotel bill in cash. There's nothing for us to go on since we don't even know whether there was an intended crime." He chewed rapidly on the cigar.

Sawyer had been quietly doodling on a legal size pad. He looked up. "I would like to know how they came by the information about the account. They had some authentic-looking documents."

"Which you don't have a copy of," interrupted Samson.

"True, but Wayne saw them, and they clearly matched the original instructions on the account."

"You said yourself that this stuff goes back to before the war. There is absolutely no trail for us to follow here, and I can't justify using any resources to check Chicago, if that's where they were from, or Holland, where this all started. It sounds to me like you just got lucky." He got up to leave.

"So there's nothing we should do?" asked Husband just to make sure.

"If you hear from them again, which I doubt, keep them here until one of us can come over. We'll do the interrogating, okay?" He shook hands wordlessly.

"Must be one of his good days," remarked Sawyer after Samson had left the room.

"Relax, he's a fine agent. We just don't look that smart, that's all," said Biggart.

"All I can say is, it makes me nervous to leave it open this way," added Husband. "Just make sure we have a complete memo on this discussion, Wayne. Circulate it to us, and then put it in the file."

The Mellon Group was an informal association of bank officers from around the country. Membership was by invitation only. The objectives of the association were to advance the understanding of new banking techniques and to share views on professional issues. Ted Biggart had been a member for four years and was now a vice president of the New York chapter. The chapter met for lunch every third Friday of the month. A speaker was featured, usually with a financial background, but occasionally, guests were invited from outside the banking world. Today, the guest was the chief economist from General Motors. His subject was 'The re-adaptation of the U.S. economy at the end of the Korean War'. Biggart was not sure who had chosen the topic, but he was convinced that it would hasten the membership's early departure for the weekend. At least, he would enjoy seeing his fellow members.

He found himself seated next to an old friend, David Sinclair, a senior vice president at the Empire State National Bank. They inquired about their respective families, reviewed their previous summer's golf scores, and commented on how dull life was in the middle of winter in New York.

"It's not really that dull," commented Biggart. "We had a strange thing happen to us this week. We've had a large deposit account on our books since before the war that belonged to a German Jew who had taken refuge in Holland. Two characters came in, trying to claim it. We had already turned it over to the proper beneficial owner. What we can't understand is how these guys ever knew about it in the first place. Then the two guys just disappeared. We told the FBI, but they didn't show much interest. We didn't look too smart."

Sinclair looked at Biggart closely. "Ted, tell me something. Was the refugee accompanied by an associate who did all the talking?"

It was Biggart turn to look strangely at Sinclair. He looked stunned. "Jesus, David, don't tell me you've just been through the same thing?"

"Yes, Ted, we have," said Sinclair with a sigh, "but we paid out the balance in the account, including accrued interest. Perhaps this is just a coincidence, but I doubt it."

"David, can I come over to your office on Monday? Let's get together on this, just the two of us."

"It's a deal. How about 9 a.m. at 155 Wall?" Biggart nodded, and turned as the chairman called for order. It was time for the guest speaker. Neither Sinclair nor Biggart heard a word he said.

Biggart had always admired the main banking hall at the Empire State National Bank. If ever a banking floor was designed to impress, this was the one. The high ceiling was painted a cerulean blue. But Biggart had other things on his mind this morning. He turned towards the back of the hall and found the bank of elevators which took him to the fifth floor.

David Sinclair had become the chief credit officer for the international division just a few months before. His office was crammed into a modest area at the end of a corridor. His name was on the door. Biggart knocked and opened the door without waiting for an invitation. Sinclair's secretary, who had been with the bank for twenty-eight years, greeted Biggart with a friendly smile.

"He's in there," she said without ceremony.

The two men shook hands and sat down around Sinclair's coffee table. "David," began Biggart, "of the two men who came into the bank, one was in his mid-sixties. He was introduced as Dr. Julius Bluhm. He was pudgy, sweaty, and ill at ease. The other, in his mid-forties, called himself Holtz. He was thin and had blond hair combed straight back. They knew the account number, the amount of the initial transfer, the works. Their story was that Bluhm was the only remaining member of the family and needed the money for his business. That's it."

Sinclair toyed with his coffee. "Okay. The reason that I reacted as I did was that we had the same combination of characters come in here a day or so before their visit to you. You may know one of our guys, named Tom Jaspers. Well, Tom brought a transfer to me for an initial; we always have a senior initial on a transfer in excess of $250,000. He explained the circumstances: a Jewish refugee collecting on an account opened before the war. As you know, we have had quite a few of these characters crop up. I asked him about his identification procedure. He seemed to have been properly diligent. We had not escheated the account simply because we have a whole bunch of inactive accounts waiting to go to Albany, and someone thought that it would make sense to wait until we have identified them all. The account was still on active status."

"Why did you think there might be something fishy about this one?" asked Biggart.

"Call it a sixth sense. It sounded too simple. Two guys walk in off the street, have good documents, play on our emotions and collective guilt, and then walk off with a large amount of money. To tell you the truth, I became so worked up about it that I asked how many dormant accounts we had lying around with balances exceeding $200,000. We found quite a few. We didn't even count the savings accounts because we have no information in those files.

"I found seven interest-bearing accounts. Two of these had been opened by a bank in Amsterdam, Hobbema and Seventer, at about the same time, 1938 or thereabouts. The one we paid out was by far the largest, however. It would make sense for them to pick off the biggest balance, because their chance of getting away with it twice at the same bank would be zero."

"That means that they knew about the other Dutch accounts?"

"It makes sense when you think of it. I wonder if they found these records in Holland during the war. Funny things happen in wartime."

"How many banks had accounts like these?" mused Biggart.

Sinclair thought for a minute and then answered, "This is something for the FBI. Maybe they'll get a little more interested this time. You know what we should do, though. Let's get Jahns and Jaspers into a room together and have them describe these two guys again, just to make sure that we don't have a coincidence. If the descriptions match, let's call the FBI."

———<>———

Biggart, Sinclair, Jaspers, and Jahns sat around Biggart's office. Coffee had been served. Biggart had taken his jacket off.

"Thanks for coming, David and Tom. Jeff Husband will be here any minute. As you know, we suspect that we have been visited by a pair of con artists, posing as a Jewish refugee and his accountant." He interrupted himself as Jeff Husband came into the room. "Good morning, Jeff, have some coffee. We just started. I was alluding to the similarities between the two visits. We would like you, Tom, and Wayne, to describe what happened when the men showed up, what they looked like, how they spoke, what they wore. We know what they tried to do. I want to understand the similarities of how they did it. Tom, perhaps you would begin?"

"Certainly. Let me start with appearances. The older man was about sixty . . ."

"Wait a minute," interrupted Husband. "I'm going to draw up two columns as you guys compare notes." He started writing on a pad.

". . . . was overweight, had very little hair, although he was not quite bald, about 5 feet 8, dressed in a black suit and a white shirt. He looked very sweaty, almost unwell."

Biggart turned to Jahns. "It's your turn."

"I would not have described the guy any differently; that's him."

"What about his voice, his inflection?"

"I don't think he said much of anything. He spoke in German," said Jaspers.

"Again, I concur completely," said Jahns.

"Okay," interjected Biggart, "let's describe the other guy."

Jaspers took the lead again. "About 5 feet 10, thin, with pear-shaped hips, unremarkable face, a few wrinkles, dark blond hair parted in the middle, combed straight back. He was wearing a non-descript dark blue suit, blue tie, white shirt."

"That tallies exactly with my recollection," concurred Jahns. "His voice was thin and reedy. He spoke very good English, but with an accent, which sounded German."

Sinclair spoke up. "This is pretty convincing. We know that they used the same kinds of documents, allegedly originating at the same bank in Amsterdam which was closed at the beginning of the war. Both of the accounts belonged to German Jews who had sought refuge in Holland. I say we call in the FBI. They have jurisdiction and can decide who else they want to bring in."

"Is everyone in agreement?" asked Biggart. They all nodded.

———<>———

The FBI office on Maiden Lane in downtown New York was typically bare and functional, underlying the serious nature of the work carried out there. Brian Samson strode down the linoleum-floored corridor into a conference room. Three other agents were already there. Without preamble and without sitting down, Samson opened a file in front of him and ran through it quickly. "You each have a description of two men suspected of fraud. One represents himself as the beneficial owner of an account opened before the war. The other guy translates into German for him. We have two cases, one at the Manhattan Bank, one at Empire State. I want you guys to talk to every major bank in New York and see whether there have been similar cases."

One of the other agents stirred. "What about banks in other cities? Like Boston or Chicago?"

Samson looked at him thoughtfully. "Good idea. John, will you call Bud Hingman in Boston? Tell him what we have; ask him to make a few calls. We'll meet tomorrow at 8.30 a.m. Let's go."

——————<>——————

They reconvened in the same conference room. Samson arrived at 8.31 a.m., greeted them and said, "Okay, let's have it."

One of the agents spoke up. "We drew a blank at the other New York banks. Boston, however, is another story. We have two cases up there, identical circumstances. The banks are really pissed that they may have been had. They want to know why a formal approach wasn't made, why they weren't notified earlier, etc. The president of Back Bay National is so mad that he's got a call in to the Deputy Director."

"I guess I had better go and deal with that. I'm going to get authority to broaden the inquiry. At the same time, I'll send around an advisory to all the banks under our jurisdiction. Nice work, guys."

——————<>——————

Samson stood in the office of the agent in charge of the New York office. This man was third in line after the Director and Deputy Director of the Federal Bureau of Investigation. He was a World War II Marine Corps veteran and had earned his law degree at Fordham in two years.

"You know that I got chewed out by Washington because you went into Boston without clearance?"

"Sir, all we did was to call Bud with a question."

"Well, you know how Bud throws his weight around, and now we have to apologize to that guy at Back Bay National Bank."

"I have a suggestion, sir. Tell the bank president to shove it up his nose. He's a sore loser, that's all. His guys paid out nearly half a million dollars to a couple of con men."

"What's the bottom line here? How much have these guys actually ripped off?"

"It appears to be about $2,700,000, sir."

"Tell me again which banks they hit?"

"Two in Boston, three in Philadelphia, and one here in New York. This is the list. We are still checking other cities. It was the second New York bank where they slipped up. They had no way of knowing that the money had been escheated to New York State and then paid out to a legitimate beneficiary. If it hadn't been for that, we might never have found out."

"What is the common thread here?"

"All of the accounts were opened by the same bank in Holland before 1940. All of the accounts appear to have Jewish beneficiaries. The Dutch bank went out of business after the invasion of Holland by the Germans in 1940."

"Okay, so obviously someone found the documents. I want you to ask Washington who our best contact is in Dutch law enforcement. We have to get them involved."

"I'll do that. You should also know that the Chicago office has been asked to assist us. It seems that the transfers out of

New York and Boston all went to Chicago area banks. Different accounts, different banks, for each transfer. Unfortunately, the funds were immediately wired out of those accounts again, apparently to an account in Panama. We have initiated an inquiry down there also. We are getting a description of the signers on all those accounts. I'm certain that they will match the description of the two impostors."

"Good. Be sure to get a record of the actual signatures used and have them checked by our handwriting experts. The similarities should be conclusive."

"One more thing, sir. There are other accounts like this that have not been raided. The balances are smaller, so these guys must have known that they had only one chance per bank to pull off this scam. They went after the biggest account at each bank. Since we don't know what other banks might have been involved, may I have your authority to circulate the details to all banks in the U.S. under our jurisdiction?"

"Yes, although I doubt that smaller banks would be involved. However, given the circumstances, I want you to send a copy to all state banking supervisors. Let them decide whether they want to include some of the larger state-chartered banks."

"We'll need to have any bank that sees these guys stall them until we can nab them for questioning. We'll need to move fast."

"I understand. But you're going too far with this. I would guess that only big banks, in large cities, were used by the Dutch before the war. What would they know about the Third National Bank of Watkins Creek? Ask Biggart which cities he would recommend, like Chicago or San Francisco. Then advise our boys in those cities. Use the rifle shot, not the grape shot, my friend."

———◇———

THE HAGUE

The new U.S. Embassy building in The Hague had just been completed. It was slightly outside the center of town, in a tree-shaded neighborhood where the streets seemed wider because of the cyclist paths built along the pavement. It was a strong architectural statement, functional yet imposing, and the proportions were pleasing to the eye.

Kees Goedkamp parked his Hillman, locked the door, and walked across the avenue to the embassy entrance. He presented his ID to the marine on duty, and walked into the reception hall. He looked again at the short memo which he had received from his boss, Mr. de Ruiter:

> "I have been informed by our friends at Foreign Affairs that the U.S. Federal Bureau of Investigation is conducting an international inquiry, and they have asked for our help. It relates to certain bank accounts opened by Hobbema and Seventer before the war. Since you are familiar with that story, I have suggested that you be the point man in Holland for them. Their contact here in The Hague is Dwight W. Scott. I understand he is an attache of some sort at their embassy. Keep me posted."

Goedkamp asked the receptionist for Mr. Scott. After a few moments, Scott appeared and introduced himself. They took an elevator to the third floor, walked down a corridor, and into a large office. "Please, sit down, Mr Goedkamp. Mr. James Belknap, our deputy head of mission, will be joining us in a moment."

Belknap entered the room. He was a tall, well-dressed man in his late forties. "Mr. Goedkamp? It's very nice of you to stop by. We should have paid you the courtesy of calling on you, but the FBI is very concerned about security since the case they are dealing with originated here in Holland.

They suggested, if you were amenable, that we restrict the initial conversation to you and hold the talks inside our embassy. Frankly, I think they are a little paranoid. Mr. Scott is not, as I'm sure you have guessed, a regular diplomat." Belknap nodded at Scott. Goedkamp did not smile. "Please go ahead," he suggested.

Scott recounted the events leading up to the discovery of the theft of a number of accounts belonging to Jewish refugees living in Holland before the war. Midway through the recital, Goedkamp began taking notes.

"So there you have it: seven accounts, in Boston, Philadelphia, and New York banks and a total take exceeding $2,700,000. The suspects appear to have been operating out of Chicago. We have interviewed the Chicago banks to whom the funds were transferred. All of them, without exception, reported that the funds were almost immediately wired out to an account, in the name of Holger S.A. at the Banco del Pacifico in the Republic of Panama. Due to Panamanian bank secrecy laws, we have been unable to get any further information. Incidentally, the descriptions of the two men match in every particular. We have circulated their descriptions quite widely, but they must feel very confident that no one could possibly link them to these accounts.

"Our question is this. The bank documents clearly originated here in Holland. Would it be possible to draw up a list of people here who might have had access to the information about these accounts? We think that this might provide us with some leads."

"It just so happens that I know one of the former managers of the Dutch bank," answered Goedkamp. "He is the person to start with. I must say, this is a most daring scheme. What surprises me is that it took so long after the war for them to try it."

"How can we contact this gentleman?"

"I will let you know. He now lives in London, but he comes to Holland quite frequently."

Back in his office, Goedkamp dialed Seventer's office number in London. He got through almost immediately. "Hello, Edu? Kees Goedkamp. You'll never believe what I have just heard from the Americans. It seems that two men, impersonating a German Jewish refugee and his accountant, have been successfully claiming ownership of accounts opened before the war at various American banks by Hobbema and Seventer. They want our help in trying to figure out who might have had access to the information. When can we talk?"

———<>———

The next afternoon, Seventer dropped his bag off at the Hotel des Indes in the center of The Hague and had the taxi continue to Goedkamp's office. It was already getting dark, due to the heavy cloud cover, and the drizzle made driving even more hazardous. Goedkamp had insisted that the two of them go out to dinner. Goedkamp, divorced after the war, had fallen 'in love', as he put it, with the best-looking woman in Holland who also knew how to cook. She owned a charming restaurant in Scheveningen.

They arrived just as the wind was picking up and walked briskly from Goedkamp's car into the warm atmosphere of the restaurant. A quantity of large oak beams had been used in the construction of the building. The walls were panelled and waxed to a warm, golden color. Small pictures and photos hung in every available space, and colored marine pennants hung from the ceiling. The overall effect was cozy and welcoming.

As soon as they had taken off their coats, a robust, blond woman emerged from the kitchen area. She put her arms around Goedkamp in what looked like a promise of greater intimacies to come. Then she welcomed Seventer warmly and led them to a corner table. She closed the shutters, blocking out the dunes and the darkness of the North Sea.

They ordered a *jonge jenever*. A little plate of cheese cubes was brought by the waiter as an appetizer.

"Tell me first of all, how are things with you?" asked Goedkamp.

"The bank has just elected me managing partner. Van Meeren is still active, however. I don't know what I would have done without him all these years."

"Do you enjoy living in England?"

"I do, very much. I feel so sorry for the Brits, though. Do you realize that they still have rationing for some things? I've heard them say, 'It makes you wonder who won the bloody war'. In spite of these restrictions, which I'm sure will be lifted before long, they manage to keep their wonderful sense of humor. London is a very civilized place to live, and, fortunately, there is nothing there that reminds me of Louisa. When I come here to Holland, on the other hand, her presence is everywhere. It's as if she and I had just walked those streets or enjoyed an evening at one of our favorite restaurants."

"What do you do on weekends?"

"Well, I often get invited to the country, but frankly, I much prefer being near the ocean. I've found a good boat, not a sailboat, a motorboat, which I use to go fishing. I keep it at the small town of Charwell-on-Sea, on the south coast. Fuel is still expensive, but it's worth every penny to have the freedom of being able to go anywhere, alone, away from everything. I even catch fish once in a while." Seventer smiled. "Next time you come over to England, Kees, I'll take you out on the 'Louisa'."

"I'd love to go with you."

"Just make sure you don't have to be back on time!"

They laughed and took a sip of their *jenever*.

"How about you, Kees?" asked Seventer, after a moment of silence.

"So-so. I'm getting frustrated by the slow progress. I've been doing this stuff for seven years. There's so much red tape. Once in a while we nail one of them, but I, for one, think that it will take another ten years to bring all of these Nazis to justice. We have at least three hundred names of people suspected of war crimes who are still unaccounted for. Anyway, how about a nice red wine with our dinner?"

They had ordered and started the appetizer before Goedkamp began to describe the inquiry from the FBI, without omitting any details. Seventer remained silent during the recital of the facts. He was completely engrossed.

When Goedkamp finished, Seventer took a long sip of wine. "By process of elimination, we can narrow the list of possible suspects," he said thoughtfully. "First of all, the only members of the staff at the bank who knew about *all* of the accounts were two of my partners, Jan ten Haave and Pim Laan. Jan lives in Apeldoorn on a war disability pension. Pim Laan went to Singapore in 1947, and has been there ever since. Our chief manager, who was head of operations, could also have collected the list, but he was deported to Germany in 1944, and died in a work camp.

"I am sure that the bank records relating to all these accounts were destroyed by Pim within days after the German invasion. It is remotely possible that one of our staff might have systematically collected the information before the invasion, perhaps to prove that he was a loyal member of the Dutch Nazi Party. I could try and reconstruct all the names of our staff in 1940; there were only thirty-four, but I simply don't see how any of them could have collected this information, let alone have made such diabolical use of it so many years later."

"We could at least reconstitute your staff list, and one by one, we could track down each of them after the war." Goedkamp didn't sound very convinced.

"Kees, the people who pulled off this incredible stunt *must* have known that the beneficial owners were dead. They couldn't run the risk of trying to claim an account which might have already been paid out. As it is, that is exactly what upset their plan, but not in the manner they had expected. The logic is inescapable. Only those Germans who were responsible for deporting Jewish families would have known that the beneficiaries were dead. The prime suspects have to be from the Gestapo or the SS."

The two men fell silent. Then Goedkamp looked up at Seventer. "Are you thinking what I'm thinking? It could be Wanstumm."

Seventer was pensive for a moment, then, a note of excitement in his voice, said, "Yes, it's so obvious. He had the opportunity to assemble the information. He had the ability to act on it. Let's suppose that he really did change his name to Galish when he worked for the Americans in Memmingen. Let's suppose he found his way to the U.S.," continued Seventer. "He had the list of accounts, but he had to work out a system to get at them. He doesn't look remotely Jewish, and he isn't the right age, so he had to find an older man to play the role of the German Jewish refugee."

"So far so good," commented Goedkamp.

"He studied banking procedures because he couldn't afford to make any mistakes. He had to understand how bankers work. What's the best way to do that?"

"Become a banker," answered Goedkamp quickly.

"Exactly. What happened after he had successfully laid claim to the money?"

"Apparently he gave instructions for the funds to be transferred to a series of small banks around Chicago, always to a different account. From there, it appears that the funds were forwarded to an account in Panama."

"I suppose I could have predicted that," commented Seventer. "Panama is the best place right now to hide money. I'm willing to bet that the company Wanstumm used there is simply a name plate on some lawyer's door, and all of the shares are in bearer form so that no one can find out who owns the company."

Goedkamp looked at his watch. "It's getting late. Can you come by the office first thing tomorrow morning?"

"Certainly. I have a lunch scheduled in Amsterdam, so an early meeting with you suits me fine."

Goedkamp was already at his desk when Seventer walked into his office the next morning. "Good morning, Kees. I was up all night thinking about it," said Seventer. "I'm sure that we're on the right track. It has to be Wanstumm."

Goedkamp nodded. "I agree. I'm going to inform the FBI that he is their most likely suspect, probably still operating under the alias of Joseph Galish, a Hungarian who may have left for the U.S. sometime after 1948. At the same time, I want to stake our claim to this guy. If this is really Heinrich Wanstumm, I want him back in Holland. I want him tried here."

"Don't you think the Americans will want to keep him in the U.S.?" asked Seventer.

"They will want him for bank fraud and grand larceny. We want him for war crimes, homicide, torture, violations of civil and human rights. Don't worry, if they don't turn him over to us, we'll kick up a huge stink. I'll have to see how we make a deal with them."

"There's something else that bothers me, Kees. The biggest Jewish accounts, by far, were opened in London. During the night, I scribbled down everything I could remember about those accounts. Of course I used our London affiliate, Mathijs Smithson, for some of the accounts, but I also opened some at the Winchester Bank. Wanstumm can't take another chance with a U.S. bank, but why wouldn't he go for a few of the big accounts in London? With two more raids, he could amass over $4,000,000. The money will be sent to Panama, and from there, who knows where it will end up? Wanstumm can live in style, perhaps under another name, in some jurisdiction with no extradition treaties."

"So what are you proposing?" asked Goedkamp.

"It's simple. I want to set the trap at my own bank in London. If you will recall, I opened several of the Jewish accounts there before the war. We also need to alert the Winchester Bank that impostors may try to claim their accounts. When they show up, the bank calls the police, and we nab them."

"That means that we have to bring in Scotland Yard. At the end of the day, they would arrest Wanstumm for a crime committed in England. Frankly, I think it would be easier to work out a deal with the Brits; they nab him, charge him according to UK law, then we get a judge there to override the charge in favor of the infinitely more serious one of war crimes. They extradite him to Holland, and it'll be curtains for our friend."

"Can't you stall the Americans? They may act too quickly. Kees, Wanstumm belongs to us, no question about it."

"I hear what you're saying, Edu, but I can't play games. I will alert the Brits immediately and tell them that you will provide them with the requisite information about the London accounts. John Hackett at Scotland Yard is an old friend of mine."

"Good. I'm returning to London today. I want to set the trap, at least at our bank. I have a feeling Wanstumm will move quickly. Shall I contact Hackett directly when I get back?"

"Please, and call me when you've set up your plan. I need to be able to reach you quickly. I have, let's see, I have your office number, your home phone number. Is there anything else that could be useful?"

"My secretary, Stella, has been around for years. She always knows where I am."

"All right, that's it then. Edu, I hope to God he doesn't slip through our fingers."

———— <> ————

NEW YORK

A telex arrived at the FBI office a few hours later. Pondexter read it quickly, then buzzed Samson's office. "Brian, you need to see a telex that's just come in from our embassy in The Hague." Samson loped down the corridor and swung into Pondexter's cubicle without knocking. He could tell from Pondexter's tone of voice that something unusual was up.

Pondexter swiveled around in his chair and handed the message to Samson.

> "To Brian Samson FBI New York Office urgent (stop) following information was obtained from Dutch police authorities (stop) most likely suspect in bank account fraud is Heinrich Wanstumm former head of Gestapo in northern Holland (stop) he is the only profile who could have had access to all information AND have known that all account owners were dead (stop) he is wanted in Holland for serious war crimes (stop) Dutch believe Wanstumm may have changed name to Joseph Galish (comma) assuming false identity of Hungarian refugee (stop) last known to have worked for U.S. Army in Memmingen Bavaria before disappearing in 1948 (stop) they have photo on file which seemed to match photo of Galish in U.S. Army personnel records (stop) all traces lost about five years ago (stop) Dutch believe Wannstumm will try to raid similar refugee accounts at London banks and have alerted Scotland Yard (stop) all this information obtained from Dutch banker named Eduard Seventer who set up these accounts before the war (stop) Seventer now working at Mathijs Smithson Dutch-owned bank in London where some accounts were opened (stop) Dutch have indicated that this is their case comma war crimes a more serious offense than bank fraud etc full stop."

"God damn it all to hell!" exclaimed Samson. "Am I reading this right? Joseph Galish? A Nazi war criminal? And the banks let him slip through their fingers!" Pondexter said nothing. He could see that Samson was about to unleash a storm.

"Tell the section that I want a meeting in 30 minutes. Call Welch in Chicago. Tell him to remain on the line. I want him to head up the surveillance team in Chicago. Call Legal Affairs; tell them we have a potential international jurisdiction issue. I want them at the meeting. Get our embassy in The Hague to obtain all the photos the Dutch have on file and get them sent here by courier pronto. Tell them to find out who at Scotland Yard has been plugged into this caper. Oh, and telex the Swiss that we have a suspect in the traveler's check affair by the name of Joseph Galish. Maybe they can lean on Wormser and get a confirmation."

Samson strode back to his office. He picked up the phone. The direct line clicked. "Good afternoon, sir, this is Samson. You're never going to believe this."

———<>———

IDLEWILD AIRPORT, NEW YORK

The international terminal was choking on the growing air traffic across the Atlantic. Facilities had become inadequate, and passengers and airline staffs had to cope with congestion and inefficiency. PanAm and TWA were planning to build their own terminals, but in the meantime, even the U.S. flag carriers had to share the restricted facilities.

Joseph Galish and Arthur Banichek entered the departure hall and headed towards the BOAC desk. Banichek was sweating profusely. He had complained of a headache and nausea since his arrival from Chicago. Galish was beginning to worry. He needed Banichek for one last trip. He turned to look at the man again. Spittle was coming down one side of

Banichek's mouth. His face was white. Galish told him to wipe his face.

"All right, you know what to do," said Galish. "I'll check in behind you so that we don't appear to be traveling together."

Banichek approached the counter. A pleasant young man in uniform greeted him.

"Good afternoon, sir. May I see your ticket and passport, please?" Banichek handed the documents over. "Is the flight on time?" he asked.

"Yes, sir, departure is at 4.10 p.m. this afternoon, scheduled arrival at 11 a.m. tomorrow morning at Croydon. And how many bags are you checking?"

"Just one," replied Banichek, placing it on the weighing machine.

Banichek stood there, feeling sicker. The agent wrote out the baggage tag and tied it to the suitcase. He then wrote out the boarding card, which he attached to the flight coupon. "There you are, Mr. Goldstein. Boarding will begin in twenty minutes. Have a wonderful trip."

Banichek stepped away slowly, pretending to be checking his flight documents. He watched as Galish went through the check-in procedure. When he was done, Banichek followed him into the departure lounge and sat several seats away from him. Galish surveyed the room. They would not be safe until they were in the air. He was certain that the police must have put an alert out on the two of them, but would they bother to check outgoing international flights?

———<>———

LONDON

Fourteen hours later, the DC6 broke through the clouds somewhere over the Thames, and made a long, slow, left-hand approach into Croydon airport. Banichek held his handkerchief over his mouth. Gray clouds scudded past the windows of the bouncing airliner, as the greater London metropolis slid by underneath them. Galish sat rigidly in his window seat, as he had done almost all the way across the Atlantic. Banichek was slumped over, occasionally moaning.

The runway rose up towards them, and the pilot made a much smoother landing than the passengers had any right to expect. The aircraft settled down to its taxiing speed. Slowly, it turned to the right, and the pilot cut his outboard engines as it arrived at the gate and stopped. Banichek was holding a handkerchief over his mouth. He looked up at Galish with bloodshot eyes. Galish leaned over and said, in a clinically cold voice, "Art, we're here. We're in England. There's lots more money here. Shape up, okay?"

Banichek stood up shakily. Galish followed him down the stairs to the tarmac and waited for him to get on the bus first. Galish followed Banichek again through the doors of the terminal, watching the man lurch unsteadily towards the end of the line waiting for an Immigration officer. When Banichek's turn was called, Galish moved swiftly to his side, muttering to the attendant, "My friend is not feeling well." The attendant allowed both of them to proceed to the same desk.

"Good morning, gentlemen," said the Immigration officer, an elderly gentleman in a gray suit. "What is the purpose of your visit?"

"I am accompanying my client, Mr. Goldstein here," said Galish turning slightly, "on a business trip. I am his accountant."

"How long are you expecting to stay, sir?"

"Four or five days. This is our first time here, and we are a little uncertain about the time we will require."

"And what does your client do, sir?"

"He is a commodities broker in Chicago. We have been invited by some English brokers to consider a joint venture. It could mean some good business for us."

"Very well, sir." Galish beckoned to Banichek, who offered his U.S. passport and landing card.

The officer checked the landing card. "This is your home address?" he asked, pointing at the card. Banichek nodded.

The man looked at the two passports carefully, and stamped them. Galish picked them up, and read, 'Good for one visit in the UK until February 4, 1954'.

"Thank you," he said. They walked to the exit, the immigration agent staring after them.

The taxi took them to their hotel on Bedford Street, near the British Museum. Galish had selected it because it seemed centrally located. The travel agent had assured him that the hotel had a good reputation. If his plan worked without a hitch, Galish would be gone in three days anyway. He had no desire to extend his stay, and when they registered at the desk, he knew he was not going to like England.

The receptionist looked at a diary. "Yes, sir," he said to Galish. "You have a reservation in the name of Holtz. Two singles. Would you mind filling in the registration card?"

Galish and Banichek each had a small room with a narrow bed along the wall. Small windows looked out on the street. It was raining. Galish opened the window to let in some fresh air. It was nearly two o'clock. It was time to make his appointments with the banks.

At 3.12 p.m., at Scotland Yard, the phone on Detective Inspector Hackett's desk rang loudly. "Inspector Hackett speaking."

"Inspector, this is James Woodruff at the Winchester Bank. You remember the case of the dormant Jewish bank accounts?"

Hackett sat bolt upright in his chair. "Yes, please go on."

"Well, it seems as if our friends may be in London. I just received a call a few minutes ago from a Mr., let's see, Holtz, wishing to make an appointment on behalf of Mr. Herschel Nussbaum."

"Good heavens! Which hotel are they staying in?"

"They didn't say. I'm sorry, I should have asked them. I've made an appointment with them for the day after tomorrow at 2.30, here at Number 3, Cornhill."

"Excellent. Now just go on as you would normally. I will be there in the morning with some plainclothes men. I promised to alert the Dutch; Inspector Goedkamp said that he might come over himself. We will need to check out the premises so that whatever conference room you use is properly secured. I will have an arrest warrant ready."

The next morning, Galish and Banichek got into a black London taxi. It was still raining. Banichek looked ashen. "Joe, I feel awful," he muttered.

Galish stared straight ahead. They were on the last leg. With their meetings at Mathijs Smithson today, then at the Winchester Bank tomorrow, they should hit the jackpot.

The cab wound through the narrow streets of the City and came to a stop in front of 32 Moorgate. Galish paid off the cabbie and followed Banichek onto the sidewalk. They should have brought umbrellas. The rain was coming down harder than ever. They hurried to the entrance of the building. The heavy door yielded slowly, and they found themselves in a small, marble-floored entrance, quite unlike the imposing halls of New York banks. A porter in uniform greeted them.

"Good morning, gentlemen, whom do you wish to see?"

"We have an appointment with Mr. Nigel Pearce. The name is Goldstein, and I am accompanying him. My name is Holtz."

"One moment, please." The porter announced the visitors on the phone. A large door opened to the right, and a tall, impeccably dressed man in a morning coat, his silver hair brushed carefully behind his ears, emerged to greet them.

"Good morning. Mr. Goldstein, I presume?" he said to Banichek.

"*Ja*, good morning," replied Banichek in heavily-accented English.

"And you are Mr. Holtz, I presume? My name is Pearce. We spoke on the telephone yesterday. Please follow me."

They were ushered into a conference room, comfortably arranged with antiques, leather armchairs, and prints of hunting scenes. They took their seats.

Galish took some papers out of his briefcase. "As I explained to you earlier, Mr. Goldstein is an American citizen. Over the last few years, he has been expanding his business in the United States. I am his accountant and representative. Here is my card. I assist Mr. Goldstein in transactions conducted in English." Galish coughed slightly and continued, "Mr. Goldstein opened an account with you before the war on the recommendation of a bank in Amsterdam. Here is the copy of their letter to you, as well as the receipt issued to him when he deposited the original funds. He now finds it necessary to use these funds as working capital for his business. He would like these funds transferred to the United States."

"May I see your documents, please?" asked Pearce. He scanned them briefly.

"They certainly seem in order. You will understand that I will have to compare them to documents that we have on file. I had a little trouble finding them, you know, rather a long time ago, all this, but we found the file just before your arrival. Would you mind waiting here while I complete the checking?" He rose, and left the room taking the documents with him. Galish frowned, surprised. Pearce had not asked them for identification. Perhaps banks in England handled things differently.

Pearce opened the door to the partners' room without knocking and flourished the documents as he strode in. Seventer was waiting impatiently.

"It's them, no question about it," Pearce stated breathlessly.

"Good. Pearce, I want you to go through the whole drill. Get their addresses, their bank in the U.S. to which the transfer is to be made, the name and account number of the beneficiary. Take their passports and write down all the particulars. Everything. Finally, and this is where you must be very careful, explain that the Bank of England has foreign exchange controls. Take a Currency Export Request in with you and have them fill it out. Tell them that it is merely routine but that we need a day to get it approved. Make sure that they understand that we cannot transfer funds without these official approvals. Ask them the name of their hotel so that we can contact them to get Goldstein's signature on the final transfer order. This will give me time to alert Scotland Yard, etc. We don't want any slip-ups. This is too important."

Pearce returned to the conference room, nervous in the role he was being asked to play. "Gentlemen, we have confirmed the account. Now I will need some information to finalize the transaction." Galish and Banichek watched as Pearce took out his fountain pen and began to fill in a blank form.

"May I see your passport, Mr. Goldstein?" Galish slipped it across the table. Pearce continued writing. The minutes ticked by.

"Can you tell us how much longer this will take?" asked Galish.

"It won't be much longer, Mr. Holtz. Please bear with me. English banking regulations are infernally complicated." He continued writing. Banicheck was becoming visibly distressed. He was sweating profusely again, squirming in his chair. The temperature in the room appeared to have risen several degrees. Galish was beginning to feel uncomfortable as well.

"Mr. Goldstein, sir, if you will just sign here, we can start the process. Mr. Holtz, perhaps you would be good enough to explain these forms to Mr. Goldstein?"

Galish pulled the forms towards him. He turned to Banichek, and started explaining them in German. He pulled out a pen and handed it to Banichek. Banichek signed where Galish pointed with his index finger. Then he pushed the papers back across the table to Pearce.

Pearce looked at them carefully again. "This appears to be in order," he said. "Now there's one last thing. You must know that residents of the United Kingdom are not permitted to transfer funds abroad. Exceptions are made for people such as you, Mr. Goldstein, who are not now, and never have been, resident in the UK. Your account is known as an 'external account'. However, in order to transfer these funds, we need permission from the Bank of England. This is a mere formality in your case. May I ask how long you expect to stay in London?"

"We were planning to return to the U.S. in a couple of days," replied Galish.

"Good. We will hand deliver these forms to the Bank of England immediately. Under special circumstances, we have been able to receive authority to transfer the funds by the following day. We will do our utmost to get this done by tomorrow afternoon. Now if you would be so good as to tell me where you are staying, we can advise you as soon as we receive the transfer authorization."

Galish thought quickly. This seemed to make sense. "We are staying at the Bedford Street Hotel. I am in Room 21." They shook hands, and Pearce led them to the main door. Banichek was so unsteady that he had to catch Galish's arm.

Pearce hurried back to the partners' room. The door was ajar. Seventer was there, stuffing his briefcase with papers. He looked up as Pearce entered.

Pearce was delighted to be playing a part in this caper. "Mr. Seventer, they are staying at the Bedford Street Hotel. I followed your instructions to the letter, sir. But why did you have me tell them that exchange control approvals could be obtained in only a day when you know perfectly well that we can't get anyone over there to approve anything for at least a couple of days?"

"Scotland Yard suggested it."

"Oh, ah, Scotland Yard," repeated Pearce. That explained everything. "Part of the plan, what?" Pearce smiled. He was enjoying this no end. Then his brow furrowed. "But when are the police arriving? Are they coming here first?"

"My dear fellow," replied Seventer, "I haven't the foggiest idea how Scotland Yard operates. I'm sure they have an elaborate plan which we are not privy to."

"Oh, quite," commented Pearce. He looked confused.

As Seventer walked out, he stopped at Stella's desk. "Would you call Mr. van Meeren at our client's office in Luton and tell him that I may be out of the office tomorrow? Tell him I'll see him when he returns on Friday."

Back at the hotel, Galish lay down on the bed. He woke up, startled, looked at his watch, and realized that it was just after six o'clock in the evening. He was annoyed with himself for having dozed off for so long. He stood up, stretched, opened his door and walked down the hall to Banichek's room. He knocked on the door. There was no answer. He knocked again, a little louder. Still nothing. He walked back to his room, tied his shoes, put his jacket on, and went downstairs to the reception.

"Could you tell me whether my colleague Mr. Goldstein, in 23, went out? He is not in his room."

The porter looked backwards to the key rack, fingered the hanging keys.

"I'm sorry, sir, it looks as if he must be in his room. I didn't see anyone go out, and his key is not here."

Galish remained impassive. "Thank you. He must have fallen asleep."

Galish walked back up the stairs. Just to make sure, he knocked on Banichek's door again. He bent down to inspect the lock, then went back to his own room, unlocked the door, and studied the lock mechanism. It was a simple enough key. First, he took a pair of gloves out of his suitcase and put them on. Then he took a penknife out of his pocket, measured the key's point of impact, went outside and closed the door. He inserted the knife blade carefully and slipped it down until he could feel the key begin to give way as he forced the bolt backwards. By pushing on the door, he was able to increase the blade's leverage. The bolt slipped back.

He moved over to the door of Room 23. The lock looked identical to the one on his door. He slipped the blade in, pushed on the door, felt the bolt give until it snapped back. He stepped into the room, quietly closing the door behind him. Banichek lay on the floor, face down. Quickly, Galish turned him over. Banichek's eyes were open but sightless. Galish didn't have to take the man's pulse to confirm that he was dead. Godammit, not now! They were so close to the biggest payout of all! Galish thought of all the money he had already paid to Banichek. What a waste!

It was almost 9 a.m. the next morning when Seventer carefully backed his Rover into a 'Permitted Parking' space. This was not the time to attract the interest of the constabulary. He was dressed in his usual pinstripe, double-breasted suit from Saville Row. He had decided to leave his raincoat in the car. Bedford Street was not busy at this time of the day. He crossed to the other sidewalk and walked into the entrance of the Bedford Street Hotel. The porter looked up from his newspaper.

"Good morning, sir."

"Good morning to you," replied Seventer. "I believe you have a Mr. Holtz staying with you in Room 21?"

The porter turned to check his register. "That's right, sir. Shall I ring him for you?"

"Please do. Tell him the bank is here."

"The bank, sir?"

"That's right."

After a few minutes, Galish came downstairs. "Are you looking for me?" he asked.

Seventer had hoped to recognize him at once, but the years had faded his memory more than he realized. The man certainly fit Wanstumm's description. Seventer's palms were moist, and he could feel his heart beating in his throat. "Good morning. Mr. Holtz, I presume?"

"That's right."

"My name is Binns. I'm from Mathijs Smithson, the bank. Mr. Pearce asked me to stop by and apologize for the delay in obtaining the foreign exchange license. Is Mr. Goldstein available?"

"I'm sorry, but he is not feeling well this morning. What seems to be the problem?"

"Just a routine matter, sir. Perhaps you would be so kind as to come down to the bank with me? We had overlooked the need for a further confirmation of the account owner's non-UK domicile. The Bank of England requires it, given the large amount involved. The form does not require Mr. Goldstein's signature."

"How long will all of this take?" asked Galish.

"Twenty minutes at the most. We can have one of our drivers bring you back to the hotel." Galish had a fleeting moment of doubt. This man was vaguely familiar. He concentrated his mind for a few seconds. No, it was just an illusion.

"Very good. Let me get my coat and briefcase. I will be right with you." A few minutes later, Galish reappeared. He went over to the reception desk. "Please do not disturb Room 23. My friend was taken ill during the night. I should be back shortly."

"Very good, sir."

———<>———

It was a busy morning for Inspector Hackett. He had to send a car to Croydon to collect Goedkamp who was arriving on the first KLM flight. A second car was to go to the airport at 11 a.m. to fetch Brian Samson, who was flying in from New York. Hackett could not understand why the Americans were always in such a hurry. Surely Samson could have waited until they had the men in jail. There would be plenty of time to sort things out.

Suddenly he looked at the case file. Two banks in London had been used by Hobbema and Seventer: Mathijs Smithson and the Winchester Bank. Hackett thought it was surprising that Mathijs Smithson had not reported receiving the same request for an appointment.

He decided to call Seventer himself at Mathijs Smithson's.

"Mr. Seventer's office."

"Inspector Hackett here. May I speak with him?"

"I'm afraid he hasn't come in this morning. Can Mr. Pearce help you?"

"Perhaps he can at that. Thank you."

There was a buzz and a click.

"Pearce speaking."

"Good morning, Mr. Pearce, this is Inspector Hackett from Scotland Yard."

"Ah, good morning to you, Inspector. Rather exciting, isn't it?"

"Isn't what?"

A brief silence.

"Er, well, you know," Pearce's voice fell to a whisper. "The two fellows showing up like that."

"What on earth are you talking about?" Hackett roared.

"But, Inspector, didn't Mr. Seventer call you yesterday? They were here. He said you were dealing with them."

"Stay where you are. I'm coming right over." Hackett slammed the phone down. As he ran out of his office, clumsily picking up his hat and coat, he shouted down the hall.

"Dobson, where are you?" Sergeant Dobson's imposing frame showed through the doorway. "Come with me."

Pearce was very nervous. He was not used to being yelled at by Scotland Yard. Hackett had burst in a few moments earlier and was now on the phone at Seventer's desk.

"Tottenham Court Station, please." He waited while the connection was made, his fingers playing an agitated melody on Seventer's burnished desk. "Hello, Hackett, Scotland Yard, here. I want four men to go to the Bedford Street Hotel on the double. I want the place closed up like the Tower of London, nobody in, nobody out, until I get there." Hackett turned to Dobson. "Stay here with Mr. Pearce. If Seventer shows up, place him under arrest. Any pretext will do. Keep him here until you hear from me. I'll send someone over to keep you company."

At the Bedford Street Hotel, the maid walked down the corridor, followed by Hackett. She took her passkey out and opened Room 21. The bed was made. Hackett stepped in, glanced at the suitcase and guessed that Holtz must still be around somewhere. The next door was 23. The maid knocked on the door. After a minute, she knocked again. Finally Hackett pounded on the door. "Police!" he thundered. Still no response. He nodded to the maid. She opened the door with her passkey. She saw the body immediately and stepped back, her hand covering her mouth.

The daytime reception clerk's name was Jones. He related that the two men had checked in two days before. The reservation for two single rooms was in the name of A. Holtz of Chicago, Illinois. He showed Hackett the registration. The name of the second man was not on it.

"Why only one name?" he asked, irritated.

"That was how the reservation was booked, sir. I had no reason to suspect anything."

Hackett made some notes in his book. "So where is the other man, this Holtz?"

"He went out this morning, sir. Another gentleman came to pick him up."

"What kind of a gentleman?"

"A well-dressed gentleman, sir, in a pin-striped suit. About six feet tall, fiftyish years old. Said he was from a bank."

Hackett stormed out, driving fast to Scotland Yard. There, he put a message out on the teletype: "Sought for questioning A. Holtz, U.S. citizen, arrived UK Croydon Airport, 15 January. Middle-aged, 5ft.10. Last seen in London at Bedford Street Hotel."

Hackett returned to Mathijs Smithson's office, having left two men on guard at the hotel until the coroner could get there. Goedkamp walked into the partners' office at the same time.

Hackett introduced himself and said, "Have you heard? I think your friend Seventer may have kidnapped Galish or Holtz, or whatever his name is. This morning. At the fellow's hotel."

Goedkamp appeared shocked. "That's impossible!"

Stella walked in the room. "Good morning, Stella, do you know where Mr. Seventer is?"

"Good morning, Mr. Goedkamp. No sir, I don't. He merely advised me last night that he would not be in today."

"Is Mr. van Meeren here?" Goedkamp asked.

"No, sir, he is on a business trip to Luton."

"Do you know where we can reach him?"

"Yes, sir. Let me try to get him for you." She left the room. In a minute, the telephone rang.

"Mr. van Meeren? This is Kees Goedkamp. I'm very well, thank you. No, I'm in London. Actually, I'm calling you from your office. Yes, well it seems that our Gestapo guy has finally shown up here. No, your colleague Mr. Seventer is not here. That's what I'm calling about. Have you spoken to him since yesterday afternoon? You haven't. I see." Goedkamp turned to Hackett.

"I'm beginning to think that your theory is plausible, Hackett. Supposing Seventer did grab Wanstumm. What would he do with him?"

"Let's ask van Meeren," suggested Hackett. It was his turn to get on the phone.

"Mr. van Meeren, this is Inspector Hackett, Scotland Yard. I know this sounds far-fetched, but would your colleague be capable of kidnapping Wanstumm? And if he did kidnap him, what would he do with him? You have no idea? Could you give me a description of Seventer's car? I see." Hackett made notes. "Well, I hate to bother you, but given the circumstances, yes, we could use your help here. Yes, at your office. Thank you. We'll see you in a while then."

Hackett knew that things could only get worse. Hackett's assistant brought in the latest communique from the FBI:

"Reurs Abraham Goldstein (stop) no USA passport issued to anyone that name (stop) Your description overweight dark-haired American male in early sixties fits about two million profiles (stop) Please advise more details (stop) Pondexter FBI New York (full stop)"

He picked up the telephone. "Send out an all points bulletin: URGENT! PRIORITY ONE! Stop and detain two males in dark blue, 1952 Rover saloon . . . Hang on . . ." He turned to Stella, "What's Mr. Seventer's car registration number? . . . The number is BRM 443. And sign it: Inspector Hackett, Scotland Yard."

Hackett reported by phone to his superior, Superintendent Galsworth. No, the identity of the man in Room 23 had not been established. Two passports had been found in the room. It was unlikely that either one was genuine.

He also spoke with the coroner, who confirmed that the body in Room 23 was that of a male in his mid-sixties. Death was apparently due to cardiac arrest, to be verified at the autopsy.

Hackett replaced the phone. "Where could he possibly take Wanstumm?" mused Hackett. He turned towards Stella. "Does Mr. Seventer have a house in the country?"

"He has a cottage on the south coast."

"Can you think why he would take the man there?"

"I have no idea. This is not at all like Mr. Seventer."

Hackett looked frustrated. "There's not much we can do right now. I've got a Priority One alert on the car. They're bound to find him."

Stella had gone into her office to answer the phone. "There's a call for you at my desk, Inspector." Hackett walked into her office. "Hackett here."

"Hi, John, this is Brian Samson. I'm at Croydon. I called your office. What are you doing at the bank? Bring me up to date."

"There's nothing much to report," he replied, annoyed at Samson's rude and peremptory approach.

"You mean the guys from Chicago haven't shown up?"

"Oh, those guys. Yes, as a matter of fact, they have. One is dead; the other has been kidnapped." Hackett could hear Samson's heavy breathing over the phone.

"I hope this isn't your famed British sense of humor, John."

"Hardly. Why don't you look for our driver who is supposed to be meeting you and tell him to bring you to 32 Moorgate? I'll fill you in when you arrive." Hackett hung up. No wonder Monty had so much trouble with the Yanks during the war.

About a half hour later, Samson strode into Seventer's office. Hackett was on the phone. Goedkamp was talking to his office in The Hague, and Pearce was pacing up and down, his normally well-groomed silver hair somewhat disheveled. They all looked at Samson, surprised at the intrusion. Hackett raised his hand in a motion advising Samson to wait a moment and then put down the receiver.

"Finally made it, I see?" needled Hackett. "Gentlemen, this is Mr. Samson from the Federal Bureau of Investigation in New York. Mr. Samson, this is Inspector Goedkamp, head of the Investigation Department, Netherlands War Crimes Commission. This is Mr. Pearce, a manager of the bank." Samson walked around, extending his hand.

"Mr. Samson," continued Hackett, "Let me bring you up to date."

The phone on Seventer's desk rang again. Hackett picked it up and listened. He began to take notes again. He dropped his pen theatrically on the desk and turned to look at everyone in the room. "That's it. Seventer's car was spotted, at a high rate of speed, south of Salisbury. Is that the road he would take to go to his cottage?" he asked Stella.

"Yes, it is."

"Think again. What is so special about the house down there?"

Stella thought for a moment. "It's a perfectly normal cottage. It's on the beach, near Charwell-on-Sea. Mr. Seventer keeps his boat at a marina there."

"What kind of boat?"

"He has a fishing boat, a cabin cruiser. He calls it his 'home away from home'."

Goedkamp suddenly stood up. "We must get down there as quickly as possible!"

Hackett picked up the phone again and dialed his office. "Dobson, order road blocks along the main road between Salisbury and Charwell-on-Sea. We have to stop Seventer before he gets to Charwell. And get the local police to stake out Seventer's cottage," Hackett cupped his hand over the speaker and asked, "Does anyone know the name of the cottage?" He continued, "Dobson, it's called 'Wintergreen'. We are on our way down there. Call me in the car when you hear anything."

———<>———

Carefully, Seventer let in the clutch and pulled out into Bedford Street. He looked over to Wanstumm. "Nice morning, isn't it?"

"Yes, very nice. Will we be at the bank very long?"

"Not more than ten minutes, I assure you."

"Do you still anticipate that you will receive permission to transfer the funds by tomorrow? Mr. Goldstein needs to get back to Chicago."

"I would imagine so." Seventer was driving cautiously. The last thing he needed at this juncture was to be involved in a traffic accident. Seventer wondered when Wanstumm's suspicions would be aroused. Would Wanstumm recognize him? No matter how many times he had rehearsed the plan in his mind, he knew that the chances of reaching Charwell with Wanstumm still in the car were minimal. Now, he was committed. There was no turning back.

Perhaps he should have let Scotland Yard arrest Wanstumm as planned. But Seventer had spent too many sleepless nights fantasizing about Biblical revenge. Too often, he had risen in the mornings, exhausted by his nocturnal confrontations. Now revenge had suddenly become a reality. Somehow, he was going to pull it off; Wanstumm belonged to him.

The Rover was now on the Cromwell Road. Seventer had been watching for any change in Wanstumm's facial expression. He saw it come.

"This does not look like the business district," said Wanstumm coldly.

"Only a little further. There's lots of traffic today, so I am taking the back way." Seventer was nattering on, saying anything to gain time, to get out of the denser traffic onto the faster moving roads.

"Pull the car over," ordered Wanstumm.

Seventer continued to drive. His heart was pounding. His mouth was dry. Could he pull it off?

"What are you doing? What's going on? Stop the car, immediately." Wanstumm's voice rose. "That is an order."

The car was now approaching the outskirts of London. Seventer was driving faster. So far, the traffic lights had been with him. His right hand came off the wheel and groped down into the pocket on the side of the door. The Belgian F. N. 34mm automatic felt reassuring. Seventer had kept it as a war souvenir. He had never imagined that he would ever have to use it again.

The crisis arrived without warning. A truck ahead of them appeared to have hit a car. All traffic was stopped. Wanstumm lunged for the door handle. Then he saw the weapon in Seventer's right hand.

"Don't try it," ordered Seventer. "I have no compunction about shooting you. Just don't move."

Wanstumm remained frozen in his seat. Maybe he could grab the gun when the man's attention went back to his driving. He had to wait for the right opportunity. Who was this man, anyway? He had not said which bank he was from.

The line of stopped cars started moving slowly around the accident. Seventer had slipped the gun back into the door's side pocket. Wanstumm studied Seventer's driving carefully. He had to find the moment when Seventer was most vulnerable. Seventer kept both his hands on the steering wheel, except when he had to change gears with his left hand. At those times, Seventer's right hand was therefore unable to reach for the gun without losing control of the wheel. Wanstumm figured that this would be the best time to make his move. He would wait until Seventer changed gears, then throw open the door and roll out of the car. Then Wanstumm realized that the car's doors were hinged from the column dividing the front and back of the car and therefore opened from the front. He could only risk making the jump at low speed.

Seventer figured that Wanstumm was looking for a chance to jump from the car. He decided to drive with the gun in his right hand at all times. He also had another worry. It was almost certain by now that Scotland Yard had found out about Wanstumm's disappearance, as well as Seventer's role in it. He had to assume that they would make every effort to track him down. They would probably send out an all points bulletin and throw up roadblocks. They might also deduce that Seventer was heading towards Charwell.

They had just passed Salisbury. Seventer decided to turn off the main road before reaching Blandford Forum. After a turn to the left, he followed a smaller road to the village of Cranborne, where he then turned right towards Wimborne Minster. He knew this little road well, and it was unlikely that the police would think of blocking the back roads.

Wanstumm was beginning to think that he might be better off to wait until they reached their destination, wherever it might be. They were moving fast, even on these back roads with almost no traffic. He eyed the gun in Seventer's hand. It was held at an awkward angle, but he could not discount Seventer's ability to use it quickly. Perhaps he should try to engage the driver in conversation to relax his vigilance.

"Where are you taking me? And who are you, anyway?"

Seventer merely smiled. As they approached Charwell, he was becoming more confident that he just might be able to pull off his plan.

Seventer looked over at Wanstumm. The man had marked creases around the eyes and from the corners of the nose curving down to the mouth, but his weight was probably the same as the day that Seventer had first set eyes on him in Gestapo headquarters, almost ten years ago. The dark, wispy blond hair still managed to cover the high forehead. The hands were quite delicate, and the thumbs were well-formed. Seventer looked down at Wanstumm's stomach; even in a sitting position, it did not protrude. Wanstumm's eyes were hooded, hardly aware of Seventer's scrutiny. Seventer felt almost amused. His end-game was under way, in the last place anyone would ever have thought of: a little corner of the south coast of England.

Wanstumm tried again. "Whatever you have in mind, you must realize that I am a wealthy man. Perhaps you should consider that."

"Money has nothing to do with it. This is about good and evil, but you probably wouldn't understand that. So you will simply have to wait until I can explain it to you."

"At least, tell me who you are."

"My name is Eduard Seventer."

Wanstumm thought of all the bank documents he had been using recently. Of course! The Dutch bank manager! The man he had searched for in Amsterdam during the war! What role was he playing, after so many years?

Hackett sat up front next to the driver. He was on the telephone. "I don't understand it. You say you have three road-blocks on the road down to Charwell? Where exactly are they?" He held the telephone with one hand, and, with the other, traced the locations on the ordnance map laid across his knees. He turned in his seat to address van Meeren in the back.

"Is there any other way Seventer might take instead of going through Dorchester?"

Van Meeren leaned forward. "Let me see the map. That is the way he always goes. I don't remember his taking any other road." Van Meeren scrutinized the map closely. What he had just said wasn't quite true. Seventer had taken a different road once with van Meeren in the car. But van Meeren had no recollection of which one it had been. He shrugged and handed the map back to Hackett.

Hackett was on the telephone again. "Make sure that the cottage is being watched. When they show up, let them go inside. Then block all the exits and wait for us."

Seventer skirted the city of Bournemouth, passed through the small town of Wareham, and took a narrow lane heading down to the village of Charwell-on-Sea. He turned left at the end of the village and headed for the harbor where he turned into a side road leading to Mellor Marine Services.

At the end of the marina ramp, he stopped and parked the car at an angle, the hood pointing towards the boat basin. From where he sat, he could see the boats, carefully docked in their allotted moorings, swaying in a fairly stiff wind. This was unusual. It was rare when a southwest wind, coming off the English Channel, felt like anything more than a gentle breeze inside the cozy haven of the marina.

He turned to Wanstumm. "I will now get out of the car. I will take the keys with me. You will get out of the car when I tell you to do so. You have nowhere to run. I will shoot you before you can run twenty yards."

Seventer continued, "You will walk ahead of me, down to the boat that I will designate. When you are on the boat, I will get on as well. Together, we will go for a ride. You are a smart Nazi with a high IQ; do you understand what I have just said?"

Wanstumm merely nodded. His eyes betrayed no emotion at all. Yet the sight of boats bobbing in the wind suddenly reminded him how much he hated being on the water. Even the tiny wooden ferries that he had taken in Holland had made him queasy. Today was different. He had to concentrate all of his physical and mental energy. He had to kill this man. Only one of them could survive.

The two men walked past the big boat hoist, onto the path leading down to one of the piers. Their feet made little sound as they padded onto the deserted wooden dock. About two thirds of the way, Seventer ordered Wanstumm to stop in front of a motor boat tied stern-first to the pier, with the bow tied to pilings.

"Step down into the cockpit," he commanded. "Now sit down on the seat facing towards me." Seventer waved the gun in Wanstumm's direction and waited until he was settled. Wanstumm's eyes never left the gun in Seventer's hand. This was going to be the most critical part of the drill. Any fumbling on Seventer's part and Wanstumm would be on him in a flash. Seventer carefully stood on the transom, then, crouching slightly, stepped into the boat. He steadied himself, then moved to the helm, to the left of which was a small door. Seventer, remaining slightly turned so that he could keep Wanstumm within his field of vision, pulled a set of keys from his pocket and found the one for the cabin door. He turned to face Wanstumm.

"You are now going down to the cabin. There is no light down there, so I want you to move slowly. You will find a banquette around the little table. You will sit down, or lie down, as you wish. I will lock the door behind you. There is no other exit from the cabin except this door. I will be at the helm, facing the door. Your cooperation will therefore be appreciated."

"Where are we going?" asked Wanstumm, hoping that he wasn't showing the panic building within him.

"To the devil and the deep blue sea." Seventer was becoming a little light-headed from the adrenalin pounding through him. He repeated, "Now please step down into the cabin."

He watched as Wanstumm moved past him towards the cabin door, ducking a little to avoid the overhanging projection from the helm. Wanstumm suddenly felt ill with terror. He had never learned how to swim. In desperation, he turned blindly towards Seventer and butted him in the stomach with his head. Seventer let out a gasp. He lashed out with his gun, hitting Wanstumm just above his left eye. Wanstumm reeled back and lost his footing as he tumbled down into the cabin.

Seventer leaned forward, his hands shaking, slammed the cabin door shut, and clicked the lock. He breathed deeply, regaining his composure. He listened for any sound from inside. Nothing.

Now he had to concentrate on getting the boat out to sea. First, he took off his jacket and from under the helm, he pulled out a sweater and an oilskin coat; he slipped them on in a practiced manner. He inserted the ignition key and turned the starter to 'on' to warm up the diesel. While he was waiting for the ready light to glow, he turned on the navigation lights and a dimmed cockpit light which outlined the instruments. Another switch turned on the compass light. He sat perched on the helm seat, watched the engine light go on, and then pushed the starter button. The diesel turned over and roared into life. He turned on his VHF radio, flipped it to the marine weather station, and listened.

". . . periods of rain and fog. Seas 8 to 12 feet. The low pressure system off the coast of Ireland will drift in a southeast direction by morning. Gale warnings for the coast of France from La Rochelle to Bayonne. Seas 15 to 20 feet in the Bay of Biscay. For the Channel west of the Solent, periods of rain and fog, turning to continuous rain by morning. Wind 35 to 40 knots southwest . . ."

Seventer was pleased. It was just what he had hoped for: high seas, rain and fog, perfect for a day of reckoning. He was in his element; the German inside the cabin was not. He got up from the helm seat and, walking in a clockwise direction, untied each line so that the last one was the windward stern line. He loved these little details. It was part of being at home on a boat.

He put the boat in gear, and nosed it very slowly out of its berth, turning carefully into the narrow channel. He spotted the first channel buoy immediately because he knew where to look. The next one, a slight dog-leg from the first, was always harder to see against the darkening background of the open water behind it. He saw the channel entrance marker, with its ten-second green flasher. As he passed it, he wondered whether he would ever see it again. But he had no regrets. This was what he was meant to do, for Louisa.

————<>————

The police Riley took the turn into Mellor Marine a little too quickly, and the rear tires skidded as the driver stepped on the brakes. The car came to a halt next to Seventer's Rover. All four doors flew open at the same time. Inspector Hackett, Brian Samson, Kees Goedkamp, van Meeren and Hutchins, a plainclothes policeman, jumped out of the car. They raced behind van Meeren down to the dock, but they knew they were too late. Even before they started down the line of moorings, they could see that one boat was missing, the 'Louisa'. They stood silently in front of the empty dock space, holding on to their hats as the wind blew in gusts.

Hackett was the first to speak. He was visibly angry. "Why didn't we think of staking out the boat? We'll have to get word out to Sea Search and Rescue." He turned to van Meeren. "Have you any idea what your friend might do out there?"

"He's been out there so often; he knows the coast well. He has even crossed over to France a few times."

Goedkamp interjected. "The weather is picking up a bit. Let's get a weather forecast. That may limit his options."

"Good idea," said Hackett. Turning to the policeman, he said, "Hutchins, get S.S.R. on the phone."

Van Meeren added, "Seventer generally stands by on Channel 16. Maybe we should try and reach him." They all looked at each other.

"Why didn't I think of it?" complained Hackett. "Do you think S.S.R. may be able to talk to him?"

"It's possible. In weather like this, a boat rolls and pitches a lot, and it throws the radio signals out a bit."

Samson spoke up for the first time. He was visibly angry. "I can't believe Seventer took off with Galish right under our noses. Now we have to organize a complicated search and rescue mission, not knowing what he's up to. What is it with you Dutchmen anyway? You're so damn pig-headed."

Van Meeren didn't need some FBI guy telling him that the Dutch were stubborn. He already knew that. The question was: would Seventer survive?

Goedkamp ignored Samson and turned to van Meeren. "Mr. van Meeren, what do *you* think your friend plans to do out there with the German? He doesn't seem like the killer type. He is too civilized. This doesn't make any sense to me."

Van Meeren searched his mind for an answer. Looking at Hackett, he answered, "Eduard hates this German, more deeply than we can imagine, but I agree, Seventer is incapable of taking someone's life. I have to believe that he has something in mind that none of us has thought of. I don't know. I . . . just . . . don't . . . know."

Silence fell on the little group. Hackett was walking back to the cars when Hutchins called out, "I have S.S.R. on the phone, sir."

Hackett jumped into the car and took the phone. "Hackett here. I'm speaking from Charwell, down at the docks. Who is this?"

"Flight-Lieutenant David Mander, sir. I understand you may be looking for someone outside Charwell harbor?"

"Lieutenant Mander, listen carefully. We have a man by the name of Seventer on his boat, the 'Louisa', a 31-foot diesel-powered cabin cruiser. He left the Charwell marina about . . ." Hackett consulted his watch, "forty-five minutes to an hour ago. We are reliably told by his best friend that he keeps the boat fueled up. He has VHF and a radio direction finder on board. We have no idea where he is going. Our reason for wanting him back, as soon as possible, is because he has made off with, kidnapped, in fact, a German Nazi, a man wanted for war crimes. The man is an exceedingly nasty piece of work. How do we get them back?"

"Well, sir," replied Mander, "for one thing, we have gale warnings for that part of the Channel. A 31-footer is going to be very uncomfortable. The 'Louisa' will be almost impossible to find unless we can make radio communication with her. It will be even more difficult since night will be falling soon. From what you say, sir, perhaps the gentleman doesn't want to come back."

"Mander, I don't care what it takes. I want those fellows back. I want a full search undertaken."

"Very well, sir. But you realize that I have to receive proper authorization. We have to launch both planes and boats. We do not do this unless lives are in danger."

"These lives *are* in danger, Mander. The German will almost certainly kill if given half a chance. They may both be drowned out there. I will stand by while you ask for the necessary clearance." Hackett handed the phone to Hutchins. "Stay with this. They are calling us back."

He got out of the car and walked back to the group. "S.S.R. is onto this. They are obtaining clearance."

"So what do we do?" asked Samson, visibly impatient.

"We have to wait. I want someone to stay here at the dock. Hutchins, you stay. I will get a couple of fellows from Charwell to come and assist you, just in case they return unexpectedly. We are going up to the station-house."

Van Meeren, Hackett, Samson and Goedkamp crammed themselves into the Riley. Hackett drove, his eyes peering through the windshield as the wipers fought the gusting rain that suddenly started to pour down unceasingly.

———<>———

Seventer had his lower back tightly braced against the helm seat and his feet pushed hard against the cabin bulkhead. As the boat lurched from side to side, he was able to adjust his equilibrium, keeping his eye on the compass. His course was south-west. Even though the compass was swinging wildly within a large arc of some twenty degrees, he always managed to bring it back to his course without overworking the rudder. He could see little of the sea around him, but the waves rising from starboard were so flecked with white foam that he was able to steer into them at an angle somewhere between the danger of capsizing and the sickening roller coaster of meeting the seas head-on.

The rain had suddenly started to pelt down in sheets that poured off the boat's hard-top and gushed down into the cockpit through the scuppers, back out into the sea. Seventer knew that with the rain and the occasional water that he was now shipping over the gunwale, whatever water did not make it through the scuppers would end up in his bilge. He had turned on his bilge pump and, judging from its pilot light, he assumed that it was doing its job. He could not risk looking over the side to see if the telltale jet of water was coming out of the seacock.

He glanced at his watch. He estimated his speed to be about six knots in these conditions. The wind and tide were diverting him from his course by about seven degrees. That meant that every hour, he would be off course by about four miles to the east. This mattered very little for what he had in mind. He needed to steer the 'Louisa' towards the middle of the English Channel, which is exactly what no one would have expected him to do on an evening like this.

He had scarcely thought about his passenger locked in the cabin below. But as the 'Louisa' bucked and reared through the growing, hissing seas, Seventer began to consider whether he ought to bring Wanstumm out on deck soon. Why wait? Perhaps something might happen to the boat before he had a chance to open the cabin door. He slowed the boat to no more than three knots, just enough to keep her in the wind. He pulled a short line from a locker and tied it around the wheel first, then experimented with tying it around the stanchion which supported the hard-top. He discovered very quickly that the waves and wind exerted a powerful force on the rudder, and he could allow very little play in the line holding the wheel. Even then, the boat tended to slew badly, so he decided to turn the boat more directly into the oncoming waves, lessening the sideways force on the rudder. The line held the wheel, and the boat's trajectory straightened out a bit. As he had expected, however, the roller coaster movement was much more violent. As the 'Louisa' headed into each successive wave, it almost stopped on the crest, uncertain whether to fall back or to lurch forward down the back of the wave into the trough preceding the next one. Seventer compensated by a small increase in engine speed.

It was time to open the cabin door. Seventer fumbled with the key. His hands were becoming numb from the cold and the icy spray. As the door opened, he looked down into the cabin. He was standing too close. Wanstumm grabbed Seventer's head and pulled him down into the cabin with him. Both men fell onto the cabin floor as the boat plunged down the face of another huge wave. Wanstumm was in better physical shape. He twisted around to slam his fist into Seventer's face. Seventer ducked aside awkwardly and managed to avoid the full force of the blow. He was suddenly sick to his stomach with anger and mad at himself for having been so stupid. If only he hadn't left the pistol upstairs in the helm's storage bin. He blindly staggered onto his feet as he felt around the cabin for something to hold on to. Wanstumm was on him with one arm around his neck, but lost his footing again.

Seventer had the advantage of knowing every inch of the boat. He moved backwards, sat down hard on the banquette, and reached for the fire extinguisher which was clipped to the bulkhead. Wanstumm tried to figure out why Seventer was sitting down. He rose on one knee, steadied himself by holding on to the table and prepared to lunge. Seventer unclipped the extinguisher and held it slightly to one side, ready to swing it into Wanstumm's face. As the boat took another wave, he suddenly saw Wanstumm's hand clutching the side of the table. Seventer swung the extinguisher down and delivered a crushing blow to the hand on the table. Wanstumm's scream was drowned in the howling of the wind. He slipped backwards onto the cabin floor. Seventer pulled himself up, quickly realizing that he had the upper hand. The extinguisher had dropped to the floor. He ran up the few steps to the cockpit. He fumbled with the door latch. It wouldn't close. The effort left him breathless. How long could he sustain a fight to the death with a man in much better shape than he was?

He saw immediately that the weather had worsened. He could tell from the howl of the wind, the hissing of the rain, and the roar of the waves. The wheel was straining against the line tied to the stanchion. He clawed his way back to the helm seat, grabbed the gun from the side pocket, and waited. Wanstumm came out of the cabin, his good hand clasping the handrail, the other hanging limply down at his side. His eyes were pin-point-sharp, yellow, flickering. His hair was hanging limply over his forehead. There was vomit on his clothes. The boat took another lurch, and Wanstumm pressed himself against the door opening. His eyes never left Seventer. A wave rose from the starboard quarter and collapsed into the cockpit. A foot of foaming water swirled around their legs. The boat rolled over to port, at an angle that Seventer judged to be at least 30 degrees. Just then, he heard a voice on the VHF radio. It was indistinct. A lot of boats would be in trouble tonight.

Wanstumm stood at the cabin door, no more than two feet away from Seventer. He looked fearfully at the waves crashing over the boat. He had begun to realize that he needed the Dutchman alive if he were to survive. But did the Dutchman need him? Suddenly Wanstumm understood why they were out there, in the middle of a tumultuous sea in the dark of the evening. This very environment was the Dutchman's protection. He was in his element, and Wanstumm wasn't. Wanstumm needed to de-escalate the situation; he needed time to think.

Seventer motioned to Wanstumm. "Move to the stern and sit on the gunwale," he shouted over the roar of the sea.

Wanstumm looked at him, fear showing in his eyes. "But the waves are washing over us. I will get swept overboard."

"Perhaps," replied Seventer. "Then again, you may be able to hang on."

"Why do you want to give me that chance?" Seventer had to strain to hear him.

"I don't. You see, the difference between us is that I cannot kill you myself. I am not a killer. You are, and the world cannot tolerate monstrosities such as you. So I have decided that nature will have to destroy you. Nature has no conscience, no qualms. It is an equal-opportunity exterminator. So here you are, and here I am, and there is absolutely nothing that you or I can do to change anything."

"So you are willing to die out here?"

"I would like the satisfaction of seeing you go first. Do you know the name of this boat? It is called the 'Louisa'. Do you know who Louisa was?"

Wanstumm shook his head. His left eye had swollen closed where Seventer had hit him with the pistol.

"Louisa Seventer-van Dijck was my wife. She died in May, 1945, as a result of your vicious and inhuman questioning at Gestapo Headquarters in Amsterdam. You tortured her. You cut off her fingers, and then you ordered her dumped on a bench in a city park. She never regained her ability to function as a human being. You destroyed my wife, like you did countless others."

"I was just doing my job for my country," Wanstumm's thin voice pleaded.

Seventer shrugged. "Oh yes, you were just following orders. It was your job to occupy Holland to protect us Dutchmen from the British. You had only the loftiest of motives. The trouble was that you could not tell the difference between good and evil."

Wanstumm said nothing.

The two men sat there, hanging on as the boat continued its wild bucking and yawing. Wanstumm almost lost his balance

as the 'Louisa' rose to meet a rogue wave, but he managed
to slide down the side of the cockpit to recover. His crushed
hand lay in his lap.

Seventer watched him calmly. He wondered how long
Wanstumm was going to hang on. He was sure that the man
was not going to slip overboard quietly. But he also knew
that Wanstumm had no way of surviving alone in this sea.
Wanstumm needed him.

The minutes went by, in a rush of ice-cold wind, roaring
waves and air-born foam. Wanstumm was calculating,
computing the odds, trying to overcome his enormous fear.
He was retching frequently. Seventer watched him, but his
mind was on the boat now. They had followed a south-westerly
course for about two hours, at an average speed of less than
six knots. The tide was still setting towards Dover, at a rate
of three knots an hour.

In his mind's eye, he saw the position of the 'Louisa' just
before he decided to turn into the wind, that is to say, to the
west-south-west. He looked at his watch. It was now 6.23
p.m. So they had been on this course for over 45 minutes. He
was almost certain that the four to five knots he was able to
maintain into the wind represented a course-over-ground of
one knot at best, what with the tide and the wind and the
waves against the boat. In all likelihood, they were probably
in exactly the same place that they had been an hour ago,
which meant that Charwell was no more than fifteen miles
due north.

But Wanstumm wouldn't know that. Seventer was
beginning to feel groggy. He had dreamed about this moment
so often, with Wanstumm on his boat. He saw that the German
was crouching in his corner, not making a move. Mother
Nature was supposed to have swept Wanstumm overboard.
With Wanstumm gone, Seventer could have turned back
towards home, his vengeance accomplished. Seventer was
exhausted, mentally as well as physically. His knee was

aching, and the side of his head was throbbing from the fight in the cabin.

As the wind started veering, it suddenly intensified in force. The line holding the wheel began to part. Seventer hung onto the wheel with one hand, while trying to untie the knot holding the line to the wheel. His back was turned to Wanstumm. He had to master the 'Louisa', get her back into the wind, correct the rpm's on the engine to balance the boat's approach to each succeeding wave, not too fast to bury its bow in the next wave, not too slow to fall back and be pitchpoled by the following wave running up to it.

Wanstumm may have thought that he had a chance to assume the upper hand. If he could get hold of the wheel, he could try to use the radio, to call for help, to explain how Seventer had been swept overboard. Under the gunwale, he noticed a long wooden handle with a nasty-looking hook at the end. It was the 'Louisa's' fishing gaff. If he could just pull it out of its rack . . . He leaned down, yanked on it, and suddenly found himself wielding a formidable weapon.

Seventer did not see the movement; the gaff was swinging around in Wanstumm's hand when the deck slid out from under him again. His useless hand could not hang on to anything. The gaff went flying like a missile. The end of the hook caught Seventer in the small of the back. He uttered a low-pitched scream.

Wanstumm pivoted as he lost his footing. He lurched forward, then sideways as the boat seemed to break away under him, and finally backwards. His head cracked against the wooden transom. His body slid into a heap, grotesquely agitated by the motion of the boat.

Seventer was hanging onto the wheel, the gaff hanging down from his back. It had pierced the fatty tissues near the top of his spine. The bucking and lurching of the boat caused the gaff to gouge an increasingly ragged wound, as it swung like a pendulum behind him. He had to get the thing out.

Holding onto the wheel with one hand, he twisted the other arm behind him. The pain made him shout. He missed the swinging handle twice, then was able to grab it. He had to find the strength to pull it out of his back without tearing the wound open even further. Each time he tried to work it free, he groaned. His shoulder was getting a cramp. He had to do it, now. With a final contortion, the hook came out but got stuck on the inside of his oilskin. Quickly he ripped open the fastener and wormed out of his jacket, keeping his knees wedged against the wheel while using both arms to pull his arms out of the sleeves. The jacket, with the gaff attached to it, clattered to the deck.

In spite of the cold, Seventer pulled his shirt and sweater up as high as he could, exposing the wound to the salt-laden air. The cold spray might slow down the bleeding. He looked down at Wanstumm's body. He knew the man was dead. Blood was oozing from his ears. A huge numbness overcame him. But now, he had to concentrate harder than ever on the steadily worsening conditions around him.

The Charwell police station was a charming old house on the main street. The street was so narrow that cars had to park at the back of the building. The Scotland Yard Riley was nosed up against the wooden railing in the diminutive parking lot. It looked out of place next to the modest cars of the local constabulary. All the lights were on in the building, a fact that only a few of the locals would have noticed since most of them had been in bed since ten p.m.

Inside, the bustle of activity was quite abnormal, particularly at 10.45 p.m. Brian Samson sat at a desk with a telephone cupped in his hand. Inspector Hackett was momentarily at a loss. He had talked to everybody he could think of. The Dutch policeman sat in a chair, tilted backwards, smoking a small cigar. Hackett was annoyed by the smell.

Nor did he like the fact that the American was spending British taxpayers' money on long-winded calls to the U.S.

The duty sergeant piped up. "Inspector, sir, S.S.R. has a fix on a boat that may be the 'Louisa'."

Hackett ran over to the telephone held by the sergeant. "Hackett here."

"Sir, this is Mander. We picked up a VHF message a few moments ago. Very indistinct. Something about heading back. That's all. The ID sounded like 'Louisa', but I can't be sure."

"Can you tell where the message is coming from with your RDF?"

"Very iffy, sir. It was too short for us to get a good bearing. But we think about due south, between fifteen and twenty miles offshore."

"What's the weather out there?"

"Lousy, sir, a real mess."

"Can you get someone out there?"

"Not before about 6 a.m., sir. We need some light to see anything. Radar won't do it; not unless it's a bloody great tanker."

"Mander, I would appreciate your getting a chopper up there at first light."

"Aye, aye, sir."

Hackett stood up. In a loud voice, he announced that he was going back down to the dock, since some contact had apparently been made with the 'Louisa'. Should anything develop, he would let them know immediately. The cigar-smoking Dutchman stood up, and said, "I'll come with you; I like it better in the open." Van Meeren followed. Wordlessly, Samson hung up the telephone and joined them.

They arrived at the dock a few minutes later. The rain had turned into a torrent. The wind came from several directions; water crept into every crease in their clothes. Van Meeren sat down on a small bench under an awning which was flapping wildly in the wind. He was looking into the distance, not registering any emotion.

Hackett turned to him, and said, "Mr. van Meeren, Seventer was transmitting on VHF, something about returning to port. Can you give me any inkling of where he went, what may have happened, anything that might be useful? We have S.S.R. all set up to search for him at first light."

Van Meeren looked at Hackett and turned away. Finally, he rose to his feet and said, "I haven't stopped thinking about it. He may have wanted to terrify Wanstumm, but I don't think he could kill him. I simply can't figure it out. But on a night like this, I can tell you he didn't get very far. Eduard is out there, quite close. I just don't know what he's up to."

"Can the boat handle a storm like this?" asked Hackett.

"The boat is only as good as its skipper," answered van Meeren. "Seventer is good."

Hackett was silent. The Dutch policeman leaned over to van Meeren and asked, "How much fuel does he normally have on board, and how long would it last in such conditions?"

Van Meeren didn't answer. A streak of white foam had suddenly appeared behind the second harbor entrance buoy. A shape disappeared, then reappeared, just a shade darker than its surroundings, nosing into the water with a long tail of frothy water behind it. Vaguely, he could make out a pale superstructure. He knew immediately that the 'Louisa' was coming in. He held his breath for fear that the gods would deny Seventer the safety of the harbor.

Hackett noticed the looks on the other faces and strained his eyes in the same direction as theirs. At exactly the same moment, they all saw a cabin cruiser slowly making its way up the channel towards the dock. Its navigation lights were on. They could not see who was behind the wheel.

Seventer managed to slip the engine into neutral just as he made his final turn into the dock. The bystanders watched, first in awe, then with growing apprehension, as the boat seemed to move slowly forward, straight for the pier at the end of the marina entrance. It was then that they saw Seventer, slumped over the wheel.

The boat was moving slowly, but unchecked, out of control. Goedkamp ran down to the pier, realizing that the only hope he had of stopping a collision was to jump onto the boat from one of the floating docks that ran parallel to the 'Louisa's' course. Goedkamp picked his dock, ran down to the end, and just as the 'Louisa' came by, he made the flying leap of a lifetime, sprawling over the rail amidships and sideways down into the cockpit. He made it to the helm with all of the speed of a desperate man. He reached over Seventer's shoulder, pulled back on the throttle and threw it into reverse. The 'Louisa' slowed and then stopped.

Van Meeren jumped onto the bow and began to tie the boat to the nearest cleat. He moved over to Seventer, who was still slumped over the wheel, a smile on his wan face. Van Meeren saw the blood-stained shirt and gently lifted Seventer up by his arms. Samson leaned over to help them off the boat. Hackett called out to Hutchins to summon an ambulance.

Goedkamp shut the engine down and turned around to check the stern of the boat. Wanstumm's body lay prone on the deck of the cockpit. One of his arms was twisted awkwardly underneath him. The blood from his ears had coagulated in hard lines down the side of his throat into his shirt collar. The face was white, expressionless. Goedkamp bent down and searched Wanstumm's pockets. He found two American passports, one in the name of Holtz, the other in the name of Velec. The wallet contained over one thousand dollars in bills. Another pocket yielded an airline ticket, a one-way BOAC flight from London to Nassau, Bahamas, with an 'open departure date'. Goedkamp reflected on that irony, smiled to himself, and stepped off the boat. His boss would be very pleased with the clean and inexpensive resolution of this case.

Samson would not go home empty-handed; two of his cases were now closed by Wanstumm's death. The Director would be satisfied.

Hackett was also pleased. His case would be closed with a certificate from the coroner. He was already rehearsing the statement he would make at the subsequent hearing. Wanstumm's death was, at worst, self-defense, at best, simply an accident.

The next day, the body of Heinrich Wanstumm, a.k.a. Joseph Galish, was autopsied by the coroner in Weymouth. He was pronounced dead from a massive blow to the cranium. Death was ruled to be accidental.

EPILOGUE

NOVEMBER, 1979

ZURICH

Bernhard Cortani finished the last drop of his liqueur and looked contentedly out of the restaurant window at the Limmat River flowing quietly below. The diminutive boats tied to little piers along the banks bobbed rhythmically, as if they were saluting the pods of ducks that rode the current down to the lake. It was a peaceful scene. It had not changed in three hundred years. Cortani turned back to look at his luncheon companion, twenty years his senior but still alert and vigorous thanks to an intense schedule of mountain climbing. Alois Hansli was the city's most sought-after lawyer, specializing in taxation and estate planning. Cortani was paying for the lunch. He was doing his homework before having to face his partners at the small private banking firm of Rachwiller, Greutz later on that afternoon. Hansli had answered most of Cortani's questions. Now it was time for the wrap-up.

"So, Alois, in all of your years of practice, you have never known an owner of a very large bank account to show up suddenly after twenty-five years when there had been no previous attempt to communicate with the bank. Is that correct?"

"It is almost unheard of. The very large amount of money you have been telling me about simply doesn't go unattended and forgotten. In my experience, when one of these accounts has been dormant for even ten years, then the owner of the account has died without making proper arrangements. In the case you have described to me, I am convinced that the account will never be claimed. You must make absolutely sure, however, that the beneficial owner of the account never issued a power-of-attorney to anyone else."

"I'm sure of it. We have searched all the relevant archives."

"Then it appears as if you will be enjoying a happy Christmas," chuckled Hansli.

"Well, you have assisted me greatly," replied Cortani, a broad smile on his face. "Perhaps I had better get back to my office. Our partners' meeting begins in one hour."

Cortani stepped out into the cool afternoon, shook hands with Hansli, and walked briskly in the direction of the Bahnhofstrasse. His bank had its office in a stern, solid-looking building on one of the side streets. The name of Rachwiller, Greutz was discreetly embossed on a bronze plaque at the front door.

———<>———

Louis Rachwiller was the bank's senior partner. At 81, he was small, thin and unsmiling. His remarkably robust health was the despair of the other partners. Under his iron rule, nothing had changed at the bank. The clients loved it. They knew that they could meet with him or one of the other partners whenever they came to Zurich, which was not very often. The average size of an account at the bank was almost four million dollars. The bank invested client funds very conservatively. And they never, ever, revealed anything about their clients to anyone.

Rachwiller came into the somber conference room exactly one minute before the time scheduled for the meeting. The other five partners, including Cortani, already sat at their appointed places. They rose when he entered. Rachwiller waved a bony hand around in greeting, sat down, and picked up the brown leather folder in front of him.

"Today, we have three items on the agenda," he stated. "The first is a review of our investment position. The second is the approval of our accounts through the end of September. The third is a review of accounts considered to be abandoned. This latter item should take us the least amount of time, and we will therefore begin with it. Bernhard, please make your presentation." Rachwiller looked at his watch as he said this.

Cortani looked at the documents in front of him. "You will note," he said, "that we have several accounts which have had no activity since 1969 or earlier. I think we know most of the clients involved, however. Two are French; all one needs to do is to read the French newspapers to know that they are both very much alive. The next one on the list is Colombian. We know that he lives in Spain; I believe our account is only one of many he has established in Switzerland. Then we have three Iraqi accounts; last year, Ibrahim al-Suweiri informed us that all three account owners were still in prison in Baghdad.

"The one account which I want to review with you this afternoon is known in our bank records as 'TRA'. The current balance is $6,986,308. It was opened in 1953 by a lawyer in Panama named Rodrigo Fernandez Lemus. The real name of the account is 'Holger S.A.', a company incorporated in Panama in the same year, 1953. Three months ago, we wrote to Fernandez asking him for any information he might have about the status of the account. He reported that he had had no contact with the owner since 1953 and sent me the following information:

> "Holger S.A. was incorporated in Panama in June, 1953. The person who signed the incorporation papers identified himself as Armando Lopez. Lopez was the sole signer. The share certificates were issued in bearer

form. He gave me a limited proxy to operate a bank
account with the Banco del Pacifico in Panama. The
annual government registration fees have been paid
out of this account. We have no other information."

"Naturally I followed up. Our Mr. Wiehlkehr was due to
make a trip to Caracas to call on his clients, so I asked him to
stop in Panama to meet with the lawyer personally. He took
Mr. Fernandez to lunch and was able to elicit additional
information. He believes that this Lopez is a native German,
and in 1953, would have been in his early forties; so he would
be nearly seventy years old today. The lawyer recalls having
asked whether there would be any other shareholders, for
instance, members of Lopez's immediate family. Lopez gave
him to understand that he was unmarried.

"I am therefore inclined to think that Lopez is deceased.
Alois Hansli cannot think of a case where an account this
large remained inactive for this long unless the beneficial
owner was permanently incapacitated, or dead. Hansli
concluded that the account could safely be considered
abandoned."

Cortani eyed Rachwiller carefully to assess his reaction.
The older man sat immobile, the mere hint of a smile on his
thin, bloodless lips. Cortani read the signs and continued, "My
recommendation, therefore, is to close the account and credit
the balance to the partnership's undivided profits account. I
further recommend that we, the partners, pay ourselves a
special year-end dividend of $500,000 each as a tax-free
distribution. The balance will remain at the bank as part of
the partnership capital."

Cortani looked around the table. The old man's face
remained impassive, the nail of a wrinkled index finger now
scratching the side of the folder in front of him. The four
other men looked at each other, read their collective approval
without saying a word, and nodded towards Cortani.

"So approved," muttered Rachwiller. "Now we shall discuss our next agenda item."

The meeting ended precisely one hour later. Rachwiller rose from his chair, wished everyone a pleasant evening, and walked with firm steps out into the corridor. The other partners listened to Rachwiller's steps recede and then turned to each other with broad smiles.

"Well done, Bernhard, a great year-end bonus, and tax free!"

"So, do we have any other large accounts like this we should look at?"

"You wonder who this Lopez really was, don't you?"

The partners' delight at their unexpected windfall gave way almost at once to their usual staid and humorless demeanor. They filed out of the boardroom one by one and returned to their small, austere offices.

CPSIA information can be obtained at www.ICGtesting.com
Printed in the USA
LVOW101732261111

256571LV00002B/12/A